THE FATE OF GLASS

A JAMES STONE THRILLER

ROBERT CLARK

*For my dear friend Jones
You magnificent gentleman
Let it never be said that you won't go above and beyond for your
friends.
Thank you for all your help with this book...
...and the following twenty to come.*

PROLOGUE

ALL MEN DIE

THEY ARRIVED BY BOAT AT A QUARTER TO ONE IN THE MORNING, and were unloaded by two. They moved back and forth in absolute synchronicity, like a choreographed dance between two large, stoic robots. I watched from the doorway. No reason to speak to either of them. Not because they didn't know I was there. They had spotted me the moment they disembarked, and had to pass me on their way in and out of the barn. But because I knew something they didn't. And telling them at this point was just detrimental to the task they were performing so well.

Because after all, who really wants to know they are a dead man walking?

They walked back and forth through the thick, dank mud, turning it into a foul soup as they retraced their footsteps to and from the boat, cradling the packages in their arms on the outward journey. No flashlights. No talking. They had the light of the moon to guide them, and nothing worthwhile to say. They shuffled past me like solemn golems. No problems. No concerns. Everything running like clockwork.

The cell in my jacket pocket buzzed. I ducked back inside the barn and pulled it out. A text message containing just one word.

'Here.'

I stopped the first guy to pass me. A hand on his chest. It stopped him dead in his tracks. His big, mellon head twisted slowly to look at me.

'How many are left?' I asked him.

'Only five.' He had a deep, lazy voice that would carry in the wind for miles if he let it, but today was little more than a whisper.

'Get them all inside quick.' I replied. 'The boss is here.'

I felt the guy tense up and shuffle away at double time. He passed his buddy on the way in and muttered something to him, which got the second guy hustled into a jog. The packages in his arms bucked about. If he dropped one, he'd know about it soon enough. He was in and out in a flash, and together with the first guy, they carried the last of the shipment in, in one haul. Go figure they'd been dragging their feet. That's what you get for hiring bottom of the barrel people. But that's also what made them entirely dispensable.

They had families somewhere in South America. But girls like that married guys like these knowing that one day they'd say their last goodbyes without realising it. And it was no skin off my back that they'd said yes to the job. They knew it wasn't legal, and they knew that a payment as high as this ran with its own risks. They could have passed up the opportunity, and it would be someone else out here about to dig their own graves.

I had clear view of the land. The ground stretched gradually up for a quarter of a mile in a one eighty degree radius in front of me, with a vertical cliff side at my back. Only one way to approach from, and that was from the front. With the cloudless sky making way for the maximum moonlight, I could see the figures approach before I could really make them out. They were high up, descending from the chain-linked fence that surrounded the site at a walk. No flashlights for them either.

Three men in total. The man on the left carried a box in his arms. The kind I'd seen too many times, and whose presence sent a shiver through my spine. The two bigger men flanked the shorter man in the middle. Not that they needed to. Because the man in the middle was without a shadow of a doubt the most capable man I'd ever met.

I stepped out into the cool night air and met them a dozen yards from the barn. Out of earshot from the two dead men. But most importantly so that with the steady incline, I was about a foot lower than the three men, and at eye level with the man in the middle.

'Boss.' I said to the man in the middle.

'Felix.' His voice was a low growl. Even in the dim light, his cold eyes pierced into me. 'Is the shipment secure?'

'Yessir. They've just unloaded the last of it.'

'And you're sure it's all inside?' The faint hint of his Haitian accent clung to his words.

'Yessir.' I said again. 'I supervised the transfer personally.'

'Good. And the men. They are inside, yes?'

'Yessir.'

'Bring them outside.'

I turned on my heel and walked back down to the barn entrance. I could see the two guys lurking inside, casting awkward glances up at the boss. As I approached, they huddled closer together. Like sheep.

'The boss wants to speak to you both.' I said. I kept my voice low, like an instruction. Just because the job was done, there was no bending the rules.

'Is that him?' The man I'd stopped earlier asked. His English wasn't the best.

I nodded.

'What does he want with us?' The second guy asked. His English was better.

'To pay you and discuss terms.'

'Terms?' The first guy asked.

'Terms. Like what you can and can't do or say. It's important to Mr Reyes that you do as you are told, understand?'

They both cringed at his name, and nodded in unison. Not the first time I'd seen someone visibly cower at the name. Domingo Reyes had the kind of reputation that followed him around like a mile-long shadow.

'He's not going to hurt us, is he?' The second guy asked.

'No,' I lied. 'Unless you piss him off or rat him out. And you wouldn't do that, would you?'

Both men shook their heads.

'Good. Now get moving. Reyes is waiting.'

I led the way, walking back out of the barn and up the hill to where Reyes stood. I heard the squelch of two sets of boots on the ground following at a reasonable distance. They were afraid, and they were right to be.

Not that it would help them.

Reyes watched the two men approach. He had the kind of unfaltering stare that felt like someone had stuck a laser beam in your face. I could practically smell the burning flesh. I stood to the side, almost like an intermediary between the two groups.

The two dead men stood there with their heads bowed like they were addressing royalty. Mexican born. Good with their hands, and even better at avoiding the cops. The type Reyes always used for this kind of job. Easy to find, and easy to dispose of. Just a couple of Beaners. Reyes let the silence putrefy, and watched the two guys squirm. When finally it looked like they were about to burst, Reyes spoke.

'You have done me a great service today.' He hissed. Only he could make a compliment sound sinister. 'The waters between Mexico and Florida are heavily guarded, yet you have managed to cross them.'

'We know these waters well,' said the second guy. The one whose English was a little better. 'We have crossed the border many many times in our lives.'

'And you have never been caught.' Reyes snarled. 'How?'

'We have the Lord's blessing. He keeps us from harm. He protects us.'

'You believe your Lord watches over you here?'

'Don't you?'

It was clear from his face that he regretted his question immediately. Reyes stepped forwards, and the guy shrunk back. Even though Reyes was at least a foot shorter than the man, his power toppled the weaker man.

'Your Lord can eat the dirt off my boot for all I care. He has no dominion over me.' Reyes growled. 'If he had any sense, he would have drowned you both at sea. But luckily for you, here you stand. Not amongst gods, but amongst men, and who do you fear now?'

He was just inches away from the bigger man. Reyes looked up at his subordinate, commanding an almighty dominance over him. The guy didn't know where to look. He had heard the stories about Reyes, packed with the mystery of an old fable about some wicked, terrible monster. He had heard about what Reyes did to his enemies. He had heard the nickname Reyes wore like a badge of honour. The Black Viper. Small and ferocious, and packs a deadly punch.

'Who do you fear now?' He hissed, emphasising every word.

'You.' The guy whimpered.

Reyes watched him cower, and nodded.

'And will your Lord smite me? Will he strike me down?'

'No, Señor.'

'You're goddamn right.' Reyes laughed. His voice echoed through the night, reverberating off the high stone walls behind us like a sadistic cacophony. As it faded away, so had the false smile on his face. 'But I digress. You have done me a great service, and I wanted you both to know that your families will receive every last cent of your payment.'

The guy with the poor English smiled and nodded in appreciation, but the second guy had clicked.

'Sorry, Señor, but what do you mean?' He asked, his voice trembling.

'I mean that your families will be paid the amount we agreed upon for your hard work.'

'But Mr Reyes, we agreed to take the money ourselves.'

'And how do you expect to get it back?'

'By boat.' The guy looked longingly in the direction of his moored vessel, no doubt wishing he was already aboard.

'My men will sink your boat.'

'Why would you do that?'

'Because you aren't leaving. In fact, you won't be going much farther than where you stand right now.'

The two men looked at each other. Confusion ripe as a peach in their faces. Reyes laughed. The two men on his flank laughed. I stayed silent.

'I don't think you understand,' Reyes snarled. 'So let me simplify things. Neither of you will leave this place alive. I'll leave it up to you who gets a quick death.'

It was the two Beaners turn to laugh, though it was clear by their tones that they knew it was no joke. Reyes joined in, his sinister cackle far surpassed those of his subordinates.

'Please, Señor. We have families.' The second Beaner whimpered. 'We promise, we will take our secrets to the grave.'

'I have no doubt you will.' Reyes said. 'And here is your grave.'

In unison, the men behind Reyes stepped forward, sidearms raised at the two cowering Beaners. The guy with the box balanced it in his hand, and propped his gun arm over the top to point at the two Beaners. Bold move.

'Better get digging.' Reyes sneered.

It clicked at about the same time with both men. The realisation dawning like the morning sun that they were screwed. Sure, they could try and run, and see just how long they could outrun a bullet. But they knew that a quick death was way more preferable than the punishment for insubordination.

The two men shared a look that I had seen a couple times

before. Not the kind of look you exchange with a cashier in the local grocery, or a work colleague at the office. This was something different. Something from a bygone era. When the shades of grey were a little more black and white. When the law of the land was kill or be killed. They were sizing each other up.

Then fixed me with their big, puppy dog eyes, like they figured I had some kind of say in their fate. I didn't respond. No point giving them false hope. No point even trying. What the Viper wanted, the Viper got.

And tonight, he wanted blood.

The first guy threw a mean right hook into his buddy's jaw. The splatter of blood and spittle visible even in the dim light. The second guy stumbled back, but retaliated fast. He wasn't about to give up that easily. He hit his opponent with a ferocious uppercut to the solar plexus, and followed up with a head-butt so strong, I could have sworn I heard the guy's nose break.

With a torrent of blood pouring down his face, the guy staggered and fell to his knees. He brought his hands up in surrender. Not that it would help. His former partner towered over him, and slammed a devastating right hook down into his jaw. The guy crumpled down and looked up at Reyes.

'Please, Señor. I promise I won't talk.' He gasped. His slurred words landed on deaf ears. Reyes looked down at the squirming mess on the ground.

'You want to live. Fight.' He snarled.

But the fight was already won. We watched as the stronger man knelt over his partner and beat him again and again and again, until what remained of his face was a bloodied, distorted mess. The survivor looked down at the body. His bloodstained fists trembled in the moonlight. Then he wept. His cries carried far into the night.

'Why do you cry?' Reyes hissed at the victor.

The guy looked up at him, his jaw shook like an infant.

'He didn't deserve to die.' He sobbed. 'He just wanted to provide for his family.'

'His family will be dead soon. Yours too, if you don't obey.'

The guy's mouth dropped open in utter shock. His face was gaunt, his eyes hollowed.

'Please, Señor. Please do not harm them.'

Reyes smiled. 'Lie down.' He said.

The Beaner looked taken aback. Figured he had misheard his

boss. But he was smart enough not to ask twice. He got down onto his stomach, then rolled onto his back. Looked like a damn fool, just lying there next to the corpse of his old buddy. His eyes were fixed on Reyes. Silent prayers danced across his lips.

The man with the box walked forwards and placed it on the Beaner's hips. It wasn't much bigger than a shoebox. Then, with one delicate finger, he flicked open the lid.

'You will want to remain calm,' Reyes told the Beaner. 'Any sudden movements might, escalate matters.'

The two goons laughed. I stayed quiet. So did the Beaner.

Reyes moved close and looked into the box. The smile on his face grew wider. He stretched out his fingers and rested them on the lid. Then he tipped it towards the Beaner's face.

Something small and sleek slithered out. The Viper's pet. The Beaner shrieked and scrambled away as the serpent writhed. Huge mistake. In anger, it rose up and stared down at the petrified man, ready to strike.

'What you see before you is an Indian Cobra,' Reyes announced. 'Although this one is from Pakistan. She is smaller than most of her kind, although don't let that fool you into a false sense of security. One bite from her can cause paralysis, and respiratory failure in only fifteen minutes. And she rarely bites just once.'

The Beaner shuddered and tried to shake the snake off of him. Second huge mistake. The Cobra took the disturbance as a personal offence. It struck down with the speed of a bullet, and caught the man in the jaw. He screamed, which only fuelled the serpent on. It struck, again and again. Rising up and striking down with terrifying speed and accuracy. Neurotoxins flooded into the man's bloodstream, burning like acid as it attacked his body.

He did not last long. His contortions faded as the venom took hold, and before long he was gone. I looked between his body, and Reyes. The goon who had carried the Cobra took a step forward, ready to reclaim the angered serpent. But Reyes stopped him.

'Don't,' he said. 'Leave it here. I have no use for it now.'

The goon nodded, and stepped back. The Cobra slid off its victim and disappeared into the night. Only once it had gone did Reyes address his men.

'Move the bodies over to the water. Let the 'gators finish them off.'

The two men holstered their sidearms and picked a corpse each.

The Cobra's victim looking much the worse for wear. His face had swollen to twice its normal size before death had claimed him. I watched Reyes' goons drag the bodies back along the track the two dead men had used, off into the night. Then I looked at Reyes.

'We are ready,' he said. 'Make the call.'

PART ONE

THE FATE OF GLASS IS TO SHATTER

ONE

DOWNWARD SPIRAL

THE LEATHER DUG INTO MY WRISTS, SQUEEZING INTO FLESH AND bone, cutting off the circulation. I could feel the fast, erratic beats of my heart as it pounded against my ribcage, desperate to escape. The gag was thick, and moist from my saliva. It rubbed against my lips and tongue, and tasted foul. It was uncomfortable on the verge of painful. But that was the point. It was all part of the plan.

My clothes were two sizes too small. They were store bought and forced upon me without consideration. The perverse choices of a man I didn't know, chosen for the sole purpose to belittle me. To turn me into an object. A toy. Not a woman. Not a human being.

The ensemble and straps made me feel claustrophobic. The air in the basement was dank and sweltering to the point where I felt on the verge of passing out. But I couldn't. I knew I couldn't. Because it was all part of his plan. The only light in the whole room burned into my face. It pierced through my eyelids and seared into my skull. I wanted to shy away from it, but with my hands shackled above my head, I was at his mercy.

Then I heard it. The muffled footsteps. The slow, calculated thud of rubber on stone. He walked with conviction, just like he always did. The steps grew louder and louder. He was close, only a matter of seconds from the locked door. I heard him stop on the other side and compose himself. This was his moment. His time to shine. He reached for the handle and swung it open. The steel screeched across the stone, following the groove dug in the ground from repeated use. Even now, after hearing it so many times, my skin shivered.

He took another brief pause as the door clanged against the brick wall, and stepped forwards into the light.

His skin was pale. Almost white. His hair, in comparison, was as black as tar. The long, shoulder-length strands slicked back under a dense film of product. His face was deathly hollow, yet his eyes shone brightly. A haunting blood red, just like his thin lips. He drifted across the room like a ghost and brought his hand up to rest his long, slender fingers on my face.

'The time has come,' he hissed. 'The blood harvest is nigh.' He pulled the moist gag from my mouth.

'Please,' I whimpered. I could feel the tears building in my eyes. 'Just let me go. I don't want to die.'

'But my child, you do. You are the sacrifice. Your blood will run through me, and make me whole again.'

He stroked his finger down my cheek. Soft. Precise. I couldn't control the trembling.

'Please, just let me go.' I begged, unable to hold back the tears. They cascaded down my face, smudging my makeup.

He watched them fall. Then his face changed completely. The hauntingly dead expression was replaced in an instant by the look of a man at the end of his tether.

'And, cut!'

The lights switched on, and the stage lit up. Michael spun on his heel and stormed away.

'The goddamn girl can't control her goddamn emotions,' he barked at the director. His name was Galloway, and he was a fat, grotesque man, with greying stubble that protruded from his plump cheeks. The last remnants of his milkshake clung to his sweaty, pot-marked lip in foul protestation. With the grace of a drunken clown, he heaved himself out of his waning director's chair and waddled over.

'What's the problem this time?' He slurred. Drunk again.

'She was supposed to say "My body will not survive this everlasting torment" but she cried like a fucking amateur.' Barked Michael as he pointed an accusatory finger in my direction.

I slipped my hand free of the bonds and stepped down from my mark.

'I was giving the character some depth,' I said defensively. 'I'm supposed to be afraid for my life. Anyone in that situation would cry.'

The director sniffed and scratched at a mole on his massive neck.

'Just stick to the script, sweetheart.' He grunted. 'This ain't Broadway, and you ain't a star. Just do your damn lines or go back to waiting tables and turning tricks.'

'You damn fraud,' I snapped. 'Don't act like this film is winning any Oscars. We're filming in a goddamn basement for Christ's sake. It's B-movie slasher soft-core at best.'

I watched as he tried to absorb the insult, but I didn't wait for a retort. I spun on my heel and stormed out. It wasn't a set. It was hardly a studio. Every single second I'd spent here had felt wrong, like I was taking a step down a dark road. I reached the top of the stairs in seconds and practically ran down the corridor towards the main reception. My body was so full of anger and emotion that I just wanted to scream and cry and punch the next moron to get in my way. But I held it all in. I had to, for now.

I pushed open the door to reception, ignoring everyone waiting around, and I barged out into the blinding midday sun. I didn't care that my casual clothes were tucked away in my locker. I didn't care that the clothes I wore made me look like a cheap hooker. I just wanted out of there. Ever since that dirtbag Galloway had offered me the role in his film, my life had turned to shit. I was under no pretences that it would be a commercial success – these films never were – but it was supposed to be a step in the right direction. Every aspiring actress had to get their hands dirty once or twice. For me, it was a little more so than others. But that didn't matter so long as it was a steady paycheck.

I strode angrily across the street to the park and slumped down on the bench furthest away from the studio. I rested my head in my hands and wept. It felt good to let some of the emotion go, even if I did feel a little embarrassed to do it so publicly. Onlookers could look and laugh. It didn't matter anymore.

Moving all the way from Brighton to Miami had been the first adult decision I'd ever made for myself. It was supposed to be the defining moment to kickstart my career. Sure, most wannabe actors and actresses moved to Hollywood, but that place felt so crowded with unrecognised talent that I would have been destined to wait tables for the rest of my life without so much as a shot at my dreams. No, moving here had been the right call. There were fewer opportunities for sure, but that meant the competition was smaller by comparison. I could find the minor roles in the indie films and make my break that way. Well, that's what I had hoped.

I knew I shouldn't have snapped at Galloway like that. He was a scumbag, sure, but he was a bureaucrat first and foremost, and a nasty one at that. We both knew that he could put a call into every studio across the city and ensure that Eva Marston never worked again. Within a week I'd be searching desperately for temp jobs in every diner up and down the beach. My future rested in the palms of his sweaty, repugnant hands, and we both knew it.

I rubbed my face with my hands. It had been a long day, and I was sure it was about to get much, much longer. Galloway wasn't in the business of forgiveness. The rest of my day – probably the rest of my time on set – would be spent kissing ass. But it didn't need to start right away. I sat with my eyes closed, absorbing the sun-rays and cherishing every moment of it while it lasted.

I slipped into a trance where nothing mattered. Somewhere deep inside my psyche, I was sat on a beach sipping cocktails in the sun. It was nice. But then a cloud drifted across the sun, and my world went cold.

I opened my eyes and stretched my muscles and conceded defeat. I walked as slowly as I could across the park, back to the front doors without appearing to dawdle. The receptionist, Kevin, had obviously watched me from the comfort of his desk. He gave me an insincerely polite smile as I walked by, but I knew he would squawk the first moment he got about how "train wreck Eva" had thrown another tantrum. He'd probably spend every second of his social life sharing my personal moment to everyone within earshot. I didn't like Kevin, Kevin was an asshole.

I pretended not to care as I headed for the doors to the studio. Without thought, I reached for my ID lanyard, but it wasn't there. I looked down, expecting to see it tucked into my pants pocket, but it wasn't. It wasn't there. Wasn't anywhere.

Typical. Just what I needed today. I walked back out of the door and across the park to the bench, hoping to see it lying discarded in the grass. But it wasn't. It wasn't anywhere nearby. I must have dropped it inside. I took a deep breath and swore to myself that I would buy the biggest bottle of red wine on the way home, and then I turned and plastered the most grotesquely polite smile on my face and walked back to receptionist *Kev*.

THE FATE OF GLASS

'Hey Kevin,' I said as cheerily as I could. 'Could you buzz me through? I think I left my badge inside.'

'Policy rules state I can't let you by without identification.' He said back, matching my fake joy.

'I know that, but I can't get in otherwise. I put it down between shots.'

'I'm sorry. I can't let you through without your ID card.'

'If it's inside, I can't show you it without getting inside.'

'Policy states...'

'I know what it states,' I said, losing my cool for a nanosecond. I paused, took a small breath, and smiled. 'Look, we both know I'm not having a great day here. Chalk it up to stress. I just need someone to take a little pity on me and give me a break. So can you please, *please* buzz me through?

Kevin's eyes warmed a little. A slither of humanity breaking through his stubborn outer shell. He gave me an honest smile.

'Policy states that anyone without an identification badge cannot be let through.' He grinned through giant, bleached teeth.

I leapt over the counter and wrapped my hands around his stupid throat.

By the time the cops arrived, I had completely broken down. The security guards had pulled me off Kevin and restrained me in their office. I had started to cry, which put the two burly security guards in a very awkward situation that neither was particularly capable of handling. They offered me coffee, but I was too far gone to respond. When the cops showed up, the guards took them aside and told them what had happened. Both officers were women. They took pity on me. They knew how it was. They'd dealt with their share of shit in this male-driven town. They drove me home, more out of courtesy than anything since dear old Kevin had been persuaded not to place charges. I thanked them, said I would take a few days off to rest, and promised not to assault any receptionists ever again.

They asked me if there was anyone they wanted me to call to come round, but there was no one. My parents were hardly going to travel all the way across the world from England to see me in a state, and I didn't want to worry them about my stupid life. I had made a point of spreading my wings by moving to America against their wishes, and I couldn't stand the thought of letting them know how bad an idea it had been.

There was only one person I wanted them to call. Quinn. But I refrained. I couldn't lead myself down that road again.

The moment the cops were out of sight, the tears were gone. The tap was switched off, replaced by something much worse. I was mad. Mad at myself. Mad at Kevin. At Galloway the drunk. And Michael the perfectionist. The city was a biased one. It was a place for the Kevins and Galloways and Michaels to get what they wanted without karma jumping up to bite them in the ass. It was a place where the Evas of the world struggled to pay their rent, and spent most nights alone in their apartment while the Kevins and Galloways and Michaels were out partying.

On top of the embarrassment I'd suffered today at work, I was locked out of my apartment. My phone, purse and keys had all been left behind at the studio. With the impending recasting sure to be headed my way, I didn't stand much chance of getting my things back anytime soon. Thank Christ for the spare key I'd left with Mrs Briggs in apartment two.

I slumped up the stairs, tapped on the door and stared at the pristinely polished number two brazened in bronze in the centre of the door. Mrs Briggs did not want for much, but she liked her world to be tidy. She was retired and twice widowed, and spent most of her retirement ensuring the apartment complex was as neat and orderly as possible. It was no surprise she had been elected chairwoman five consecutive times in a row. I liked Mrs Briggs. She had taken a shine for the plucky girl from England who had come all the way to America to follow her dreams. She shared my love for golden years of cinema and often offered to give me a lift to work so we could discuss the classics.

So it came as quite a surprise when she opened the door and scowled at me.

'Miss Marston.' She said through pursed lips.

'Hello Mrs Briggs,' I said, noticing the hostility in her voice. 'How are you today?'

'Perturbed,' she said, bluntly. 'I didn't sleep much, thanks to a certain *someone*.'

'Oh, I am sorry to hear that. I've had a tough day too.'

'Yes, I did happen to see the police car.' She eyed my outfit with utter disdain. 'I expected more from you.'

'No, it wasn't anything serious,' I said. 'I was robbed. A thug stole my purse, and the officers were kind enough to escort me home.'

THE FATE OF GLASS

Mrs Briggs softened up slightly at my lie.

'Oh,' she said. 'I suppose you will need your key.'

'If you wouldn't mind, that would be great.'

She shuffled away, returning moments later with the key I'd given her shortly after I'd moved in. She handed it over.

'I hope they catch the ruffian,' she said. 'And do please keep the noise down tonight.'

And with that, she closed the door in my face.

I frowned. I hadn't made any noise last night, none at all. I'd had a glass of wine with my meal and fallen asleep on the couch beside Mr Whiskers. I'd woken up an hour before my alarm was due to ring and spent the morning doing yoga. At no point had I been loud. But then, Mrs Briggs was a fussy woman and had many times stormed around the apartment building demanding residents to quiet down. I supposed eventually I would be one of her victims. Nevertheless, I climbed the stairs to my apartment and stuck the key in the door.

I should have spotted it immediately, but a whole host of other matters occupied my mind, so I didn't notice that the door was already unlocked. I didn't see the torn mail that I'd left unopened on the counter before I went to work, or the open cupboards that I'd not used for several weeks. I made it all the way through to my bedroom before something finally clicked in my brain.

Mr Whiskers wasn't there.

Every day since I'd adopted him, Mr Whiskers had met me at the door and rubbed his long black coat against my ankles until I fed him. It was our daily routine, our afternoon greeting. Sure, I was a couple of hours early, but that had never stopped him in the past. To him, my return meant the immediate arrival of food. It didn't matter to him how early I got back. I glanced around the room for him.

'Mr Whiskers?' I called. Usually, he would come trotting up when I called his name, but there was nothing. Had I left a window open? No, I hadn't touched the windows for ages. The air-con was more than enough to suffice. Besides, Mr Whiskers wouldn't risk his life by jumping out a window. He was probably curled up in some corner, bathed in the midday sunlight.

'Here, Mr Whiskers.' I called. I searched under the bed, in the wardrobe. The bathroom too was empty, as was the kitchen and the living room. All that remained was the spare bedroom. That had been Quinn's domain. These days I didn't feel the need to go in there, but that wouldn't bother Mr Whiskers. The door was slightly ajar. *I didn't remember leaving it open.* I pushed it gently.

Then I screamed.

The room was completely ransacked. Countless wide holes dotted around the drywall. The bed was upturned, and the mattress was ripped apart, scattering the innards across the room. But there was some much worse that drew my attention.

In the centre of the room lay Mr Whiskers.

His body had been cut open, and his guts strewn across the tattered mattress. His blood had soaked and splattered across almost every surface. His wide eyes stared up at the ceiling, cold and empty.

Something behind me moved ever so slightly. I barely noticed it. If not for my peripheral vision, it would have gone undetected. The shadow slipped forwards, and I felt a hand grasp around my mouth.

'Scream, and you will die like your cat,' a male voice growled. I felt a knife press against my throat. 'Do you understand?'

I nodded slowly.

The hand moved from my mouth, but the knife didn't.

'Good. You ought to get dressed. We're going to go for a little drive, Miss Marston.'

TWO

THE BURNED MAN

My body trembled. The straps around my wrists were tight, but even they couldn't contain the shaking. The wooden arms of the chair squeaked as they wiggled against their joints. Maybe one day I would shake them so much I could break free, but I probably wouldn't live that long.

The room was large and empty like an abandoned office space. The only light came through the large floor to ceiling windows that ran the length of the room to my left. No curtains. No need for privacy. No one would have a good enough view of the room to see what was happening inside. Through it, I could see the street. It was quiet, with only a couple of cars driving by in the time I dared to look.

'I'm going to ask you this one last time, Eva. Where is Isabella Reyes?'

I looked up at the man before me. He was Hispanic. Maybe mid-thirties. Maybe older. He was at the end of his patience, but he was hiding his anger well. His nostrils flared as he waited for an answer. But it was an answer I couldn't give.

'I don't know an Isabella Reyes,' I trembled. 'I've never heard of her before.'

'Don't lie to me,' he barked. 'I know just as well as you that you know her. You know her real well. I've seen the pictures. Don't you lie to me.'

'I promise you. I'm not lying. I would tell you if I knew. Please, please just understand.'

He slapped me hard across the face. The skin stung. I whimpered.

'You think this is bad?' He shouted. 'Can you even understand just how bad this is going to get? My boss, he's coming here right now. If you want all this to stop, you tell me what you know. But you better hustle. Otherwise he's going to bring holy hell down on you.'

Tears ran down my face.

'I promise you,' I cried. 'I've never met Isabella Reyes.'

He swung his fist again and struck me in the cheek. My neck snapped sideways.

Down below, twin headlight beams twisted towards the building as a car pulled off the street into the lot, and a small stream of light crept up and reflected against the roof. It lingered there for a moment, then vanished. Not long enough to alert anyone to our presence, but enough for the Hispanic man to give me a look that chilled me to the bone.

'Look's like your time's up.' He said.

I pulled against my restraints. Not intentionally. An involuntary act. As if my body knew what was approaching, and wanted any alternative. The restraints didn't budge. I was shackled to this fate. There was silence, broken only by my erratic breathing. My eyes locked on the door to the hallway. I felt like an antelope waiting for the lion to approach, knowing it was out there somewhere. The elevator out in the hall whirred into life and began its descent. There was a pause of about ten seconds, and then the pulleys and counterweights reversed, and the elevator ascended. I heard the jovial ping as it reached its destination, and the doors slid open.

And then footsteps.

With the only light in the room coming from outside, the rear corner of the room had swamped in shadow. A lone figure stepped through and looked across at the Hispanic man. He was tall and well built. He stood for a long moment in the shadows. Then he walked into the light.

I couldn't mask the gasp that escaped from my mouth. I had expected fear, but nothing of that magnitude. His face was horrendously scarred. The skin had warped and tensed across his skull from severe trauma, almost certainly an egregious burn. His features grievously distorted, yet the wounds looked fresh, so much so that I couldn't believe he wasn't in enormous pain. What little remained on his cheek was stretched back, leaving a crooked half smile. His

THE FATE OF GLASS

right eyelid was all but gone, which made the eyeball look in danger of falling out. He was bald, but I doubted that was through choice. His walk was firm and confident, like the pain from his wounds no longer afflicted him. Or maybe he was too strong to let it show. He wore a midnight blue suit, shirt and tie that looked like it cost more than most of the houses in the city.

The Hispanic man didn't look directly at him, but from his expression, he too feared what he saw. The burned man stopped a few feet short of my chair. He observed me.

'So this is the one?' He asked. His voice was cruel. His warped mouth extended some of the words. The S's elongated into a serpentine hiss.

'There's been a mistake' I begged. 'You've got the wrong person. I don't know any-'

'Speak when spoken to,' the burned man hissed. 'Or you will regret it.'

My jaw shook. I didn't speak again.

'Did you search her apartment?' the burned man asked of his subordinate. 'Did you find anything?'

The man named Marco shook his head.

'She claims she doesn't know where Reyes is,' he said. 'But it's her. We searched. Doesn't look like she has been there in a long time. But we found photographs of the two together in her apartment.'

'So she is useless?'

'Hard to say. My gut says she hasn't had any contact with Reyes for a while. Especially not since her old man split. The place was like a shrine to her.'

A shrine?

The burned man looked at me.

'You. Your name is?'

'Eva Marston.' I whispered.

'Eva. I'm going to take a page out of my father's book. He liked to offer people a choice. give them some control of their fate. He found it worked well. So I'm going to give you two choices. Your first choice is to come clean and tell me everything you know about Isabella Reyes, where I can find her, and I will let you go. Or you keep up this tired charade, and you and I are going to go for a ride out to one of my warehouses. I will drill holes through both of your hands and hang you up on a hook, just high enough so that your feet can't touch the ground. Then, I will cut out your tongue and leave you with my rats. They love to eat, especially when they're hungry, and they haven't eaten in a long time.'

He forced a smile.

'So, Miss Marston, what is your answer?'

I trembled. My mind was a scrambled mess.

'Please, I don't know. I'm sorry. I'm so, so sorry.'

'She's stalling,' Marco huffed.

The burned man cracked his neck. The tight skin stretched and split slightly. A trickle of blood ran down from his chin and under his collar.

'Then option two it is.' He hissed.

He lurched forward and grabbed hold of my wrist.

'No, please,' I screamed. 'I don't know anyone called Isabella. Please, just let me go.'

He ignored my pleas. His grip was deathly cold. I tried to wriggle free, but his fingers dug into my skin, and the straps were too tight. Marco approached from behind and grabbed hold of my throat. His hands were warm and sweaty. A stark contrast to his boss.

Together, they untied my binds and threw me down onto the ground. I landed on my front, and my face slid against the carpet. I had to escape. What the burned man described was a fate worse than death. I scrambled to my knees, but before I could make a move, I felt something cold press into the base of my skull.

'Make one wrong move, and I will blow your pretty little head across this whole damn room.' It was Marco. His free hand grasped at my shirt, and he pulled me to my feet. A quick nudge to the back of the head was a clear message. Cooperate, or this gets a lot worse. I tried to force my mind to oblige and willed myself to take another step.

I heard the buzz of a cell phone.

'Stop.' Marco ordered.

I did as I was told, and out of the corner of my eye, I glanced back. The burned man pulled the phone from his jacket pocket and answered the call. He didn't speak for the duration of the thirty-second conversation, but I could tell it was bad news. His eyes flared, and his jaw tightened. The skin on his face stretched and turned white. He ended the call and thrust the phone back into his pocket.

'Things have escalated,' the burned man growled, emphasising the last word with a hiss. 'Stay here with the girl. Don't let anyone in this room without my consent.'

His bright eyes seared into my soul.

'It seems you've caught yourself a break, little girl. Perhaps if you can survive the night, then maybe we can have our fun in the morning. My rats will *love* to meet you.'

My stomach turned at the thought.

Marco clipped me with the gun and ordered me back to my seat. As he tightened my bonds, the burned man stormed from the room. I couldn't control the tears. They trickled down my cheeks and down onto my lips. I was going to die for a person I'd never even met.

I wept quietly as the elevator descended, and the headlights danced across the ceiling and out of view. I was going to die before I'd even had the chance to live. There were so many things I wanted to do. I'd never been to Paris, or New York, or even Hollywood itself. I'd never seen my name up on the big screen or heard the crowds scream with delight when they saw me. I was going to die and be replaced in Galloway's dreadful film and be forgotten about before the dawn came.

'You don't have to do this,' I said quietly. 'Please, I don't know anyone called Isabella. You know that.'

'Shut the hell up, unless you want me to do to you what I did to your cat.'

My throat closed up. The sight of Mr Whiskers, dead on the bed, sent a tidal wave of emotion through my body. I wanted to scream. I wanted to strangle this vicious man to death.

'He did nothing to you!' I gasped, unable to hold back the tears. 'He was the sweetest, friendliest cat. And you murdered him.'

I watching his thin mouth twist into a smirk. Slowly, he turned away from the window and glared at me.

'Shit happens.'

THREE

WHERE MONSTERS LURK

I sat at the bar and drank alone. No one bothered me. No one asked if they could join me. It wasn't that kind of place. No tipsy singles searching for love. No tired couples enjoying a drink together after a long day at the office. They would avoid this place like the plague, seeking refuge in classier establishments across the city where the good vibrations made up for the jacked up prices. This was a place of solemn silence where strangers sought solace in the bottom of a bottle.

A group of sedated sheep, all unaware of the wolf among them.

It was only my second beer, yet it was to be my last for the night. I didn't want to go any further, and as much as my body craved the idea of just letting go, I knew I needed to stay sober. I had the van outside, as always, and while I wouldn't be swanning off on some major excursion, I didn't want to risk being pulled over. These American beers weren't as intoxicating as the stuff back home, but even so, two was my limit for tonight.

It was my third night at the bar. The first had been a little daunting. From the outside, the bar had a distinctive end-of-the-road feel to it. The stone was a dark charcoal colour, as though it had suffered through a fire but not given up. The windows had bars on the outside, and the glass was tremendously unclean. Even the palms trees swaying gently in the breeze looked haggard and exhausted. Dressed in a pair of denim jeans, a charcoal coat and a plain grey t-shirt, I doubted I was going to fit in well.

I was right.

THE FATE OF GLASS

On the inside, the bar looked even more dismal. The room was dank and smelt of stale cigarettes and regret. The hanging lights let out a weak yellow glow, as though afraid of exposing the patrons below. It reminded me of a prison. Each gang huddled up around tables in every corner, ready for combat. I'd attracted the attention of almost every patron, which in a place like this was the last thing you wanted. But after I'd sat down and ordered my drink without causing a major ruckus, those wandering eyes had returned to their drinks and left me be.

The only difference between that night and the following two was that I'd attempted to engage the bartender in conversation. That was what you did, right? Especially in America. They were supposed to be a chatty bunch. Not here. The portly woman tending the bar whose namesake hung over the door had been as loquacious as an old boot and had ended my attempts with a shutdown that packed as much punch as a shotgun.

'Don't ask questions, sweetheart.'

So I'd sat and drank my two beers every night and watched everything and nothing until it was time for me to depart. No more questions. No more disturbances. Just watching and waiting and drinking.

The other main difference between the first night and the third was the gang that lingered at the back of the room. They were a lively bunch. Young and dangerous. They were heavily tattooed and had bright, wild eyes. They twitched and jerked like only those on drugs seem capable of. The man in the centre of the table locked eyes with me and held it. He gripped his drink so hard, I was surprised the glass didn't smash.

But they paid me no mind, so I returned the favour. The bartender's vigil did not waver once. While she busied herself with the other patrons, I felt her gaze linger over me like a spotlight in a prison. But she had burned the bridge of communication herself, which was fine by me, so long as she didn't realise who I was. I sipped my beer right down to the dregs, wishing I could chance a third, and nudged a thick glass ashtray back and forth across the bar like a bored kitten. It seemed tonight was going to be a right off as well, just as the previous two had been. That was a shame. I didn't know how much time I could waste coming back to this place without any progress. Time waits for no man, and the same can be said for nemeses.

Was it nemeses, or nemisi, or nemisises? None sounded particularly right, but such was the English language. Frequently nonsensical.

I could feel the eyes of the young gang on me. They didn't like a stranger in their midst, that much was clear. Their eyes followed me everywhere I went, which wasn't exactly far. Only one trip to the bathroom in the two hours I was there. They talked amongst themselves, just like every other gang in the bar. I could feel my welcome becoming outstayed. I was just about to finish my drink and leave when something finally happened.

The leader of the young pack pulled out his phone and stared at the screen. I couldn't see what it said, nor the muffled command he gave to the others at his table. Out the corner of my eye, I saw him get to his feet and drop a sizeable wad of cash down on the table for the others. They looked at it in glee, with some patting him on the arm in appreciation. With an overtly ridiculous swagger, the young man made for the door. As he approached, I finished my drink, dropped a crisp twenty on the bar, and moved from my seat at the bar.

He was no more than a couple of feet from me, his attention elsewhere. He barely noticed as I staggered sideways into him, knocking him off his stride.

'Yo watch it, asshole!' He barked at me. He was several years younger than me, no older than a teen.

'Sorry,' I slurred. 'Must've slipped.'

He looked at me with the disdain one gives a drunken fool. His response was his middle finger raised tall and proud just inches from my face. I shooed it away like a fly and smiled drunkenly at him. He turned and headed for the door once more, his friends at the table chuckled to themselves. There was no fight to be had with the drunkard.

I gave the leader a head start before I followed. I clutched the item in my hand. The art of pickpocketing was one I'd learned a long time ago, back when I was just a cheeky school kid with a flair for the risqué. It was a skill that had come in use on many occasions in my adult life, especially since everything had gone to shit. Be it a wallet or a passport, or some cocky kid's phone, it had saved my arse more than once.

And got me in the shit a few times as well.

But the kid hadn't realised, yet. His was a flip phone, which made it small, and easy to go unnoticed. I watched him push through the exit and saunter away into the night unaware that he had

THE FATE OF GLASS

just been robbed. He moved slowly, enjoying the evening breeze as he made his way over towards a battered convertible with the roof down. He made it halfway across the lot before he stuffed his hand into his pocket and realised what was missing.

I held back and leaned against the side of a van parked up in the lot. My own van was up on the street about one hundred yards from where the kid was having an internal crisis. If I needed to get to it in a hurry, I could. But for now, I just lurked in the shadows and watched with mild contempt. The kid patted at each of his pockets in turn, then looked around on the floor to see if he had dropped the phone. Having no luck, he swore to himself and headed back towards the bar.

I didn't bother to wait for him to make it the whole way inside. He wasn't about to turn around halfway and give up now. I slipped around the rear of the van and headed for his car. I reached it as I heard the distant thump of a door being forced open. I figured I had about a minute, maybe two if the kid tried to get one of his friends to call the phone. I slipped the phone into my trouser pocket and swung open the passenger door of the convertible. It wasn't locked. No need when anyone could just climb inside. The kid probably relied on his street credentials to dissuade people from attempting to carjack him.

But not me. I sat down on the worn leather seat and opened the glovebox. I just needed something, anything that could point me in the right direction. I had the phone, which was a good start, but phone numbers meant nothing without a location. There was a whole lot of crap stuffed into the small compartment, most of which was better suited in a rubbish bin. I threw aside the heaps of garbage, searching for something of use. I found a working plastic lighter, which I pocketed. But there was no notebook or hastily-scribbled address on the back of a sheet of paper. In my pocket, I felt the phone vibrate. I pulled it out and saw that there was a new message on the screen.

Jorge, it's me. You got the stuff? Call me back. CJ

I returned the phone to my pocket, so this guy was called Jorge. Always good to know a name. *Well, I'd feel sorry for you Jorge if you weren't such a prick.* I stuffed the contents that had spilt out into the footwell back into the glovebox and looked around. I rummaged under the seats - an act I instantly regretted as my hand touched something damp - and checked the small storage compartments in the doors. Nothing. That was a disappointment. I really could have used a win. I swung open the door and climbed out.

And spotted Jorge himself storming back across the parking lot.

He had noticed me. The lot was not all too dark, and my actions not all too subtle. He stopped briefly as the shock of the moment caught up with him.

Then he ran towards me. Fight, not flight. As he ran, he pulled something out of his trousers and held it up in front of him. There were no prizes for guessing what it was. It wasn't the first time I'd come face to barrel with a firearm. The first time had been accompanied with heart-stopping shock, and while the experience had not exactly grown any fonder over the years, it had at least become a little more predictable.

'Yo, what the hell do you think you're playing at?' Jorge barked behind the safety of his pistol.

'Sorry,' I said. 'I've always wanted to have a go in a car like this. And I've got to say, yours was an enormous disappointment.'

'You think you can come around here messing with people's stuff. You've got a lot of nerve.'

I watched the man behind the trigger stare furiously into my eyes. His body was twitching. Not enormously, but enough that the pistol in his hand wobbled. Definitely on something. Drugs made people erratic, which at the best of times was an inconvenience, and at the business end of a pistol was practically a death sentence. This close, it was remarkable just how young he looked. He had to be somewhere in his late teens or early twenties at best. The body had run the marathon of puberty and was in a heap a couple of yards over the finish line. Even so, his mind still had a way to go before it reached true maturity. If Jorge was a smart man, he'd understand the ramifications of committing murder, even if I was a globally-hunted terrorist.

But he was also high, so clearly he wasn't in the business of making smart decisions.

'You know, you really should clean it out once in a while.' I said. 'Or are you just more comfortable living in your own filth?'

That got him riled up. I could see his eyes flare with anger.

'Get down on your knees.' He snapped.

'You first.' I replied nonchalantly. The key was establishing dominance over him. He was boisterous enough to hate being talked down to. He figured waving a firearm in my face gave him power. I needed him to know he was wrong. From the tip of his pistol, he was about three feet away from me with his finger on the trigger.

I stepped forwards and closed the gap by a foot.

'I ain't here to take orders from you.' He snorted. His nostrils flared.

'I tell you what, I'll do what you want if you answer a riddle.'

'You think this is a game son?' He snapped. He wanted me scared, and the lack of fear was starting to seriously piss him off.

'Come on, it's a good one. What's the one thing you can eat that eats you back?'

His expression changed again, this time from anger to confusion. The confrontation wasn't going how he'd expected.

'I don't know, a shark?' He said eventually.

'A shark? Are you kidding me?' I laughed. 'Come on mate, since when could a shark eat you while you were eating it? I'd expect more from a child.'

He thrust the pistol forwards until the cold metal was just inches from my face. Big mistake, but I wasn't in the clear just yet. I had to move half a foot to be clear of taking a bullet to the face, and all he had to do was squeeze his finger a fraction.

'Yo, you better show some respect.' He growled. My tactic was working. The mixture of drugs and rage was clouding his judgement.

'Where's all this aggression coming from man? Is this because I stole your phone?' I asked. 'You know, you should have said something if you wanted it back.'

'You took my cell?'

'Well, yeah. You weren't using it were you? I can give it back if you like?'

Slowly, I moved my hand across to the pocket I had stashed his phone. My coat pocket swayed as I brushed the heavy object tucked deep inside. I pulled out Jorge's phone and held it up.

'Yo give it back!' He shouted at me.

'But of course.' I smiled, tossing the phone in his direction.

It bounced off his chest and dropped to the ground just a few feet to our right facing upright. Jorge scowled at me. I slipped my hands into my coat pockets.

'Sorry,' I said. 'Butterfingers.'

His body moved like clockwork, nice and predictable. He took a half-step back and knelt down, using his free hand to reach out for his discarded phone. I waited until his eyes broke contact with mine, then I moved into action.

Because Jorge's phone was not the only thing I'd stolen in the bar. The weight of the thick glass ashtray was about that of a house brick, and about the strongest improv weapon in the bar that wasn't bolted to the ground. Getting it out of my coat pocket took less than a second, and I used the gaining momentum to swing it around into Jorge's weapon with as much force as I could muster. It slapped into the side of the pistol right along the grip, which meant that not only did it cause the firearm to carrell out of my way, but it also crushed the young man's fingers between the two solid objects.

Jorge let out a yelp that only heightened his canine demeanour and let go of the weapon. The pistol clattered away, coming to a stop under a nearby vehicle. Jorge, shocked and angered, tried to scramble to his feet. He would need to show a lot more bravado to win this fight now that I'd bereft him of his firearm. But sadly, he was not destined for that fate. With a backward swing of the arm, I brought the heavy ashtray crashing down into his left cheekbone. It was enough to knock him back off his feet.

'You fucking psycho!' He shouted, scrambling away from me.

'Oh come now, Jorge. There's no need for name calling now, is there?'

He glared at me as he finally got to his feet. For a second, I thought he wanted to go for another attack, or run back inside and call on his friends for backup. I took a step forward, raising the ashtray up to put the young fool in his place, and the thought of retaliation died about as quick as it had appeared.

'You best be running along now,' I said to him, allowing him space to make it back to his car.

He didn't need telling twice. Without another word, he skirted around, keeping a sizeable distance away from me, and jumped into his battered convertible. As he screeched away, I heard him shout the word "Puta" at me. And just like that, Jorge raced from sight. He hadn't even bothered to pick up his phone. I took both it and the discarded pistol, stored both in my coat pockets, and hurled the ashtray out of sight. Then ran down the road towards my van.

Because I wasn't done with Jorge yet.

FOUR

ON THE HUNT

ONE MIGHT WONDER THE PRACTICAL BENEFITS OF TAILING AN erratic man high on drugs who'd just shoved a dangerous firearm right in your face. It would be a relatively astute concern, given the circumstances. It's certainly one I considered in the prelude to said decision. I had to. It's a considerable risk, after all, to give a man already content with the idea of murdering a particularly intrusive stranger a second chance to do the deed. But in this circumstance, the pros outweighed the cons.

I'd come across the enigma that is Jorge just three days ago. Finding him had been both a coincidence and a blessing in disguise. The man himself was hardly anything special. A jumped up dealer at best. But he was a branch, strong and full of life, ready to be climbed.

Miami was a remarkable city. I'd never given any thought to visiting during my former life as a regular guy, but upon my arrival, I was pleased that the circumstances hadn't taken me to the arse end of nowhere instead. Even in November, it was warm, bright and vibrant. My nights asleep in the back of the van had been comfortable, to say the least.

The van had been a wise choice made many weeks ago. The biggest problem with being a fugitive was the constant fear of being recognised. The name James Stone was still too toxic to go unnoticed, even in a city I had no affiliations with. Staying in motels or eating in restaurants spiked that likelihood tenfold, but in the comfort of my secure van, I felt safer than I had in months. Bought from a guy whose waist stretched further than his morals, the white Chevy was definitely not worth the six thousand dollars in cash that I'd paid. He'd probably thought I was some idiot Brit who hadn't worked out the exchange rate on the flight over the pond, and I was more than happy for him to keep thinking that way. Little did he know that money was of no issue to me. It was but a drop in the ocean of my current funds.

All two million dollars, minus a couple thousand dollars of change for handling any impromptu payments, was not actually with me at the moment. I didn't want to risk some little prick busting open the van while I was out, and discovering a fortune big enough to swim in. So the remainder of the cash sat in a nondescript holdall tucked inside a padlocked gym locker on the outskirts of the city, where it would remain safe until I'd finished my business here.

That kind of money doesn't simply fall into your lap. It was the reward of chaos. The fallout of an explosive endeavour that had started when a wild-eyed stranger sat down opposite me in a diner outside New York and had ended with an actual explosion. Her name was Nicole, and she had looked at me with a smile that I knew would get me into trouble. Yet for some reason, I let her into my life with all of her unique baggage, both emotional and physical.

The physical took the rather surprising manifestation of a rucksack packed full of stolen cash, and the emotional baggage brought the problems that typically follow such a fortuitous circumstance. Over the course of just a couple of weeks, I came to realise just how damaging she was. The two million dollars had been hers by the law of thieves. Stolen from her now-deceased psycho ex-boyfriend, who had in turn purloined it from his now-deceased psycho ex-employer, I too had taken up the mantle of thievery, and snatched it from Nicole as the dust settled. Chivalrous? Perhaps not, but Nicole had denied her right to the money when she sold me out to the man who had brought me to this country. Changing her mind halfway through did little to grow back the end of my finger, which that had severed at my reunion with a madman.

His name was Ramiro Salazar, son of the reviled Hector Salazar, and he was every bit the bastard of his father. He had squeezed me into a crate just small enough to ensure insanity, and shipped me across the planet to America. All so that he could subject me to his perverse desires and torture me with his friends. Escape had come by chance, and as I'd fled the city, I thought I'd seen the last of his soulless eyes. But that was not to be the case.

Which brought me back to the matter at hand. Why follow lovable buffoon, Jorge? It's simple. He was my gateway to Ramiro Salazar.

In the fallout of his father's demise, Ramiro had to make a choice. Either he could succumb to the near-fatal burns he had received as his father's house was destroyed, hole up and try to recover before his next plan of action. Or he could frantically struggle to regain control of his father's empire.

Hector Salazar, as I had learned from online articles in the weeks following his demise, was a ruthlessly tenacious businessman for over fifty years. Across his lifetime, his empire was valued at around one billion dollars. Every single cent coated in blood. Most came from trafficking drugs. Cocaine and methamphetamine. But it hadn't stopped there. Arms, counterfeit goods, and even humans, all adding to his considerable wealth. His power was tantamount to no one. The FBI, DEA, and CIA had all taken a run at him over the years, yet somehow, he had thwarted them all, time after time, like they were nothing. The American Pablo Escobar, although in truth, Escobar had been the Colombian Hector Salazar. No one came close to him. For over half a century, he had been untouchable.

And I had taken him out with a sippy cup.

No sooner had his body turned cold did his empire come crashing down. Miami had always been his city. He had built it with his bare hands. You couldn't count the number of local businesses that had risen to success on his coattails. It was the beating heart of his entire operation, and it all went into cardiac arrest a second after his own heart gave in. The newspapers had squawked about the whole affair. It was hardly a subtle phenomenon. Hector Salazar had ruled with an iron fist. His men in equal parts feared and respected him. Part of this came from the control and respect he gave to those closest to him. His lieutenants had been trusted with not just Salazar's life, but his empire too.

But before the ink was dry on the newspapers, his lieutenants had disowned him. The king had been usurped, and there was a throne ripe for the taking. So much for honour amongst thieves. The bonds forged over fifty years were broken, and the fight for the crown had begun. But not everyone sought after crumbling remains of the Salazar empire. Those people had either been fast enough to jump ship or wavered long enough for the authorities to come knocking. The cops had gone over the remains of the Salazar estate with a fine comb and used his death as the collateral they needed to make some serious waves with their prosecution. That ripple had worked its way down into every echelon of the Salazar empire, taking everyone with it.

No place was this fact worse than in the town he had built himself. In the weeks since his death, there hadn't been a day where the ongoing power struggle in Miami hadn't made the newspapers. If Ramiro Salazar was anywhere, he would be right in the heart of the conflict. He was not the kind of man to shirk his birthright, no matter how sore his wounds were. His was an ego of unsurmountable heights. His father had spent a lifetime building an empire, and now Ramiro had to step up.

I had heard the whispers of his arrival. People spoke of the burned man like he was some kind of myth. The horribly disfigured man that had swooped in from the North to take control of the ashes. Some knew he was the son of the late Hector Salazar, but most had no idea. That made him a wild card. A ghost. And as it turned out, tracking down a ghost wasn't the easiest thing in the world to do.

Which was why Jorge was so important. He was young and brash, which made him equal parts cocky and moronic. He stuck to ideals born out of fantastical notions of loyalty. He must have watched the Godfather on repeat as a child. He had observed the people in the uppermost echelons of the Salazar empire turn on one another and had looked on them with great disdain. He wouldn't turn his back on the adopted family that would have sooner shot him in the face than given a pat on the back. He watched and waited for the son of Salazar to return. And when he did, Jorge shouted it from the damn rooftops.

I'd stopped at the bar by happenstance. After a series of failed attempts to track down the man in question, I wanted a beer, and I wanted anonymity, which came no better than in a sleazy establishment such as Bennett's Bar. I'd sat down and taken my first sip when Jorge and his cohorts sauntered in. They were in deep admiration of their leader, who bragged openly about getting to meet the man himself. I hadn't paid them any mind until the name Salazar made my ears prick up and the hairs on my neck stand to attention. I knew I couldn't walk right up to them and ask, nor did I see any chance to pursue them as a group. Both ran the risk of calling undue attention to myself, which was the last thing I wanted.

The name James Stone struck fear into a lot of people all across the globe. The reporter who had lost his way in Afghanistan and

THE FATE OF GLASS

returned to England years later a traitor was a story I had fought to dispute. Fabricated evidence, false testimonies, and lots of bad luck was a difficult fight to win singlehandedly. I left the Middle East a tainted man, and had it not been for a series of unexpected circumstances, I would be dead. My name besmirched, my family betrayed, my life destroyed.

Yet here I was, a wanted man in a foreign country, thousands of miles from a family I didn't know whether or not were still alive. I was here by the grace of a God I didn't believe in, following a doped-up teenager that I'd just hit in the face with a glass ashtray.

I wasn't sure where my unknowing guide was taking me. Poor Jorge might just be heading home to lick his wounds. If that were the case, I figured I might as well pop in and have a lovely chat with the begrudging lad over a cup of tea regarding the whereabouts of his beloved employer. I had been known to be somewhat charming when push came to shove, and without the backup of his cohorts, I was sure I could get Jorge to open up.

The clock on the van's dashboard said it was quarter past nine in the evening. The sun had set, the streetlights were on, and there was little to see out of the window that their golden glare didn't reach. That being said, I could already tell that we were moving in a much more affluent area. Bennett's Bar had been a place for low morals and meagre paycheques. But the further we drove, the more apparent it became that the people nestled comfortably behind the thick walls and bright windows that past by in a blur were not the sort who frequented such seedy soirees. Nevertheless, Jorge weaved through the meandering streets towards an unknown destination.

Tailing the young man was a ludicrously easy task. A few drinks, a couple of joints and the burning rage of a battered ego does not a wise man make. Even if Jorge was furtively searching his rearview mirror for signs of a tail, I was confident that he would not spot me. He hadn't seen me arrive or depart in the van, and as far as he knew, I was just some random jerk who he'd picked a fight with and lost. So long as I hung back and hid behind the anonymity of the van's headlights, he could no sooner discern me from any of the thousands of vehicles on the road in Miami. All I had to do was keep him in my sights, and let him lead the way.

I was sure that wherever it was he drove to, it was a destination chosen of conscious thought. His actions weren't those of a man blowing off steam driving aimlessly through the night. The twists and turns he took through the evening streets were calculated.

That calculation came to fruition twenty-seven minutes later. The building was far from what I expected. Not another seedy hangout. A lavish block of apartments with massive floor to ceiling windows stretching across the five stories. The view from the upper floors must be spectacular on a morning, with the Easterly sun rising up over the North Atlantic Ocean. That view alone must have skyrocketed the value of the property.

Jorge pulled his convertible up to the kerb just a stone's throw from the driveway but kept the engine running. I hung back and waited. Was he waiting for someone? That question was answered moments later when the snarl of an enormous black Mustang shattered the sleepy evening silence and pulled out of the driveway and onto the street. The mammoth vehicle slowed as it passed Jorge, then bellowed as thousands of tiny horses under the hood kicked into life sent it galloping towards me. It shot by in an instant and disappeared long before the sound of the powerful engine faded away. An expensive car for a wealthy neighbourhood. Both my van and I stuck out like a pair of sore thumbs in a place like this, as did Jorge and his busted old convertible.

I glanced back to watch him pull into the recently vacated space and climb out. With renewed swagger, Jorge hustled over to the door of the building and waited patiently for someone to let him in. From the van, I could just about make him out. It looked like he was speaking, probably via an intercom, to someone inside. A fact I was doubly sure of when the door swung open a few seconds later, and he sauntered through the dimly lit entrance alone.

I switched off the engine but did not follow. There was no point, yet. Jorge was unlikely to leave soon, and even if he did, I would have ample time to resume my pursuit. But I had a feeling that my time following the idiot had come to an end. Whatever his reason for coming to this place, I felt it held more importance to my mission than any other place he could have gone. He certainly didn't live here, not dressed like an imbecile. Instead, I climbed out of the driver seat, walked around to the rear doors and got in.

The inflatable mattress took up most of the available space, and what was left was taken up with my provisions. Dozens upon dozens of canned goods and bottled water had been bought in bulk at a large chain camping store on my way to Miami.

To keep the van's battery from draining, I'd bought a small LED light, which I'd fixed to the ceiling with a little duct tape. I switched it on and pulled Jorge's pistol and phone from my coat pockets and placed them on the mattress. The gun had a full clip, always a bonus, and the phone's battery had around half of its charge remaining.

Getting into the building was going to be the tricky part. The relative calm of the surrounding neighbourhood meant that any loud approach was off the table, not that I would have opted for such anyway. There was no telling who was inside or how many. Just because I had one guy's gun, that didn't suddenly mean I could go in guns blazing and expect to walk away without a scratch.

Well, not with my weapon being so gosh darn loud at least.

I had taken a few liberties with my mobile home. I wasn't a savage after all. The midday November heat was still enough to make an Englishman irritable, and opening the windows was apparently an open invite for the entire city's population of flies to come nosing around. To counter that issue, I had a roll of fine wire mesh that hung down across the open window, barring all from unwanted entry. But it served a greater purpose now, so I pulled it free.

Just because I was a wanted felon, it didn't mean I didn't have standards. I liked my mobile home clean. That went for the tins of food too. Once used, I would clean them out. You could never know when a small collection of seeming useless rubbish would suddenly find a purpose. While the cans would have to wait for their time to shine, the steel scourer I used to scrub out the leftover food scraps was about to have its five minutes of fame. I took one of the bottles of water, drank half, then used the other half to wash free any scraps of dirt from both the mesh and the scourer.

With a knife, I cut the bottom fifth of the water bottle free, then cut a small circle into the centre of the base. Next up, I rolled up the mesh into a cylinder that fit snugly into the mouth of the water bottle, which I then reinforced with a strip of duct tape so that it didn't lose its shape. I nestled it into the bottle, and packed the scourer into the remaining space, and taped the bottom fifth of the bottle back into place with the cylindrical mesh role sticking out the hole I'd cut. Once satisfied that the whole thing was secure, I took one of the bullets from the magazine and dropped it down the tube. It fell through with no resistance. Good.

The mouth of the bottle slid comfortably onto the muzzle of the pistol, which with another strip of duct tape, secured the rudimentary contraption with ease.

And there it was, a poor man's silencer.

FIVE

SHIT HAPPENS

The night was dark, yet there was an electric energy in the air. Like an excited crowd before the main act, something big was coming. I crossed the street and clung to the shadows between streetlights. Even though Jorge was out of sight, it didn't mean there weren't cameras watching me. I tried to act natural. Just a man out for an evening stroll. Nothing special. My clothes were far from the sort adorned by those tucked up inside the multi-million dollar homes that lined the streets, but that didn't matter. It wasn't a crime to dress on a budget. With the pair of mirrored aviators tucked into the neckline of my t-shirt, and the baseball cap pulled low on my head, I could blend easily into most suburban scenes. Anonymity at its finest.

I tucked the stolen pistol in my coat pocket. Makeshift silencer pointed up. To a passerby, it looked like I'd done nothing more than place an empty bottle in my pocket. Their surprising depth had been the deciding factor for this particular coat. You never knew when you needed to conceal something easily.

I walked casually, head bowed, by the building Jorge had entered. The ground floor of the structure was taken up by a row of four garages, all locked. Aside from Jorge's convertible, there was only one other car parked up. It was a light blue, five-door Chevrolet. Not the sort of car that sat well next to something as shabby as Jorge's wreck. If the building was a block of apartments - as the series of garages would suggest - then there could be any number of civilians inside. From a quick scan, I couldn't see any cameras

THE FATE OF GLASS

around the building. I figured there would be a small one above the front door to give the tenants a chance to see who was ringing their bell.

Through the large windows, I couldn't see any signs of life. No lights on. No movement. *Strange*. If the building was a block of apartments, there should be something, even just the glow of a floor lamp to give the impression of occupancy. The hour was late, and most people would be winding down for the night.

I walked across to the front door and looked at the small console beside the handle. Sure enough, there were sixteen available buttons, yet in the space next to each where one would expect to find the name of the resident, there was nothing. The building looked new, but not enough to still be vacant. Which meant knocking on the front door would be a problem.

Nor was I getting around to the back of the property without a lot of trespassing and a high degree of danger. The houses on both sides had built up walls that stretched high above my head. A straightforward, effective form of security. And I could see why. The house prices here were steep, and I had no doubt the contents inside were just as valuable. But it also meant that a tall wall was the least of my concerns if I tried to cross by. Security systems had turned into the stuff of science fiction in recent years, and I was no master of their intricacies.

The gleam from the streetlights reached far enough to cast a dim light over the front of the building. Anyone walking by would spot me, and could call the cops if I started trying to tamper with the front door. The same went for the garage doors.

So I needed to change my tactics. Perhaps it wasn't a case of doing the heavy lifting myself. Jorge had been competent enough to understand how to open a door. All I needed to do was get him to repeat the process. I looked at the two stationary cars parked outside the building. Of the two, Jorge's car looked easiest to steal, but was that any good if it didn't attract inside attention? I could make it to the next state before Jorge realised it wasn't parked up outside. The Chevrolet was newer, nicer and probably came at a higher price. The kind of people who bought something like it probably didn't revel the thought that someone might come along and steal it. They would probably spring for the available extras, like a loud alarm system.

Which was good for me.

I hustled back up to the van and climbed inside. I grabbed the duct tape and peeled off a small strip, stuck it to the back of my hand for safekeeping, and snatched up the lighter I'd knocked from Jorge's car.

Plastic lighters were a genius invention if you knew how to use them. I removed the flame guard from the top of the lighter and slid the ratchet to the right, increasing the flame height to the maximum. Then I lifted the ratchet up, disconnecting it, and slid it back left to minimise flame height, before pushing it back down into place. I repeated the process, again and again until the gas began to leak without help.

Back out of the van, and hiding beside the Chevrolet, I took the strip of tape and placed it over the lower body of the lighter, then taped it onto the front left tyre with the metal end pointed down, and struck a light.

With no dedicated light pointing over it, the building entrance was poorly lit. It was a run of the mill, hinged door with a thick sheet of glass running down the length of it on either side. Standing on the outside, you would have to pull the door towards you to open it, letting it swing left towards the tall brick wall separating it from the house next door. As such, there was a small gap in the recess to allow the door to swing open wide without bouncing off the wall. A space, as it happened, just big enough for a fully grown man with a silenced pistol to hide and wait.

With a steady stream of leaking gas to keep it going, the flame of the lighter burned strong. The small flickering flame was barely noticeable. So with no one to object to its existence, the flame stood proud and stoic in the evening air, steadily melting the plastic that contained the small deposit of flammable liquid.

It was, as they say in the business, an accident waiting to happen.

The explosion was louder than I had anticipated for such a small device. The burst of the tyre sounded like miniature canon fire, and echoed through the evening sky, drowned out only by the piercing car alarm that came a split second after the rubber had shred into a million little pieces. Even though I had expected it, I winced at the abrupt disruption. Across the street, I saw a couple of windows light up as nosey neighbours sought the source of the sudden sound.

It was just a matter of time. I kept myself pressed up against the wall behind the door and waited. It took less than a minute. Out of the corner of my eye, I saw automatic lights flicker on, illuminating hurried movement in the corridor. The door burst open, and a man ran out into the open. It wasn't Jorge. This guy was older. The short hair on his head flicked back and forth as he scanned for some sign of attack. I caught the door handle and held onto it until the new guy moved over to his car. He knelt down beside the burst tyre and swore.

Tough luck mate, but as the Pope said, "shit happens."

I didn't wait around for him to get over his loss. I ducked in through the open door and, once satisfied there was no one else loitering in the corridor, hustled as stealthily as I could deeper inside.

If I hadn't been before, I was now certain that the building was designed as a block of apartments. Along the left side of the entrance was a series of sixteen mailboxes. They had that untouched, pristine look of a forgotten relic in a lost city. Opposite them were two elevators, both of which were stationed on the ground floor. I left them be, and took the door for the staircase. The automatic lights flicked on in the stairwell as the motion sensors detected movement. Not ideal for remaining hidden, but their presence also meant that this particular space was dormant.

I moved up to the first floor and opened the door as gently as I could. Again, the lights flickered on in mild desperation to cater to their newly arrived guest. But as no one burst through any of the doors lining the hallway, I figured that this was not the place I wanted.

I moved up to the floor above. As I approached, I caught sight of the faint glimmer of light peeking through a thin window just above the door-handle. *Here be monsters*. I peered through the meshed wire glass for any passersby. Nothing. As carefully as I could, I twisted the handle and heaved the thick fire-resistant door inwards.

I slid out through the smallest gap I could make, and edged into the all too accusatory glare for the strip lights mounted on the ceiling. The hallway snaked around the corner and ran down what I guessed to be the centre of the building. With two doors on either side of the corridor, spaced out wide enough to give each prospective tenant some distance from their neighbours, I could see the nearest door - which faced out towards the street - had been left wide open. All other doors remained closed. It didn't take a genius to guess which room piqued my interest.

I slid the pistol and makeshift silencer out of my pocket and - after ensuring the silencer hadn't dislodged enough to truly roger me in the midst of battle - brought it up ahead of me. The absurdity of the creation was not lost on me, but if it gave me the edge, that was fine by me. Keeping my body pressed up against the wall with the open door, I edged quietly forwards. The cry of the car alarm had died, leaving in its wake an eerie silence and the constant high-pitched ringing in my ears. Years of havoc and explosions had done wonders for my eardrums. Even so, I was sure I could hear noise emanating from the open door. Not conversation, but some disturbance. Agitated movement. Shuffling footsteps. Hurried furtive breathing. The sounds made by those that know something is coming for them.

But they couldn't know it was me, and I had no idea who *they* were. Other than my dear pal Jorge, there was no telling who was in there, or how many, or how pleased they would be when a man wielding a bottle-laden pistol disturbed their equilibrium. But standing around in the hallway burdened with doubt was accomplishing nothing. I took a step forward and swung my arm and pistol through into the room. With most of my face tucked behind the safety of the doorframe, I peered into the room.

There was but one person inside. A young woman in a chair. Her wide eyes looked at me with pure terror. Her mouth was open, but no words escaped her. The shock had claimed her entirely. She was not a combatant. Nor was she there of her own free will. I could see bonds strapped tight around her arms, holding her to the chair.

I moved closer. No point in hiding from a captive. I lowered the weapon slightly, enough that I could bring it up if some clown jumped out of the shadows.

'It's okay,' I mouthed, not wanting to make more noise. 'I won't hurt you.'

She was visibly trembling. This was a new world to her, and not one she was happy to be stuck in. I remembered that feeling well, and knew just how hard it was to adapt and react. I repeated the same silent sentence again as I took another step into the room. She shook her head wildly and nodded towards the door in the corner of the room.

In there, she said with her eyes.

I nodded in understanding and brought the weapon up again. I crossed the empty room to the door and placed my free hand on the handle. Three, two, one. I took a deep breath and pushed it open.

'Yo, what the hell?'

It was Jorge. He sat on the porcelain throne with his trousers around his ankles. The definition of a shitty situation.

'Hello, sunshine.' I said, pointing the pistol at his head. 'You know, there's an idiom warning against this very thing.'

He jumped in his seat and bashed his knee against the edge of the bath. It was a small bathroom. Just wide enough to fit a tub lengthways inside. A glass partition ran down from the ceiling to the edge of the tub, turning it into a shower when needed.

'How'd you get in here?' He barked.

'You're not exactly in a position of power here, so let's leave the questions to me, okay?'

He shuffled uneasily on the toilet, but with his own pistol stuck in his face, he had little option but to comply. It was a mightily misfortunate situation for him. One that I relished. His cocky bravado had come back to bite him right in the arse. His bargaining chips were inexistent. I shuffled into the room to face him head-on. My back pressed up against an unmarked sink. I kept the pistol pointed at his head the whole time. Best to keep any thoughts of rebellion in the toilet where they belonged.

'Let's have a little chat, shall we?' I said, fully aware that the guy whose tyre I'd just exploded could be on his way back up. 'First things first, who is she?'

Jorge glanced through the open bathroom door at the young woman tied to the chair. Her eyes flashed back and forth between the two of us.

'Just some bitch,' was his less-than-apt response. It earned him a swift kick in the shin.

'You want to try that answer again?'

'I don't know man. I ain't supposed to be here, you know?'

'Then why did you come?'

'Because you stole my piece, yo. I had to bounce.'

'Yeah, that was pretty stupid of you. So why did you come here of all places? Don't try and fool me that this is your home.'

'I ain't saying.'

'Jorge, you don't seem to be grasping the gravity of this situation. I don't know if you've ever been shot, but it's something you'd want to avoid. So let me give you the benefit of the doubt. Answer the question, or I'm going to shoot out your kneecaps.'

His eyes pierced into me. I returned the gesture.

'Yo Marco said this was the joint,' he said, gestating in a way that only one can when high on all kinds of substances. 'This is where the serious shit happens, you know?'

'That made no sense whatsoever. You know that, right? Who's Marco for a start?'

'He's my guy. He gives me the shit, and I sell it.'

'And who does he get it from?'

But before he could answer, there was a disturbance. In the hallway, I heard the faint ping of an elevator summoned. Jorge glanced towards the door. I took the opportunity to swing the door to a slither of a gap. The young woman remained stranded all on her own. The footsteps grew louder. With the pistol pointed at Jorge's head, I pressed my finger to my lips, condemning him to voluntary silence.

SIX

THE PATH OF MOST RESISTANCE

I HEARD THE FOOTSTEPS OF THE MAN I GUESSED TO BE MARCO breach the threshold. His demeanour was calm. Not relaxed, but neither was it agitated. Not that of a man who'd concluded that his tyre had been a casualty to help a stranger gain entry to the very building he was guarding.

'Yo, Jorge, where you at?' he shouted.

Jorge's eyes flashed back to me, waiting for some direction.

'Call him in here,' I whispered.

'I ain't doing that.'

'You are if you don't want a bullet in the leg.'

His eyes had an air of vacancy. Voluntarily zombified. Scrunched up behind his tanned, youthful eyelids, he still knew how to pack a whole lot of aggression into them.

'I'm in here.' He called through the tiny gap.

'You taking a shit?' Marco called back.

'Nah man. But you got to come in here, yo.'

'Man, I ain't going nowhere near you if you're taking a dump. This is serious.'

'I ain't playing man,' Jorge insisted. His eyes barely left mine. The fermenting rage held just at bay. 'You got to come in here and see this.'

'Not a goddamn chance.' Marco called. 'Now get out here and help me deal with this bitch.'

Jorge held up his hands in attrition.

'Try harder.' I mouthed.

'He ain't listening to me. He ain't coming in here.' Jorge replied a little too loudly.

Marco noticed.

'You talking to someone in there?' He asked. He moved closer.

'Nah man. I just need you to see this,' Jorge replied, although the lie was evident in his tone.

I couldn't see Marco, but if I were him, that would be the moment where I pulled out my weapon. From what I'd seen, he was a tall guy of average build. Nothing special, but nothing you'd dismiss in an instant either. And there was no telling from his physical state how skilled he was with a weapon. I pressed myself up against the sink so that any rogue bullets fired at the door would not hit me.

'Who you in there with, Jorge?' Marco asked. His tone had changed.

'No one, man. I'm alone.' But there was no mistaking the panic in his voice.

'Then come out here.'

'I can't do that, you know? You've got to come here.'

'And there is no goddamn way I'm stepping foot in there. So get out here now, or the bitch takes a bullet.'

A stalemate.

Jorge glanced at me. Still horribly stoned, but sober enough to recognise what was going to happen next.

'Marco,' I called, hoping vaguely he would reply with *polo*. 'It is Marco, right? Listen, pal, as hard as it might be to believe, what with me sneaking into your place and pointing a gun at your buddy's head right now, but I'm not here to fight. I just want to talk.'

'Whoever the fuck you are, you better get out here right now, or this puta is going to die.' Marco shouted in retort.

'Who?'

'What do you mean *who*?' he snapped. 'This bitch. I'll fucking kill her, man!'

'Right, and why is that my concern?'

Marco took a second to reply.

'Because you came here for her,' he said, but the doubt was clear in his voice. 'But you didn't count on the two of us being here.'

'That's a wonderful story and all,' I replied. 'But I've never met her before, and I couldn't care less about whether or not you shot her. So you don't really have a leg to stand on right now, do you? No offence, lady.'

'I don't want to die.' She gasped. The accent was English, which I wasn't expecting. She had that American look to her. Her voice shook, but it was good that she had the strength to speak.

'Shut up, bitch!' Marco snarled at her.

'Don't call me a bitch!' She snapped back. Whoever she was, she had some fight in her.

'How about we all drop our weapons, well, you drop your weapon first, then we can talk for a while before we part ways?' I said, knowing the suggestion would go down like a fart in a church.

'I've got a better idea, you let Jorge go and come out here, or I'll cap this bitch.' Marco barked.

'Don't call me bitch!' the woman shouted, this time louder.

'I tell you what,' I said. 'I'll let Jorge go if you can answer this riddle, okay? Jorge couldn't get it, but he's not exactly the brightest spark, is he? What's the one thing you can eat that eats you back?'

'Yo, you better jump this fool,' shouted Jorge with a feeble attempt of bravado. 'He stuck a bottle on his piece, yo. Like, I don't think it will even work no more.'

He smirked at me with glacial eyes.

So I shot him in the leg.

The weapon was still as loud as thunder contained in the tiny bathroom, but compared to the ear-splitting boom that would have occurred without the extension, the improvised silencer worked a treat. A double victory. A small win for my invention, and a magnificent defeat for Jorge's ego. His cry of pain far surpassed the noise of the weapon.

'Jorge is taking a time out for bad behaviour.' I called out, watching as the steady trickle of blood oozed out between his clutching fingers.

'You son of a bitch!' Jorge screamed.

'Watch your language,' I snapped back. 'Unless you want a matching set.'

'This is your last chance to come out, man,' Marco shouted. 'I mean it. You've got till the count of three.'

He won't shoot her.

'One.'

She's his hostage. Why would he go to all the effort of taking her just to kill her now?

'Two.'

You can't back out now. He's not going to do anything.
'Three.'
I was half right.
Marco fired two shots that hit their target less than a millisecond later. But they were not fired at the woman.

They were meant for me.

The two rounds smashed through the bathroom door, sending a billion tiny splinters cascading into the enclosed space, and dug into the white and grey checkered tiles on the adjacent wall. The surprise of the attack sent me into an involuntary flinch. I recoiled my gun arm slightly as the minuscule fragments of door bounced against my face, and I closed my eyes instinctually to save myself from permanent blindness. It couldn't have lasted more than a second, but that was all Marco needed.

Before I could recompose, Marco threw himself at the bathroom door. With all the force he could muster, he kicked it aside, which sent it jettisoning straight towards me. My gun arm took the brunt of the attack, which knocked the weapon out of my grasp and into the tub. But the door wasn't finished there, as the weapon tumbled out of reach, the inch-thick slab of solid wood slammed into my face.

I staggered back, all but defeated by what felt like taking a speeding train to the face, and fell into the small slither of space beside the sink. Blood trickled down from my nose to my lip, leaving the foul taste of iron in my mouth.

In the confusion, Marco had forced his way into the bathroom. He swung the bathroom door shut behind him, leaving nothing between the two of us but the growing tension. He held his pistol in his right hand. Pointed at the wall. That didn't last for long. My stance was hardly that of a fortunate person. I was trapped down beside the sink, but the cramped quarters benefitted as much as it hindered. With both hands outstretched to the sides to stop my fall, and my feet bent into a semi-awkward kneel, I heaved myself forwards into Marco's midriff. With my left hand, I snatched at his right wrist, pushing the limb and weapon up towards the ceiling. Marco retaliated with a wild bullet. It smashed into the bulb, plunging us into almost complete darkness.

With three fully grown men, it was - for want of a better phrase - a shit show. Jorge scrabbled to his feet, but with his trousers around his ankles, and the torrent of blood gushing from his wounded leg, he was a complete and utter hindrance to the situation. Marco and I tussled like drunken dancers, bouncing off the wall and the sink, and

Jorge himself. His uninjured leg thrashed at us, unconcerned whether it hit friend or foe.

I focused most of my efforts on the pistol in Marco's hand. A rogue bullet could put an end to everything. But that was far from my only concern. Marco was a tough opponent. His left fist landed a series of crippling blows into my stomach, and for all I tried to retaliate, I was much, much stronger with my left fist, which was occupied with the struggle on the weapon. It was all I could do to endure the tirade.

And throw my forehead into the centre of his nose.

I felt the crack without seeing much of the attack and saw the vague shadow of Marco's head flick backwards, followed a moment later by a sound all too similar to that of a pigeon flying straight into a window. The glass partition. With all the strength I could muster in such a small space, I thrust both my hands forwards into his chest.

Game over.

Marco collapsed into the bathtub. A cascade of razor-sharp glass fragments rained down. Some escaping the porcelain tub, most not. With the almost complete lack of light, there was no telling how severe Marco's wounds were, but no one would bet in his favour.

I picked up my pistol and fumbled around in the dark for Marco's. A small shard of glass sliced into my hand like it was warm butter. I winced and swore, glad that a small cut to the hand was the worst of my injuries. I found the second pistol in the tub beside a limp - yet somehow alive - Marco, and snatched it up.

I darted from the room before Jorge could make another audacious move, and ran past the bound woman towards a switchboard at the front door. I found the switch for the light hanging centre stage in the main room and flicked it on. An all too abrasive yellow glow stretched into each corner of the room, attacking the dormant darkness that had settled before.

I swung open the bathroom door, allowing as much light as I could to get inside. Marco did not look good. His blood had already begun to fill the bathtub, sending a steady stream of the crimson substance down the plughole. Marco's face had turned a ghostly white. Had it not been for the feeble rise and fall of his chest, I would have thought he had already gone.

Jorge groaned. His eyes locked on his fading comrade.

'You need to call an ambulance, yo.' He yelped from the toilet.

I pulled out Jorge's phone and held it up so both could see it.

'I will, but first, you need to answer some questions.' I said, looking into the weakening eyes of the dying man.

'Fuck you.' He groaned.

'By all means, feel free to die here while your buddy takes a shit. There are worse ways to go I guess, but not many.'

Marco pierced his lips together. He didn't want to die. Hell, I didn't want him to die. He couldn't be much older than me.

'Three questions for three numbers,' I said. 'Then I'm out of your hair. Promise.'

Reluctantly, Marco nodded.

'Excellent. First, why do you have that woman tied to a chair?' I pointed back into the room.

'She knows where Isabella Reyes is.' Marco said through gritted teeth.

'Okay, that's your first number. Two to go. Who is Isabella Reyes?'

'She's the daughter of Domingo Reyes.'

'Who?'

'The Black Viper. He thinks he runs this city, but...' Marco stopped to cough. I could see the blood dribbling down from his lips. 'He ain't shit. This ain't his town. It never was.'

'Why do you want his daughter?' I asked, but Marco glared at me.

'You said three questions.' He hissed.

'Well, you're not a genie, are you. So if you want help, you better answer that as well.'

'Collateral.' He groaned. 'To put Reyes in his place.'

Marco's eyes rolled into the back of his skull, and he deflated. Question time was over. I watched his chest rise and fall. Not dead. Yet. I thumbed the buttons on the phone.

'Nine nine nine,' I said. 'No wait, that's the England one, isn't it. What's yours again?'

'Nine one one you psycho!' Jorge spat.

'That's right. I knew I was close.'

I dialled the number and waited for the response.

'Nine one one, what's your emergency?'

I explained the situation, then relayed the address from Jorge, and hung up.

'Now then Jorge. My advice would be to keep your buddy conscious for as long as possible, okay? And don't move him before the paramedics arrive.'

'You fucking puta!' He snapped at me, spitting on the floor at my feet.

'I'll leave the door open for the paramedics.' I said with an annoyingly polite smile, before turning to leave the two to their survival.

The young woman stared at me with panicked eyes. Just because I'd thwarted her kidnappers, that didn't make me her ally. I walked over to her and knelt down before her.

'Are you okay?' I asked gently. 'They didn't hurt you, did they?'

She shook her head.

'Good,' I said. 'Do you think you could walk? We need to get out of here.'

'I think so.' She replied.

I untied her restraints and helped her to her feet.

'What's your name?' I asked.

'Eva. Eva Marston.'

She was visibly shivering. The night was cold, but not enough to warrant such a response. Most likely the shock had sent her body into overload, and this was the response. Even so, I picked up a coat off the counter that I guessed belonged to Marco, and wrapped Eva in it. She smiled at the gesture. Progress.

'Come on, Eva. We need to leave.'

'Shouldn't we wait for the ambulance to arrive?' She asked. 'And the Police?'

I shook my head.

'We can't rule out the possibility that these guys don't have backup on the way. I want to get you as far away from them as possible. But I promise you I'll keep you safe, okay?'

'There was a man,' she muttered. 'He only just left. He wanted to, he wanted to kill me.'

'Then I'm taking you home now. Come on.'

I fed my arm under her shoulder and practically carried her from the room, leaving Jorge and his endless slew of profanities behind us. I called the elevator, and we rode it down before Eva had the strength to speak again.

'You weren't really going to let them shoot me, were you?' she asked timidly.

'Of course not,' I replied. 'But they had to think I didn't care whether you lived or died. That way shooting you would achieve nothing. And if they believed that I hadn't come here for you, then it would be just a waste to go through all the effort of capturing you just to kill you when a stranger shows up.'

'So did you come here for me?' she asked.

'Well, no. Honestly, I had no idea what was here. I followed that guy Jorge on a whim. Call it a happy accident I guess.'

'Their boss, he wanted to kill me,' she said. Her jaw was trembling, elongating the words. 'He said he would cut me open and feed me to his rats.'

'I won't let him do that. I promise.'

'He didn't believe me. He kept saying I knew where this woman was. He said I had photos of her. But I've never heard of her before.'

I pushed open the door and walked out into the fresh evening breeze. Using the hubcap of the destroyed tyre, I propped open the door for the paramedics. When I turned round to see Eva, she had tears rolling down her face.

'This Isabella Reyes?' I asked. 'You've never heard of her before?'

'Not once. I don't know anyone with that name. I don't know where they think I know her from, or where these supposed photos are. I didn't know what to do. They were going to…'

She didn't finish the sentence. Didn't need to.

'It's okay, now.' I reassured her, putting my arm around her shoulder and easing her back towards the van. 'They can't hurt you now.'

'His face. It was so burned. He looked like a monster.'

That stopped me in my tracks. Practically stopped my heart. I turned to look at her. I barely noticed my hands clasp her shoulders.

'This guy,' I said, not registering the urgency in my voice. 'The guy with the burned face. Did you get his name?'

'That other man, Marco. He said he was called Salazar. Ramiro Salazar.'

SEVEN

SO CLOSE

I HAD MISSED HIM BY MERE SECONDS. I WAS ARMED. I WAS PARKED up in a secure and easily escapable position, and looked directly at him as he drove away. The chance of a lifetime. Pissed away. I could have stepped out and emptied the clip into his face until there was nothing left of him, and be long gone before the cops arrived. I wanted to scream and swear and smash the whole place to smithereens, but I couldn't, because Eva was staring at me with fear in her face.

'Too bad I didn't get here a minute earlier,' I said as jovially as I could to mask the bitter disappointment. 'I've been meaning to have a chat with him. But there's always next time.'

She was shaking. A real, visceral fear was rumbling through her and rocking her to her core. I let go of her arms and gave her a false, warming smile.

'You're English?' I asked, and she nodded meekly. 'Where from?'

'Brighton.'

'That's cool. I went to Brighton once with my wife. It's lovely.'

A small smile broke out over her face, but it quickly disappeared.

'You're not mad at me, are you?' she whimpered.

'No. No, of course not. It's not your fault you got mixed up in this. Nor is it your fault I didn't run a couple of stop signs to get here faster. Just take a couple of deep breaths, and relax. I'll get you back home, safe and sound. They won't come looking for you anymore.'

'You can't promise that.'

'You said it yourself, they didn't want you. They won't risk any of their men going after you. You're free.'

'I don't believe you.'

'Then let me show you. I'll get you back home and show you that you're safe, okay?'

She nodded reticently.

The night air had a distinctive chill to it. I ushered her across to the van, opened the passenger door for her, and she climbed in. I stared for a moment at the spot where Ramiro Salazar had driven right by me, and fought hard to suppress the fire that raged inside.

There's always next time.

Don't be so sure of that.

I eased the van out onto the empty street and headed North, away from the apartment building.

'I'm James,' I said after I'd put a couple blocks between us and her captives. 'It's a pleasure to meet you.'

She smiled.

'Do you want to give me your address?' I asked.

She told me her address. Her face had turned pale. The shock of the situation had caught up with her. No amount of reassurances were going to get her out of that. I had thousands of questions for her, but they would have to wait, so I snaked across the city towards the address she had given. Gradually, her colour came back, and she slowly recanted the tale of how she had ended up within spitting distance of Ramiro Salazar.

'They took me from my apartment,' she said after a long silence. 'That guy Marco, he broke in and... and killed my cat.' She paused. I glanced at her and saw more tears in her eyes. She forced them back and carried on. 'He put me in his car and told me if I screamed he would cut out my tongue. Then he took me to that place, and started asking me questions.'

'About Isabella Reyes?'

She nodded.

'I've never even heard that name before. But he said he'd found proof of the two of us together. I was so frightened.' She choked up again.

'It's okay,' I said. 'Just rest for now. We're nearly home.'

Eventually, I found her apartment. It was a large red brick apartment building sat amongst a dozen of its ilk. She thumbed in a six-digit code into a keypad, and after the gate swung open, I drove down to the car park beneath. Eva pointed to a vacant lot, and I parked up, and together we climbed the stairs to her apartment.

The door was unlocked. Undoubtedly the people who had taken her didn't care much for home security. I went first, gun in hand. I didn't expect any resistance, but Eva needed the song and dance all the same. One by one, I ticked off each room until there was one room left.

'Don't.' Eva said as I placed my hand on the door handle. She sat on the sofa, still wrapped up in Marco's coat. The room wasn't cold by any means. It was a sign of comfort.

'I need to make sure it's clear.' I said.

'I don't like to go in there.'

'I'll be quick. I promise.'

She nodded meekly, and I opened the door.

The room was far from what I'd expected. What I'd expected was an overtly tidy room full of the same sort of things I'd found around the rest of the apartment. What I hadn't expected was the site of a murder.

The blood had gone pretty much everywhere. Splatters reached high up the rear wall and had left nasty stains on the carpet. It wasn't fresh. The cat was still there. The sight of its cold body laying there was haunting. I didn't feel so bad about Marco anymore. If he was capable of doing something like that to a house cat, he deserved a slow and painful death. The smell was starting to become pungent. I crossed to the window and cranked it open. Didn't want it to permeate the whole building. I took a pillow case and rested it over the body. A little respect for a beloved pet.

I fulfilled Eva's request and didn't linger inside. She sat on the sofa. Her body was tense. Her mind raced. She looked at me, but not *at* me. Her mind was elsewhere, on the people that had invaded her privacy, and the burned man. I hadn't seen the damage to his face, but Nicole had described the horror that remained. I couldn't imagine how frightful it would be to see that monstrosity for the first time.

'Do you want something? Food? Coffee?' I asked gently.

'I'm okay.'

'You should eat something. A sandwich at least, or a banana?'

She nodded gently. She was a small woman. Petite, some might say. The mouse brown hair that stretched a little over her shoulders was bedraggled like she'd climbed through a thick bush before being captured. She reminded me of a girl I had a crush on in school.

The kitchen and living room were all in the same space. A waist-high counter separated one from the other. It made the whole place feel very spacious, yet compartmentalised. No doubt it was a big selling point. But for someone haunted by demons, the voluminous space only left more places for something to hide.

I busied myself with the preparation of a sandwich. Eva didn't exactly opt for the opulent lifestyle. There was a pack of ham that was a week out of the sell-by date, and a loaf of bread that was eagerly trying to become penicillin. I scavenged what I could, and placed an adequate sandwich and cup of coffee in front of Eva a few minutes later.

She ate slowly and quietly. Between each bite was a moment of contemplation. Her mind wandered down avenues it needn't traverse, and with every internal step, she got ever more exhausted. I walked over to the window and looked out at the street. The city was still brimming with life, even at half past ten at night. Dozens upon dozens of cars and bikes and pedestrians flowing around in a perpetual farrago. No one lifted their eyes to the apartments above. No one watching. The door was locked. No one was getting in.

'Do you have a laptop?' I asked eventually. Eva looked up. She hadn't finished her sandwich.

'In the bedroom. Why?'

'That guy Marco said they wanted this Isabella Reyes to use as collateral to put her father in place. I'm curious who he is. Maybe it will help piece together why they came for you.'

'Did they give you his name?' She asked.

'Domingo Reyes, but they called him the Black Viper as well.'

She took a long, thoughtful pause, drinking in the new information.

'I recognise that name. The Black Viper.' She said, getting to her feet and walking through to her bedroom. A moment later she returned with the laptop. She sat back down in her seat and leaned forward. I sat down on an old wicker armchair and waited for her to speak.

'There,' she said after a minute. 'Domingo Reyes. The Black Viper.' She twisted the laptop around to face me. On the screen was a newspaper website. Small flashing advertisements danced around the edges, luring the reader into their lair like a twenty-first-century succubus. In the centre of the screen was an article, accompanied by an image. It was of a stout Hispanic man in his late fifties. His small, copper-coloured eyes pierced through the screen, as though he knew two strangers were watching him from the comfort of an apartment. His hair was short and jet black, with the odd grey hair poking through like a weed in a garden.

It was a picture taken in motion, and from the looks of it, one taken without permission. Domingo Reyes was mid-walk when he had spotted the paparazzi snapping his photo. He wore a lean black suit with a beige shirt that was unbuttoned past his collarbone, to allow for his thick chest hair to breathe. Behind him followed two men. Bodyguards perhaps. Reyes was at least a foot shorter than them but had accommodated by adding some serious bulk to his upper body. To take a punch from him would be to dance with death.

'Who is he?' I asked.

'He runs drugs I think,' Eva replied, spinning the laptop back around to face her. 'He's wanted by almost every law enforcement agency in the state, but any time they get close, he manages to worm his way out of an arrest. It says here he's the most dangerous man in Miami. They call him the Black Viper because apparently, he kills people with poisonous snakes.'

'Venomous snakes.'

'What?'

'It's a common mistake. Venomous snakes are the ones that harm you by injecting venom when they bite, not poisonous snakes.'

'You know a lot about snakes, huh?' she mused.

'Know your enemy.'

'Wait, are you saying this guy Reyes is your enemy, or snakes are?'

'Let's say both and leave it at that.'

'Oh,' she said. 'Well yeah, he uses venomous snakes to kill his enemies. Allegedly that is.'

'And I take it he's not the kind of guy you run in the same circles with?'

'I don't think I've ever come across him in my entire life. I certainly would remember those eyes.'

'And you can't think of any time you might have taken a photo with his daughter?'

'If I did, it's certainly not something I'd hold on to. I don't have a clue who she is.'

Eva rubbed her hands into her face, massaging the exhaustion that had settled in the wake of the adrenaline. It was late in the evening of quite possibly the longest day of her life.

'I should get going.' I said, heaving myself out of the wicker armchair.

'Oh, do you have to?' She asked, looking uncomfortable at the thought of being alone. 'You could stay the night if you want? On the sofa, of course.'

'You'll be safe,' I replied, feeling the exhaustion myself. 'They won't be coming for you again.'

'You can't know for sure. What if that man with the burned face, what if he blames me for, you know, what happened?'

It wasn't beyond the realms of possibility.

And it sure as hell beat another night in the back of a van, constantly waking at every passing car.

The sofa looked invitingly comfortable.

'Okay, yeah. I'll stay the night if that's what you want.' I said, stifling a yawn.

Her face relaxed slightly, and she even managed a smile.

'Thanks,' she said. 'I've got a throw in the bedroom you could use.'

She got to her feet and headed back towards her bedroom, laptop in tow, and returned a moment later carrying only a beige throw. I took it from her with a thanks and got settled down on the sofa. It was warm from the heat of her body. I laid the throw over my clothes. No point taking them off if I needed to leave in a hurry, or if one of Salazar's men came bursting through the door. Eva stood back and watched me get settled.

'You're going to be alright,' I reassured her for the umpteenth time. 'No one is coming to get you.'

She nodded, but I knew I hadn't assuaged her doubts.

'Goodnight James.' She said before heading to her room and closing the door behind her.

Goodnight Eva.

It was wonderfully quiet in the apartment. The double-glazed windows did a stellar job of blockading the noise from the busy streets outside, leaving me only with the faint hum of the pipes in the ceiling, and the constant faint ringing in my ears. I settled down and stretched out. I knew that getting a good nights rest was going to be critical to the next couple of days.

Almost killing my biggest lead was maybe not the wisest choice I had ever made, but at least the evening had not been a complete waste. I knew Salazar wouldn't be heading back to that apartment building. The paramedics would have notified the police. They had to whenever there was a gunshot victim. So the cops would have torn that place apart, leaving Ramiro Salazar with no option but to put as much distance between himself and the building as possible.

But that was okay, because I had a new plan now.

Eva seemed like a nice person. From what I'd seen of her apartment, she had charming taste in decor. Except for her choice of cushions. It felt like someone had stuffed a football into a cushion case and figured it would suffice. No matter which way I positioned my head, it jammed into my neck. Sleeping on it for several hours would not be a fun experience. I discarded it to the floor and searched around for something else I could use. My hand brushed across the coat I'd stolen for Eva. It was bulky, yet folded down it would make for an altogether better sleeping experience. I wrapped it lengthways, then again widthways.

I could feel something in the pocket. Nothing noteworthy if you were to wear the coat, but notable if you decided to use it as a makeshift pillow. The object was slim, yet firm, like a card, or a folded up piece of paper.

Or something else.

I unfolded the coat and stuffed my hand into the inner breast pocket, and retrieved the item. Or items to be precise. The light in the apartment was dark after Eva had switched off the lights, but there was enough of a glow from the streetlights outside that I could see what I held in my hand.

Photographs.

Six photographs, all of two women standing close together. Three of the images looked like a third party had taken them. In these, the two women squeezed together and beamed into the camera lens in front of a backdrop of memories. The beach, a theme park, and finally, a pier. The other three photos had been taken by holding the camera out and twisting it around to face them. These photos looked like they had been captured one after the other, showing a steady, intimate scene. The two women once again smiled into the camera. Heads close together. In the next image, they looked at each other, glowing in each other's radiance. And in the final photo, they were deep in an embrace. Lips pressed tightly together.

The first woman was definitely Eva. The other had to be Isabella Reyes.

Clearly they didn't know each other well.

I knocked on the bedroom door. She couldn't have fallen asleep yet. It took her a short while to open the door.

'What is it?' She asked, blinking away a fresh set of tears.

'I think I know why those men came for you.' I said.

'But I have no idea who this Isabella Reyes person is,' she said, sounding exhausted from the constant accusations. 'I've never met her before in my life.'

'I'm willing to bet that might not be true.' I held out the photographs, image facing down.

She took a long moment to recover, but eventually, the curiosity stole over her. She had to know who the mysterious woman was, and why she had suffered on her behalf. She opened her eyes and looked at the photographs.

Her expression changed in an instant.

'That's not Isabella Reyes.' She said slowly, and cautiously.

'They were the photos Marco had in his coat pocket.'

'It can't be,' she said. 'Her name is Quinn. Lizbeth Quinn.'

EIGHT

A.B.Y.B.

It had lasted sixteen months. Sixteen long months of pure elation. The most intense, breathtaking and heartbreaking months of my life. She had been my drug, and she had spirited me away from the world on a rollercoaster of ecstasy. All because of one shitty day, and one impulse decision.

I'd been acting for less than a week. The hours were long, and the director was a complete ass. Nothing compared to that arsehole Galloway, but still not exactly the image I'd built up in my head of what it would be like. They'd had me in this scene that required me to be hoisted up on a cross, ready to be ripped apart by a perverse nightmare clown. It had been physically and mentally exhausting, not to mention wholly embarrassing. By the time I'd left, I had no desire to go back in the following morning. I wanted to pack up, head home and find a simple job in the ass end of nowhere, where the customers were simple, and the living was cheap. But first, I'd wanted a drink.

I found a bar close to the studio that had that no questions asked kind of feel. Dour vibes for dour patrons. I'd taken a seat on a stool at the bar that had been torn apart and fixed up more times than anyone cared to remember, and ordered a double vodka and tonic. I wanted to feel numb, and I wanted it fast. The bartender had obliged and moved on without feeling the need to do a little prying into the life of the newest floozie to set up shop. Good. I didn't want company. Not from him at least.

'Rough day?'

I turned to see who had spoken. I hadn't even registered someone had sat down beside me. I caught eyes with a woman who I could only describe as breathtaking. She had the kind of captivating eyes that would send a thousand soldiers to their doom. Her jet black hair was tied up, revealing a faded neck tattoo that trickled all the way down her right arm to her knuckles.

I realised I was staring.

'Rough week.' I'd replied without really thinking what I was saying. Her eyes lit up as she caught my foreign accent.

'English?' She asked.

I nodded.

'You're not the type of gal who searches for answers at the bottom of a bottle.' She said, her eyes transfixed onto mine, ensnaring me.

'What gave it away?'

'You've got a kind of innocence to you,' she said with a gentle smile. 'You're better than a place like this.'

'Says who?'

'Says me. You're not like these other losers. They spend so much time here, they're practically part of the woodwork.'

I looked around and had to agree. Most of the other patrons slumped in their chairs, lost to the outside world. I couldn't stop the smile that stretched across my face.

She smiled at me, and something in that smile reached deep inside me and grabbed hold in a way no one else ever had before. I sat and drank with her late into the evening, hoping that I'd think of some smart way to impress her. Yet after my eighth drink, I could barely stand, so she had called a taxi and taken me home.

The following morning had felt like waking from a nightmare, only to realise that the horrors were true. I'd embarrassed myself in front of the first person in the city I'd genuinely felt something for. I'd walked out of the bedroom, looking and feeling like a zombie, only to find her asleep on the couch. She opened her eyes, brushed the hair from her face and smiled at me again.

And I knew I was done for.

I drifted out of the past and looked at James.

'She told me her name was Lizbeth Quinn,' I said, rubbing away the remaining tears that lingered on my cheek. 'Although most people called her Lizzy.'

But to me, she was always Quinn. It sounded like the name of some kickass crime fighting detective. *Call me Quinn.*

'And you never had any idea she went by another name?' James asked. He was a big guy, maybe six foot. Framed in the doorway, he looked slightly intimidating. *Who the hell was he?*

I shook my head.

'Never. She didn't like to talk about her past, and I never really pushed her.' That was partly true. I had pushed, but she pushed back. So her past was her past. Her demons were her own.

Never mine.

'What about any family members? Her mother, or any siblings?' He probed.

Again I had to shake my head.

'She told me she was an only child, and her mother died when she was little.'

'Who raised her after that?' He asked, still standing in the doorway.

I looked down at the photographs in my hand. I'd hidden them so long ago I almost forgotten they existed, yet I knew every tiny detail of each like they had been taken yesterday. And each felt like a dagger to the heart. I looked down at the face of Quinn.

'I don't know,' I said, feeling like an idiot. 'She never told me. I figured it was her dad, but she didn't tell me anything about him. I figured he was either dead or in prison. Never *this*.'

Life with Quinn was like nothing I'd ever felt before. It hadn't taken long for us to become an item. She had a carefree, bohemian attitude that I was immensely envious of. She didn't care what people thought. Didn't care what people said. She did what she wanted, and she got what she wanted. And she had wanted me.

She had wanted me. And she had got me.

Every single moment we were together was beyond anything I'd felt before. I felt like I'd lived my life in black and white, and now I could see colour. It felt cheesy and cliche and ridiculous and utterly unbelievable. After a couple of weeks, she'd moved out of her apartment and into mine. She'd taken over the guest bedroom for her artwork, and had packed in her job to go self-employed full time as an artist. I was surprised how well she had done. Almost immediately, she was making money from her art. Enough to live comfortably off. It was magical, seeing her at work, and knowing that she was living her dream. Her success fuelled my own, and before long I had gone from being an extra to starring in supporting roles in a couple of television movies.

Our relationship grew and grew. I shared every bit of my life with her, and she took it all in without judgement. I told her about my family back in England, and how I missed them. I told her how they disapproved of me moving to America to be an actress, and how that had spurred me to going ahead with it. I told her how I had gotten so close, how I had almost moved to Hollywood, but bottled out at the last minute and stuck with Miami instead.

Quinn said I'd made the right choice. The people in Hollywood were superficial. She said how much she loved my stories, and how she wished she had stories to share for her own. She didn't like to talk much about her family. She never told me how her parents had died or how it had affected her at such an early age. Anytime I pressed her for information, she would grow cold. I hated the cold. It filled my mind with doubts. I couldn't imagine my life without her in it. My heart was hers, and the thought scared me beyond belief.

'What about friends, did she ever introduce you to anyone you think might be involved with her father?' James asked.

'Why does that matter?' I asked.

'Because Isabella - Quinn, she's in danger,' he said. 'Those men want to use her as collateral to get to her father. They want to put him in line, and if he's half the criminal the world thinks he is, she is in real danger.'

I hadn't thought about that. The burned man had threatened me. He had no qualms putting me through unspeakable things so that he could get to Quinn. What would he do to her to get her father to cooperate?

'I met a few of her friends at parties. She had a couple of close friends that she would hang out with, but I wouldn't think any of them would work for a drug dealer.'

But then, I would have never thought Quinn was involved in that world. How well did I know her?

It hadn't been perfect every minute of the day. Sure, we argued, just like every couple does. Sometimes it was the small stuff. *Don't sweat it, right?* We usually worked past it in a couple of hours and made up for it in the usual way. Sometimes it was worth getting into an argument just to make up.

But sometimes it went worse than that. Sometimes it felt like a rift had appeared, fracturing the equilibrium in a way that just wouldn't ever mend. Not properly at least. Those were the worst times. Those were the times I felt like I had slipped into a void that I would never return from. It was those times that I pushed her for information. I just wanted her to let me in. I had bared all to her. I was naked, exposed, vulnerable. Yet I felt completely safe. I felt like she was the only person in the world who saw the real me, and would go to the ends of the earth to make sure that never changed.

I wanted her to feel the same way, which meant she had to break down the wall she had built around herself. Too many bad experiences had hardened her. She couldn't hurt the same way again. But her battle-hardened facade was more than I could handle. I needed her to let me in, but every attempt pushed her away.

We would be together, but we would never be one.

'Anyone you think she knew well enough to live with, or someone who might know where she is?' James asked.

I tried to focus, but my mind was a mess. I had woken up that morning to a normal life. Nothing out of place. Now, I felt like something big had changed, something that would never slot back into place. My life forever disrupted. A broken bone, healing distorted. Quinn had drifted in and out of my life like a storm, and left me to pick up the pieces. And now, all this time later, it felt like it had happened all over again.

Did her friends feel the same way, or was I the only one who felt the brunt of her destruction? Did the others laugh off her eccentricities as though nothing mattered? I knew one man who would. One guy who Quinn had always bonded with. One guy she said really got her.

'There was this one man,' I said, trying to remember as much as I could. 'Greyson something-or-other. Used to talk about owning a couple of bars that were the place to be. He liked to talk about all the movie stars and singers that showed up. Quinn lapped his stories up as much as the rest of them. He was the only person she talked about. I think in a way she idolised him.'

'That's a start,' James said with a smile. 'And you know where to find him?'

'I… I guess so. Quinn took me to a party at his house. He might know where she is, if he's still there. It was a couple of years ago now.'

'It's better than anything we've got,' he said. 'We'll go in the morning and see what he knows.'

'We? Why would you want to help?' I asked.

'I think Quinn might be able to help me.' He replied.

'How?'

'That can wait. We need to get some rest. We'll talk more in the morning, okay?'

I nodded, and he headed back to the sofa. I closed the bedroom door and climbed back into bed. The photographs still clutched in my hand. I stared through the darkness at them, recalling the memories. My fingers thumbed the faint smudge of ink on my wrist.

We celebrated our one year anniversary in our typical fashion. I went overboard, hiring a luxurious hotel suite, and paying for a meal in a five-star restaurant. Only the best for Quinn. She bought me a card, inside of which she had written the most romantic thing I'd ever read.

Always be yourself, beautiful.

I had cried tears of joy as I read the message over and over again, making an utter fool of myself right there in the restaurant. She had smiled back at me, ignoring the inquisitive looks from the surrounding tables. In that moment, it was her and me. Adrift in the depths of space. Just us, together, alone. It was all I ever wanted.

A week later, I was walking back from a long day shooting when I passed a tattoo parlour I'd walked past a million times, and I'd been unable to resist the urge to step inside. An hour later, I was rushing home with the letters A.B.Y.B. tattooed on my wrist. I'd never even considered a tattoo before, but the thought of seeing the look on her face when I showed her it was too much to resist. A.B.Y.B. *Always be yourself, beautiful.*

She'd been out when I arrived back at the apartment. I sat and waited, making a casserole for both of us. It was one of her favourites, and I wanted to do something nice for her. The skin on my wrist stung from the needle, but it was a pleasant pain. It made me feel alive. It made me feel in control of my life.

But the hours passed, and the casserole went cold and hard, and my calls went straight through to voicemail. I didn't want to go to bed without her, not tonight.

It was early in the morning when finally she came home. She was angry, and high on god knows what. She stormed in and slammed the door behind her, no doubt waking up Mrs Briggs downstairs. The track marks on her left arm were clear as day. Her beautiful eyes had glazed over, and even though she was looking at me, I knew she wasn't really there.

It hurt to see her like that. It wasn't the first time. She didn't want to talk about it. It was her problem, not mine, as she liked to tell me. I tried to talk, tried to tell her about my new tattoo, but she didn't care. She called me a dumb bitch and smashed the glass of water I brought her on the floor.

She slept in her art room, while I lay alone in our bed.

And rubbed the fresh letters on my thumb.

A.B.Y.B.

NINE

ALL THE KING'S HORSES

MORNING IN MIAMI BEGAN WITH A YAWN, AS THE DULL EVENING sky succumbed to the encroaching morning sun. I watched the midnight blue gradually lighten like a watercolour painting as shades of orange permeated the enormous canvas. It wasn't until it settled into a peaceful baby blue shade that I finally climbed off the sofa and stretched out my stiff muscles. I rubbed my hands through my beard. It was a couple of weeks long at this point. Exactly how I liked it. Without a couple of millimetres worth of thick brown hair protruding from my face, I looked like a child. Even so, it could do with a little bit of a trim to stop me looking like I was homeless.

I could hear Eva moving around in her bedroom. I took the opportunity to use the bathroom before her. She had a few towels hanging on a rack beside the shower. I figured I could use one, what with having saved her life after all. A few minutes later I returned a clean man. It had been a while since my last proper shower, although I had managed to fashion one using a hosepipe and a punctured water bottle before I got to Miami.

By the time I left the bathroom, Eva was making food. She looked at me, giving me a slightly awkward smile that aptly acknowledged the peculiarity of the situation. We ate fried eggs and toast with a side of black coffee in relative silence, and once Eva was ready, we headed down to the parking lot and climbed back into the van.

'So, Greyson what's-his-name,' I said as I fired up the engine, 'Where did you say he lived?'

Eva gave me the address and I navigated through the busy streets, watching as the city prepared for another long day at the proverbial office. Traffic was slow and tedious, and Eva didn't seem in the mood for much conversation.

We weaved through the tapestry of city streets in the vague direction of the building we had met in just hours before. Whether Eva had pegged onto that fact, I didn't know. She sat and watched the tirade of passing vehicles in a trance, occasionally breaking free to offer directional advice. I let her have her moment, I knew how precious they were.

It took the better part of an hour to get to the house. It wasn't much to look at from the outside. Sure, it was a two-storey villa with two flash sports cars parked outside, but that was where the expense ended. The neighbourhood was okay at best. The garden had been left to transform into a wild jungle, littered with an unhealthy amount of trash. It looked like a school kid's homework project on the impact humans had on the world. I parked up on the street, and we walked up the driveway to the front door. A sizeable ornate door handle sat loud and proud in the centre of the painted wood. It was a copper penis.

'I'm just going to knock.' Eva said, rapping her knuckle on the door.

'Good call.'

It took a long minute before someone responded. I could hear the gentleman shouting something inaudible to another person. As the door swung open, I caught a woman from somewhere inside the house shout *asshole*, yet the person standing before us didn't acknowledge it.

He was a man in what I guessed to be his forties standing in the doorway in a pair of tight leather trousers that left nothing to the imagination, and a bathrobe covered in cigarette burns. His dyed blonde hair sat like a dishevelled island on the top of his skull, with only the meekest amount of stubble stretching down past the temples. He wore a pair of purple-tinted sunglasses that did little to cover the exhaustion in his eyes. A cigarette hung limply from his lips, threatening to fall loose at the slightest provocation.

'Who the fuck are you?' He asked, pushing his sunglasses just down his nose to observe the intruders at his door.

'Greyson?' Eva said in a surprisingly jovial tone. 'Grey, it's me, Eva. Lizbeth's friend.'

He took a moment, during which his eyes ran across every inch of her body.

'Oh, little Lessy Quinn.' He said, almost dropping his cigarette in the process. I caught the slight look of disgust on Eva's face. So did Greyson. 'Oh calm down darling,' he said with a look of exasperation. 'You know she didn't give a shit about that name. Lizbeth, lesbian. I don't need to spell it out for you, do I? Lessy practically came up with it herself. She knew how to take a fucking joke. So what are you here for?'

'We were wondering if we could talk to you about her.' I said. Greyson eyed me again behind his sunglasses.

'Oh yeah? And what the fuck would I want to do that for?'

'Perhaps if we could talk inside?' Eva asked. 'It's important.'

'If it's so fucking important what's this fucker doing here?' He asked, looking at me. 'For all I know he's a fucking cop.'

'I can assure you I'm not a cop.' I said.

'You're English too are you? What, you fucking breeding over here now?'

'Don't you Americans have a law that if you ask if someone's a cop, they have to tell you the truth?' I asked, ignoring his comment.

'That's fucking made up.'

'Well, it was worth a shot. But I can promise you I'm not. I don't even know if Brits can become American police officers.'

'If you try and fucking pull anything I swear to fucking christ I'll fucking have you.' Greyson snapped.

'Well see there you threatened me,' I replied. 'So if I were a cop, I'd have to arrest you now, wouldn't I? Yet here you are, free from custody.'

He scowled and stormed back inside.

'He's a charming guy.' I whispered.

'Don't sugar coat it,' Eva muttered. 'He swears more than he breathes. I always hated him.'

We followed Greyson inside. I wasn't worried about the possibility of him recognising me. The news stations had gotten bored of my story weeks ago, and Greyson didn't strike me as the kind of guy who cared about anything outside his own ego.

The interior of his house was about as recklessly savage as the way he dressed. A large cracked mirror hung in a gold-rimmed frame over a fireplace adorned with empty bottles and condoms. The mirror itself had a red stiletto sticking out of the centre. Shards of mirror littered the shag rug beneath it. Greyson threw himself down onto a red leather chair that looked more like a throne than a standard household object. He did not invite us to sit.

'So what the fuck has Lessy gone and done now?' He asked, pulling a joint from his pocket, and using a lighter fashioned into the shape of a bullet to light it. Within seconds the smell of marijuana filled the room.

'We're trying to find her,' I said. Greyson was an ass, but I suspected he would be more straightforward with a stranger, and I could tell by the way he dismissed Eva that he saw her as nothing more than a clingy ex. 'We believe she might be in danger.'

'What the fuck is this? *We believe she might be in danger?*' He mimicked my words with an abrasive English accent. 'You must be off your fucking rocker if you think Lessy wants your help.'

'Why do you say that?' I asked, ignoring his mocking tone.

'Because Lessy Quinn is a fucking force of nature, alright? Well, ask me, and I'd say she's gone the same way as her mother.'

'Her mother died in a house fire,' Eva said defensively. 'It was an accident.'

'Accident my ass.' Greyson rebuked. 'You really think she'd have died if she wasn't jacked up on ket? She sat there and roasted like a fucking pork chop until her eyes popped like popcorn. Once a crack whore, always a crack whore, you know?' He looked at me as though expecting me to agree obediently.

'Well, lucky for us nobody did ask you.' I replied calmly.

He looked at me with cold discontent.

'Fucking cunts the pair of them.' I could practically feel Eva recoil at the word. 'What, you don't like cunt, darling?' He blew a big cloud of smoke towards Eva. 'Grow the fuck up. It's a fucking word, alright? You've got one, haven't you? What else would you call it? Besides, Lessy always knows what she's getting herself into. She lives to lose control.'

'So you don't know where she is?' I asked.

'Why should I? She was a dealer and a good laugh when she had a gram in her, that's it. I bought a bit of coke off her, and sometimes we did horse together. Sometimes we mixed the two and made some whiz-bang, yeah? That was Lessy. Go hard or go home, except what do you do if you haven't got no home? You just go harder and harder till they put you in the ground.'

'Please Grey,' Eva said. 'I'm really worried about her. Some serious people are looking for her. I just want to help her.'

'Oh, I'm sure you fucking do. I'm sure you want to help and

kiss and make up, don't you? Like I said, I don't know where the fuck she is. If she's not dead already, she probably has the fucking sense to stay hidden. Those people are serious shit.'

'Which people?' I asked.

'The ones that follow her around like fucking lapdogs. The ones she gets all her fucking drugs off. I've seen the way they watch her. That big guy, the black one that stands there like her fucking shadow. I wouldn't want to get on his bad side. Well, maybe I do. It's been a while if you know what I mean.' He winked at me through his sunglasses and took a long drag on his joint. 'Scary fucker, but I bet he'd know a thing or two in the bedroom.'

'Did you catch his name in between these thoughts?' I asked.

'What's the matter, getting jealous?' He blew another cloud of smoke towards us, then shook his head. 'We never talked. Like I said, the guy was a like a bodyguard or some shit. He wasn't big into talking with Lessy's cohorts.'

'Okay, well what about…'

But Greyson interrupted me.

'What the fuck is this, twenty questions? Jesus fucking Christ how many times do I have to tell you I don't know where the fuck Lessy is. She's an adult. She doesn't need some boy scout and the neediest fucking ex in the world hunting her down like some kind of criminal.'

'I'm not the neediest ex.' Eva said defensively.

'Darling, you are. I've heard the stories. You need to take a fucking chill pill, alright? Lessy doesn't want you anymore, alright? You were a phase. Girl's probably had farts that lingered longer than you. Okay? So just drop it and move the fuck on.'

He finished his joint and flicked the remainder into the fireplace. No sooner had it come to a rest between the empty beer bottles did he pull out a dirty pipe and light another flame on his bullet lighter. I watched him heat what I guessed to be crack, and inhale the outcome. He savoured the release behind closed eyes. In his silence, Eva took the chance to retort.

'I don't know what Quinn told you about me, but what happened between me and her was personal, alright? That means it's not your place to get involved.'

'Christ, are you still here?' Greyson groaned. 'Do the words *outstayed your welcome* not mean shit over in jolly old England?'

'Hey, I was talking to you!' She snapped back.

'Oh my God, blah blah blah. Don't make me get the muzzle.'

Eva scoffed, but it was clear there was nothing more we were going to get out of the miserable bastard.

'Come on Eva,' I said, putting my hand on her shoulder to quash any thoughts of jumping across the room to jam her thumbs in his eyes. 'Let's leave before he makes an embarrassment of himself.'

I ushered her back down the hallway towards the front door. No sooner did Eva step back across the threshold did I hear the sound of Greyson calling from the other room.

'Hey, London boy, come 'ere.'

I sighed and turned, leaving Eva behind. Greyson hadn't moved. The pipe hung between his loose fingers. He didn't stir as I approached.

'What do you want?' I asked, resisting the urge to kick him in the crotch.

'That bitch is like a noose,' he said, staring at the ceiling through his sunglasses. 'She clung to Lessy like a leech. She thinks she knew Lessy better than anyone, but that ain't true. I was the guy she would come to when that psycho got too much.'

'That doesn't sound like a question.'

'If someone hurt Lessy, I'd know about it,' he said with a subtle tone to his voice that I would have sworn was genuine affection. 'Wherever she is, she's there for a reason. She likes her alone time. What do you call it, she's a recluse. She ain't right in the head, you know? She fucking saw her own mom burn to death. Can you imagine how fucked up that would be? All the king's horses and all the king's men can't put that fucker back together again. So wherever she is, she's there of her own free will.'

'I'll keep that in mind.'

'You fucking Brits are all the same. So fucking polite. You ever just tell someone to fuck off?'

'When I need to.'

And with that, I turned and walked through the front door, leaving Greyson to his euphoria.

TEN

ESCAPE FOR THE SOUL

I STORMED OUTSIDE AND STARED UP AT THE BRIGHT BLUE SKY AND swore at the world. The sun seemed too bright, like it was mocking me for having such a terrible time with its splendour. There should be storm clouds, and rain, and thunder. That would be more appropriate.

'Can you believe that guy?' I snapped. I turned around, expecting to see James behind. But he wasn't there. He was still inside. Letting Greyson fill his ears with more secrets and lies. I swore again and stomped Greyson's lawn into submission. The grass was too long, and littered with empty bottles and cigarette butts. Another reason to hate the guy. He couldn't even clean his lawn.

It didn't take long for James to reappear, but in that time my mood had soured. I felt like a bullied kid at school with everyone laughing at me. I had hated it then, and I hated it now. Why people chose to be so ruthlessly cruel was beyond me. Not once had I ever done that to another person, but for some reason I was always the brunt of everyone's attacks.

As I heard James approach, I spun on my heel and glared at him.

'What did he want?' I snapped.

'Nothing, he was just rambling.' He said, a little defensively. I knew I should apologise, but I didn't. No one was going to apologise to me. Why should I break the mould? I turned and headed back towards the van. James fell back.

'I hate that guy. Can you believe what he was saying?'

'Don't worry about it,' James sighed. 'He seems like the kind of guy who likes to stir the pot. Don't take it personally.'

'How can I not?' I snapped. 'God, I told her everything about me. What did she keep secret?'

'More than that arsehole in there is letting on.' He insisted, giving one last look at Greyson's dreadful abode. 'Don't let one bad encounter ruin something special for you, okay?'

But that was easier said than done. Our relationship had been a perfect glass vase. Beautiful to behold. But delicate. One drop was all it had took to shatter it. I had scrambled around, picking up the pieces, and with bloodied fingers I had tried to rebuild. But it would never be the same. There would always be pieces missing, and the cracks were too clear to hide. The lie I'd always told myself was that only I could see them. Clearly, that was not the case.

'What about that man he mentioned, the mysterious black guy. Did you ever meet him?' James asked.

'I don't know anymore. I need a drink.'

So off we went in search of one. James drove again, putting as much distance as he could between us and Quinn's past as possible before we found a suitable place. It was a bar, because James figured coffee was not the type of drink I had wanted. He was right, and a couple of minutes later I sipped on a brand of whiskey I didn't recognise over a handful of rapidly melting ice cubes, and looked into the gloomy void ahead.

'Try to think,' James said after he took a pull on his pint. 'A tall black man following her around must have stood out, right?'

'You don't know her. She liked to meet the most eclectic people. It was part of her charm. She seemed to attract them.' I said, picking at an old sticker on the table.

'But if this guy was working for her father, he wouldn't be like the others, right? He would be remarkable just by being unremarkable.'

But the more I thought about her, the more the wound opened. Time had healed nothing, and the pain was just as fresh as it had been on the first day.

'Why am I even doing this?' I snapped. 'Why am I going to all this effort for her? If the tables were turned would she be here doing this for me? No. Of course she wouldn't. I could barely...'

But then I stopped. Somewhere in the deepest recesses of my mind, something arose. A memory I'd long forgotten about. The details were scrambled, their message distorted like a fading dream. I focused on it. Tried to peel it away from the fog, up to the surface.

A forgotten trip upstate. A spontaneous decision. And an argument.

'Actually, there was something.' I mused.

The memory came back to me. It had been so sudden at the time. Like the idea had come to her in the moment, and she had been powerless to refuse it. Quinn had described it as an escape for the souls. I didn't know what that meant, but it sure as hell beat watching reruns of whatever daytime drama was on TV. And it was her idea, which meant she would be in a good mood. Quinn liked to get her way, and I had no problem seeing her happy. We hired a rental car for the weekend and headed out. Quinn took the wheel. It was her plan after all. She knew where we were headed.

It took the better part of the day to snake up North. We ate pizza from a roadside vendor and drank warm soda from sun-heated cans and watched the city drift away like a forgotten dream. We made jokes and shared simple stories and sung along to the radio. She smoked cigarettes and let her jet black hair dance in the breeze. It was a dream. Just me and Quinn escaping the world.

'What is this place?' I asked as we turned off the freeway and headed down onto the quiet backwater roads.

'It's a surprise. Just you wait, we're nearly there.'

I wasn't sure what to expect. We had headed up into Citrus County to a place called Ozello, about seventy miles north of Tampa, with our noses pointed towards the Gulf of Mexico. Not the kind of spot you went for a relaxing getaway. The air was humid, and there was a real stink to everything. The roads were cracked and beaten from years of abrasive sunlight, which slowed the final stretch of the journey to almost a crawl. When finally we stopped, it was beside what looked to be a trailer park caravan on stilts.

I went to climb out of the rental car, but Quinn stopped me.

'Not yet, sweetie,' she said with a look on her face I'd seen before. 'I'll be right back.'

She left me inside and climbed out of the car. She lit another cigarette as she approached the house, and bashed her fist on the door.

A man appeared, I could only just make him out. He stood with most his figure tucked inside the domicile, but even so, I saw he was tall and black. Immediately, I could tell the conversation they had was heated. Quinn's stance turned from one of relaxed confidence to that of a cornered mutt. My window was down, though at first, it was impossible to tell what they were arguing about.

That began to change as the exchange escalated.

'You can't stop me coming up here, Felix!' Quinn snapped. 'I've got every right.'

'Like hell you do! If he found out you'd been here, do you know what he'd do?' The big man barked back.

'He doesn't give a damn about me.'

'Oh, you really think that? He's made every effort to save your ass, but if you're gonna come up here and start poking your nose where it don't belong, he'll just as easily kick your ass out to the kerb. So get back in your car and get the hell out of here.'

'We're not leaving.' Quinn shouted defiantly.

'We? Who did you bring?' The big man stuck his head out and looked right at me. It was just a moment, a flash, but in that, I saw a man with unbridled rage etched into his face. 'You stupid son of a, what the hell are you playing at? What do you think your…'

But the man lowered his voice. I could hear his deep, bass voice reverberating across the empty space, but the words were masked beneath it. Quinn seemed to follow suit. Their argument continued for several minutes, all the while I sat and waited patiently, feeling like somehow I was intruding. When finally she returned to the car, her jovial mood had dissipated.

'We're leaving,' she snapped, sticking the car into reverse and spinning us around to face the other way.

'What was all that?' I asked, but I knew what the response was going to be.

'It ain't none of your damn business, okay? Just leave it. I don't want to talk about it.'

And with that, we left. No more talk of Ozello, or the caravan, or the man named Felix. We spent the rest of the weekend down in Tampa in some dirt cheap motel. Quinn acted like nothing had happened, and I played the part too, yet something felt off. After the weekend, we headed home and went back to our lives, and the awkward memory of our weekend getaway drifted from my mind.

Until almost three years later when I relayed the story to the man who had saved my life.

'And this Felix chap, you never heard of him again?' James asked from the driver seat of his beat up old van.

'Never. Quinn made it clear it was off topic. I figured it was just easier to keep quiet. We had enough to argue about.' I said, staring out into the traffic once more.

'And Ozello, you said it was somewhere up north?'

'Near Tampa by the Gulf. Maybe five hours or so by car.'

'Okay then,' he said. 'Well, we better get going if we're going to make it there before sundown.'

ELEVEN

ANOTHER DAY IN PARADISE

'When I was twenty-five, I got hit by a bus. Just stepped off the sidewalk right in front of it. I didn't see it coming. Chalk it up to juvenile stupidity. I spent three weeks in intensive care. Nearly died. But you know what, it was the best thing that could have happened to me, because it gave me clarity.'

I cracked open the beer in my hand and looked at the man in front of me. He was six, maybe seven years my junior, and he was shaking like a leaf. Couldn't blame him. I would be if I were in his boots.

'It made me focus on the important things in life,' I continued. 'Made me cut the fat. Anything that wasn't in direct correlation to my goal had to go. I won't say it was easy. Hell, you ever tried to tell a honey that she's got to get steppin' because she's holding you back? It ain't easy. It ain't straightforward. But it was a necessity to get to where I wanted to be.'

I took a long pull on the beer, savouring the refreshing taste before I continued.

'You see, I wasn't content with a simple life. I ain't gonna do a nine to five down the local Walmart. I wanted something bigger, something better. So, I went out and got it. You dig?'

The younger man opposite nodded nervously.

'Good. I knew you'd get it. You know, you and I are quite alike, don't you think?'

He opened his mouth, but no words escaped him.

'We're both men with aspirations,' I continued. 'We looked at the pie and decided we wanted a bigger slice. We both used unconventional means to get what we wanted. Took the road less travelled. I sought out opportunity through a partnership with Domingo Reyes. You found it through putting your hand in his pocket.'

That got the guy in a real state. His legs buckled beneath him and he dropped to his knees like he was in prayer. No god was going to save him today.

'Please Felix, I can explain.' He trembled.

'I ain't here to listen to excuses.' I interjected. 'It's your own damn fault you decided to take more than your fair cut. You put your hand in another man's pocket, you best be willing to lose that damn hand. So shut your goddamn mouth and listen.'

Tears ran down his terrified face. Did he have no shame?

'You fucked up.' I continued. 'You made the decision to take a cut off the top. Not me, not Reyes. You. You wouldn't crash your car and blame it on the manufacturer, would you?'

He shook his head.

'Exactly. You'd man up and take responsibility for your actions, which is exactly what you will do now. So I'm going to give you a decision. Right or left?'

'Right or left what?' He asked.

'If I wanted to elaborate, I'd have done it already. Make your choice. Right or left?'

He mulled the decision over. Right or left. A binary choice. One or zero. Ying or yang. Yes or no. At the end of the day, it wasn't a difficult choice to make. It wasn't like I was asking him to pick between which of his daughters he wanted to save.

'Left.' He said eventually, which was exactly what I had expected, because it wasn't a fifty-fifty decision. It's a loaded question, depending on your history. Like asking right or wrong. Unconsciously, you want to pick right, because you want to *be* right. Right or left has a multitude of answers. Are you right or left-handed, for example. In this case, his decision probably came from the two boxes between the two of us. Two identical wooden boxes about the size of a shoebox, but cube-shaped. Nothing to discriminate one from the next, other than the predetermined biases. So the young guy had weighed up his biases and picked left.

So, left it was.

I drained the last of my beer and got up from the armchair. I put the empty bottle down on the box on the left and turned to leave. The young guy watched me, unsure as to what would happen next.

Curiosity would seize him eventually. It always did, and it didn't take long. Eventually, he would move the beer bottle and lift up the box and see what lay beneath, and then he could see the consequences of his choices. He could feel the whole weight of them. After all, it wasn't like we'd made him pick between which of his daughters he wanted to save.

Because we had taken the decision away from him.

His screams caught up with me halfway up to my office, though they didn't last long. A nine millimetre round saw to that.

I closed the office door behind me and slumped down into the plush leather chair behind my mahogany desk and rubbed my hands hard into my face. I didn't want to think about what lay beneath the two boxes. I had seen enough to get the picture. Chavez had set it up before I arrived. His stomach was stronger than mine.

On a scale of one to ten on just how reliable a guy can be, Chavez was high up there. An eight or nine. The type of guy who asks no questions and always gets results. But he was a constant reminder of just how far I had come. Sometimes, I wasn't sure whether he was there to aid me or sent by Reyes as a watching eye. I knew I would never shake the feeling that one day, I might be the one looking down the barrel of his Beretta. But for now, I couldn't dwell on it. Domingo Reyes was a mercurial man, but it was always best to stand beside him than against him. After all, there was a reason they called him the Black Viper.

In the seventeen years I had known him, Reyes had never wavered in his deadly approach to problem solution. More men, women and children than I cared to think had died at his command, sometimes by his own hand, sometimes others. Sometimes mine. If someone had told me when first we met what Domingo Reyes would make me do, I would have turned down his offer and fled the state. But at the age of twenty-six, seven million dollars was a hard thing to pass by, and the same juvenile stupidity that had made me jaywalk right into the path of a bus blinded me against the horrors of going into business with one of the country's most dangerous criminals.

Seventeen years and countless millions of laundered dollars later, and here I was, the Viper's second in command. Right at the forefront of his empire. And there wasn't a thing I could do but smile and obey like a damn hound.

The cell in my jacket pocket buzzed. I fished it out and answered. No reason to look at the number. Only three people in the world had my number committed to memory. Rule one of the Viper's business guide. Memorise cell numbers.

'Yes?' I sighed into the receiver.

'Jackson, is it done?' The voice was Reyes. He called me Jackson when he was impatient, which was almost all the damn time.

'The problem is taken care of.'

'Then why haven't you called in?'

'I was just about to.'

'Spare me your excuses.' He snarled. 'I want results.'

Which elicited another involuntary sigh from my mouth. I caught it just in time to not broadcast it down the line. Truth was, the news was bad. Even with the problematic thief dealt with, income was down. Way down. Only a fifth of the weekly intake had made its way to me, and it wasn't likely to get any better. With the DEA, FBI and every other three letter acronym government agencies in the country crawling down our necks, everything was going to shit. Product manufacture had all but ceased. No product, no sale. That which was still in circulation was either getting snatched up by the DEA or stolen by rivals and customers alike.

A shitty situation for a crumbling business.

'It's not good.' I said hesitantly down the line. 'We've had another four pushers picked up in the last twenty-four hours. They're cleaning shop. At this rate, we won't have enough product to last the end of the year. And then there's Salazar.'

'Hector Salazar is not a concern anymore.'

'But his son is. Ramiro is causing problems. He's drawing attention with his actions.'

'Ramiro is a child. He doesn't understand this game, just like his father. Leave him to his toys.'

'Sir, we need to think about damage control. We're facing problems on all fronts, and without a plan, we won't last much longer. We need to discuss how much are we willing to lose?'

'*We*?' Reyes hissed. 'Did *we* start a business together? Did *we* create an empire from nothing? Use that word again, and I will show you how much your life means to me.'

I bit my tongue and resisted the urge to backtalk. It was my club that laundered his money. It was my life that was on the line day after day, all while Reyes hid in the shadows like a damn puppet master. I wished I had another beer. Actually, I needed something stronger.

THE FATE OF GLASS

'I don't give a damn what happens to the piss ants crawling the streets. I want an update on China.' Reyes snarled.

Of course. The new venture. It was all the old businessman had talked about for weeks. Truth was, everything was on course, yet Reyes had barely turned his attention to anything else since it began. The cracks weren't starting to show, they were already there, and tearing everything apart.

'Everything is on track.' I replied, searching my mind for anything remotely interesting to disguise as an update. 'I spoke to Chang just this morning, and he assures me everything is in order.'

Reyes huffed into the receiver. His agitation was evident even across the line.

'Sir, I need to know what we do about Salazar.' I insisted. 'If he continues…'

'If he continues he will face swift justice.' Reyes barked. 'But until I see that child as a problem, I won't waste my breath discussing it. I want an update this evening.'

And with that, he ended the call.

I dropped the cell on the table and rubbed my hands into my face, massaging the muscles. From the bottom drawer of my desk, I retrieved a bottle of single malt whiskey. A birthday gift, and an ever more frequent last resort. I didn't bother with a glass. I took a long pull from the bottle and held the liquid in my mouth, savouring the burn.

Everything had changed just six weeks ago. The house of cards had taken one gust too many, and tumbled. Ever since Domingo Reyes' old business partner Hector Salazar had gone and got himself killed, there was no going back. No amount of wealth and affluence would make a lick of difference when the might of the government puts you in the crosshairs.

They had come at him hard, attacking every part of his life, business and personal. The luxurious, thirty thousand square foot estate he had bought and fortified all those years ago had been the first casualty. Now valued at an eye-watering sixty million bucks, the enormous residence had been vacated the moment the sirens started up. The three-thousand bottle wine cellar, the fourteen guest bedrooms, and the nine-hole golf course had been thrown to the mercy of the vultures and abandoned. Even his prize collection of exotic snakes remained. *Thank God.* I couldn't stand the slippery little bastards, or what Reyes used them for.

Sure enough, the cops had come. And those filthy beasts had

torn the damn place apart. Hell, even Homeland Security had come for a slice of the pie. Warrants that were previously declined were suddenly approved, and the locusts had swarmed the building with a furtive bloodlust. And when a man can't save his own home, what is left?

From safe house to safe place, the old man had run. The Viper forced into hiding. If his enemies knew, they would jump on the remains like a pack of hyenas.

Not that any of that mattered to Reyes anymore. His sights were set higher.

I sighed to myself and returned the bottle to the drawer. As it slid shut, my cell buzzed again. A text message.

Can't wait to see you tonight. B.

The sight of her message melted some of the ice around my heart, and I couldn't help but smile. All of this was for her. It hadn't always been, but she had come into my life and recalibrated my focus. Where Reyes had centred my mind on money and power, B turned it away. She gave it purpose. Something money couldn't buy. This deep into the game, you started to notice the voids money couldn't fill. Then life became all about filling them. She filled them.

Me too. Might be late, but will see you when I can. F.

I typed the response, hit send and deleted both texts from my phone. A precautionary measure, but a necessary one. Even a burner phone could be stolen.

I returned the cell to my jacket pocket and got up. Hopefully, Chavez and his men would have removed the fresh corpse by now. The boxes too, and their contents. The thought turned my stomach and sent a shiver down my spine.

Just another day in paradise, I told myself.

TWELVE

THE FLIGHT OF THE MANATEE

THREE HUNDRED AND FIFTY MILES WAS A LUDICROUSLY LONG DRIVE. That's about five thousand, three hundred and sixty football pitches, or forty-three thousand, three hundred and thirty Double Decker buses. In fact, from our starting point outside the bar, we were closer to Havana than we were to the small town of Ozello. These were just some of the facts I had time to consider as I forced the tired old van up the state, and they didn't make the journey any less tedious.

The journey took slightly over seven hours. This was in part due to the heavier traffic in the city slowing us down, but also because I wasn't ready to leave immediately. I wanted some answers, however relevant they may be, on where precisely I was committing spending the better part of a day travelling to. We drove back to Eva's apartment, parked up, and climbed the stairs back to her quiet abode. While Eva packed an overnight bag, I borrowed her laptop and typed Ozello into the search bar.

Ozello, as I learned from the first link I clicked on, was a small unincorporated community right here in Florida. It sat in the middle of Citrus County. According to the internet, there was a whole lot of nothing there, except for swampland, and in the winter months, migrating manatees. Besides that, there was little to learn of its wonders. No random sites blurting out all kinds of intel on Lizbeth Quinn, or this mysterious Felix fellow, or Papa Reyes.

A quick search of Citrus County was more of the same. Of the seven hundred and seventy-three square miles of occupying space, almost two hundred square miles consisted of water. The two most notable things to happen there in the one hundred and thirty years since it started were the dwindling citrus industry, and the discovery of a large phosphate deposit, which had been mined up until the First World War, then left to be reclaimed by mother nature. Besides that, even the might of the internet could not glean any information to its worth. Not ideal, but I felt better for not going in blind, or spotting any obvious signs of warning.

So back to the van we went, and turned our eyes to Ozello.

At first, we clung to the coast. The North Atlantic Ocean watched us for most of the first two hours, before finally dropping away as we moved further inland. From there, we passed by the city of Orlando as we headed north. Sophie and I had considered Orlando as the destination for our honeymoon. In the end, it had come down to costs. We simply couldn't afford to save up for our first home, and splash the cash for flights to America. I felt a strange pang of guilt at the thought that I'd made it here without her.

We stopped three times along the way. Three times at service stations to fill up tanks and empty bladders. Eva was a quiet passenger. She slept for a long stint of the drive, comfortable enough in the knowledge that the further we drove from the city, the safer she was. When she finally woke, she spent most of her time wrapped up in her thoughts. She was the polar opposite to Nicole. Nicole would have done everything in her power to fill the van with noise.

But as all things did, eventually, the end came. As the clock on the dashboard showed quarter past five in the afternoon, I stopped a couple of miles short of our destination at a roadside diner that looked downtrodden and dishevelled. Inside, I spotted a catatonic waitress glued to the television screen. We got out to stretch our legs and eat something that wasn't pre-packaged.

It was hard to tell whether the waitress was confused to see another living soul, or annoyed to be dragged from her reverie. She dropped a pair of menus on the table and poured coffee for both of us before we'd had the chance to give her a smile, and returned only when Eva waved her down. We ordered our food. Chicken salad for the lady, and a cheeseburger for Sir.

'Do you think it's worth us finding someplace to stay the night?' Eva asked as the waitress dropped two plates of "food" in front of us. 'Or have you got a plan?'

'I suppose it can't hurt to get an early night. Although there might not be anywhere nearby to stay.'

'What should we do?'

'You're not a snorer are you?' I asked her.

'Not that I'm aware.'

'We could sleep in the van. That's what I've been doing.' I took a bite of the burger. I'd certainly eaten worse meals, but not many.

'What's your deal?' Eva asked, looking up from her meal in search of an answer. 'Living out of your car, beating up strangers. I mean, don't get me wrong, I'm glad you saved me, but you have to admit it's not a normal life is it.'

'It's a long story.'

'We've got time.'

'It's not interesting. I came here to get away from the world.'

'I don't believe you.' She said, taking in a mouthful of chicken salad. 'You've got a kind soul. I wouldn't peg you as the kind of man to just up and leave home to get into all kinds of trouble over here.'

'You did.'

'Trust me, this was not part of the plan.'

I took another bite of my burger to avoid an immediate response. Didn't work.

'Come on,' Eva urged. 'You've practically found out everything about me in the last day. You think I go around talking about my past with Quinn to everyone I meet? So it's a sore subject, I get that. But after everything we've been through, I'd hope you would at least be upfront with me.'

I swallowed the mouthful. She wasn't about to get the whole story.

'What do you know about that guy with the burned face?' I asked her.

'Nothing,' she said, looking out the window as though expecting to see him there.

'There's no one out here,' I said gently. 'Salazar and his men are hundreds of miles away. No one has been following us. I checked. And if he were, he would have done something by now.'

'How do you know?'

'If he knew I was here, in the middle of nowhere, he'd be on me like a tonne of bricks.'

'What happened between the two of you?'

'You don't want to know.'

'I do,' she insisted. 'You saved my life back there. I know you didn't do it for me, you weren't there looking for me, but you saved me. I owe you big time. I just want to understand how you came to be in the right place at the right time.'

The right place at the right time.

'It's complicated.' I said.

'Try me. I'm an actress. I eat complicated for breakfast.'

I looked from my half-eaten burger through the dirty window. Were there monsters hiding out there? Probably. There were monsters everywhere, if you knew where to look. I took a long pause, searching for the right words.

'Ramiro Salazar is the son of Hector Salazar. I don't know if you've ever heard of him?' Eva shook her head. 'He's a bigger deal here than back home, so it's probably for the best. He wasn't a good man. He thought I knew things, big things, that would change the world. He got it in his head that if he could track me down and catch me, he could make me tell him what I knew, and in turn sell it to the highest bidder.'

'What sort of information did he think you knew?'

'That's even more complicated,' I said again. 'He told his son to track me down by any means necessary and squeeze the information out of me. Ramiro found me in Europe. I was in a bad way. I wasn't exactly expecting someone to kidnap me. He forced me into a box and shipped me across to Manhattan.'

Eva's eyes widened.

'I don't know how long I was there,' I continued. 'Weeks at least. Ramiro and his men, they did things I'll never forget. They tortured me, physically and mentally, beyond the point where I prayed for death. But they never once asked me to tell them what I knew. That made it so much worse. If I knew that I had something they wanted, I would have told them. I didn't want to be in that place. I'm no soldier. I was never trained to withstand that kind of torment. I would have cracked had they given me the chance. I don't know if it was some kind of tactic. Hector had asked his son to find me, but they didn't seem interested in what I knew. I didn't know what they wanted, or how long they would continue the torment.'

'How did you get out of there?'

'Ramiro slipped up. He had this kid. Well, not a kid. The guy was probably in his late teens or early twenties. He wanted to be like Salazar, but he didn't have that psychopath's attention to detail. He messed up, and I managed to use that to escape.'

'So you're trying to get your revenge?'

'Sort of. Ramiro Salazar may wear his scars for all the world to see, but what he did to me is far worse. I just want to stop him from doing something like that to someone else. He's a monster, through and through. No one should have to go through what I did. But in terms of revenge, I guess I already got that.'

'How so?'

'Those burns on his face. He has me to thank for that.'

She placed down her knife and fork. The look on her face was one of complete shock.

'Just to be clear, I didn't go at his face with a blowtorch or anything like that,' I said, trying to undo some of the damage. 'I just blew up his house. It was karma that did that to his face. I was in there too, you know, and I came out fine.'

'When was this?'

'About six weeks ago.'

'I think I remember hearing about it. The police said there was an attack, right?'

'Correct. Hector Salazar had a lot of enemies, and they came calling. But anyway, that's a story for another time.'

I took another huge bite of the burger. The police had never mentioned my involvement. Most of the evidence had gone up in flames, so as far as the world was concerned, James Stone had nothing to do with Hector Salazar's death. Eva didn't touch her food. An awkward silence drifted over us like a bad smell.

After what felt like an hour, she spoke again.

'So how does all this tie into finding Salazar? You can't expect to find him up here, can you?'

'No,' I said, swallowing the final mouthful of burger. 'That's where Quinn's dad comes into play.'

'How so?'

'Well, you know that thing you read said he was into selling drugs and the like? Well, I think he and Hector Salazar were in business together. After Hector died, this massive empire of his was suddenly without a leader. Ramiro couldn't seize the reins because he needed medical attention, so everyone down the hierarchy had a choice to make. Pack up and get the hell out of dodge, or step up and take charge. I think that's precisely what Reyes is doing. The way the newspapers talked about him, he ran Miami. And now with him out of the picture, he's decided he wants it all for himself.'

'So how does that help you find Salazar?'

'Because I know him. You don't go through what we went through without learning how the guy works. He won't be willing to just give up what he sees as his birthright that easily. He wants it all because he has the ego for it. He's addicted to control. He wants to have it all, so that's why he's here. His father started it all in Miami. It's the heart of the whole industry.'

'So he's here to fight?'

'Exactly. He's here to take back the city, which means he has to go through Reyes to get it.'

'You think that the enemy of your enemy is your friend?' Eva asked.

'You got it in one. If I can find Reyes, I can use him to lure out Salazar. Then I can end this once and for all.'

We finished the meal and were back in the van before six o'clock, and ate the final few miles for dessert. Eva took the news of my encounter with Salazar pretty well, at face value at least. Whatever it had done to her internally was anyone's guess. She had suffered a similar fate, albeit a damn sight easier than mine. But it wasn't about the scars. They healed with time. It was about the lasting effect it had on the mind. The nights I woke in a cold sweat, thinking that Salazar was right there, watching me sleep. His continued presence in the world haunted me. His ruthless tenacity put nothing off limits. Be it a month or a year or a decade, I couldn't be certain that one day he would be there again, ready to pick up where he left off.

Which meant he had to die.

THIRTEEN

OZELLO

THE NIGHT WAS STILL YOUNG, SO WE DECIDED THAT INSTEAD OF heading straight to bed, we would see if anyone had heard of the mysterious Felix. The internet had done a great job of explaining just how strange a place Ozello was. Of the houses we passed, each was propped up by a series of ageing supports. Flooding in the Citrus County was a serious affair. Hurricanes were known to favour the Gulf of Mexico, which put this small backwater settlement in the line of fire. We pulled up at the first house with the lights on and climbed out.

'Game plan?' I asked as James switched off the engine.

'Go in guns blazing and take no prisoners.'

'Yep, that seems like the only option. But if for some reason that doesn't work, what shall we do?'

'I guess we just see what people know. This is hardly the sort of place that sees a lot of action. Surely someone took notice.'

The door was slightly ajar, and the faint sounds of music came from within. I knocked, and the door swung inwards slightly.

'Hello?' I called inside. The music died down, and I could hear someone approach. A large, grubby man appeared in the gap. His face was damp with sweat, and dirt clung to every inch of skin.

'Somethin' you need?' he grunted in a thick southern accent.

I straightened up and gave him a wide smile.

'Hi there,' I beamed with false enthusiasm. 'I'm looking for someone, Lizbeth Quinn. You heard of her?'

He shook his head.

'Ain't no one by that name round here.'

'Do you know if someone around these parts might know? It's important.'

'You guys cops?' He eyed me suspiciously.

'No. Not cops. We're just friends of her is all. We're trying to find her.'

'She ain't here.'

'Okay, what about someone called Felix? He's a big guy, African American. Know anyone by that build?'

He shook his head.

'Ain't much in the way of them folk round these parts.' He grunted, closing the door in our faces.

We walked back to the van and climbed in.

'You get the feeling he knew something about Felix?' I asked.

'He dodged the question.' James replied, pulling back out onto what counted as the country road. 'But if this place is linked to Reyes, I'm sure his reputation precedes him, if you know what I mean.'

'Maybe they're afraid to talk.'

'Then how do we make them talk?'

How indeed.

'I've got an idea.' I said. 'Come on, let's find someone else.'

It didn't take long to find the next place. It was a decrepit fish and tackle store. Unlike the other structures, it wasn't propped up on supports. Instead, it sat on the bay atop a rickety pier that had begun to degrade at the far end, silhouetted in the fading light against the seemingly endless ocean.

The bay was enormous. I had no idea how far it stretched before it finally met solid land, with only a smattering of miniature islands dotted in between. Back when the phosphate mining industry was still booming, I wondered if they would have shipped out the product, or followed the long, winding the roads. Shipping would be quicker, and cost-effective, but ran the risks of sinking, or piracy. Those smaller islands would make the perfect cover for someone wanting to stage a heist.

Or for someone wanting to smuggle something in.

From the window of the store, I could see the owner hustling around inside. He was a fresh-faced guy, maybe mid-thirties. He looked up from his business as we approached.

'We're closing,' he said bluntly. 'You lookin' to buy somethin'?'

THE FATE OF GLASS

'Maybe,' James said, taking the lead this time. 'But I've got questions first.'

'This ain't a library, you know? I've got a store to run.'

'Not if you're about to close up you don't. Come on, it'll be quick.'

He sighed again.

'A'right. Go ahead.' He mumbled.

'Felix sent us,' I said, looking at the grumpy store owner. 'He's concerned that someone has been talking. We're here to make sure everyone is on the same page, okay?'

The owner pushed off the counter and pressed his back against the wall behind him. The various hooks and bait that hung down were pushed aside.

'Ne'er heard of 'em.' He croaked. 'Ain't anyone here by that name.'

There was something in his stance. He looked naturally defensive – an unfortunate trait for a store owner – but there was hostility there. He arched his back slightly. It was an instinctual reaction, like two bears fighting over a mate. His subconscious wanted him to appear bigger and more ferocious than he was. Quinn herself had a similar trait. I only saw it a couple of times in her, usually when family was mentioned.

'Bullshit. You know exactly who he is,' I pushed. 'Just like you know who's been sending you a little something extra to keep your mouth shut.'

He shifted slightly, moving his weight from one foot to the other.

'My business is my own.' He snapped. 'Everything here is legal. I don't have to answer your questions.'

'You want to bet on that?' I snarled, channelling my inner Quinn. She always knew how to get her way. 'Or do we need to come back here in a couple of days and see just how well you're doing after Felix finds out you won't cooperate?'

'Okay, okay.' The store owner huffed. 'I do as I'm told, okay? I haven't said anything about anything. I keep my mouth shut and I make sure I stay away.'

'Stay away from where?' I asked.

He looked between the two of us.

'The old mines. Like I was told. I don't say nothin'. Promise.'

We were back in the van a minute later. James had got the cowardly store owner to give us directions, and we hadn't stayed around to watch him piss his pants. James drove. We were told to head back out of town, then turn left at a small fork we had dismissed on the drive in.

'Well done,' James said as he bumped down the old dirt track. The van bobbed and weaved through the grooves. It was clear the road wasn't used much, but enough for the track to remain visible. 'What made you think of it?'

'It was simple really. When I came here with Quinn, she argued with this guy Felix by one of the houses. He didn't seem too concerned about making a scene until he spotted me in the car. Why would anyone be like that if they had something to hide, right? This place is too small to hide anything. I figure everyone here knows, and gets paid to stay quiet.'

'Smart.'

'Thanks.'

The road dipped down into a thick field of reeds. They stretched high into the sky, blocking our field of vision. The track was low and waterlogged, and the tyres of the van sunk down into the mud. James fought for control and barely managed to save it from getting stuck.

'We should back up,' I said, looking hesitantly at the track. 'This is the last place we'd want to break down.'

'Agreed.' He threw the stick into reverse. The van struggled, the wheels spun into sludge. Slowly, we retreated up the track, and James found a spot to pull off onto solid ground.

'Looks like we're on foot for the rest of the way,' James said. 'You don't mind a bit of mud do you?'

'It's not the mud I'm concerned about.' I replied as we stepped down onto the squelching soil, 'Out here you've got to watch out for snakes. They hide up on the reed tops to sunbathe.'

'You're kidding me, right?'

'Try not to get in their way and you'll be fine.'

Reluctantly, James stepped forwards. I followed close behind. The murky, putrid water seeped into my shoes. It was silky and bitterly cold. We followed the track through the reeds. They rose high above our heads. The air was cool, but the smell was foul and stagnant.

Eventually, the reeds died away as the land rose up again. The temperature rose as James's snake fear subsided. We followed the track for about a mile, skirting around the edge of the bayou before moving slowly inland. The only thing to be mined around here was phosphate. If Quinn's father had interest in the old mine, perhaps he had found a new pocket of the resource. I fed the theory to James, and he shrugged.

'Could be,' he said. 'Seems out of character for a guy who dedicated his life to selling drugs.'

'If he doesn't own the mine, it would be stealing though, right? Not too much of a departure.'

'Sure, but I'm still not sold on it. Phosphate mining contaminates water. If he was reinstating the mine, the wildlife around these parts would suffer, and there would be an army of animal rights supporters and naturists swarming the place with pickets and pitchforks.'

'You mean naturalists?'

'What did I say?'

'Naturists.'

'Oh god. Nobody would want that. Although the bugs would have a field day with all that bare flesh.'

I laughed, and then stopped when I spotted something up ahead.

A mesh fence glistened in the last glimmers of sun.

It was new. Maybe only a couple of months old. There were only minimal signs of wear and tear, and the thick wooden posts dug deep into the land were fresh. The mesh was thick and tough and topped with barbed wire to deter trespassers. A good job, but a rushed one. Whatever the reason for it's erection, it hardly shrouded the contents in a clandestine mist.

James hoisted himself up to get a better view inside, not that it made much difference. Through the links, the mine was clearly visible. First and foremost, it was clear that Quinn's father was not using it for its original purpose. The land had been dug out decades ago, and nature had reclaimed it. If Reyes wanted to mine every last rock from the earth, he either hadn't started the process yet, or had found a new, subtler way to do it.

'You don't happen to have a spare bolt cutter on you?' James asked.

'Oh yeah, I've got one in my purse,' I said bluntly. 'Not got one in the van?'

He shook his head.

'Didn't plan on a spot of trespassing today. Otherwise I would have.'

The track followed the fence around to a spot further along where the track steadily descended. At the centre of the crater were notable signs of tyre tracks. They cut through the untouched grassland, leaving dark trail marks in their wake. But besides the disturbance, there were no signs that anyone had been here for years.

'There's a gate round there,' James said, pointing towards the spot where the track ran down. 'Maybe we could squeeze through there.'

'What do you think they're doing?' I asked.

'Beats me,' James replied. 'Whatever it is, they didn't want people snooping around.'

We followed the track around, keeping the fence on our right, and reached the gate a couple of minutes later. A metre long length of thick steel chain was wrapped around the latch. James gave it a shake, and the gate wiggled, but there was no way either of us would be able to squeeze through the gap. The top of the fence too was lined with more barbed wire. James took off his coat.

'If I can cover the wire, we should be able to climb over.' He said, eyeing the gate.

'James, this isn't right. We can't start trespassing. What if someone's in there, or if someone turns up? They'll call the cops, and we can't exactly excuse our actions, can we?'

James looked through the gate, then threw his coat up over the top, covering the barbs.

'Wait here,' he said. 'And keep an eye out for anyone. If someone shows up, you tell them we got stuck, and we were looking for help.'

Before I could object, he heaved himself up and over the gate, and landed with a thud on the other side. I watched him jog down towards the bottom of the excavation. As he grew smaller and smaller, it put the whole operation into perspective. The site was massive. Easily a square mile devoted to the age-old mine. In the twenty-first century, a dig of this size would have been a breeze. One hundred years ago, it had to have been dug out with blood, sweat and tears.

At the bottom, I could see what appeared to be an ancient barn built up against the far side of the excavation. Whatever lay inside, I couldn't tell. For such an old structure, it held up surprisingly well. In a storm, a place like this had to flood like crazy, yet the barn had managed to survive time after time. I watched the tiny figure of James reach it, and look around. He tried the barn doors to no effect.

He was there for a while, trying to find some way inside. I paced around, lost in my thoughts, waiting for him to return. I played through a series of scenarios if someone turned up and started asking questions, and how I'd handle it. These ranged from a simple conversation easily defused by flashing some charm and playing the victim, to fleeing from a raging madman with a shotgun. I wore down the grass pacing back and forth.

This all came so easily to James. He didn't seem to care about ramifications. He could jump a fence and stick his nose in other people's business without a second thought. He didn't care about threatening a stranger to find out what they knew or shooting a thug in the leg to save someone's life. If I had been in his shoes, could I have done that?

Quinn could have. She was tenacious. She didn't care what the world thought of her. She didn't care what she did, so long as it suited her. She didn't care about lying to me for over a year.

I felt the familiar twinge in my chest. The heartache had burned through me like a corrosive acid. I'd barely managed to eat or drink after she left. I let everything go. My job. My friends. My life. I became a shell of my former self. Even the memories of that dark chapter of my life hurt to recall. Quinn had completely destroyed me. Why was I trying to find her now?

Because of James. A man I'd not even known for more than twenty-four hours. I'd spent more time in the company of people I hated, yet I had put my trust in James, and followed him across the state to dig up bad memories. I didn't even know his last name, or where he grew up, or why he was here in the states.

Had I made a mistake in trusting him? He was a nobody to me. For all I knew, he was a serial killer who had lured me across to some secluded remote spot to slice me up and eat me. He could have done the same to Quinn. This whole adventure could be a charade.

I watched him jog steadily back up the hill towards the fence, and minutes later he dropped down beside me.

'Any trouble?' he asked.

'A band of mercenaries turned up, but I fought them off. What did you find?'

He shook his head.

'Whatever it is, it's been there a long time. That barn down there is ancient. There's a big lock on the door, and from what I can see inside it just looks like a bunch of old mining junk.'

'So it was a waste coming here?'

'Maybe,' he said. 'At least we've got something to go on. If

Reyes bought this place, there'd be a record of the sale. We might be able to track him down that way.'

'And if he didn't?'

'Then we can look up your pal Felix and see what he knows.'

He smiled. I didn't reciprocate.

'Come on, let's head back to the van,' he said. 'Last one there buys the sandwiches.'

'Oh, I'm avoiding bread at the moment. It's a diet thing.'

'You're no fun.'

We headed back the way we came, following the track around with the fence on our left. The weather hadn't changed from before, but a slight breeze had picked up. The cold air felt good on my skin. We didn't talk as we walked back to the van. James was deep in thought. I wanted to talk to him about his life, but I couldn't be sure the topic wouldn't spook him. I was becoming more and more certain he was a criminal. If that was the case, I could probably look online and find it out for myself. So I kept my mouth shut. I would find out for myself.

We trudged down into the field of reeds. The surrounding water looked deep. One wrong move and you'd be in up to your waist. James's fear of snakes would go into overdrive if that happened.

'Should be just around this corner.' James said as we neared the van.

'Then where to next?' I asked.

'Back to Miami, I guess, unless you want to have a crack at some of the other residents.'

'I'll be fine,' I huffed.

'You alright?' he asked as we turned the corner.

But I didn't answer, because two armed men stood beside the van.

FOURTEEN

TROUBLE

It was immediately obvious they were a threat. Both men had rifles slung over their shoulders. The guy closest had opened the passenger door and was searching inside. His partner was walking around to the back. The rear doors were open wide. Neither man had noticed us. *Yet.*

'Who are they?' Eva asked.

'Well, I'd guess they aren't the welcoming party.'

'What do we do?'

'Nothing yet.'

I waited for them to make the first move. They were about one hundred feet away, and for all I knew they could just be a couple of friends out hunting, although I doubted it. My bet was the store owner had made a call shortly after we left. I made a mental note to go back and break his nose.

'If something happens, dive into the reeds. I'll draw their attention, and you try to get out and take their vehicle.' I said.

'What if they come after me?' She asked. I could sense the fear in her voice. I took the pistol I'd stolen from Jorge out my coat pocket and discreetly passed it to her.

She held it like a bowl of hot soup. Never held one before.

'Just point and shoot.' I said. 'Aim for the chest. It doesn't matter if you just wound him. You just need to get out of there.'

She slid her hand around the grip. Didn't look thrilled at the prospect.

'Don't you need it?' She asked.

'I'll be fine without. We don't want a fight. There could be more men out there. We just need to get past them.'

The guy checking out the passenger side door climbed out and looked around.

And spotted us.

He shouted something to his friend. From the back of the truck, he ran around and stood beside his buddy. They didn't call out to us.

'Should we say something?' Eva whispered.

'Invite them over for tea?'

'I'm serious, James.'

I could sense their next move. Like a coming storm, the clouds were rising, the thunder rumbling.

In unison, they reached for their weapons.

'Now!' I shouted.

The two men swung the rifles around on their straps and brought them up to face us. Together, we darted left into the swamp as a round of gunfire soared behind us. Immediately, the water rose up to my hip. Eva was smaller and sunk deeper. Quickly, she hauled the pistol out above the waterline and held it up in front of her. The mud was thick beneath our feet, and traversal was much, much slower. Our only advantage was the distance between us. I grabbed hold of Eva's wrist and heaved her alongside me.

'We need to move, fast.' I whispered. 'Get out of their line of sight.'

Every step was slow and laboured. The armed men had to be close. No sooner had the thought entered my head did another round of gunfire burst through the reeds. Seeds rained down on us, but the bullets were high over our heads. It confirmed two things. The gunmen didn't realise how deep the water was, and in the dim light, they couldn't see exactly where we were.

I crouched down, so only my head was exposed. The water smelt of something sinister, and was full of debris. I pulled Eva down too. With her dark hair, she was almost completely hidden so long as no one saw her face.

'Stay down.' I breathed.

I cupped my hands down into the muddy dregs by my feet and scooped up a handful. I splashed the gooey substance on my face, and did the same to Eva. She recoiled, but didn't resist. Only the whites of her eyes and the exposed pistol stood out. She looked close to vomiting.

'Go that way,' I gestured towards the van. 'If you hear movement. Stop, and stay out of sight.'

'What if you don't come back?' She asked. Her voice trembled.

'I will.'

'But if you don't?'

'You can make a speech at my funeral about how I died valiantly.'

She nodded timidly and bobbed away. Within seconds, she was lost amongst the reeds.

I heard a loud splash as one of the gunmen jumped down into the swamp. I pushed away from my spot and moved further back. The smart money would bet on the two men splitting up, and they had. One would act as a lookout. The other would be the hunter. A smart move.

But it was also mistake number one.

It made things easier for me. So long as the sniper couldn't pop my head off, I was sure I could take down his buddy. I stayed low and listened to the sounds of the water. Only the last dregs of light stretched into the sky, and barely any of its glow permeated the swampy battlefield. The swamp water felt like I'd jumped into a foul-smelling cup of leftover tea. Cold and dreadfully unpleasant.

The hunter was moving closer. I caught glimpses of movement through the reeds, but there was no telling whether it was him, or the gentle breeze, or a terrifying swamp creature. I focused on the noises. The sound of disturbed water. The squelch of boots in thick mud. He had to be close, but it was hard to move much myself without drawing attention my way. Slowly, I eased forwards, taking care not to disturb my surroundings. The sniper would be tracking his partner, and would likely recognise the signs of another person wading through the swamp. Any sudden movement could be deadly.

Up ahead, the reeds parted, and I caught my first sight of the attacker. He was a big guy. Probably similar in build to myself. His skin was tanned from many days labour in the sun, and his hair had a sun-dyed look. He held his rifle up out ahead of him and turned in a steady arch as he waded along. It was another smart decision. Submerging the weapon ran the risk of blocking the barrel, or clogging the firing pin. But it also put him at a disadvantage. A rifle in close quarters was a terrible weapon to use. The simple act of pointing the muzzle at a target would take longer than a pistol.

In his current trajectory, I would remain at his nine o'clock and steadily move round to seven. I was in his blind spot. But he had to be going that direction for a reason, and I would put money on that reason being Eva.

I moved in behind and followed the path he had forged through the swamp. He was just a few metres ahead and was still aiming his rifle up at where he thought our heads would be.

Almost fully submerged, I used my hands to propel through the silt in near silence. The gunman was struggling in the swamp, which made my approach much faster. I was just a few feet away. The gunman moved, disturbing the water around him. Something down by his side moved. It was small and sleek.

A snake.

It scuttled through the water with freakish ease, right towards my head. A satanic look in its cold, black eyes.

I couldn't stop myself. I leapt out of the water and brought my arms up to defend my head. The rush of water startled both snake and gunman, and both reacted. The snake altered its course and disappeared in a flash.

The gunman, however, was more of a problem. He heaved himself around through the sludge and had the gun pointing in my direction much faster than I had expected. I threw my hands up and grabbed hold of the barrel, and he fired a reactionary shot over my shoulder.

The gunman was no pushover, and had a solid grip on the weapon. But his feet were not on terra firma. I heaved the rifle backwards, out of his grip. He fell forwards, and we crashed back down into the murky water.

The first thing to hit me was that the swamp tasted awful. The second was that the man attacking me was as agile as a fox. He knew that in such close quarters his rifle was useless, so he let go. As my body sunk into the acrid sludge, he slipped his hands around the butt and the barrel of the rifle, and pressed it lengthways into my chest.

Under the water, I was useless. I heard a round of muffled gunfire from above the water. The sniper was taking pot shots into an uncertain battlefield. I scrunched my eyes tight shut. Thick, dirty water flooded up my nose and burned my nostrils. Involuntarily, I gasped, and the vile fluid flowed into my mouth. My stomach twisted, and I had to fight the urge to gag. Desperately, I pushed back against the rifle, but it was useless. His weight trumped mine. He had my torso pinned.

But not my legs. I hauled them up and wrapped around his waist like a big goddamn satanic snake, and used every ounce of core strength I had to heave him onto his back. His body was immensely strong. But my legs were stronger. He fought against the assault. Either he could let go of the weapon to untangle my legs, or he could pray he was strong enough to hold on till I drowned.

The need to breathe and vomit was unbearable. I could feel my strength waning. I gave one last enormous heave and pulled my legs down. He caved and flopped back. Like a human seesaw, as he descended, I emerged. As my head broke free of the ghastly slime, I gasped wildly. I couldn't have had more than a couple of seconds left.

But as my body relaxed, the gunman went into overdrive. With no weapon to occupy his grip, he wrenched my legs off him and burst up out of the water like a filthy, wrathful merman. As a cascade of miasmic water arced through the reeds, he lurched forward and threw his arms around my waist, and once more I plummeted back into the swamp.

Neither one of us was winning awards for style. I needed out of the situation, fast. With my balance ruined, all I could do was leapfrog backwards to get out of his reach.

The hunter changed tact. He wanted to ride me like a bronco into the afterlife. He pounced forwards and threw his weight down on me. He knew how to fight dirty, but so did I. I swung my arms around him and pulled him into a bear hug. My tactic put his face right down in the swamp water and left him with little option to retaliate without giving up his position on top.

He conceded and bucked around. Once again I was upright, with my arms trapped beneath our combined weight. Neither of us had our heads above the water, and if nothing changed, it would come down to who could hold their breath the longest. I tried to wiggle free, but without much room to manoeuvre, I was shit out of luck. Our heads were just inches apart, and he was trying desperately to use the lack of space to his advantage. His forehead blindly jutted forward, aiming at anything close enough to become a target. I tilted my head back as far as possible, leaving only my chin in his range.

I wiggled my knees up to my chest, gaining more stability, and squeezed the hunter as tight as I could. Using my legs as a springboard, I launched up, pivoting on the top of my ankles. At the same time, my arms and back muscles tensed long enough to lift the hunter up off of the ground. As we neared the peak, I let go of the man and slipped my arms free. He collapsed back into the sludge, which stunned him enough to give me a second's head start.

I pushed up and swam out of his reach. But once again the hunter was on point. He rose up out of the water and pounced at me.

And his head exploded.

I'd caught the rifle just in time, and twisted it into the direction he leapt from. I squeezed the trigger instinctively, and the bullet rocked down the chamber and a split second later caught the guy just below his right eye. He crashed down into the swamp as blood protruded from the fresh wound and tainted the murky water.

I breathed a sigh of relief.

One down. One to go.

FIFTEEN

STAND OFF

THE HUNTER FLOATED FACE DOWN IN THE SWAMP. FRAGMENTS OF skull and brain matter drifting outwards like a live-action Jackson Pollock painting. Whether it was the sight of such an unpleasant mess or the excessive amount of swamp water I'd inhaled, but I couldn't hold back. My stomach contracted, and the burger I'd enjoyed earlier came rushing back up to the surface, along with a pint of swamp water. I flopped backwards away from the mixture of skull and sick, clutching the rifle like a life vessel.

The rifle was one I recognised. The M14 rifle. Designed and mass produced between the fifties and sixties, during which time over one and a half million were built, and had a part to play in almost every war since. A weapon for just about every occasion, including a one on one in a Florida swamp.

But the chances of it lasting much longer was not something I was willing to bet my life on. The first bullet had already been locked and loaded, so the likelihood of a misfire was minimal. Anything short of a slug stuck halfway down the barrel was not going to be much of a problem. But as the spent shell ejected, it left a snuggly little void for the Floridan lifestyle to flood in and occupy. Putting my faith in the second bullet hitting its mark was not as comforting as I would want, so I needed a plan.

Mr Sniper was still out there. No doubt he had heard the disturbance, which meant either he knew his buddy was dead, or I was. The longer the ensuing silence, the more likely it was the former. Sooner or later, he had a decision to make. He could jump in and try to keep the party going himself, stay where he was and keep taking potshots at every Stone or snake that drifted in his way, or he could count his losses, retreat and call for backup. Only time would tell which he went for, and I wasn't about to wait to find out which it was.

I moved left, keeping the track and the sniper somewhere on my right. If I could get further down the track, I could get behind him and take him by surprise. High risk. At any point, he could turn round and put a bullet through my face. But high reward. If he saw my rifle aimed at him, he might have the sense to know he wasn't going to win.

All that changed a second later. Through the reeds, a woman's scream broke the silence. Eva.

I threw caution to the wind and heaved myself towards the path. If Eva was in danger, I had to help. I didn't care about making noise. I didn't care about snakes or whatever malevolent beasts lurked nearby. Sludge sloshed and splashed as I forced my way back to the road. As I neared the track, the reeds thinned, and I had a better view of the scenario.

The second gunman had heard my approach. He fired a warning shot into the reeds.

'Come out here with your hands up.' He shouted.

I waded out and climbed back up onto the track. My clothes and skin were black with foul-smelling mud. I probably looked more like a swamp monster than a human. The gunman eyed me cautiously. He had his weapon raised, just not at me. Eva, trapped between the muzzle and the side of the van. She was equally filthy, though the look of fear resonated through the mud. The gunman was about six feet away from her. The muzzle of the rifle was out of her reach.

I held the stolen rifle with the end pointed down to the ground. It too was caked in muck. I had zero faith in it working.

'Drop the weapon and put your hands up.' The gunman called out. I kept hold of the rifle.

'You not hear me?' He shouted. 'I said drop the damn weapon.'

'I've got a riddle for you.' I said. My voice was calm like I was talking to him from across the table in a bar or restaurant. 'What's the only thing you can eat that eats you back?'

He didn't bite. Not in a playing mood. He edged closer to Eva, gun at her head.

'I'm serious. Drop it now, or she gets it.' He barked.

'Gets what, your witty repartee?'

'I won't ask again. Drop the rifle.'

So I did. The weapon was no good to me anyway. He knew it. I knew it. A satellite photo from a thousand miles up would know it.

'Hands up.' He shouted across to me.

'Why?'

'Because I said so.'

'Lot of people tell me to do things. Doesn't mean I listen to them.'

'I'll shoot her.' He insisted, poking the weapon at Eva like I hadn't seen it before.

'No you won't.' I said. 'You would have done it already if you were going to.'

He lunged forwards towards Eva and thrust the rifle in her face.

'You want to test that theory?' He shouted. 'Put your damn hands up now.'

I raised my hands slowly. Only halfway, and as slow as I could do it, just to piss the guy off. He pursed his lips together and scowled at me.

'Walk slowly forwards.' He ordered. 'Don't try any funny business.'

'Like clownmanship?'

'What?'

'The art of being a clown. It's funny business, right? I've never given it a go.'

'Quit being a smart ass and walk here.'

I took a step forwards. Slow and calculated. I was aiming for a pace fast enough to comply, but slow enough to annoy the gunman.

'Hurry up,' he barked. 'We ain't got all day.'

'It's this gosh darn mud. It's everywhere, and it's surprisingly heavy. You'd be amazed at the lethargy I'm feeling.'

'The what?'

'The lethargy. The lassitude. Come on man, the inertia. Didn't you learn the Queens' English in school?'

He brought the rifle round to face me instead.

'What are you, a damn dictionary? Shut up and hustle.' He used the rifle to gesture me over, meaning that the gun wasn't facing at either me or Eva. I looked over at her and hoped she had the same thought in her head.

'What can I say, I just have a fondness for words. They're the backbone of our...' I stopped, buckled and winced. 'Sorry, I've got a rock in my shoe.' I knelt down on one knee. 'I'll just be a moment.'

'Damn it, get your goddamn ass up off the floor.'

He took a step forward, putting Eva out of his field of vision. I looked at her and willed the thought into her head. Whether it was telepathy or similar-mindedness, I didn't know. Eva slipped her hand into the back of her trousers and pulled out the pistol. She pointed the weapon at the back of his head.

'Drop it.' She snarled.

Not expecting such an abrupt turning of the tables, the gunman turned his attention off me and looked right down the barrel of the gun.

'I'd do as she says,' I said to the outnumbered gunman. 'She's not in the mood for henchmen. This one guy killed her cat. He's in the hospital now.'

He dropped the weapon, and I moved up. When I was close, I took his weapon.

'Thanks for that.'

'Asshole.' He groaned. His face was grubby up close. His skin was in dire need of a clean, and his attempts of shaving the hair that spread almost up to his eyes and halfway down his neck were woeful.

'I'll let you have that one since I just gave your buddy a third eye.'

His eyes flared.

'I tell you what,' I said. 'I'll let you choose whether or not you live. Does that sound fair to you?'

'Kill me or don't,' he growled. 'You are going to die.'

'Well, that's pretty bloody philosophical for this time of day. How about we assess our current predicaments, and think about what's best, instead of talking about the futility of life, okay?'

'I ain't going to tell you nothing.'

'Excellent. I'm glad you're being so cooperative. So, if you don't mind, who sent you to kill us?'

'You stupid? I just said I ain't telling you nothing.'

'Oh I heard, but I don't think you understood what you said. It's a double negative, you see. You said you wouldn't tell me nothing, ergo you'd have to tell me something. Progress, you dig?'

'I ain't saying shit.'

'Again, that's good news. I don't want shit. I want answers. So step to it, won't you? We haven't got all day.'

He scowled and tried to move, but stopped when he felt the business end of the rifle jab him in the gut.

'I don't think you want to die,' I said. 'If you did, you wouldn't have come all the way out here to the arse end of nowhere at the behest of someone else.'

'I tell you anything, and I'm a dead man.'

'And here I thought this rifle shoots gummy bears.'

'A bullet to the head would be a gift compared to what he would do.'

'Who?'

'I can't say.'

'You can. There's no one out here to overhear. You tell me who sent you, I'll let you go. I'll even tell your boss when I see him that I shot you in the head.'

I watched his face. The internal cogs of doubt were twisting in his mind. I walked over to the van and retrieved a small stack of cash I'd kept for reserves, and held them out to the disarmed gunman.

'There's about a grand there. It's all yours. You can get yourself on a ferry to Havana, a motel for a couple of nights, and still have change to spare. You got family?'

He nodded.

'Call them when you get there. Tell them to meet you. You can start all over again.'

He paused. Weighing up the pros and cons. Not that there was much of an argument to make. He could live or he could die. He made his mind up fast.

He reached out for the money.

'Answers first,' I said, keeping the gun on him. 'Why did you come here?'

'We got a call from one of our people. They said someone was snooping around these parts. No one goes up here or starts asking questions about it on accident.'

'By accident.'

'What?'

'On accident is an oxymoron. It implies an intention to the accident.'

'A what?'

'Never mind. You were saying?'

'We get the call when people start asking questions. We act on it if they start mentioning names. We bring guns if they come up to the mines.'

'What do they want with an old mine?' I asked.

'I ain't paid to ask questions,' he repeated. 'Haven't been on site since day one. I get paid a lot of money to stand around and watch a dead end road.'

'So who's paying you?'

'I don't know. Never seen the boss. I only ever meet one of his guys.'

'And you've never tried to find out who employs you?'

'I heard whispers, you know? The guy who pays me, he's smart. He don't let anything slip. Guy called Felix Jackson. He's about the only guy I see going in and out to the mines.'

'See now that's more like it,' I said with a smile. 'We're getting somewhere now. What else?'

SIXTEEN

SAINTS AND SINNERS

THE LAST SLITHER OF LIGHT FADED FROM THE NIGHT SKY AS JAMES retrieved a pack of cable ties from the van and bound his captive's arms behind his back. He was completely caked in the foul-smelling swamp sludge. Once the guy was secure, James patted him down, taking a clam phone and wallet. The phone he dropped onto the passenger seat of the van, the wallet he flicked open, and pulled out a driver's license.

'Shaun is it?' James asked the gunman.

'Yeah.' Shaun replied.

'Shaun, I'm James. I'd say I'm pleased to meet you, but what would be the point in lying, right? We both want to get out of this place pretty sharpish, so let's not dilly-dally. First things first, where did you park?'

'We blocked the track just back there when we saw the van,' he said, pointing over his shoulder down the track we had all driven in on.

'What kind of vehicle is it?'

'Dodge Ram pickup truck.'

'You got the keys?' James asked.

But the other guy shook his head.

'He has them.' He nodded his head back into the swamp.

James sighed.

'Well isn't that swell.' He groaned.

'You didn't have to kill him.' Shaun muttered.

'And you guys didn't have to try and kill us either, did you?'

James responded. 'Don't get in a sulk because you lost.' He left Shaun kneeling in the mud and walked over to the van. A moment later he returned with a towel. He handed it over to me. 'Here, you can use that to get some of the gunk off you.'

'Don't you need it?' I asked.

'I've got another. Besides, no point cleaning myself before I go for another swim. Now if you'll excuse me, I've got a corpse to plunder.'

He turned and headed back towards the murky water. Within seconds, he was lost to the darkness. I listened to the sound of splashing water grow ever distant as he waded away. In truth, I was glad to have a little time alone. Well, alone from James at least. The gunman, Shaun, had spotted me emerge from the swamp almost instantly. The wild look in his eyes and the way he waved the rifle around had been terrifying. Now as I watched him kneel impotently in the dark, it felt like he was a different creature altogether. Subdued by another. James, once again, had saved my life. Yet the blasé way he acted was starting to wear thin. He seemed incapable of reasoning with those who stood in his way. He lacked sympathy, and he threw sarcasm around like it was going out of style.

Without thought, I exhaled noisily, which drew the attention of my former captor.

'He's going to kill me.' Shaun said in a hushed tone.

'He won't,' I replied, unsure why I was sticking up for a man I barely knew. 'He just wants to make sure you don't call for help. Then he'll let you go.'

I attacked the thick grime clinging to my clothes and skin with the towel. Most of the foul substance fell away, congealing in a large puddle on the ground, but anything shy of a thorough shower was never going to do the job. And there goes a couple hundred bucks worth of clothes. That kind of stench would never leave.

Shaun eyed me cautiously.

'Why're you helping him?' He asked me.

'It's mutual. He saved me, and he's helping me find someone.' I replied.

'You really trust the guy?'

'Like I said, he saved my life.'

'That's gotta be a first for Stone.'

I stopped towelling myself down and looked at the kneeling captive.

'What did you call him?' I asked.

THE FATE OF GLASS

He let out an uncomfortable chuckle.

'You don't know who he is?' He probed. 'Seriously?'

His eyes bore into mine. The look full of contempt.

'Tell me.'

But no sooner had the question escaped my lips did I hear the sound of splashing water close by, and the dishevelled figure of James appear in my peripheral.

'Christ that stinks,' he called out, shaking the excess water from his body like a dog. 'Remind me never to do that again. I think that smell will haunt me for the rest of my life.'

He approached me and held up the set of keys.

'You can drive, right?' He asked.

I nodded in the darkness, staring at the man I knew nothing about. He smiled at me and held out the keys.

'Mind moving their truck out the way for us?' He asked. 'Then just toss the keys in the swamp or something.'

'It's Jimmy's truck!' Shaun objected.

'Who?' James asked.

'Jimmy. Jake's brother.'

'You're saying a lot of names at me without giving any explanations.'

'The guy you just murdered. It's his brother's truck. He needs it for work.'

'Well, if Jimmy wants his truck back he'll have to come and get it. That's not my problem.'

James turned his attention back to me.

'You better get going,' he said. 'I want to get out of this place before it's too late.'

I took the keys from him without another word, turned and hiked back up the track in the direction we had come from. I couldn't shake the feeling in my gut that something was wrong. James Stone. I knew that name, but why?

I found the pickup a short ways away. It was a broad, silver beast. I'd known a lot of guys swoon over trucks like this one, but I never saw the appeal. I thumbed the button on the key, and the lights flashed in response. I swung open the driver side door and looked around inside. The driver had left his coat hung over the back of the seat. I pulled it off and rested it down so I didn't track mud across the upholstery. I started the engine, and jacked the seat forward so I could reach the pedals comfortably, and twisted the vehicle off the track. Once I was satisfied there was enough space for another vehicle to pull past, I switched off the engine and climbed out. I didn't throw the keys. I wanted answers first.

I walked back down the track towards the van. As I approached, I saw James had hauled Shaun to his feet. I hung back just far enough to stay out of their way. James retrieved the money he had promised and stuffed it into his pants pocket, but he kept Shaun's hands tied.

'You've got a few miles hike until you get back to town. As much as I'd like to trust you, you did shoot at me, so I don't. I'm not going to untie you, so try not to fall over or think too much about the itch on your nose.'

'I don't have an itch on my nose.'

'You sure about that?'

Shaun twitched the muscles in his face.

'Now like I said, use that money and get your family out of the country. Your boss will kill you if he finds out what you've done. Don't forget you and your partner just got beat.'

'What you did to those people…' Shaun started, but James cut him off.

'You'll want to learn to hold your tongue if you want to see the dawn, okay?' he snarled. 'I've been pretty bloody liberal with kindness. But don't think for a second that I'll keep that going.'

'You're going straight to Hell.' Shaun spat back.

'Then I'll see you and your shit-head friend there, won't I? I tell you what, whoever gets there first can get the first round of drinks in, yeah?'

James gave him a pat on the back and sent him begrudgingly on his way. Shaun shuffled up the track in my direction. His eyes were glued to mine.

'Don't trust that guy,' he whispered as he passed me. 'He's no saint.'

I turned and watched the man follow the track until his figure faded into the blackness. Behind me, I could hear James busy himself with his van. The piercing glow of the interior light spilt out into the night. I stared at the looming shadow that stretched out before me.

'We better get going,' James called after a couple of minutes. 'If we're lucky, we could maybe find a motel or something to get a proper wash.'

I didn't move. I didn't reply. I waited until he noticed, and came over to check on me.

'Hey, are you okay?' He asked. Again, I ignored his question. I felt his hand on my shoulder, and I recoiled. 'What is it?' He asked, stepping in front of me to look at my face. 'I know this kind of thing can be awful, okay? If you need to talk about any of it, you know I'm here…'

'Who are you, James?' I asked.

'What?'

'It's a simple question. That guy Shaun recognised you. He was afraid of you. Who are you?'

'Trust me, that's anything but simple. Look, let's just get out of here, then we can talk.'

'I'm not going anywhere with you until you explain. I'm not an idiot. I know you've got to be some kind of criminal. Tell me why some stranger would be so scared of you?'

'Just drop it, okay? I don't want to talk about it.'

I pulled the pistol out and held it by my side. He saw me do it. I could see the look on his face change.

'What are you doing?' He asked cautiously.

'I'm not going anywhere with someone I don't know.' I said, stepping back slightly to stay out of his way in case he made a move for the weapon. 'I've put a lot of trust in you. I told you about the deepest secret of my life, okay? I don't exactly go around sharing that kind of info with everyone I come across. Whatever it was, I want to know.'

He rubbed the palms of his hands into his eyes. Whatever it was that he was keeping secret, it weighed on him heavily. I took the opportunity to skirt slowly around him so that I was in between him and the van.

And the stolen phone.

'Look, I want to tell you,' James said. He was facing away into the swamp with his back to me. 'I want to be honest about it. But it's hard. The media blew it out of proportion. There's a lot of hyperbole, and it's not like I can just go and tell my side of the story.'

'What did you do, James?'

'Please, can you just put the weapon down first?' He asked, but I shook my head.

'You need to tell me who you are, right now.'

He turned to look at me. His eyes were sore.

And then he told me.

With every word he spoke, I felt like a toxic cloud swept over the world until I could barely register what was real anymore. It seemed impossible. Incomprehensible. How could I be so stupid? His face had been over every newspaper and television screen for months, and yet I had let him into my home. I'd left him alone while I slept. I'd shared my most intimate and vulnerable secrets with him as though he was my friend. I'd exposed myself to a monster. *The* monster. The way the papers had spoken about him had made him seem inhuman, like the man standing before me should be part beast. A werewolf, or Wendigo, with peeling skin and bloodthirsty eyes.

Yet somehow, what stood before me was worse than all that. Because he was real.

'Calm down.' He said. He held his hands out. I staggered backwards and struggled for air. He took another step forward.

'Don't.' I gagged. 'Stay away from me.'

I pointed the gun at him.

He nodded and stepped back.

'Please, just let me explain,' he said. 'I'm not the guy they say I am. It's much more complicated than that.'

I needed to call the cops. I needed them to take him away.

'I'm not a terrorist. I'm just a normal guy. Please, I just want to talk about it. I promise I won't hurt you.'

He took a step forwards.

'Don't come any closer.' I screamed.

He retreated pretty quickly.

'You don't have to do this Eva,' he raised his hands in the air. 'I'm not going to hurt you. I want to help you. Quinn too.'

'Don't you say her name. Don't you dare.'

'Please, just put the gun down, and we can talk. Just give me five minutes I'll explain.'

'I don't care. You're a psychopath. I don't want to hear any of your lies.'

There was a flash of something feral in his eyes.

'You don't know what actually happened to me.' He snapped. 'Not the bullshit they put on the news. The real stuff. You haven't a clue. If you're too stubborn to listen, then fine. But don't forget the fact I've saved your life twice now. Don't act like that doesn't count for anything.'

He lowered his hands.

'Shoot me if you have to.' He snapped. 'In fact, I implore it. I'd rather a quick death than what the rest of the world wants for me.'

'Keep your hands up.'

'Why? If you won't listen, then I'm not going to comply either.'

He walked away towards the swamp and ran his fingers through his filthy hair. I ran across to the van and snatched the stolen phone from the seat. I flipped it open and dialled.

'Nine-one-one,' said a female operator. 'What's your emergency?'

'I need help. Please, just send the cops.'

James spun around. The look on his face was one of horror.

'Wait!' He yelled.

I ignored him. He was just a few yards away. I ran as fast as my legs would carry me, with the phone pressed against my ear. The adrenaline surged through me, pushing me faster than I'd ever run before. I could hear James behind me. He was close. He would catch me, eventually.

'What's your location?' asked the operator.

'I don't know. We're near Ozello. Can't you just track this call?'

'We can do ma'am, but it will take a while.'

'Please just hurry. James Stone, he's here. He's chasing me.'

'Eva, wait!'

He was gaining on me.

I didn't stop.

'Stay calm and keep your distance. We are dispatching officers, but it will take time for them to reach your location. Stay on the line with me until they arrive.'

'He's right behind me. I don't have time.'

'Ma'am, just…'

James caught me by the shoulder and snatched the phone from my hand. He threw it to the ground and stomped on it.

'What the hell did you do?' He screamed.

'If you're going to kill me, go ahead and do it. I'm not afraid of you.' I spat.

'I would never hurt you. Never. If you would have just listened to me.'

'To what, your lies? If you think you can stand here and convince me that you aren't the man the whole world says you are, then you're deluded. I've heard the stories, I've read about what you've done, to your family, your country. And that tape. You're a monster.'

He glared at me.

'Don't you dare accuse me of harming my family!' He shouted.

'Everything I've done, everything I've sacrificed has been for them.'

I fired a shot at him. The bullet grazed the skin on his arm. He staggered backwards and looked at me in horror.

'Back up,' I yelled. 'I'm taking the pickup.'

'Like hell you are.'

'I'll shoot you in the stomach. You can die slowly for all I care.'

He scowled at me and backed away. I kept the gun pointed at him all the way up to the pickup, and only once I was inside did I lower the weapon. I fired up the engine once more and backed away. Clutching his wound, he swore at me.

A final gift from the monster, James Stone.

SEVENTEEN

BETRAYAL

I STOOD AND WATCHED UNTIL EVA WAS OUT OF SIGHT, AND THEN I screamed. A loud, visceral howl. I didn't stop until my throat was sore. I stormed back towards the van and threw my fist into the frame. I hit it, again and again, beating the metalwork out of shape. I couldn't feel. I couldn't think. Rage was all I had.

From beyond the darkness of my mind something awoke. The shadow stirred. He slithered silently across the void, as he had done countless times before. His arms reached up and wrapped around my shoulders.

'In a sulk, are we?' he hissed.

Finally, I stopped, and the pain gushed through me. My knuckles were sore and bloodied, and the wound on my arm throbbed. But worst of all was the pain inside me. I dropped to my knees and rested my head against the wheel arch.

'Piss off. I don't have any bloody time for you.' I shouted.

He laughed.

'How many times must we wander down this path of self-destruction?'

I looked across at him. He wore my face, my clothes, like doing so gave him some sort of authority over me. But he was nothing more than a fragment of a tortured soul. He had named himself the Wolf. Come to prey on the weak. Perhaps he was more a mutt.

'Call me all the names you like,' the Wolf said. *'It is merely a sign of fear.'*

'You know,' I spat, scowling into a pair of eyes I knew didn't *exist. 'For a moment I thought "maybe I've got over being totally fucking insane and seeing visions", but no, here you are like a bad case of haemorrhoids that just won't quit.'*

His poison filled my mind in moments like this, aiming to take over. Not that I would let him. He had no control over me. He would never have control over me.

'Another woman has come and gone,' he growled. 'Did you love this one too?'

I ignored his taunts.

'She was terrified of you, did you see? The fear in her eyes. That is your only legacy. You will forever be nothing more than that. She thought you were a monster.'

'Is this whole act supposed to achieve something?' I snapped. 'Perhaps you think that you can bore me into submission?'

'What I want is for you to understand your destiny,' the Wolf growled. 'There is a long road ahead, James. One that you must take. Regardless how long you decide to fight it, you will reach the end. Filling your life with these menial tasks can only prevent it for so long.'

'Then humour me,' I spat. 'Tell me exactly what it is that you think I'm supposed to do? Go back and save Sophie and Peter? I'm trying to.'

'Don't make me laugh. They aren't part of our plan.'

'Then what is?'

'Deep down, you know what it is.'

'You're completely useless, you know that?' I spat at him.

'And you seem oblivious to the fact that we are one. Everything I know is already ingrained inside your mind. If you won't acknowledge that fact, then I cannot help you. You have been given a free ticket to drop all of this nonsense. Eva has gone, she will not help you with your trivial plans. Now we finally get the chance to drop this ridiculous endeavour that started when you arrived in this God forsaken country.'

'I won't stop until Ramiro Salazar is dead.'

'And what will that achieve? He has forgotten all about you. You are a mistake in his past. Nothing more. He is not a threat. Neither is Domingo Reyes. Don't poke the bear, James. Both of these men will destroy you if you go within a mile of them.'

'Have you forgotten what the Salazar family did to me?' I shouted. 'No, of course. You were silent for that entire ordeal. You hid in fear right from the moment they took me. That was your *perfect opportunity to take control. I was weak, afraid and alone. I needed help, even if you were all I had. But you thought we would die there, and you were too much of a coward to support me.'*

That got him to shut up.

'What, now you're lost for words?' I shouted. 'You're more than happy to berate me, but you were too afraid to feel what real pain feels like. Can you even for a second contemplate that level of fear? You want me to work with you towards some stupid goal, but when I needed help, you wouldn't lift a damn finger. So, unless you've got something helpful to contribute, kindly piss off and leave me alone.'

And he did, just like he always did. The familiar whisper disappeared into the wind, and once more I was alone.

Time was of the essence. I had to act faster than I had in a long time. I jumped up into the van and swung it around to face the way Eva had fled. It was highly likely that we were both about to take the same track out of Citrus County, and it was entirely possible she had stopped anywhere along the route to wait for the police, but running the risk of driving right by her was one I was willing to take. Leaving the van and heading out on foot was not an option, and I had to use every second of darkness to my immediate advantage.

I pushed the van as hard as I could. The tyres struggled in the thick, sloppy mud, but I didn't hold up. I had to get as far away from here as possible. Eventually, the track gave way to the potmarked tarmac track I'd followed in just hours ago. With the headlights on, I floored it back the way I'd come, bidding the strange little town of Ozello a less than fond farewell. I didn't stop until I made it back to the highway.

Then I pulled over for a renovation.

One of the main reasons I'd sprung for a white van was the ubiquity factor. Vans were everywhere, white vans especially so. You could see one hundred pass you by and not know whether if you'd seen the same van one hundred times, or one hundred vans once. I leapt through to the rear, heaved up the bed and grabbed two thin plastic oblongs. License plates. They were easy enough to come by. All you had to do was wander into any long-stay car park of an international airport and take your pick. You could be long gone before someone realised what had happened. Next, I grabbed the role of duct tape, and a large black aerosol can that I'd not yet had to use.

I climbed out and swapped over the plates in mere minutes. That was the easy part done. Next up was adding a little something extra to throw off anyone keeping an eye out for suspicious white vans in the area. With the duct tape, I tore off a series of footlong strips and stuck them onto the side of the van in the outline of the letters TLNT. The letters didn't have to make any sense. That was the beauty of it. TLNT could be the name of a plumbing business or extermination service or any of a million different possibilities. What it did was mask me. It made me look legit. Just another self-employed guy off to work.

With the spray can, I coated the space I'd laid out inside the strips of duct tape with a fine layer of black paint. Not enough to do a brilliant job, but enough to ensure a quick dry with minimal dripping. The mud was still a problem. I considered taking it through an overnight car wash, but someone might remember, or at least have a surveillance camera that would. The same went for borrowing a garden hose. It made me look suspicious. For the time being, the mud would have to stay. I tapped my foot impatiently as I gave the paint time to dry, then peeled off the strips of duct tape, and marvelled my quick job.

But not for too long, because time was slipping away.

As hard as I tried over the next hour, I couldn't take my mind off Eva. By now, she would have been picked up by the police, which meant that a BOLO for a white male covered in mud driving an equally dirty white van would be in full effect. Within the next twenty-four hours, any surveillance camera within a one hundred mile radius would be scrutinised. My van would be picked up as a potential suspect, and then the real hunt would begin.

On I drove, following the highway back down the state in the direction of Miami. On the horizon, clouds formed. The air felt powerful like it was building towards something catastrophic. The news on the radio warned about an impending storm ever since I'd arrived in Miami. The residents knew how to survive the damage, and hopefully, I would be long gone by the time it hit.

I kept going long into the night, unable to relax while knowing that any one of the bright lights in my rearview mirror could be an approaching police car. Yet with each that passed, I remained a free man. Not that that made me feel any better. The lack of police response filled me with a different kind of dread. Eva had to have spilt the beans on our escapades by now. Even the most inept of police departments would by now have searched the area I was last seen, which meant DNA would be swabbed, tyre tracks studied, and what remained of Jimmy's brother heaved from the swamp. Yet so far not a peep had been made by any law official to stop my progress south.

Why was that? Was Eva really locked in conversation with some police officer to comb through every fine detail of her small stretch with me, or had some other fate befallen her? If it were the latter, what could that be? CIA? FBI? Or was it Salazar or Reyes that had got to her?

'You shouldn't have told her,' The Wolf said. He sat beside me in the van, watching the sprawling sea of tarmac that stretched ad infintum ahead of us. He voice lacked the sinister undertone that had become the norm.

'You sound disappointed,' I replied. 'If I didn't know any better, I'd say you miss her.'

'If either of those monsters got their hands on her, then you're to blame. You didn't have to tell her.'

'Well, in sight of hind, if I'd thought it would put her in more harm, I wouldn't have.'

'That hardly excuses you.' He scowled at me.

'You're very quick to judge. If you want to contribute your opinion, don't always wait until after the shit's hit the fan to speak up.'

'I shouldn't have to,' he said. 'Like you're always quick to remind me, you're in the driving seat. I'm just here to advise.'

'Well, by all means, advise away,' I said as I yanked the van out to overtake a particularly tedious driver. 'I'm not exactly inundated with options right now, am I?'

The Wolf paused for a moment.

'I've got nothing.'

'Oh wow,' I replied sarcastically. 'Thanks for that wonderful insight.'

'What do you expect me to say?' He snapped back. 'We're of the same mind. Of course, I'm going to think the same as you.'

'Then leave me alone until you can think of something useful. Unless you want to take a turn driving through this hell hole?'

He gave me a patronising smile and disappeared.

I drove till I was beat. Outside a place called LaBelle, I pulled off the highway, and nosed the van down a small track lined with trees, finding a secluded spot where I could pull over. My eyes were raw with exhaustion, and my head felt like television static. I switched off the engine and crawled into the back. I flopped down on the mattress in my foul clothes and fell asleep in seconds.

I wasn't sure how long I slept for, but when I woke, it didn't feel like enough. The sun was up, which meant it was time for me to move, and to make a hard choice.

As much as it pained me to admit it, it was time to bid my farewells to my mobile home. I just couldn't run the risk of carrying on in the van. Eva would have given a pretty apt description, and although my alterations might have thrown them for a while, they would be no match for the sheer might of the American police force. One white van had entered Ozello, and one white van had left. Changed plates and hastily added logos only did so much.

I followed the track as far from civilisation as I could take it, then pulled off and forced the van across a field into a small stream at the far side. The place was practically untouched. The gentle trickle of the water lapped playfully against the tyres. The lowered riverbed hid the van from sight, and the thick trees above hid it from passing helicopters. It could be weeks before anyone stumbled across the van, by which time I could be anywhere in the world.

Or I could be dead.

I washed off as much of the residual swamp mud as I could in the stream, packed the leftover cash and enough rations to get me through the long day ahead, then hiked back up the way I'd come. I stopped to give the van one last look before it fell from sight. It had been an excellent vehicle. It had been a safe, comfortable home for over a month. It would be sorely missed.

Even through a thick layer of clouds, the November weather was still far hotter than my British body was used to. I was battle-hardened on rain and sea breezes. I'd have my jumper off at five degrees Celsius. The weather in Florida was easily triple what I was used to. I followed the road into the city and found a small store that had just opened for business.

I bought a white t-shirt with a faded floral design on the front, a pair of light grey linen trousers and a thin, maroon jacket to top the ensemble off. Combined with a new baseball cap, sunglasses and some cheap sneakers, I looked like a normal person again.

'That outfit suits you, sir,' said the overly enthusiastic boy on the counter. 'Although it won't be long until the storm gets here.'

'How bad do they say it's going to get?' I replied in my finest American accent.

'Oh, real bad,' he said with a sheepish smile. 'Word is Hurricane Joyce is going to come straight through this town.'

'Hurricane Joyce. I wonder why they try to humanise hurricanes by giving them names?' I mused.

'Oh, it's not to humanise them, it's to make sure people don't get confused. Folks used to think they were named after people who died on the Titanic, but that's not true. It's just so warnings don't get all mixed up.'

'Well, you learn something new every day.'

'Never seen one in person though. Not that I want to, mind. Pops wants me to head back up to his tonight. He's got a bunker in the backyard. Built it himself. He says no one should stick around these parts. He's a worrier, you know? But I'll be fine. Besides, it's an awful lot of money to get out there.'

I passed over the cash and then passed him an extra one hundred dollars.

'Go up to his place.' I said. 'Don't let him worry. Hey, what's the one thing you can eat that eats you back?'

The store clerk shrugged.

'A little food for thought. Don't hang around here for too long, kid.'

He thanked me profusely as I left. I threw my old clothes in the bin and left the store. I found a small library and ducked in to use the computer. It was an archaic device, circa nineteen-ninety-something, but it had a connection to the internet, which was all I needed. It took me a total of three and a half minutes to find out the information I needed, and I was out before the librarian got back from her rounds.

I stopped the first passerby and asked for directions to the nearest car lot. She was an older woman who walked with the confidence ingrained into those who've known their locale their entire lives. She recounted a list of available places, with her own personal reviews of each. There were four in total, the seediest of which was a twenty-minute walk. I liked seedy. Seedy implied fudged records that conveniently got lost on the way to the tax man. Seedy suited me.

An hour later, I was back on the road. The salesman had been almost a carbon copy of what I'd pictured in my mind. To say he was overweight was an understatement. He was suffering from some serious corporeal decrepitude. He sold me a weathered beige car that looked more like a hearse than a family vehicle. I paid six hundred dollars, but it wasn't even worth one hundred. He smiled through labyrinthine teeth as he swindled me from my not-so-hard-earned cash, and we parted ways all the more enlightened by the exchange. The only risk with a man of his greed would come when word of my presence spread throughout the town. If he put two and two together, the vehicle would be as useless as the van.

But for now, it didn't matter. I had somewhere to be, and so long as it didn't break down on me until I got there, then I didn't care. I couldn't help but feel that life was about to get harder. If Eva had made it to the cops, she would have told them everything she knew about my intentions. She knew I planned to head back to Miami. But it was a big city, and she had no idea where exactly I was heading. Which was good. Because I knew exactly where I needed to go.

And where to find Reyes' right-hand man.

EIGHTEEN

HIS FATHER'S LEGACY

I STARED AT A MARK ON THE CARPET. A SMALL, DARK PATCH. No bigger than a nickel. What was it, blood? I knelt down and rubbed my thumb against it. Wasn't damp. Figured it was all that remained of the thief. His body, as well as those of his wife and kids, had been incinerated. Their ashes scattered under the freeway. Now all that remained of the guy was a tiny blood splatter on my floor.

Go figure that would be my downfall. The one blemish on my entire business that the cops would spot, and then my whole world would come crashing down a little faster than it was already. I poured a little of my beer on the spot and rubbed it in with the sole of my shoe. That would have to do. Never thought I'd be cleaning up blood in my own club. Is this the life I wanted? The great Felix Jackson, a glorified janitor.

'What made him change his mind?' Chavez asked. He stood by the door. I took a pull on my beer and pondered the question.

'Serendipity, brother.' I sniffed. 'Don't question the logistics.'

The VIP lounge had been rearranged to suit the needs of the Viper. Gone were the clusters of leather seats and glass tables, replaced by a rudimentary layout. Two identical chairs, spaced six foot apart, lit only by the glow of the club's most decadent feature. The hanging aquarium had been put it at the request of Reyes, and had cost an eye-watering sum well into the millions. Why he wanted it, I wasn't sure, but it had certainly drawn quite a crowd. Night after night, hundreds of excitable drunks filed in to ogle at the spectacle thirty feet above the dance floor.

The greatest view was saved for the lucky few who made their way to the VIP lounge. The back wall had been built from reinforced glass, providing an unbeatable view of my own personal ocean. The subtle cerulean glow flooded the quiet space, amplifying the silence while it lasted. It wouldn't last. I knew they were on their way.

Domingo Reyes had been so resolute about his decision to shut out his former partner's heir. Ramiro Salazar was nothing to him. He wasn't part of the plan. Yet, something in the old man had changed, and without warning, he had told me to arrange a meeting between the two men. No reason requested, no answer offered. The Reyes way.

'Do you think this is a good idea?' Chavez asked.

'It's not our place to ask.' I replied. 'We're just here to stop it turning into a bloodbath.'

'And if it does?'

'Then we shut it down on the spot, you hear? I ain't letting my business go down because Salazar can't keep his cool. You put a bullet in his head if he so much as looks at Reyes the wrong way.'

'As you say.'

'Good. Reyes should be here soon. Go and wait for him, will you?'

Chavez nodded and left. Both Reyes and Salazar would be entering through the back via the private exit installed during the building's renovation all those years ago. Another of the boss's demands, and one that had come in use more times than I could count. It felt like something out of an old spy movie, but it was a necessity in this business. There was no telling who was going to come knocking.

The cell in my pocket buzzed. Instinctively, I pulled it out and answered it without looking at the screen.

'Go for Jackson.' I said.

'I like it when you talk like that.' It was B. I recognised her voice immediately. But where normally it brought warmth, today it made my stomach drop. 'My big boss man.'

'I can't talk now.'

'I just wanted to hear your voice. I missed you this morning.'

'I know,' I said. 'I had to shoot off.'

'We were going to get breakfast together.' The disappointment was clear in her voice.

'I'm sorry. We can reschedule it for another day.'

Reyes would be there any minute. He couldn't know.

'I don't want to have to reschedule with you. We're supposed to be in a relationship. You need to put in time with me.'

'I can't talk about this now.' I insisted. Out in the corridor, I could hear movement. 'We'll talk tonight, okay?'

'Whatever.' She said, hanging up.

I slipped the cell back into my pocket as the door behind me opened. Three men appeared. Chavez up front. Some heavy I didn't recognise at the back, and Reyes in the middle.

'Boss.' I said with a nod, handing him the glass of whiskey I'd prepared in advance. Reyes returned the nod and took and took the glass from my hand.

'Where are we with China?' He asked.

Again with China. There were more important things in play than that.

'Everything is on track.' I said. 'We've managed to secure transport out over the gulf as per your request, and I've been assured they have a flight chartered in Mexico to take the shipment. We don't foresee any problems.'

He moved away to the reinforced glass, watching the vast array of life floating by.

'Sir,' Chavez chimed in. 'He's on his way up.'

'Good.'

It didn't take long for him to arrive. The terms of the meeting had been strict. No more than four men each, yet I knew neither party would actually abide. It came as no surprise then when seven men entered the VIP lounge. Six smartly dressed thugs crowded in like a hive, protecting their leader. As they approached, the hive separated, making way for the burned man.

Ramiro Salazar looked worse than shit. In fact, shit would be an upgrade for him. The skin had warped to hell from his eye down to his chin. The flames had twisted his mouth into an elongated smile. He looked more like a viper than Reyes. He wore a sharp black suit, shirt and tie, with matching leather gloves, all no doubt hiding more of the damage done to him at his father's compound.

His ferocious eyes caught me, but I resisted the urge to look away. I'd seen enough monsters to know not to fold.

'Did you know that the great white shark has one of the strongest senses of smell of any living creature?' Domingo Reyes said. His back was still turned. His attention on the wonders floating inside the aquarium. 'If there were but a single drop of blood in one hundred litres of water, a great white shark would be able to detect it. They are nature's born hunters. They are unparalleled in their skill. They could rip apart a fully grown human male in mere seconds, yet we do not respect them. We catch them and cage them and put them on display. I think that says more about our species than any of our greatest achievements, don't you think?'

'I do hope you haven't brought me all the way up here to give me an ecology lesson,' Salazar hissed. His stretched lips distorted his words. 'If I were you, I would have started with an apology.'

'On the contrary,' Reyes replied. 'I came here to explain the gravity of the situation. But if all you came here for was an apology, then you're shit out of luck, Rami.'

'Do not call me Rami.'

'Why not? That is what your father used to call you, am I right?'

'Not for a long time.'

'Even so, I think it's important to remember where we came from. You are the bastard son of an immigrant, are you not?'

'Hector Salazar built this city with his own bare hands.'

'Well, he tried. I was the one who gave him the tools. Without my help, he would have spent his life digging in the dirt.' Reyes turned to look at his adversary. His frame silhouetted in the glow of the aquarium.

'You expect me to be impressed by all this?' Salazar sneered. Every word he spoke was elongated and hissed like a serpent. I could almost feel the burning rage searing through his pores. 'This vulgar display of wealth will not sway me, for it is not yours. Every cent you ever earned belongs to my father. Every single inch of it is mine by rights. It was my father's legacy. It was never yours.'

'Sure, it was Hector's product that started our enterprise, but it was my contacts we sold it to. He was production, I was distribution. The reason we became so successful is that we both understood that. I let him think we were equal. I let him dream that I had plucked him out of the jungles of Panama because he was unique. That assumption kept him loyal, and it will keep that tongue in your mouth if you honour your father's so-called legacy.'

'Do you really think my father didn't read you? He saw through this façade decades ago. He learned about each and every one of your contacts, and he forged his own dealings. He played you like a damn instrument. You have been redundant for years, old man. The only reason he kept you alive is that you were an obedient little dog.

You played right into the palm of his hand, and you didn't even realise it.'

'And yet, which one of us is still alive? The revered Hector Salazar is known throughout the world. He had a target on his back from the moment he arrived in the USA. Yet somehow, he managed to survive for decades without succumbing to his enemies, do you know why that is?'

'Because he was smart.'

'Not nearly smart enough. He survived because of me. I have been his shadow long before he appeared on the America's shit list. I made him the centrepiece of the whole organisation, all so that I could continue to keep our business afloat. I protected him, time and time again. I stopped every two-bit cop or crook from putting a round between his eyes. Hector Salazar was a figurehead. Nothing more.'

'You take that back.' Ramiro growled. 'You would have been nothing without him.'

'And now he's dead. Killed in his own home by some young punk who got too big for his own boots. And look at you. Tell me Rami, does it hurt? Can you still feel the heat eating away at your skin?'

Reyes looked him dead in the eye. The pain was clear as day. The fire still raged. He was mesmerised by it. Consumed by it.

'Do you really think you could run this empire in your condition?' Reyes spat. 'Since Hector died, the spinning plates are falling. Everyone is running for the hills. Your father's legacy is cracking, all because he got too complacent and got killed by one of his men.'

Ramiro snapped out of his trance.

'You sound afraid, Domingo.' His voice was full of menace. 'Have you finally realised you can't do all this alone? You talk the talk about spinning my father around your thumb, but the moment he's gone and you want rid of his empire.' He moved closer. His lizard face inches from Reyes. 'You are a coward. You cannot do this all by yourself. You never could. That's why you roped my father into this world in the first place. You wanted a scapegoat to take the heat, and now you can't stand it yourself. But trust me, I know a thing or two about heat.'

He smiled, and for a moment I felt Hector Salazar smiling at Reyes from the grave.

'You're out of touch, Rami.' The Black Viper spoke quietly, yet every word was loaded with power. 'Those pills you're on must be scrambling your brain. Your father was a tool. A means to an end. Don't think for a second that you're owed so much as a dime.'

Ramiro smiled again and walked away towards the exit. His men followed, bunched in close around him. As he reached the door, he paused.

'My father was fond of giving people a choice. I'm sure you knew that. So, to honour his memory, I'm going to give you two choices. Pack up and leave this town before dusk. You forget about this empire, and leave with your tail between your legs. Or you stay, and you pay the price for disgracing my father and being so audacious to assume you were his rightful heir.' He looked at the silver wristwatch around his wrist. 'It's nine fourteen a.m. That gives you eight hours and forty-six minutes to run as far as those arthritic legs can carry you. Otherwise, you'll feel the vengeance of the Salazar family.'

Reyes laughed.

'I'll be seeing you, Rami.' He leered.

Salazar huffed and stormed away, his men in close pursuit. Chavez and the heavy followed to make sure Salazar didn't tear my club apart. As the door swung shut, I couldn't help but wonder why Reyes had called the meeting. His only objective it seemed had been to antagonise the man. And while it was not beyond Reyes to do so, it did seem unjust.

I watched the Viper turn again to look out into the aquarium and waited for him to speak.

It didn't take long.

'I received a call this morning.' He said, his back turned away from me. 'Who do you think it was from?'

'I don't know, sir.'

'The sheriff up in Citrus County.'

I didn't respond. A response wasn't in my best interests.

'I pay my men a lot of money to keep a boundary between me and those on the ground. I pay *you* a lot of money to shield me. Yet, I found myself on the line to the sheriff of goddamn Citrus County telling me that someone was sniffing around.'

If the call from B had made my blood turn cold, Reyes' words made it glacial.

'Sir, I…' I started, but Reyes cut me off.

'Why do I feel like this is the first you're hearing about this?' He snarled.

'My people up at Ozello know to contact me at the first sign of trouble.' I insisted. 'If someone is up there, they know to call me immediately.'

'And yet, they didn't. Would you like to know why?'

I didn't speak. Just waited for the Viper's words to sting me.

'Because they are dead. The Citrus County sheriff called me this morning to let me know there was a situation. Said he's got a girl in custody and two people missing. Your people. The sheriff told me he took a little drive and found what was left of one of them floating in the swamp up near our site. Said he went up there after a girl came to hand herself over to the authorities. Said he was sorry. I asked him why. Said he'd had to call the FBI. Asked him why again.'

He took a long sip of his whiskey, letting me stew in the moment.

'Because the girl he picked up said the guy who killed your man was a fugitive. Went by the name of James Stone.'

Which set alarm bells ringing off in my mind like World War Three.

'The Brit?' I said, trying to stay calm.

'The Brit. The same goddamn Brit that blew up Hector Salazar and his compound. The same goddamn Brit that caused all this mess in the first place. So tell me, Felix. Why is the guy that killed Hector Salazar snooping round my business?'

'I don't know.'

'You don't know. Congratulations, Felix. You just became the dumbest fucking person in the state.'

He finished the whiskey and threw the glass aside. It smashed into the wall. Tiny shards of glass rained down onto the carpet.

'I shouldn't be in the dark about what's going on in my own city, yet here I am.' Reyes shouted. Rage evident on his face. 'I don't care what James Stone wants, I want him out of the picture, you understand? Same with this girl that handed herself in. You shut this shit down, right goddamn now.'

'Yessir.'

'And I want someone watching Salazar.' He barked. 'I want him unstable. I want him making mistakes. Sooner or later, he'll show his hand, and we will see what he's capable of. But under no circumstances is he or anyone else allowed within a hundred miles of Ozello, understand?'

'Yessir.'

NINETEEN

ANYTHING SHY OF THE APOCALYPSE

I WAITED ALONE IN THE CITRUS COUNTY POLICE STATION FOR OVER an hour. After I'd arrived and explained myself to the all too confounded receptionist just how dire the situation really was, I had been ushered away into a corner office to wait for someone to come and speak to me. But it was clear from the air in the room that no one was going to take me seriously. To them, I was nothing more than just a dumb city girl lured out by a handsome stranger into the middle of nowhere. A story told a thousand times to an audience of deaf ears.

Finally, the sheriff came a knocking. He was a wide guy with wise ideas. He handed me a cup of stale coffee and sat his fat ass down behind the desk.

'Miss Marlon, was it?' He grunted. 'My name is Sheriff Vasey here of the Citrus County Sheriff Department. I apologise for the delay. You see, around these parts we like to take reports of homicide real seriously. I've taken a ride up to where you described to my secretary and found the body. Now, I know you must be real shook up about the whole thing, but I need you to write up your witness statement. We've got pens and paper at the reception. Take all the time you need.'

'It's Miss Marston. Eva Marston.' I said.

'That not what I said?'

'No. And I want to know what you're going to do about James Stone.' My body itched with urgency. My knees danced on the spot.

'Oh, right. We've put in a call about Mr Stone. A representative from the Federal Bureau of Investigation is on his way to come talk to you about that. He should be here shortly.'

'But James Stone is out there,' I leaned forward in my chair, angry at the lack of interest. 'He could be anywhere by now. Surely you should have people out there looking for him.'

'Ma'am, I understand. But we are under strict instructions. This is a matter for the FBI now. Their representative will be here within the next few hours, and they will discuss the issue with you. We are forbidden from taking this matter into our own hands. So please, if you would care to wait in reception until they arrive…' He tailed off with the sentence and returned his attention to the stack of paperwork mounted on his desk.

I sat in the chair waiting for an apology, but when none came, I got up and walked away. The reception area was milling with strangers. They gave me a foul look as they caught my rather repugnant odour. I took a notebook from the reception, then sat and wrote down every slither of information I could think of from the past forty-eight hours that might help the authorities find James. The receptionist took it and dropped it onto her desk with an air of complete and utter disinterest. I wanted to shake her and scream in her face how urgent the situation was, but instead, I sipped a fresh cup of coffee ordered from a machine tucked into the corner of the waiting room, and watched the door patiently.

The FBI representative arrived fifty-nine minutes later. It was immediately clear he was with the Bureau. He sauntered in through the sliding glass doors and took his sunglasses off like a model on the catwalk. His suit was light grey and tailored to fit his muscular physique. He strode by the long line of patiently waiting visitors and flashed his badge to the woman at the reception, and she pointed towards me.

'Eva Marston?' He enquired. I nodded. 'I'm Agent Jonah Miles. Could you please follow me?'

Even his name fit the catwalk. He strode away back in the direction I had come, so I got up and followed him. He had a fast pace, and I struggled to keep up. We walked past the office of Sheriff Vasey and into a vacant room at the far side of the precinct. Once inside, he gestured me to sit and squeezed in the chair opposite.

His skin was dark, and his hair was short. He was well groomed, but his aftershave was overbearing. He pulled a recording device out of his jacket pocket and pressed the record button. After a brief introduction recorded on tape, he asked me to detail my interactions with James Stone.

And so I did. I began my story for the second time that day, starting with my departure from work, all the way up to the moment James revealed his identity. Agent Miles remained silent for the duration, occasionally jotting down notes. When I came to the end, he smiled and then reviewed his notes. I sat awkwardly, wishing I had a glass of water.

'So, you said James Stone rescued you from Ramiro Salazar's men.' Agent Miles said. 'Do you have any reason to believe he may have orchestrated the kidnapping to gain your trust?'

'Not that I can think of.'

'Not because of your relationship to Isabella Reyes?'

'I don't think he knew about that until afterwards, and I never knew her by that name. She told me she was Lisbeth Quinn.'

'She concealed her identity from you?'

'I guess so.'

Agent Miles raised his eyebrows and looked down at his notes. Didn't take a genius to guess what he was thinking.

'And did James Stone mention to you how he managed to track you down?'

'He followed one of the people there, I think. He didn't elaborate.'

Agent Miles made another note on his paper.

'What can you tell me about James Stone's relationship with the Salazar family?'

'I don't know much,' I said. 'He told me he was responsible for the burns on Ramiro Salazar's face, but besides that, he didn't talk about them.'

'And he didn't discuss the rising feud between Reyes and the Salazar family?'

I shook my head.

'On the record please, Miss Marston.'

'No,' I said. 'He kept his cards close to his chest.'

'Right.' More notes on the paper. 'So when he told you about Ramiro Salazar's burns, were you not suspicious of his motives?'

'I was, but I didn't know the whole story. I still don't.'

'But you decided not to call the police at that point?'

'I didn't know enough about the situation.'

More notes.

'And did James Stone tell you about how he arrived in America?'

'No.'

'He was shipped across from Europe in a crate at the behest of Hector Salazar,' Agent Miles said. 'We had agents at the docks ready to pick him up, but we were unable to locate the specific crate. We have been attempting to locate Mr Stone ever since. Besides a few sightings, you are the only person we have been able to get reliable information from.'

I didn't know what to say.

'But, Miss Marston, I'm struggling to understand your motives. Why would a woman with no notable history of violence suddenly team up with a known terrorist and travel across the state?'

'I didn't know he was a terrorist.'

'You didn't see any of the news coverage from his time in Afghanistan, or England, or Europe, or even over the last two months in America?'

'I don't watch a lot of television.'

'Or read the newspapers?'

'I don't know what to say. I didn't recognise him. When he told me earlier this evening, I put two and two together. I honestly didn't realise he was the same guy until then.'

'Why did he decide to tell you about his past?'

'I asked him.'

'And he told you, then and there?'

'Well, yes. I told him I wouldn't go any further with him unless he told me who he was.'

'So you did suspect him?'

'I thought he might have some sort of criminal history. I just wanted to make sure he wasn't a serial killer.'

'But you were happy to travel across the state with him?'

'No,' I was getting impatient. Agent Miles stared blankly into my eyes. 'He'd just killed the guy with the rifle, and disarmed the other, and I wanted to know what sort of man he was. I never expected his answer to be so... awful.'

Agent Miles added to his notes. My foot tapped against the carpet.

'Am I keeping you from something?' He said without looking up.

'No, I... sorry.' I stopped my foot. Agent Miles finished his notes.

'So from the moment he freed you from Ramiro Salazar's men, you spent approximately twenty-four hours in his company?' He asked.

'Yes.'

'In your personal opinion, where do you believe he will go next?'

'Back to Miami would be my guess. If he wants to find Domingo Reyes, he'll head back there. The whole thing with the mines was a dead end. He had an urgency to his plan like he didn't want to hang around any longer than necessary.' I glanced at the clock on the wall. 'He could almost be back there by now. You should call ahead and warn them to be on the look for him.'

'In due time, Miss Marston.'

He wrote another note.

'Interview ended,' he said before hitting the record button again. 'Thank you for your time, Miss Marston. I'm going to ask for someone to arrange your travel back home. An officer will be there when you arrive to ensure you get home safely.'

He stood up out of his chair.

'Are you going to catch him?' I asked hastily.

'Don't you worry, we'll find him. It's what we do.' Agent Jonah Miles said before he left.

Sheriff Vasey drove me to the Bus Depot, and bought me a ticket on the government dime. He chaperoned me right up to the moment the coach lurched lackadaisically out onto the open road. I slumped into the faded velvet seat beside a man who smelt far too strongly of fish, and stared out of the window at the parked cruiser. The Sheriff watched from the driver seat. His expression null. Just glad to have me out of his life. The feeling was mutual.

My vision slipped into a trance as the coach hauled ass down the highway. I looked at everything and nothing. The world was a blur of colour. Cars flashed past in the other lane in a nanosecond, in and out of my life in less than a heartbeat. Just like James. Just like Quinn.

I tried to steer clear of those thoughts. But they were like the tide, never too far away, always returning. I had nothing but the ever-changing view from the window, or the prospect of forced conversation with strangers to distract my attention, but neither option was strong enough to deter the coming storm of emotion that lurked in the depths of my mind. They would come again, just as they had before, just as they always would.

THE FATE OF GLASS

I resigned myself to get catastrophically drunk when I got home. I didn't relish the prospect of drowning my sorrows in a bottle of wine, but today I just didn't care. I would head straight from the depot to the twenty-four hour liquor store a block away from the apartment. I'd buy six bottles of red wine, and drink until I passed out. No more James. No more Quinn. They were ghosts in my life. A vision in a rear view mirror.

But the thought of Quinn plagued my mind for the entirety of the six-hour drive. The coach stopped a couple of times along the way, and to my relief, the fish man got off at the first opportunity. He was replaced by an elderly woman who offered me a cupcake which she produced from the depths of her enormous handbag. After I picked the dust bites from the top, I tucked in. It tasted surprisingly delicious.

The taste lingered in my mouth right up to the moment the coach pulled in at the final depot. The coach lurched to a stop, and one by one, the passengers stood up, collected their luggage, and departed. I waited until the end, not through choice, but because the elderly woman beside me dithered long enough to allow everyone behind us access first. I descended the steps and stretched in the cool evening breeze.

'Miss Marston?' The coach driver called. He was standing at the rear of the coach, helping people with their larger luggage that had been stored underneath the sitting area. 'There's an officer waiting for you inside.'

I thanked him and reluctantly headed towards the sliding glass doors ahead. I didn't need a chaperone. The further I got from Ozello, the safer I had begun to feel. Even though Miami had last seen me almost hung and fed to a rat colony, I felt like the worst of the danger had passed.

The officer was a man in his late forties dressed in a smart pressed uniform. He was clean-shaven, and his hair was well kept and blonde. He spotted me as I approached and walked towards me, cutting the commute in half.

'Eva Martin?' he said with a loud booming voice.

'Yes?' I said without correcting him.

'I've been assigned to take you home. If you could come with me please.'

I followed the officer back to his car. A Crown Vic. Like a gentleman, the officer opened the door for me, and I climbed inside. A minute later and we were out into the busy dawn traffic. I watched the dazzle of warm orange lights pass me by as the cop drove me home. The shops we passed had signs in the window detailing massive sales before the storm arrived.

'They say we could have a category four hurricane.' I said to the officer.

'Yes ma'am.'

'Will we be okay?'

'Anything shy of the apocalypse, we will survive, ma'am.'

He took a left just before the intersection and nosed the cruiser into an alleyway.

'Is this the way home?' I asked cautiously.

'Just a shortcut, ma'am.'

The cop drove the length of the alleyway and pulled out on the other side, avoiding a mass of stationary cars waiting in line. Impressive. He pulled out onto the street, then paused and pulled over. He pulled out his cell and stared at the screen for a moment.

'What was your address again, ma'am?' he asked.

Besides today, I don't think anyone had ever called me ma'am. I gave it to him, and he nodded at his screen as though it had answered him instead, and pulled back into traffic.

I tried to focus my mind on something positive. What would be the next step in my life? Acting wasn't working, and the love had died for the craft long ago. I could teach. Those who can't do, after all. My drama teacher in school had inspired me to act. Perhaps that was my destiny. Finding the next George Clooney or Julia Roberts. There was no shame in that.

The cop pulled into another alleyway.

If I decided on teaching, I needed proper qualifications. Going to my parents and declaring myself a moulder of young minds would perhaps win them over to the idea that I hadn't failed my dreams. That could work.

I barely realised the cop had come to a stop.

Through the meagre light, I could just about make out the space we were in was surrounded by high buildings. Dumpsters lined the surrounding walls, which were spaced out into the shape of a courtyard. There was no exit up ahead, only the way we had come.

'Is everything okay?' I asked. But the cop didn't reply. Instead, he opened his door and got out. I tried the handle to the door on my right. Locked. Designed to stop criminals escaping. Same with the door on the left. My heart was racing. What the hell was going on?

Then, out of the shadows, people emerged. Not one or two. Ten.

They rushed towards the car, weapons in their hands. I screamed and shuffled back towards the centre of the rear seat. But it was no use. Both doors swung open as the figures approached and arms stretched into the car. I screamed again, lashing out at the flailing hands. But as I did, others grabbed me from behind. I kicked and writhed, but it was no use. The figures were too strong. Their numbers too many. They forced me to the ground, and something hard was forced into my mouth. The barrel of a gun.

'Scream, and you will die, ma'am.' The officer snarled.

PART TWO

THE FATE OF A ROSE IS TO WITHER

TWENTY

VIVAZ

ANOTHER DAY HAD COME AND GONE IN THE GLIMMERING metropolitan. Eighteen million Floridians woke up, went to work, argued with their co-workers over who drank the last of the coffee, ate lunch, and watched the clock as it crept achingly slowly towards five o'clock until, finally, they could head home. Some of those eighteen million people snuggled up on the sofa with a hot drink and a reasonably engaging programme on the television. Some of them hit the gym, or went out for a run, or walked their dogs. Some of them met up with friends or partners for a couple of drinks at their local bar. Some of them visited loved ones. Eighteen million people. Eighteen million stories. Not one of them the same.

Not one of them like mine.

I stood in line amongst a throng of luxuriously dressed strangers all exuding the same electric excitement. In their midst, I was one of them. My hair was tidy. My beard cut back into something vaguely resembling order. For the first time in God only knows how long, I wore a suit. It was a slim black affair that tucked into my physique in all the right places. I wore a navy blue tie, and a white pressed shirt. The glare from the streetlights reflected off the black brogues adorning my feet. I felt, for once, like a regular guy. Nothing special here, move along.

The line shuffled a couple of feet forwards as another few people up front moved inside. The queue stretched halfway down the block. For a Friday night, there was no better place to be, apparently, yet I could think of a million different places I'd rather be.

I had arrived back in Miami shortly after midday. My new car rattled and whined the entire journey. It was by no means an outstanding car, yet in that stood its beauty. It was remarkably unremarkable. Neither black nor white. Somewhere in the middle. Unnoticeable. Another car amongst the rest. A drop in the ocean. It granted me anonymity in a land where I was the enemy, which made it perfect for my needs. I drove my bland disguise straight into the belly of the beast, searching the streets for what I needed.

The line moved up, granting me my first look at the abrasive neon signage above the main entrance to the club. The word Vivaz shone out a bright pinkish light that snaked around in a groovy font indicative of the memorable eighties Miami. The building was a monolith of self-obsession, easily bigger than any of the surrounding buildings and far more lavish. It had to have cost millions to build.

And they say subtly is dead.

The couple in front of me moved up to the front of the queue. The guy on the door checked their ID and waved them in. Then it was my turn. In the UK, I was pretty accustomed to being ID'd. My early adult years had been spent in and out of pubs, clubs and supermarket alcohol aisles. My youthful skin accompanied with lithe, bushy hair did not a man make. I'd taken to seeking out younger staff members in the hope that they might take me for someone at least in the same ballpark of age to that I was aspiring to be.

But that was before Afghanistan, before Fadhil, before Salazar. With a thick beard and enough faded scars visible to show I'd been around the block a couple of times, the bouncer was satisfied that I had earned a drink. His eyes spent just a couple of seconds giving me an ocular pat-down before he took an obligatory step back, and granted me welcome.

If the outside of the club looked ludicrously expensive, it was nothing compared to the interior. Every inch of the place screamed its wealth with the shrill nature of a rapacious harpy. It rubbed this fact in my face like a displeased owner would to a dog that has urinated on the carpet, albeit with less anger or disgust. The bar stretched the length of the club, way down to the far end where a wall-length mirror reflected it back on itself, giving the illusion that the alcohol and the good times never ended, which of course they would, eventually. Hundreds upon hundreds of liquor-filled bottles lined the wall, each contained in a separate, individually lit alcove made of frosted glass which rose up behind the bar to the mirrored ceiling high above.

The club was packed to breaking point. Robotic people fuelled by electronic music and drugged by the illusion of the dance floor partied their lives away under an array of coloured flashing lights. The floor itself made up of hundreds of LED squares, each about a square foot in size, all glowing in a spectacle of ever-changing light to sucker those around into a sense of deluded wonder.

But the most incredulous and expensive addition was not at eye level. For that, you had to turn your head to the heavens. An enormous aquarium suspended over the mass of dancing strangers, illuminated to give the people below a view of inside, an enormous array of tropic fish of all colours and sizes weaved through the water like a peaceful current.

The enormous construction felt like a twenty-first-century wonder of the world. Right there next to the pyramids. Every inch of it a testament to human ingenuity. But - just like the pyramids - it had a darker side. I hated to think how many fish had died at the expense of a good night out. And whoever was stuck with the monumental task of cleaning it hadn't even done a good job, a small object drifted against the glass. It looked like a bag of some kind. A small smudge on a captivating canvas. I stared transfixed into the glass prison. Someone had condemned those beautiful creatures to this terrible fate.

And that was the man I was here to see.

I approached the bar and ordered a drink. A bottle of beer that was light on the alcohol and light on the taste, and moved straight to the dance floor. I wasn't exactly in my element in such an environment, but it's what people do. I weaved through the thick tapestry of gyrating strangers until I found myself a spot on a red LED square. It quickly changed to yellow as my feet planted themselves firmly on top of it, then continued its path through the colours of the rainbow like a disinterested child trying to pick their favourite. The pack squeezed in, trapping me in a quagmire of dancing zombies. Swallowed by the rhythm of the night. The heavy bass reverberated through my body with every thump of the drum. I lifted the beer to my lips and took a long swig, catching a glimpse of the caged beasts above. Each in our own prison.

The song ended, and another began. A blast from the past. Jackson Five pumped nostalgia through the speakers, and everyone cheered. I had to admit, I was relieved to hear something good for a change.

I took another sip of beer and let the music flow through my body. I let the dance floor claim another victim. It felt good to let go, just for a while. Dancing here. Free from the world. It was something I hadn't experienced in a long time. No one was looking for James Stone in a nightclub. No one looked at the smartly-dressed man dancing and thought *"he must be a criminal."*

A quick stop off at an end-of-the-road type motel earlier in the day had given me a little more chance for rest, and provided the amenities to spruce up. A lukewarm shower rid my body of the final clinging remnants of swamp water, and a pair of store-bought scissors worked my hair into shape. After a quick detour to the finest retail store I could find within a couple of blocks of the motel, I bought my suit and turned myself into something resembling a presentable human male.

The song ended, replaced by new age garbage. The moment ended. The spell broken. I let reality wander back into my life, and scanned the horizon of bobbing heads in search of something useful.

Towards the back of the club were a row of plush booths sat on a raised plateau, granting those who rested there a chance to glance out over the crowds of dancers like spectators at a colosseum. I squeezed through the mass in their direction.

In a dark corner towards the back of the club, a door opened. Three smartly-dressed Asian men staggered out. They had the lasting look of elation etched into their faces. Each man looked a little unkempt in their presentation. Ties were off-centre, shirts slightly untucked. These were men who had experienced something a little *extra* tonight. A VIP lounge perhaps?

They looked the sort. Men with more money than sense. I watched the men drunkenly lurch towards a group of attractive young women dancing together. They spotted the men approach and formed a tight circle to block them out. The VIPs started talking loudly at them, but two well-built men came over and ushered them back towards the door they had just come through.

I moved closer. There was no one guarding the door, and no signs strictly forbidding people from going inside, but neither was there anything that foretold that this was a place of elite status. Surely in a club like this, the whole point of a VIP lounge was to be seen by those not worthy of entry. Whatever lay on the other side of that door was something more than a place for very important persons.

'That place is off limits, sir,' said a calm male voice from directly behind me. I jumped slightly and turned to see who had spoken. A waiter, judging by his attire. He held a heavily-burdened drinks tray on the palm of his left hand, level with his shoulder. His expression was strictly business. The Jeeves of Vivaz. 'It leads to the staff area.'

'Okay,' I replied, not really knowing what to say. 'Thanks.'

'Are you looking for someone, sir?' The waiter asked.

'You wouldn't happen to know if the manager is in today?' I asked.

'Do you have a complaint you wish to make?'

'No, I just...'

'The manager is unavailable. However, I see you are low on your drink, sir. Would you like another?'

I nodded, drained the last of my drink, and handed over the empty bottle and a twenty dollar note. I didn't expect to see change. Jeeves smiled and disappeared into the crowd as though they were nothing more than apparitions. I stayed put, and shifted my body so that I could watch for Jeeves to return while ensuring that I would catch any movement from the staff door. The waiter returned with incredible speed, extending the fresh beverage on his tray like an offering to the Gods. I took the bottle and gave him a fake smile that I hoped clearly portrayed my dissatisfaction at receiving precisely zero change. Jeeves nodded and disappeared just as quickly as he had appeared. I took a swig of beer and glanced one last time at the door. It would take more than a polite denial to stop me.

I figured the easiest approach would be to make a scene. Managers don't like people "making a scene," especially in front of so many paying customers. If I caused enough distress, someone would have to come for me. The only problem with that was whether or not they would haul me deeper into the beast, or throw me out on my arse. It was a gamble to say the least, and if the manager was who I suspected, I figured I was more likely to be taken out back and decapitated instead.

Okay, so not that, but what else? I could trigger an evacuation. Pretend there was a fire or a bomb threat. That would get everyone out fast, and it would provide enough commotion to sneak through the door. But clubs didn't tend to leave fire alarms in places drunken idiots could trigger them, and I was just as likely to get behind the bar as I was to get through the staff door. Besides, panic usually led to a police presence.

Right, what else?

I took another gulp of beer and tilted my head back to look up at the fish. They were such beautiful creatures. Such an array of colour. They swam around, mixing together like watercolour paint. It was mesmerising. It was disorientating.

I blinked and looked away, but the colourful image had fused in my vision. As I looked around, the crowd of moving strangers mixed in with it, distorting everything. The bottle slipped from my hand. I heard it smash on the floor like a distant echo.

I took a step back, at which point my brain seemed to switch to low-power mode. Everything seemed to slow, yet I knew it hadn't really. I felt a rushing sensation behind me, and I realised I was falling.

What came next was perhaps the most surreal experience of my entire life. I was falling, but not through any real space. My body had already come to a stop against something softer than a floor or a wall. This was something different, like an ant falling from atop a giant, I could feel myself spiralling away into the deepest recesses of my mind. I threw out my hands and saw from what felt like a million miles away the hands of James Stone mimic my actions as though they were joined together by strings.

'What is happening?' It was the Wolf. His voice echoed through the haze. Distant, yet close at the same time. 'What have you done?'

I ignored the voice and struggled to grip onto something, anything that would prevent me from slipping further. I felt a pair of hands shove into my back and heard a heavy American accent shout out.

Like some kind of celestial puppeteer, I tried to twist my human vessel around to see where the hostility had come from, but the action only served to send every solid shape in my vision through a tumble-dryer. All I could make out was a pair of bright blue eyes on a swirling face.

'Get out of my way.' The Wolf snarled.

He spoke through my mouth. Commandeering the sinking ship.

The face before me frowned and disappeared into the murky, swirling darkness.

'What are you doing?' I shouted at the Wolf. My voice was weak. The words mumbled and merged together.

'We need help. We need to get out of here.' The Wolf replied. He

spoke with confidence, much more than I could. His grip on my conscious was strong.

We took a step forward. It was difficult, but we managed it. We didn't fall.

'Good,' he said. 'Keep going.'

Did he know how much control he had? We took another step, and another, and another. We fought against the fog in our brain. Trying to focus on the people in the crowd.

'The door.' *I slurred, my voice far weaker than his.*

'Leave it. We need to get out of here.'

But that was easier said than done. Up ahead was trouble. Suited men. Dressed all in black. All big, brawler physiques. All short haired. All stern-faced. They weren't partygoers. They were staff. They pushed through the crowd towards us, drifting in and out of focus like subjects under a lens.

'Don't stop,' *the Wolf snarled.* 'We have to move.'

We stumbled left, towards the bar, and away from the men. The crowd condensed. Harder to cut through. We scrambled at the blockade of drunken idiots, trying to separate them. They didn't budge.

Arms grabbed our shoulders and pulled us backwards.

'Fight, James. Don't let them take us.'

We shook free from their grasp and lurched forwards, using the spectators as a shield to prevent us from falling flat on our face. We slumped into a short guy, who pushed us away, and we stumbled around to face the men. The Wolf swam into existence beside me. It was unsettling to see my face on his body. He looked uneasy. Unsure in us.

'I'm not unsure, I'm trying to figure this out,' *he said. Our mouths moved in unison. Unaware of the consequences of his words.* 'The guy on the left is favouring his left leg. Kick it, and you might be able to take him out.'

We pointed at the leg.

The guy on the left shifted his weight and advanced.

'Or not, I guess.' *We said.*

I tried to focus on the three men. Every movement twisted and distorted. I wanted to throw up. I wanted to fall down and give in, but failure wasn't an option right now. The man in the middle was already on the move. He pounced forwards and pinned his hand around my throat.

We struggled against his grip, but it was useless. He was much stronger than us.

'Don't give up, James.' The Wolf said.

'I...can't...'

'Hit him. Pull out his eyes. Crush his throat.'

I crawled at his hands.

'Punch him, right now.'

'I...'

The Wolf lashed out and struck the man across the face. The force was incredible. Vastly unexpected by all parties. He relinquished his grip and staggered backwards.

The Wolf didn't let go. He held my fist in place. Shock etched on his face. He had control.

But he didn't have long to savour the act, as a moment later I was punched in the face.

TWENTY-ONE

THE WOLF OF WAR

When I was a child, I had trouble sleeping. There was something about lying there with the dark of night creeping into every corner of my room that would push my mind into an unstoppable tirade of fear. I would be trapped inside my mind, drowning in a sea of terrifying thoughts. I would dread the setting sun like it was my last day on Earth.

My mum took me to the doctors. They prescribed drugs. Referred me to specialists. I visited psychiatrists and hypnotherapists, tried meditation and studied self-help techniques. There was no cure. Even now, I sometimes feel the sensation writhing around inside my body. Something deep inside trying to poison my mind with fear and doubt.

I've come to understand that it is the Wolf. The part of me with which I live in a constant battle with. He gave himself that name. Stolen from an old Cherokee story about a man who had two wolves at war in his mind. One that represented love and peace. The other fear and anger. He believes that he is the latter. The wolf of war. Locked in an eternal battle. He believes it makes him stronger, separates him from his human coil. Yet he is nothing more than a shadow. He is fear.

In the end, it was the ticking of a clock that sent me to sleep. The passing of time is infinite. When I am long dead and forgotten, and the world is nothing more than a burnt crisp, time will move ever onwards through the endless void. Somehow, that knowledge soothed me. Whatever happened didn't matter, so why should I fear it? I would listen to the ticking clock, and fall victim to its hypnotic rhythm.

I could hear a clock somewhere nearby. I kept my eyes closed and listened, adjusting my head and drowning out everything else in the room so that it was all I could hear. Tick, tick, tick. The passing of time is infinite. With my eyes closed, the clock seemed louder.

I could sense him waiting for me. He lingered nearby, listening to the tick tick tick of the clock. He wanted me to address him, but I wouldn't.

A door opened, and the sound of several pairs of shoes slapped against the floor drowned out my ticking clock.

'Get this fool up and bring him downstairs.' One of them said.

Two sets of footsteps moved close and lifted me up out of my seat. Something cold slipped across my wrists. Handcuffs. Only as I was forced forwards did I open my eyes.

He looked at me. Using my own eyes against me.

'We need to talk.' The Wolf said.

I ignored him.

The man who had spoken walked ahead of me. I didn't recognise him from the fight, but even trying to recall the events of the day seemed hazy. Whatever they had given me had done one hell of a job on me. With the other two men behind me, we walked in single file down a long flight of narrow stairs and through storage room after storage room, each filled with boxes of bottled alcohol.

The Wolf skulked in my wake like a shadow. Ever watchful.

The door ahead opened as we approached, revealing a luxurious private bar room. An eerie blue light cast dancing patterns on the ceiling, which I realised was coming from the levitating aquarium. Through the reinforced glass, the enormous expanse of water floated calmly. Almost ethereal. Piercing lights down below cut through, casting shapes into the otherwise lightless room.

A sleek, well-stocked bar stood unmanned opposite the door I had entered through. The light flickered against bottles of expensive liquor standing in solidarity against the rear wall. Two wide chesterfield sofas sat facing one another in the centre of the room, one with it's back to the window, the other a pool table.

The two men behind me forced me down onto the sofa facing away from the window into the deepest recesses of the occupied space. I counted sixteen men, all dressed in suits far more expensive than the one that adorned my body. For the most part, they stood with their backs to the wall, neither watching me nor the door at the far end of the room that opened just moments after I sat down.

A fierce beam of light spooled into the room, silhouetting a single figure in the doorway. He was a large man with the kind of physique that can shut down an argument before it's even begun. He absorbed the moment for a while before walking confidently towards me. He needed no introduction. I knew who he was from my research.

Felix Jackson.

He fixed me with a cool, relaxed stare. Not the usual response when people see me, but Felix was not an ordinary man. He was something else. He stood there in a casual black suit, unbuttoned over a midnight blue shirt with the collar open down to the third button. He stood and absorbed the moment like a businessman clocked off for the weekend absorbs the endearing draw of his favourite bar. I could see him drink it all in like that first cool, refreshing pint of beer. Intoxicating the senses, if only a little. He let it lapse over him before he finally spoke.

'The man of the hour. The indomitable James Stone,' he said with a deep, cool voice. 'To what do we owe the honour?'

'Oh, you know. Just passing by,' I said. 'Thought I'd see what all the fuss was about. I was a massive fan of Miami Vice as a kid. Wanted to get a couple of souvenirs for the family back home.'

He chuckled to himself and moved towards the bar. He reached over the counter, collected a bottle of beer from behind the bar, and twisted the top off with his hand. He flicked the bottle cap towards me. It fell short and clinked against the rim of the chair.

'I'd offer you a drink, but you're not a guest, and I don't want to waste stock.' He said nonchalantly before walking to the opposite sofa and sitting down. He settled back and crossed one leg over the other like he was amongst friends, and took a long swig of his drink. 'Besides, you probably don't need anything else rattling around in your body. We pumped you with enough sedatives to take out a gorilla, and let me tell you, you do not want to start screwing about with that shit in your system. Even if you were out for the count for, what?'

'Seven hours.' The man who had led me into the room said.

'Seven hours?' Felix laughed. 'Shit son, you can't handle your cocktails, can you? Most guys we hit up with that stuff are back on their feet in six. I think the record is five and a half.'

'What can I say, I had a light lunch.' I said calmly.

'Seven hours.' He said to himself. 'Damn, we managed to empty the tank out while you were sleeping. That's some strong shit if the noise didn't bring you round. You really didn't wake up?'

I shook my head.

He laughed again and took another long pull on his beer. When he lowered the bottle, I could tell the conversation was headed in a new direction.

'So, tell me, James - you don't mind me calling you James, do you?' Felix didn't wait for a response. 'Tell me, James. I get a call early in the morning - well, yesterday morning now - from one of my guys upstate saying there has been an *accident*.' He raised his hands to mime air quotes for the word accident. 'They tell me that some guy's been sniffing around, asking questions and shit about things that didn't concern him. My guys upstate know how I like my beauty sleep and don't want to bother me, so they take a little initiative, they try to plug a leak. They're smart. Actually, smart ain't the right word. They've got at least one mostly functioning mind between them. Enough to know when to shit, and when to get off the pot. They follow the guy when he goes off on his own to do a little snooping around, and that's when their "days since accident" counter spirals all the way back down to zilch. So they get on the phone and make a call that I am sure they didn't want to have to make. But like I say, they know when to pick the right answer between two shitty situations. Calling me up will mean a whole lot less hurt than trying to cover it up, you dig?'

The ethereal glow from the tank glistened against Felix's teeth as he flashed a smile.

'So they make the call, and they hope I've had my beauty sleep, and they own up and accept they made one big ass mistake.' He continued. 'And I'm talking real fucking big here. Like a meteor the size of Tallahassee smashing right into your backyard big. They tell me they fucked up, and I tell them they better apologise to their families because they're about to spend Thanksgiving digging their own graves. But then they tell me something that makes me hang on the line a little longer. They tell me that they recognised the fool who came sticking his nose where it ain't concerned. They tell me that the guy who kicked their asses and put a bullet through one of their guy's heads was none other than that fancy old British terrorist they'd seen on the newspapers. The one that killed all those people in Europe.'

THE FATE OF GLASS

Felix leaned forwards, grasping the bottle in both hands.

'And I found myself thinking, why on Earth would the man who tried to destabilise his home country's government want to go snooping around someplace thousands of miles from home where he don't belong?' His eyes bore into mine. 'Why would someone who already danced with the devil want to test his luck again?'

A silence descended on the conversation as Felix waited for me to respond. His unfaltering eyes fixated on me.

'Maybe he expected a better reception the second time.' I said, holding an equally cool stare. 'But you know, shooting a guest up with gorilla tranquilliser isn't usually the best start to a healthy relationship. Didn't your daddy teach you to court like a gentleman?'

'Didn't your daddy teach you to recognise when you ain't welcome?' He snarled back at me.

'He was too busy teaching me how to fish.' I said. 'And I never really got the hang of it.'

'Then let me spell it out for you. If someone points a gun in your face, you don't ask them to borrow a cup of sugar. You get the fuck out of dodge with your tail between your legs.'

'How can you know whether I came around for sugar, or to save your life?'

'I don't need the power of foresight to know that if a wanted terrorist rocks up on your front doorstep, he ain't come bearing gifts.'

'Maybe not frankincense or myrrh, but a little gold did no one any harm.'

'Tell that to Midas.'

I looked out through the window.

'What time is it?' I asked.

'Almost five in the morning.' Felix said as he checked the lavish gold watch on his wrist.

'How close to five?'

'Close enough. Why, you got a breakfast date?'

'Something like that. You know, it doesn't hurt to give the benefit of the doubt in unusual circumstances.'

'You're still breathing aren't you?'

'Just about, but you know what they say. Fool me once, shame on you. Fool me twice, you're just a terrible person.'

'Oh is that how that goes in England?'

'More or less.'

'Well ain't that something.' He took another pull on his drink. 'So you Brits just think you can come around another man's house when you ain't invited?'

'Only when you've got a brew on.'

'A what?'

'Only when we've got something important to discuss.'

'And you've got something so important that you just had to make a scene in my club?'

'Well, I'm not the one who filled me up with tranquillisers, am I?'

'And you didn't have to kill one of my guys.'

'When did I kill one of your guys?'

'In Ozello.'

'Oh right. Well that's not my fault. He started it.'

Another silence.

'Well, it's a moot point,' I said. 'We could spend all night here arguing who killed who, and who shouldn't have drugged who with gorilla tranquillisers. But I sure know I can't really be arsed with that, and I'm sure we could think of a million better ways to spend the early hours of the morning, so what say you to skipping the macho chess match and having an actual conversation?'

Felix smiled at me and finished his drink. He placed the empty bottle on the floor beside the sofa and stood up. The two men beside me hauled me up out of my seat a moment later.

'I take it you noticed my aquarium?' He asked, walking past me to stare out through the glass into the swirling mass.

'So that's a no to a proper conversation then.' I said as the two men forced me around to look through the window. 'But since we're ignoring each other now, how about a riddle. What's the one thing you can eat that eats you back?'

Felix gave me a look somewhere between annoyance and genuine confusion. It didn't last long, and he did not answer.

'Did you know, it takes over two million litres of water to fill it. My aquarium. That's two billion cubic centimetres of water. Two thousand metric tonnes of liquid suspended over hundreds of drunk idiots.'

The two men beside me ushered me towards Felix until I was standing right beside him, staring through the glass. It was empty, save for the flecks of fish that drifted in the manufactured current. The object I'd seen below was still there, sliding listlessly along the bottom.

'Can you even comprehend just how many complications I could have with this?' He continued. 'If any one of a million things happened - a cable snaps. The glass breaks. Hell, some fool comes in here with a semi-automatic and fires straight up at the damn thing - then hundreds of people would be dead.'

He slapped a large hand on my shoulder.

'And that's not even including the fish, or the logistics of cleaning something that big. Like right now, we had to empty the club a couple of hours early and get a crew in just to take the fish out and move them into separate containers before we can drain the whole thing in the morning. We have to do that every damn month so that we can get some structural engineer in from the state department to sign off on it. It's a logistical ass fuck from start to finish. But we do it. Do you know why?

'I'm not one to comment on the rectal preferences of other men.' I said.

'We do it because it's what the boss wants. And what the boss wants, the boss gets.' He looked me dead in the face. 'What, you think I don't already know what the hell you're doing in my club?' He asked with the kind of tone that told me it was a rhetorical question. 'I know you came here hoping to get close to Reyes, but I've got news for you, kid. That ain't gonna happen. Not tonight, or tomorrow, or next fucking year.'

'If it was a no from the start, why indulge me with all this?' I asked.

'Why do you think I go through the monumental pain in my ass of emptying and refilling this aquarium when I know that at any point, it could all come crashing down, figuratively and literally?'

'You like the thrill of semantics?'

'No. This, James, is just one of the many things I'm responsible for. One of thousands. Tens of thousands, probably. It would be enough to make most men go insane. But I do it, because I can, because Domingo Reyes *knows* I can. He puts an awful lot of trust in me because I am willing to take the burden away from him.'

Felix turned and walked away from the window. I followed him with my eyes.

'He's going to want to hear what I have to say.' I said.

'Actually, he isn't. In fact, you won't get within a mile of him, ever.'

'Then I'll ask you again. Why indulge me from the start?'

'Serendipity, brother.' Felix said. 'All my stars just aligned right before my eyes.'

From an inner-jacket holster, he pulled out a handgun and pointed it right at me.

TWENTY-TWO

BARGAINING CHIPS

I LOOKED AT THE INDEX FINGER RESTING AGAINST THE TRIGGER. николаевич Not twitching in panic. Not squeezing carefully in anticipation. No fear. No emotion. More of a business transaction than a killing act.

The man behind the gun held it steady. How old was he, late thirties, early forties? The lighting didn't help make an educated guess. He had the look of a man with years of experience, and it was hard to believe Reyes would put his trust in a young man. His eyes were black and void of emotion. This wasn't the first time he held another person's life in his hands, and it wouldn't be the first time he'd crushed one to dust. He was a killer for sure. A savagely successful businessman, the road he'd taken to get there was paved with the bodies of his enemies. He didn't look like he'd lost any sleep over that fact.

'There are parts of my job that I wouldn't wish on any man,' Felix said. 'But the price of loyalty comes with the best reward of all. Trust. The boss has faith in my capacity to make decisions based on his best interests, because I've proven that his best interests are my best interests. It ain't been an easy ride, as you can imagine. I've done things that would make the Pope turn in his grave. But it gives Reyes the freedom he requires to continue running this town, and it lets me act on his behalf. So when I see a convicted criminal saunter into my club, my first thought isn't opportunity, its deceit. I look at you, and I just have to ask myself, why would someone like you be so audacious to think he can come up in a place like this and expect to get treated like an equal? What motive could you possibly have?'

'You think I've been arrested?' I asked.

'Not unless you've managed to smooth talk your way out of jail time. I know you ain't wearing a wire. We checked you over the moment your head bounced off the dance floor. And I know you haven't got a cavalry of cops hiding up your ass. So no, I don't think you've been arrested.'

'Then what motive do I have?'

'That's not a question I have to answer,' he said. 'I'm not the one with the gun pointed at them.'

'Reyes and I have mutual interests.' I said, looking more at the weapon than the man brandishing it. 'You know I'm the one that killed Hector Salazar. You probably know that it was his son Ramiro who snatched me up and brought me to America in the first place. I never asked to come here. I never wanted any of this. And all I want is revenge on the man that brought me here.'

'Hector never did know when to quit.' Felix said. 'We all knew it was coming. Every time I saw him, I could see he wanted something more. It's almost as though running the most successful and lucrative business in America wasn't enough for him. He wanted the next level. He wanted power, control, like no one man could ever get. He wanted whatever it was they say is locked up in that head of yours to get him there. His ego was too big for him. His son is the same way.'

'Sounds like I can help you.' I said. 'Our interests seem mighty aligned for two people on either side of the fence.'

Felix smiled at me. For a moment I thought he was about to lower the weapon. I thought wrong.

'And that's where your whole plan is ass backwards.' He said. 'Don't get me wrong, I can see the thought process behind it. Hell, I might have made the same decision had I been stuck with your luck. But you and I are headed in opposite directions.'

'How so?'

'Because James, you cut the head of the snake and got blood all on the linens. You made worrying over whether two thousand metric tonnes of water was going to drop on a bunch of people's heads look like child's play. The moment you blew up that old fool's house, you condemned a whole economy of trade to death along with it. Do you have any goddamn clue of the chaos that you caused? Can't you see the ripple effect? You turned a profitable business, literally putting food on the table for hundreds of people, and keeping even more than that out of a life behind bars, and you blew the whole goddamn thing sky-high.'

He took a step forward, aiming the gun at my heart.

'You think Reyes gives a damn about Ramiro Salazar? That clown can run around here acting like he owns the place, but what he can't seem to comprehend is the fact his father's empire is done. He lacks both the leadership and common sense to stop it from turning to ash in the wind. He can have it. All of it, or what's left of it at least. He'll get what's coming to him soon enough. Ain't nothing you or I can do about it now.'

'You're willing to leave it up to chance?' I asked.

'This ain't a game of chance. It's the law of the jungle. Ramiro ain't got a clue what he's doing here. He didn't live in this world like Hector or Reyes. He didn't build his fortune out of the dirt. He was born into this world with Benjamins lining his pockets. The jungle knows, and it's waiting to go in for the kill. All you've accomplished in coming here is slipping the noose around your own neck.'

I saw his finger tighten around the trigger and felt the two bodyguards by my side shift out of the way. At this range, Felix wasn't about to miss. Even a child could make that shot. But a pistol that size had to be packing some serious oomph, which for a change worked in my immediate favour.

'I wouldn't do this if I were you.' I said.

'You wouldn't shoot me right now if you had the chance? Don't make me laugh.'

'Oh, I'd shoot you, but not here. Not unless I had the IQ of a toddler.'

'Flattery isn't your strongest suit is it?'

'What type of gun is that?' I asked.

'A Glock.'

'Looks serious.'

'As a heart attack.'

'Except a heart attack doesn't run the risk of cutting right through me and leaving a nice crack in the glass behind me, does it?'

His eyes glanced past me towards the small ocean twisting ceaselessly behind me.

'You're right, that would be reckless. So tell me, James, where would you like me to shoot you?'

'Tip of the finger if you have to.'

'Where geologically?'

'I hear the North Pole is nice this time of year. But hey, who am I to fret over the well-being of your aquarium when you can't even be bothered to clean it properly?'

A flash of anger crossed his face, but only momentarily, for as quickly as it came, it morphed into a grin.

'James, if you've got something to say, how about you cut the shit and just say it?'

'Oh, so when I'm the one with the audience, I have to cut the proverbial fat?'

'If you don't mind losing a couple of teeth, be my guest. Tell me in explicit detail what the problem is.'

I held his gaze for a couple of seconds. The Glock stayed right where it was, pointed at my head.

'Bottom right corner closest to the exit.' I said, nodding at the aquarium. 'You should be able to see it better if you turn the lights on downstairs. Otherwise, it might be hard to make out.'

Felix didn't move. Instead, he fixed one of his men with a look, and the guy took the bait. He moved wordlessly over to the window and looked out into the watery cosmos. It took him a couple of seconds to locate it.

'There's something in there.' He said eventually.

'What is it?' Felix asked.

'I don't know. A bag, maybe? It's hard to tell.'

'To call it a bag would be a gross understatement.' I sniffed.

Felix leaned in close.

'You better tell me right now what it is my man is looking at.' He snarled.

'You know, there's one thing that really strikes me about this country.' I said. 'You can get your hands on anything here without much work. Want a new car, pop down your nearest dealership. Need a singing toilet seat, stroll on down to Walmart. Got a craving for a block of C4? Well, that's not so easy, but it's not impossible. Seriously, it's pretty alarming how quick it is to come by.'

That got their attention. In one swift movement, seventeen arseholes squeezed tighter than a hangman's noose.

'I like C4,' I continued. 'It really gets the job done, you know?'

'You're bluffing.' Felix hissed.

'You need to vet your cleaning crew better. It's amazing what you can do with a little confidence and a jumpsuit.'

The Glock was mere inches from my face. The man behind it

fixed me with a seething stare. I could see him weighing up the pros and the cons. Could I really get into his club - past his security - with a bomb? They had patted me down, removed me of my personal belongings, and found no detonator.

But there's more than one way to set off a bomb, isn't there, Felix?

'How close to five did you say it was?' I sneered.

He fought the urge to look at his watch. Kept to burning a hole right through my skull with his eyes.

'All this to sit down with a man who doesn't want to see you?' He said. His voice barely more than a whisper. 'I don't buy it. You're a dumb son of a bitch, but you ain't *that* dumb.'

His men weren't so confident. I could see them looking around at each other, checking watches. The looks on their faces didn't spell confidence.

'Can't be more than a couple of minutes left.' I replied.

'I could wait here all day.'

'Want to bet?'

The seconds ticked down in my head. Fifty. Forty. Thirty.

'Let's say for a moment that you're right and that little package in there goes off. What's to stop me from shooting you right where you stand?'

'I suppose there isn't.' I said. 'And to be honest, I didn't think we'd be cutting it this close. Maybe a bullet to the head would be the smart move. So long as you're sure that it's the only package I placed.'

His face was a picture. Thought after thought running through his mind like ticker tape on steroids.

'You're a very easy man to find, Felix Jackson.' I continued. 'A quick internet search was all it took to figure out your home, your place of business. The world wide web will be the death of us all. And I've had a whole day to waste.'

He lowered the Glock. Couldn't take the pressure anymore. He looked down at his watch. I did too.

The minute hand was only one away from showtime.

'If even one single ounce of C4 goes off anywhere in this city, I'm going to skin you alive, you understand?' Felix barked. The cool facade evaporated like a puddle on a hot summers day. 'You think you can come to my club - hell, my country - and pull this kind of shit, then you've got another think coming. I don't know how you do things in England, but here in America, we take this shit seriously. So you better be prepared to suffer the consequences if that package goes up, because they are going to be some big, fucking, consequences.'

'In my defence,' I said. 'I would like to point out that if you hadn't shot me full of gorilla sedatives, we could have avoided this part of the plan. That's really on you for thinking I wouldn't come to your house without a plan B. But as a dear friend once said, you don't become a globally hunted terrorist by stumbling through life, do you? Wait, was it that? Hell, I can't remember. It was something to that effect, you know.'

The seconds ticked down.

'Still, a little time left if you want to have a go at my riddle.' I snickered.

Three. Two. One.

And then...

TWENTY-THREE

TRIAL BY FIRE

EIGHTEEN PAIRS OF HELD LUNGS WAITED IN ANTICIPATION. EIGHTEEN minds racing through a cluster of theories, deducing at speed whether the stranger in their midst was telling the truth. Only time would tell. Seconds ticked by at a glacial pace. Each charged with the energy of an atom bomb. One Mississippi. Two Mississippi. Still, there was silence. Three Mississippi. Four Mississippi. No ear-splitting detonation. No panes of glass shattering into a billion tiny pieces. Just a whole load of awkward tension. A bomb or a bluff? That decision was starting to take shape.

I burst out into laughter.

'Oh man,' I jeered. 'You should see the look on your face.'

Felix was the first to regain his cool. The smile that had adorned his face returned, bigger than before.

He laughed. 'I'll admit, you nearly had me there. What was it, a lump of clay, a dirty diaper?'

'Beats me. I didn't put it there. You've just got rubbish cleaners is all.'

Felix raised the handgun back up to my face.

'And it does beg the question,' I continued, trying to ignore the weapon inches from my face. 'Why would someone so sure of their convictions be so quick to panic about one man?'

'Precautions got me where I am today.' Felix said, more as an assurance to himself than an answer to my question.

'Even so, I had you worried there. I can see the beads of sweat on your face right now.' Felix resisted the urge to wipe his brow.

'You believed me, didn't you? You had some faith in me sneaking into your business, your home, your life. Digging under the surface and getting you where it hurts. You knew I could do it, which can only mean one thing.'

I let him take the bait. He couldn't resist.

'And what might that be?' He snarled.

'You're afraid. Of me. Of Reyes. Maybe even Ramiro Salazar. You've built a nice sandcastle for yourself, but it won't stop the tide from washing it all away. You can surround yourself with bodyguards as long as you like if it makes you feel secure, it won't mean a thing when that first wave comes crashing down. It took me less than a day to find you with just a library computer and a bit of ingenuity. Imagine what someone with proper resources and manpower could do. You think Reyes will protect you, or will he feed you to the wolves?'

Felix said nothing. Just looked right down the barrel of the gun into my cool, calm eyes. There was no emotion on his face. No smile. No anger. Nothing. He could have been carved from stone, and I wouldn't be able to tell. He held the pistol steady. Then he lowered it. Slowly.

'You know, you're probably right.' He said. 'Why waste the bullet?'

He nodded to his men, who slipped back alongside me and wrapped meaty hands around my upper arms and lifted me up like a bag of shopping. Felix spun on his heel and headed for the door. Strong, steadfast strides. My chaperones followed, dragging me along like the dead weight I intended to be. At the door, Felix took a right, up a flight of stairs to the floor above, and through the room directly above the one we had been in moments before.

It was a dark, utilitarian space, designed for use over statement. Along either side of the room were large shelving units lined with empty glass tanks, with an assortment of canisters and diving gear hung up at the end. A foul stench clung to the somnolent space. It was a stench I was immediately familiar with. One my childhood had reeked of. Fish.

A large structure protruded from the centre of the room like a wart jutting out of a clean face. Even without any clear signposting as to its purpose, I could already tell what it was. The guy on my right let go of me, headed for the structure and knelt down beside it. His hands outstretched, and grasped a handle, and heaved the giant hatch door open.

I stared down into the cold, glistening pool.

Trial by fire. Or in this case, trial by water.

'You're making a huge mistake.' I said, not taking my eyes off the hatch door. 'All I want is to talk to Reyes. I've no beef with him, or you.'

'Reyes doesn't need help from people like you,' Felix said. 'He has built an empire up from the ground all by himself. He didn't have to rely on the kindness of strangers to get him where he wanted to be, and now is no different.'

'You're so sure of yourself that you won't even ask him?'

'What makes you so sure we haven't discussed you already?' He chuckled. 'Credit where it's due, you already passed over his radar, and he made the call. He wants you out of the picture.'

Anticipating resistance, the man on my left tightened his grip on my arm. With my hands cuffed, there was little I could do to cause a scene. Felix sniggered at my feeble attempts.

'Then he's as dumb as the rest of you.' I snapped, losing my cool.

'You strike me as a man who likes his facts, Mr Stone. So let me give you a little one. The average person can hold their breath for around two minutes. If you can stay alive for double that, I'll let you meet Reyes. I'll go find him from whichever rock he's hiding under, and you can tell him what you really think.'

'A funny thing to say from his right-hand man.' I said. 'If I were a gambling man, I'd say you're losing your grip on the top spot.'

Felix snorted.

'Throw all your luck on that if that's where your priorities lie.' He sneered. 'But I'd be more concerned about the matter at hand if I were you.'

The man behind me laughed and shoved me forwards.

'To sweeten the deal, the tank is, as of an hour ago, empty.' Felix continued. 'I don't mean *empty* empty. Don't get your hopes up. I'm talking about the fish. We get them out of there every few days to clean the glass. Like I said, it is one Jesus goddamn logistical nightmare, but at least you don't have to worry about being eaten alive.'

The water below was crystal clear. Below, the club was dark and still. The night had ended, and the partygoers had dispersed like forgotten ghosts.

'Take a deep breath James,' Felix leered. 'You're going to need it.'

He crossed the space between us and placed his hand on my chest. He gave me a wide, perverse smile. A smile that showed exactly how much he was going to enjoy watching me squirm. The blight of our species, the desire to hurt. I could see the muscles flexing in his shoulders. He was savouring the moment.

But not for long.

The door burst open. A younger man, maybe in his late twenties, dressed in similar attire to the rest of Reyes's men, rushed into the room.

'Boss,' he gasped through laboured breaths. 'We've got a problem.'

Felix let go of my chest and spun around.

'Spit it out.' He snapped. Impatience burned through to his core.

But the younger man didn't need to reply, because down below, beyond the aquarium, Felix got his answer. A chorus of gunfire rang through the nightclub. I could see the flashes of automatic fire popping in and out of existence through the deep water like mysterious sea beasts lurking in the depths.

Felix watched it too.

'Salazar.' He hissed.

'That sandcastle of yours isn't looking so strong now, is it Felix?' I smirked.

He glanced at the younger man, then at me, then at the flashes of light far below.

'You two,' he barked at the guys behind me. 'Wait here with him. If he so much as smirks, you put a bullet in between his eyes.' He received two grunts of acceptance, then turned on the newcomer. 'You, gather the men. Get the call out. Get everyone in a ten-mile radius here in goddamn double time, you hear? You get them here yesterday, goddamnit.'

The younger man nodded and ran from the room. He gave me one last piercing look.

'Can you hear the waves?' I cooed. 'They're so close.'

He didn't have time for an argument. He didn't have time to craft a witty response. Instead, he followed his subordinate from the room and slammed the door shut behind him.

An awkward atmosphere drifted across in the dark space similar to that between a teenage couple, unsure what to do with each other. Except instead of the possibility of a budding romance to look forward to, I was stuck here with two big, burly guys. Both clearly spent a lot of time working out. It was probably a part of their

THE FATE OF GLASS

contract. *Must be six foot tall, built like a brick shit house, and dumb as a football post.*

They didn't look particularly intimidating now. Clearly, neither man had been an actor or poker player in a past life. They both telegraphed their feelings right across their faces, and right now they were anxious. In their shoes, I'd probably feel the same. They were trapped upstairs while their brothers in arms fought to the death down below. And if they lost, then Salazar's men would make their way upstairs and deal with them too.

Not that I was thrilled at the prospect either, but at least my situation seemed marginally more positive. My chances of survival had risen from zero percent to about five percent. I could work with five. Five was my jam.

'Well ain't this a coincidence?' I said in a mockingly relieved tone. 'Salazar's guys attack the place right after I tell Felix just how much of a darn nuisance he is. Small world, huh?'

'You heard the boss,' Snapped the smaller of the two men. 'One more word and I'll blow your brains out.'

He stood on the right, and looked to be the younger of the two. Looked like he had a couple of cards short of a deck as well. His brain hadn't fully matured to the point of restraint. I chose to ignore his request.

'Hey, you guys like riddles?'

'Stop talking.'

'What's the one thing in the world that when you eat it, it eats you back?'

'I won't ask you again.' The younger man snapped.

'Seriously, you're not going to try? It's really not that hard when you think about it.'

'I told you to shut up.' The younger man barked.

'You'd be amazed at the answer, seriously.' I continued.

He raised his fist to hit me into submission.

Just like I hoped he would.

I darted right, missing the fist by a proverbial mile, and threw my weight off the back of my heel. I brought my forehead down right into the centre of his nose. The bone splintered under the tremendous force, and he teetered backwards, clutching his face. He tripped over the open hatch door and collapsed into the corner of the room.

Which gave me a window of opportunity. Both of the men were armed, and all I had at hand were my good looks and dazzling charisma, which weren't going to win me any free passes today. My eyes darted around the room for something I could use. Hanging beside the glass tanks was a rack of diving gear. I lignored the charging second guy, and lunged for one of the small oxygen canisters. It was the size of a small fire extinguisher, which made it an excellent blunt object to use. And if it was full of pressurised gas, it might make the other guys hesitate. An explosion would definitely kill me, but they were close enough to take the blast as well.

I grasped the closest oxygen canister in my hands and swung it wildly behind me. And just in time. The thud of the canister as it collided with flesh was almost unnecessarily loud in the small area, but the guy's cry of pain was louder. As I turned my head, I caught the sight of a small black object sail through the air, and land with a splash into the open hatch. One gun down. I'd caught him seconds from executing me in the back of the head. Score one for me.

And in an ideal world, that would have been the end of it. But this an ideal world was not. No sooner had his firearm hit the surface of the water did the guy attack. He was older and had that chiselled quality only the most battle-hardened possessed. He'd been in more than his fair share of rodeos, and he'd come out on top more than once. It was an intimidating look, had it not been for the moustache and long dark hair that made him look like he belonged on a Beatles album cover.

He lunged forward and threw his uninjured fist in a mean roundhouse into the side of my face. I mimed an almost pitch-perfect arch through the air as the guy's gun had travelled just seconds before, and came to a resounding end on top of the first guy. Too occupied by the ludicrous amount of blood exploding from his nose, the impact came as quite the shock to him. As his head ricocheted against the floor, he let out a groan that had an all too familiar night-night quality to it. At least that was one guy taken care of.

But Sergeant Pepper was still up and ready. As I scrambled to my feet still clutching the canister, he leapt at me and threw his massive fist into my right cheek. The force knocked me off balance, and I relinquished my grip on the oxygen canister. I heard it clatter away, and splash down through the hatch. But it gave me back the use of my hands. As I stumbled, I reached out and grabbed a handful of his shirt, pulling him over with me.

Which would have been alright, had it not been for the open hatch behind me.

TWENTY-FOUR

ONE MINUTE

I REGISTERED THE LOOK OF FEAR IN THE OLD MAN'S EYES AS HE realised where we were headed. Hands outstretched, he lashed out for an anchor to prevent him from falling. Except the only thing in his reach that matched that description was the hatch door. His hands latched onto the handle, and as I splashed down into the tank, I pulled the guy down with me. Suddenly his anchor wasn't so cooperative. As he fell, our combined weight heaved the door towards us, and the old man wasn't quick enough to realise his mistake and let go.

And as the massive steel hatch door slammed shut above us, our only way out went with it.

Felix had been right on the money. Well, right on the money to an extent, if such a paradox could exist. The average person could hold their breath for two minutes. What he hadn't included was the fact that those people did so under ideal circumstances. Good overall health. A low heart rate. The ability to resurface if they weren't fond on the idea of drowning. And preferably not while in a frantic fight for their life.

Add in a smattering of stressful circumstances, and that average trickles all the way down to about half that time. At one minute, you'd rather stick a fork in your eye than hold your breath a second longer. One minute was not a long time. One minute was not my jam.

But I could make it work.

The older guy struggled. He bucked and flailed, marred only

slightly by the resistance of the water. Neither of us had prepared for submersion. But I figured I had the edge on him by being at least a decade younger than him. That had to count for something. Preferably a couple of seconds at least.

He twisted around in the water to look up at the closed hatch door. His buddy was still up there, which meant his best bet was to leave the way he'd come. But turning his attention away from me wasn't in his immediate best interests, and we were past the point to let bygones be bygones.

I let go of his shirt and brought my hands up and over his head, slipping the chain of the handcuffs around his neck. With all my strength, I squeezed my hands together, tightening the chain into his skin. The shock of it made him gasp. Bubbles escaped from his mouth as he struggled to break free.

Below, I could hear the faint thumps of gunfire. Underwater, they sounded unthreatening, like a dozen people knocking on doors halfway down the street. Though if just one bullet sailed skywards, they could likely bring about Felix's logistical nightmare. And probably my death along with it.

Ten seconds down.

The fear was starting to set in with the other guy. His brain was coming to the same calculation as mine. He was vastly underprepared for underwater warfare. He knew it. I knew it. And he knew he had to do something about it fast. So, like any animal backed into a corner, he fought back. He let go of my wrists and moved on to his secret weapon. Tucked into a holster in his trousers, he pulled free a second pistol.

Guns and water do not typically go hand in hand together. Back when pistols relied on the spark of gunpowder to ignite a reaction, you had about as much chance of killing someone with a gun underwater as you did by throwing the ammunition at them by hand. Modern pistols, however, did work, albeit not all that well.

Most important thing to remember is that friction is king. You point a gun at someone underwater, they better be nice and close. Otherwise, the bullet's trajectory isn't going to be worth a damn. To put it simply, there's a reason why amphibious weapons existed.

But it wasn't a concern for the other guy. He had fact number one on his side. Every vital organ in my body was within that two-foot radius. All he had to do was aim the gun somewhere behind his head and fire, and I would be a distant memory.

He dragged the gun up through the water and flailed it wildly beside his head. With my hands bound, I wasn't in the best situation to easily grab the gun out of his grasp. Doing so would mean I would have to let go, and letting go was as good as a death sentence in itself. The gun wasn't pointed at my head, but it was close.

All the same, I threw my head the other way, trying to put as much space as I could between me and the barrel of the pistol. He sensed the movement and twisted the gun towards me.

Then he fired.

The bullet nicked me in the neck, just below the jaw. A flesh wound, though it was enough to shock my body into expulsion. Precious oxygen burst from my lips and bubbled up to the surface.

Twenty seconds down.

I forced my mouth shut, swallowing the mouthful of putrid salt water, and hoping there was still enough fight in me to keep going. Blood pulsed from the wound and diluted in the water, creating a red cloud around our heads. The sight of it gave the other guy hope. He couldn't tell without turning around whether or not I was dead, which wasted further seconds as he attempted to see.

I, on the other hand, went on the full offensive. Gone was the time for jovial underwater struggle. With all the force I could muster, I tightened my grip on his throat, and wrapped my legs around his chest and squeezed tight. He was going to die down here. The only question was whether I would die first.

My leg muscles have always been a hidden strength of mine. The muscles tensed and crushed into his ribs, forcing him to a point where his body couldn't cope. He dropped the pistol, and it sunk like a stone down towards the base of the tank. He knew his time was up. His muscles relaxed and the fight drifted out of him.

Thirty seconds down.

My lungs ached, but not as bad as my neck. The salt water tickled my wound like a thousand tiny knives, which only made the need to breathe all the more excruciating. The older guy had to be dead by now, or at least unconscious, which was good enough for me. I slipped my hands free, pushed off the motionless body, and looked around. I needed out fast.

With shackled hands, my ability to swim was handicapped. Adopting a slightly restricted breast-stroke manoeuvre, I swam up towards the closed hatch. Even unlocked, I knew my chances of moving it were slim. It looked enormously heavy, and with nothing to anchor myself to, I knew pushing it would be almost impossible.

I got up close and pressed my head and hands up against the

hatch. With all the effort I could muster, I threw my legs back and forth. At the same time, I worked every muscle in my torso and pushed at the hatch with my hands and face. The hatch groaned but didn't move at all. Not even an inch. Nothing. Nada.

Forty seconds down.

I could be there all day and not make a damn bit of difference to it, so with the hatch above me as good as a death sentence, I needed to get creative. But an empty fish tank offered little in the way of imagination. Unless the dead guy had a grenade in his pocket, I had no idea how I could forge a new exit.

I looked down at his body. He had already drifted listlessly down and come to a stop star-fished against the glass base. Below him, the blurred flash of muzzle fire lit the room like blinking stars. And floating right beside the body was something special.

The oxygen canister.

A lot of pressure in an oxygen canister.

I spun in the water and kicked off the hatch door - which still didn't bloody budge - and shot like a lazy torpedo down towards the body and the canister. From below, the tank looked big. Inside, it was enormous. My legs flailed back and forth, pushing me onwards. The seconds ticked horribly by, and the canister remained tantalisingly out of reach.

Fifty seconds down.

As I struggled closer, I noticed the dead man floating a couple of feet from the base of the tank. Beneath him was his pistol. I heaved the corpse aside and snatched up the weapon with the desperation of a starving man with a sandwich. If I could penetrate the glass, my chances grew a little better. Even if the fallout was a fall out of a fish tank suspended thirty feet in the air that was equally likely to kill me.

But the laws of underwater gunfire hadn't magically changed in the last thirty seconds, which meant I'd have to be pretty damn close to an exploding object to get the desired outcome. Luckily for me, I had a shield. A big, meaty shield.

One minute down. All done and dusted.

The dead guy came to a rest about a foot from the canister. I hoped his body would direct most of the blast down into the glass, but an underwater explosions expert I was not. I had no idea how big an explosion the canister would make. Even with my arm outstretched, my body was going to be within five feet of the blast point. Meatshield or no, that wasn't a fun place to be.

But time doth wait for no man, and the pain in my head was making me woozy.

I hauled the corpse over the top of the canister. I tucked myself in behind as much as I could. Eased my hands around to point at the canister. Felt the clink as it hit the barrel tapped against it.

I pulled the trigger.

And nothing happened.

One minute, ten seconds down.

The gun was spent. Water had made it as useful as a chocolate fireplace, and with it went my last chance to survive.

I couldn't stop my lungs anymore. They needed air and were too damn stupid to realise that wasn't an option anymore. Salt water flooded into my mouth and down my throat and into my lungs. The pain was excruciating. Like someone had lit a bonfire inside me, and let white-hot flames tear every precious inch of me apart. I dropped the gun and scratched at my throat like it would do anything. It was useless. I was going to die. A bullet to the head would be a mercy now.

But as that thought flickered into my panicked mind, a slither of rational thought snuck in with it.

The pistol.

Not the useless one that had cut my neck. The first one. The one I'd knocked into the tank moments before I fell in after it. Desperately, I glanced around for it and saw it lying dormant several feet away. With everything I had left, I kicked out and snatched it up in my tortured hands. It had to work. It just had to. My life depended on it.

I hauled myself back behind the corpse and thrust the gun down towards the canister.

One minute, twenty seconds down.

I pulled the trigger again.

While I was in Afghanistan, a soldier told me that the best way to survive a grenade is to be nowhere near it when it detonates. However, if you are unlucky enough to be close to it, the way to minimise being hit by shrapnel is to lay down at least fifteen feet away with your feet pointed towards the blast. The casing of a grenade is built to fracture. At the point of an explosion, these pieces of shrapnel burst out in all directions.

Underwater, the situation is different. Like the pistol, the ignition causes a pressure wave as the reaction bursts out with frightening force. With a grenade, this pressure is about a million times more intense. On land, this pressure wave dissipates quickly, as the uninterrupted air can compress and expand easily. Although we weren't on land, and it wasn't a grenade. Underwater, the pressure is a brute. It travels through the water until it comes into contact with something it can compress.

The moment the bullet penetrated the shell of the canister, the whole thing exploded like a dying star. A wave of pressurised oxygen burst free with unbridled force, hitting the corpse face on and tearing him apart like warm butter in a blender. The guy was lucky that he was already dead because that had to hurt.

An explosion, however, doesn't only go one way. It expands in every direction to cause maximum damage. A well-placed grenade could take down a brick wall, blow up an armoured vehicle, or decimate a glass pane.

The glass used in the aquarium was strong. It had to be. The health and safety boffins had lost countless nights of sleep worrying over the logistics of the thing. Then the lawyers had drafted documents in advance for the shit storm that would entail if something happened to the glass when the club was packed. They would blame the manufacturer of the tank, accusing them of malpractice. So the manufacturers had made it as sturdy as possible. They'd thrown everything at their disposal at it and slapped a big old sticker of approval on the product. They'd probably said it could survive an explosive tank shell.

In the coming weeks, those lawyers would be pulling out those documents, because the shit storm had come.

And in defence of the manufacturer, the canister only cracked the glass. The pressure had hit it with the force of a tsunami, and it had taken it like a champ. But you can't hit something with that much force and expect it to proverbially shrug it off. The glass split in the shape of a lightning bolt about a metre and a half long. That would have been the end of it had the whole thing been empty, and a team of specialists could have been paid to come in and swap it out for another small fortune. But unfortunately for them, the tank wasn't empty.

Under two thousand metric tonnes of water, it was a lost cause.

It was all over in around eight seconds. The explosion rocked through the water with the boom of a jet engine. It burst my eardrums and reverberated through to my soul all within the first second. The cracked glass managed to hold out for a good two more seconds, by which time the intense weight of the water became too much, and it gave way.

Two billion cubic centimetres of water, a trillion tiny shards of glass, two flooded pistols and two bodies dropped the thirty feet from the base of the tank to the dance floor below in the final five seconds. As the ground rushed up to meet me, I lost consciousness.

TWENTY-FIVE

SEIGE

On my eighteenth birthday, my brother Sam took me out for my very first night out. My mum was pretty relaxed about what we did at home, but even so, Sam thought it best that he took me out to experience the wonders of a busy nightclub for my birthday. We started out with what he called "pre-drinks" at the local pub down the road from home before we moved on to the main attraction. I remember being giddily excited as the bouncer on the door checked my newly minted ID and let me through. I remembered doing shots with Sam at the bar before ordering a double vodka and lemonade and moving to the dance floor.

And that's about where my memories checked out for the evening.

Didn't forget the hangover the following morning.

That skull-crushingly dreadful headache had returned with added panache. I didn't know where I was, or why I seemed to be lying face down in about an inch or so of salt water. All I knew was that if I opened my eyes, the melted remains of my brain would likely ooze out onto the floor. So I just lay there, semi-submerged, and tried to figure out where I was. The stench of salt water and fish reminded me of my childhood on the North Sea with dad, but unless I was on the world's calmest waters, then I figured I wasn't out on the boat again.

Besides, that wouldn't explain all the shouting.

Dozens of boots splashing down in water soundtracked a series of angry voices, and it didn't take a genius to figure out who it was.

THE FATE OF GLASS

'Police, put your weapons down and surrender.'

And then it all came back to me. The club. The tank. The explosion. The fall.

I opened my eyes a crack. The room was dark, lit only by a couple of lights high above the morning glow through the open double doors, and the roaming beams of a dozen flashlights. Heavily armoured police officers swarmed into the club, assault rifles raised at the remaining few survivors of the assault. Some threw down their arms in surrender, but not all. Those cocky few hidden behind meagre cover clutched their weapons. Whether they planned to go down guns blazing was none of my concern. All I wanted was an escape.

The torrent had swept me across towards the bar. The guy I'd used as a human shield was a couple of feet away, lying on his back. His face and torso had been torn apart by the blast, leaving a wholly unpleasant sight to behold. A large jagged piece of canister protruded from his cheek. The sight of it turned my stomach.

The closest police officer was standing on the other side of him, weapon pointed at one of Felix's goons hiding behind a pillar in the back of the club. He was a big guy, beefed up by an inch of body armour. He had his back to me, but he was close enough that any noise I made was going to attract his attention.

He was inched sideways. His eyes on his target. The goon behind the pillar had that manic look that people get when they realise their only option left is going to get all kinds of bloody, and he was getting ready to clock off. The other cops swarmed through the room, clearing up where they could. Eyes flickered across every body, living or dead, with fingers twitching on triggers. Any movement was about as clear a death sentence as you could get.

The cop took another step left, moving right in front of me. His legs momentarily blocked my vision from the cornered goon, which meant two things. One, the cop had a clear shot. And two, the guy was all out of time.

The goon moved with the speed of a rabbit with a firecracker up its arse to face the cop and opened fire. A maelstrom of bullets shot across the empty dance floor in a wide, chaotic arch, hitting everything in a ten-foot swipe, including the cop. The Kevlar took the brunt of the impact, except for the bullet that smashed into his visor. He dropped like a guy shot in the face, by which I mean he went flying. He landed with a splash right on top of my meat shield, head tilted back to look directly at me, or at least it would have been if there was any face left over.

If it was any consolation to the cop, his killer didn't last much longer than he did. The round of gunfire came in terrifying unison from almost every other living person in the building. The guy took a torso-load of lead in the first fraction of a second, and was ripped in two in the second. He dropped to the floor a disfigured mess.

It didn't take long for the survivors to react. The pretence of escape disappeared right before their very eyes. One of their number had killed a cop, which tarred them all with the same tainted brush. So, like a chain reaction, those remaining few returned fire. They decided to fight fire with fire, which meant only one thing. They were going to get burnt.

It couldn't have lasted more than a couple of seconds. The gang members were backed into a corner. They were unprepared, underdressed, and up against staggering odds. The officers were suited and booted, and trained for situations just like this. They cleaned up the rabble in mere moments. Every single one of Reyes and Salazar's survivors dropped like the soul had just jumped right out of them. And the whole thing was over as quickly as it had started. One nil to the system.

But as the officers returned to their sweep, guns barrels still sizzling, there was one small difference.

I'd noticed it the moment the cop stepped in front of me. A minuscule movement off in the darkness to my left, right in the sweet spot of my peripheral. Had I looked right at it, I doubted I would have seen. But fate had played its cards the way it had, and I'd been paying just the right amount of attention.

A figure shifted in the darkness. Crouched low behind an overturned bar stool, I noticed the slight movement as the figure blocked a slimmer of light reflecting off the stool's metal stand. Probably a million to one odds that the stool had come to rest exactly there. Right where the dim light from the open door caught it in just a way to reflect the meagre glow at my exact spot. Just in time for the figure to move perfectly across the beam of light, breaking it just enough for me to notice. Million to one odds.

I shifted my head to look directly at the figure. With the nightclub lights shut off, he was in almost perfect darkness. I could tell by his shape that he was a big guy, yet in good enough shape to stay low and move light on his feet through the shallow water without attracting undue attention. He edged silently towards the bar with the grace of a stalking panther and leapt over the chest-high counter as the cop killer was ripped asunder. The burst of gunfire was enough to illuminate his face for a millisecond.

Felix Jackson, making a run for it. The guy was too tenacious to go out like one of his lackeys.

As the remaining gang members opened fire on the cops, I heaved myself up, ignoring the throbbing pain in my neck and back, and hurled myself sideways over the counter. I landed on my hands and knees with a loud splash that I hoped was hidden under the orchestra of gunfire. Felix was up ahead, bent double, and hustling as fast as he could towards a door at the far end of the bar. I hoisted up onto my feet and followed suit.

As he reached the door, Felix offered a fleeting glance behind him and spotted me in an instant. Not that I was trying to hide from him. I wanted him to know I was coming, and there wasn't a damn thing he could do about it. He shouldered the door open as the gunfire came to an end, and disappeared through it a moment later.

But I was hot on his tail. I made it to the door before it swung shut, and squeezed through the gap.

Which opened me up to a cheap attack.

Felix's colossal fist smashed into my temple as soon as I crossed through. His swing was weakened by the angle he had to attack from. Kneeling low, my head was around four foot off the ground, which put me at the height of a small child. If I had to guess, Felix wasn't in the business of punching children, so his attack was less experienced. All the same, I slumped sideways into a set of office drawers by the door and fell on my arse.

'Jesus Christ, are you trying to get caught?' I hissed.

'You're dead. You know that, right?' Felix snarled back. 'You just caused tens of thousands of dollars' worth of damage. I'll cut your fucking head off.'

'You want to keep your voice down?'

'Screw you.'

I scrambled to my feet, narrowly avoiding another swinging fist, and darted into the space ahead of Felix.

'Shut up, and maybe we can get through this, okay?' I whispered. 'Now, how do we get out of here. There's got to be a back-door or service exit, right?'

'Like I'm going to help a son of a bitch like you.'

'Oh, you want to go at it alone? You won't last two minutes by yourself. I know what I'm doing, okay? This isn't the first time I've run from the cops, and if there's one thing I've learned it's that you don't want to do it alone.'

'I don't need your help. Get out of my way before I snap you in two.'

'I'm not your enemy. All I want is to help Reyes get rid of Ramiro Salazar which, if I'm not mistaken, is going to be his priority after what just happened. We don't need to fight on this.'

He lunged forward and pushed me aside, which was answer enough, and set off at a run through a side door. With no desire to wait around for the cops to come and turn me into a bullet piñata, I took the liberty and followed him out.

Having never been a police officer in a past life, I didn't know the ins and outs of siege tactics. But if you put a gun to my head and asked me to explain how it worked, I figured I could hazard a pretty close guess. A building this size had to have more than one exit. Those very same health and safety chaps that bitched and moaned about the levitating fish tank would have demanded any patrons of the club had a plethora of choice when it came to escaping the club in the case of a raging fire breaking out on the dance floor. That meant that any cop worth a buck was going to slither around the building and stick their tentacles in every available exit, so long as they got there first. Which also meant that the window of escape was dropping rapidly.

I couldn't have been unconscious for long. Not face down in two inches of water. I guessed the cops had been waiting for their chance to strike on the club, and when Salazar's boys rocked up tooled to the arms, they were eager to strike. But a small battalion of cops was not an easy thing to conceal, especially in a busy city like this. My bet was that the main bulk of law enforcement had just barged through the front door, looking for a grand-scale Mexican standoff situation. The unlucky ones would be sent to scope the exits and pick up any stragglers. One or two at most was my bet. And they would have a good number of exits to keep an eye on.

So long as backup didn't arrive first.

Whether Felix had put those pieces together was anyone's guess. He moved with incredible delicacy for someone built like a tank wrapped up in a two-grand suit. I followed as deftly as I could. From back the way we had come, I could hear the sounds of the armed officers sweeping through each room like a virus. They were on a bloodlust. Shoot first, ask questions later.

'You better know where you're going.' I hissed at Felix.

He ignored me. Wherever it was he was headed, it wasn't a back door. He crossed an eerily quiet kitchen and through a door at the back, I was surprised to see him climbing a set of stairs. He had to have some kind of plan. I took the stairs three at a time, arms poised in front of me lest I trip. The sounds of muffled shouts came from below. A single shot fired out, followed quickly by a cascade of retaliatory fire. Clearly, we weren't the last men standing.

And Felix didn't seem keen to share that title. At the top of the stairs, he darted through the door straight ahead and swung it shut behind him. I reached it a couple of seconds behind, but it was no good. As soon as my hands touched the door handle, I felt something very solid thud against the other side. I threw my weight into it, but it was no use. He had wedged it shut.

I glanced around quickly, looking for another exit. The room appeared to be a rudimentary rec room. A haggard sofa sat looking utterly defeated up against a set of old lockers, with a dishevelled coffee table tucked up against it. The growing noise from below took the stairs down off the table. The bastard had trapped me.

I ran back to the door and pushed every ounce of plucky, tenacious Brit into it as I had available. It didn't give. There had to be another way out. I looked around for something, anything. No windows. The room was lit only by a hanging light, swaying gently in the breeze.

'How is there a breeze?'

Up above the lockers was a ventilation shaft. It had to be maybe a foot and a half wide at best. That would work.

I jumped up on the sofa and hauled myself as high as I could onto the top of the lockers. They groaned and squealed under my weight, but held steady. With both hands, I pulled at the grate standing between me and freedom. It was bolted in place, but not very well. As I tugged against it, the bolts wiggled. I let go and worked at them, one at a time. All the while feeling the heat in my toes as the cops drew closer. I worked the first free, then the second. The metal dug into my skin. I ignored it. Just kept working.

The third bolt came free.

I heard footsteps on the stairs.

All out of time.

I yanked the grate free.

And heaved myself inside.

TWENTY-SIX

ASH AND BONES

IN ALL MY DAYS, I'VE BEEN IN A LOT OF TIGHT SPOTS, BUT FEW quite so literal as this, which was saying something. I wiggled forwards like a frantic worm, stopping only once I was sure I was inside. I let go of the vent grate, and laid it down gently so that it didn't make a sound. Back in the room, I could hear frenzied sounds of the SWAT team approaching. Shoulders barged against the barricaded door, followed quickly thereafter by the decisive blast of a shotgun, and the explosion of splintering wood. No messing around.

Much quieter, I wriggled onwards feeling more like a distressed seal than a John McClane. There was no light inside the vent, and it smelt of something I didn't want to linger on. The flow of air guided me forwards like a mole in a tunnel. My clothes snagged against the seams where the sections of vent connected, and more than once I shuffled head first into a corner. I was literally running blind. Well, semi-literally, on account of the fact I couldn't run. Shuffling blind.

As I squeezed around an impossibly tight corner, I caught sight of my exit. The light of dawn crept through spinning fan blades mere metres away. A loud crash behind me told me the cops had managed to get past Felix's blockade. At least they wouldn't be squeezing in the vent after me. The fan moved at a steady speed. Thankfully not a hand-severing velocity. I worked my way towards it and slowed the blades to a halt.

Peering through I could see the building opposite looming close, a wall of giant grey bricks. The close proximity likely meant below me was some kind of service alleyway for the nightclub. I figured there was a cop or two guarding the exits, but not definitely. Not if the backup was still on its way.

But as I looked down, I knew it was a no go. The ground was at least twenty feet below. If I pushed the fan free and slithered out, I would be going down head first onto solid concrete, and I was all out of luck when it came to spine-breaking falls for the day. I needed another way out.

I found one after several long minutes wiggling around in the dark. It wasn't the way I'd entered. Intact grate. And lacking in fans, feds, and twenty-five foot drops. All was quiet on the other side. I repeated the process of jimmying the grate free, this time from the inside, and wiggled out. As my face bounced off an unsuspecting desk lurking below, I felt the immense relief that I hadn't risked the other exit, combined with sudden and immediate regret that I hadn't had the foresight to put my hands out in front of me and soften the fall. The ensuing headache did little in the way of raising my spirits.

I got up and crossed the office to the door, and pressed my ear up against it. All quiet. I opened it and peeked out. All clear. I slid out, keeping close to the wall, and moved along the corridor. Somewhere above, I could hear hurried footsteps running around. Cops probably. I found the stairs, and ascended so that I was on their level. I could hear them sweeping room by room. At any moment, they could burst through the door and shoot me. I didn't stick around to give them a chance.

I swept through the room and into the next as quietly as I could. Felix had gone upstairs for a reason. Unless his plan was to hide in a safe-room, or on the roof, then he had to have a plan to escape, and I wanted in. Neither of us would last long on the streets without a real idea of just what the hell we were going to do.

I opened the next door, exposing a long corridor quite like the one Felix had led me through when he planned to drown me. At the far end beside another staircase, I spotted the back of a cop as they disappeared through an open door. I thanked my lucky stars he was facing the wrong way.

I hustled quickly down the corridor and up the staircase. As I'd guessed, it led me straight into the very same corridor I'd walked along with Felix. Not wanting to wait around and be spotted, I moved into the room we had spoken in with all his goons. The room was empty. With the aquarium in ruins, the private bar looked far less mystical. Felix wasn't there. Nor was he in any of the nearby rooms. I opened door after door, finding what appeared to be small booths, like a changing room, but much more exotic. A chic maroon velvet coated the walls, with a leather armchair facing the far wall. Didn't take a genius to figure out what happened in there.

I abandoned the door to door search, and ran down the corridor for the door at the end. As I swung it shut behind me, I saw the head of a cop climbing the stairs.

But it was the sound of rustling behind me that got my attention. Felix was bent over a large office desk, looking at a bundle of papers spread wide across the desk. As I entered, he looked up, pistol raised.

'You're like a damn plague.' He said, lowering the weapon.

'We need to move. The cops are right outside.' I whispered, looking for another exit. Nothing. Not good.

'In a minute.'

'We don't have a minute. It won't take them long to figure out were in here, and I don't know about you, but I don't fancy our chances of taking on a small battalion. So unless you've got some kind of secret passage… oh, you do.'

As I spoke, Felix pushed on a section of wall directly behind him. It swung open, revealing a hidden passage. He exhaled and swept all the paper into one stack, then dumped the lot into a metal bin beside his desk. With a match from his desk, he sparked a flame and tossed it onto the pile of documents.

'This way.' He said.

He held it open for me to go first. I did and Felix closed it behind us quietly, then slid a heavy deadbolt lock in place. No way anyone was getting through there in a hurry. The passageway was uncharacteristically narrow. I doubted the health and safety boffins had been pleased with that. If they knew about it at all, that was. Felix squeezed past, leading the way along, then down a tight staircase. It felt like we were walking in between the walls. The purgatory of the building. The space between the in and the out.

We took the stairs all the way down to the ground floor, not that there was anywhere else to get off at. Felix unlocked the door at the bottom using a control panel on the wall beside it. The door swung open automatically, allowing the glow of the morning light to creep inside.

'Fancy.' I said.

'Shut up.'

We stepped through, and the door swung shut behind me. There was no exterior handle. No snazzy keypad or anything. It just looked like a slab of steel in an otherwise unremarkable brick wall. We were in the alleyway I'd seen through the ventilation system. It was much thinner than I'd thought. I doubted any vehicles were coming up and down here in a hurry. Not if they wanted to keep their wing-mirrors intact.

'This is where we part ways, brother.' Felix said.

'Not without your boss's location. I'm not giving up on this.'

'You're going to have to. He ain't wasting his time on you or anyone. You want to live, you better disappear on the breeze.'

'Listen, dick.' I snapped. 'I didn't come here to almost drown and then walk away empty handed. You said if I survived, you'd take me to him. Be a man of your word.'

'Actually, I said if you could last four minutes, I'd arrange it. I didn't say shit about you blowing the damn thing up.'

'Don't get caught up in the semantics. You owe me this.'

'Like hell I do.' Felix snapped. 'One minute you're talking about Salazar being a danger, then the next he comes and starts a fight. How am I supposed to know you didn't orchestrate that yourself?'

'If you think Salazar would go anywhere near me and let me live, you're as dumb as a rock.'

'What I know is that you are bad news. I ain't spending another minute near you. I certainly ain't putting Reyes in harm's way.'

'He doesn't give a shit about you, or anyone, so why are you covering for him? I don't care if he lives or dies, I just want Salazar gone.'

'No, you listen. Don't you get what's going on here? Reyes doesn't have time for your bullshit. You've got a real one-sided view of this thing, and this ain't the world you think it is.'

'What the hell does that mean?'

'It means, the battle is already over, man. The war is lost because you went and blew up a goddamn building. Don't you get it? You gave the cops everything they needed to shut this shit down. So this feud between Ramiro Salazar and my boss, it ain't there anymore. Reyes couldn't give a shit. There ain't nothing left to rule over but a pile of ash and bones. Salazar can have it.'

'So what, Reyes is just going to give up everything like that?'

'Who said anything about him giving up? It's survival of the fittest, brother. This a changing world. You've got to adapt or die.'

'Sounds like he's got quite the plan figured out.' I said.

'That ain't your concern. You want Salazar, you better figure out another way to get to him.'

'That doesn't sound like the Reyes I've heard about. The Viper didn't get his reputation by turning the other cheek. He got it by being relentless, by never giving up. I can't believe a guy like him would want the man actively trying to usurp the business he's spent his life building up to keep breathing.'

'Like I said, Reyes is looking to the future, not wallowing in the past.'

In the distance, the sounds of approaching sirens echoed in the morning breeze.

'That's my call to leave, brother.' Felix said. 'Take my advice, get out of here before someone cuts your head off.'

He spun on his heel, but as he did, something caught his eye. A flash of movement off in our peripheral. His right, my left. Big enough to spark our inner feral instincts. In unison, we turned towards it.

An officer stood in the mouth of the alleyway. A woman, maybe five foot. A slim build. All on her own. Bad odds for her, two on one. Had it not been for the pistol in her hands, pointed right at us, and the swathe of backup close by.

'Hold it right there,' she said with the tone of an army sergeant. Not her first rodeo. 'Put the weapon on the ground and put your hands behind your head.'

Felix didn't drop the pistol. He kept it low, finger on the trigger. Not a threat. Not a submission.

'I said, drop the weapon and put your hands behind your head.' The officer snapped.

Again, Felix didn't move. Was he itching for a fight? Slowly, I lifted my cuffed hands up over my head, and placed my palms one over the other on the back of my skull. At least that way if shit hit the fan, she wouldn't shoot at me first.

'Sir, drop the weapon.' The officer commanded, and finally, Felix did as he was told. Gently, he knelt down and placed his weapon on the ground. As he stood up, he brought his hands up with an air of mocking attrition, like it was some kind of game. The cop didn't like it. She was maybe fifteen feet from us. She closed the gap by half in a matter of seconds. Gun pointed right at Felix's face.

She swapped to a one-handed hold on the weapon and reached for her radio.

'This is Officer O'Neil. I have two suspects in the alleyway behind the club. One armed, one in cuffs. Requesting immediate backup.'

Bad. Very bad.

'Copy that, on my way.' Said a voice through the radio.

Very, very bad.

'You don't have to do this.' I said, instantly regretting opening my mouth. Officer O'Neil looked directly at me with that searing glare only cops can manage. She looked me up and down, compartmentalising my description in her mental bank, running it against all the other young, white males of my size and height that she knew to watch out for. It was only a matter of time before she put two and two together.

'Shut up and get down on your knees.' She said to both of us. With no other available options that didn't involve getting shot, we did as we were told. As soon as knees hit concrete, O'Neil closed the gap. From her belt, she pulled a pair of plasticuffs free. The first set she slapped on Felix. Arms lowered one at a time around his back. Cuffs slipped up to his wrists. Pulled tight. Then she moved on to me.

'Who put these on you?' she asked, looking at my metal cuffs.

I nodded at Felix.

'Why?' she asked.

'Long story.'

All the same, she slapped on the plasticuffs. No assumptions made here. As she tightened the straps, a second cop turned the corner. Clad head to toe in a couple of inches of reinforced riot gear, it was hard to tell if it was a small man or a woman. The tactical shotgun in his or her hands was pointed at me, and he or she strode towards me with dire conviction. I watched the shotgun barrel get to within a foot of my face.

'Get down on the ground.' The masked cop said. The voice was undeniably female, although the helmet muffled the dictation. I did as I was told. No reason to agro a cop with a shotgun in my face. Carefully, I dropped onto my shoulder, then flopped onto my stomach. This was it. The end. Escape was hardly an option when all I could do is wiggle on my chest for freedom. Both cops knew it. As soon as Felix dropped down beside me, I saw the two women lower their weapons. The battle was won.

'Cover me while I pat them down.' The first cop said. She stowed her pistol in the holster and knelt down on top of Felix. Starting with his ankles, she carefully checked up his thighs, searching for anything suspicious. After the legs, she moved to his torso and ran her hands confidently across his back and sides. From the pocket of his jacket, she retrieved a phone and a wallet. Nothing out of the ordinary. She threw them across to the discarded pistol.

Satisfied Felix wasn't packing anything other than a sulk, the cop moved on to me. Her knee pressed down into the small of my back, squishing me into the concrete. I groaned as the air was knocked out of me.

'Shut it, scumbag.' She snapped.

'If you could just move a little to the right.' I gasped. 'So I can keep breathing.'

Which pissed her off something rotten. In a flash, she had her pistol out and pressed into the back of my skull.

'I told you to shut the hell up.' She barked, letting the thrill of the moment get the better of her. The pistol squeezed against my head, forcing it down. I scrunched my eyes shut.

At which point, I heard something loud and unexpected, followed by something that sounded somewhere between the cry of a fox, and the grunt of a professional tennis player. Then something heavy crashed down into my head. At first, I wasn't sure what the hell it was. But as I struggled free, and saw just what had happened, I wasn't sure whether what I'd seen was real, or the aftermath of being shot in the back of the head.

The peaked black hat came to a stop upside down right beside Felix's belongings. The golden insignia sparkled in the morning sun. The officer slumped down between Felix and me. Over her unconscious body, I saw Felix struggle up to his knees, and look up at the other officer. She towered over both of us, shotgun held in her hands like a baseball bat.

'What the…' He started, but didn't get any further than that, because the masked officer struck him in the centre of his face with the butt of the shotgun. He went down like a joke at a funeral. As Felix's eyes rolled into the back of his skull, I saw the shotgun rise up again, preparing for another strike.

But then she paused and lowered the shotgun. The weapon hung in one hand as she reached up and pulled the helmet from her face.

Which was when I was sure I was dead, because there was no way in hell that the face I was looking at was real. She looked down at me and smirked. The familiar twinkle in her eye flashed momentarily. Those eyes. Wild and dangerous. The kind of eyes that make you agree to pick up a hitchhiker you just met. The kind of eyes that make you gamble your life to save. It couldn't be real. It just couldn't be.

'Long time no see.' said Nicole Green.

TWENTY-SEVEN

REUNION

MY EYES MET HERS. THOSE IMPOSSIBLE, WILD EYES. THE LAST TIME I had seen her, she was recovering in a bed in her uncle's house all the way in Nebraska from a succession of gunshots, burns, cuts and abrasions. She was not, could not, by any stretch of the imagination, be right in front of me. This was another trick, a game the Wolf was playing on my mind to make this whole thing a little easier to compute.

'Not me,' the Wolf whispered in my mind. 'She's the real deal.'

'If you're done gawping like a jackass, we've got to move.' She said. She bent down beside the unconscious officer she had just brained with the shotgun and fished out a set of keys. Tucking the shotgun between her thighs, she shuffled towards me and unlocked my steel handcuffs. With the plasticuffs, she used a pocket knife. I just watched her, dumbfounded.

'Hey asshole,' she said, clicking her fingers an inch from my eyes. 'Get it together. We've got to go.'

'How?' Was all I could manage at that moment. One minute I'd been contemplating an extradition to Britain. Now this.

'We can talk about it later. We need to hustle. Take your tie off.'

'Why?'

'So we can stuff it in this pig's mouth and stop her complaining when she wakes up, unless you want a dozen cops climbing up your ass?'

I didn't. Breaking myself away from the revere, I pulled my

THE FATE OF GLASS

sodden tie off and wrapped it around the cop's mouth. It wouldn't stop her ability to shout, but it would dampen the noise enough to stop people overhearing her objections. As I tied a quick knot around the base of her skull, Nicole used one of the plasticuffs to secure the cop's hands behind her back. She did the same with her feet.

'Drag her over there,' Nicole said, gesturing towards a bin the size of a small hatchback. I did as I was told, still numb from everything. As I tucked her in the shadows, Nicole pulled the visor back down on her helmet. 'Come on, we've got to move.'

'We need to take him.' I said, looking at Felix. He was spread-eagled on the ground. He looked out for the count. Going down on your head like that tends to have that effect. I snatched up the belongings the cop had removed from his person. The phone, the wallet and the pistol.

'No way. We'll stand out too much. Just leave him.'

'I can't. I need him.'

'I don't give a shit. He's too big to carry, and he ain't going anywhere fast like that.'

'You shouldn't have knocked him out then.'

'Are you seriously giving me shit for saving your life? Don't think I didn't notice your lack of gratitude.'

'Thanks, but I'm not leaving him here.'

'Why? What's so important about him?'

'We can do this later, just help me, will you?'

She let out an unnecessarily audible sigh and moved over to Felix. Moving the shotgun to her left hand, she knelt down and slipped her free right hand under his arm. I did the same on the other side, and together we hoisted him up. He felt like he weighed the same as a small elephant. Moving him anywhere was going to be a serious problem. Nicole had come to the same conclusion. With no care for his health, she dropped Felix like a sack of potatoes and strode away.

'We can't give up.' I groaned.

'And we can't haul his fat ass out into a street full of cops. If you need this guy, you better come up with a solution fast.'

'How did you get here?' I asked her.

'I took a cab.'

'How'd you get those clothes?'

'What, you never charm a cop out his pants before?'

'Can't say I have. Look, we can't stay here. We need to move before someone figures out what's happening. What was your plan to get out of here?'

'I don't know. I just winged it.'

'You've got a car though? A getaway vehicle?'

She shook her head.

'Please tell me you're joking.'

'I didn't plan on this, alright? I managed to take out one of the cops by luck in the first place.'

'I cannot believe you, Nicole.'

'Oh, by all means, go hand yourself in if you want. I'm sure you'll make a fantastic prison bitch.'

I looked up and down the alleyway. At one end - the side Nicole and the cop had come from - the road was alive with police action. I jogged the other way, down into the belly of the alley, but it went nowhere. Just ran straight into a dead end around the corner at the rear of the club. No escape there, unless I wanted to risk my luck with the cops inside. I jogged back to Nicole.

'We need to steal a vehicle.' I said.

'Yeah, no shit.'

'Can you get one of the police cruisers?'

'Not without someone noticing.'

'Then isn't it great you decided to come in fancy dress.'

'Why can't you do it?' She snapped.

I held my arms out to my sides. Water dripped onto the concrete.

'Why are you so wet anyway?' she asked.

'He tried to drown me.' I said, pointing at Felix.

'Why?'

'Because trying to kill me is the newest craze, aparently. Now go and get us a car.'

'Come with me.'

'No.'

She handed me the shotgun and pulled off the bulletproof vest. She exchanged it for the shotgun. The unconscious officer's hat had fallen off as she collapsed. Nicole fished it up and placed it on my head.

'Take the jacket off, and you'll blend in.' She said.

'My clothes are soaked.'

'So? No one is going to notice.'

To be fair, she had a point. The vest was tight, and the hat perched awkwardly on my head. But combined with the rest of my black suit, I did look more like an officer to the untrained eye.

THE FATE OF GLASS

Unlucky for us, there were a lot of trained eyes out in the street. High risk. Perhaps too high.

Nicole fished out a pair of aviators from the officer's body. They hid the fear in my eyes. Together, we heaved Felix up beside the cop. At least that way anyone walking by the alleyway wouldn't immediately spot the bodies.

The sun was hoisting itself higher in the sky, and daylight had claimed most of the land. As we reached the mouth of the alleyway, my stomach dropped. Police cruisers ruled the street. Two menacing black trucks were parked up by the front door to the club. SWAT vehicles, no doubt about it. Of the two-dozen people I could see, all of them were law enforcement. Impromptu barriers had been erected at either end of the block. Behind them, a throng of nosey civilians had amassed, eager to watch the events.

Four older, dirtier cars that Salazar's men had pulled up in stood abandoned in the street as their owners lay dead inside. The cops themselves were busy with the proverbial red tape. They moved in and out of the nightclub, dealing with the aftermath inside. No one gave us a second glance.

There weren't a whole lot of options around us. We couldn't exactly carry a body past the perimeter and down the street for the nearest cab.

Nicole said, 'We have to take one of those cars, it's our only option.'

'Are you mad? Someone will see us.'

'So? We're cops. We can do what the hell we want.'

'Even drive an unconscious criminal out of a crime scene in a piece of evidence? That's going to look majorly suspicious.'

'Newsflash, James. Whatever we do is going to look suspicious.'

'Then we take one of the police cruisers.'

'And if the keys aren't in?'

'I've hot-wired a car before, so have you.'

'Want to bet cop cars aren't rigged to stop that kind of shit?'

'Okay,' I said. 'What about one of the SWAT trucks?'

'If you want a death sentence.'

'It was just a suggestion.'

'Make better suggestions.'

'Then we risk taking a police car. It's our best bet.'

The officers hustled about, busying themselves with official police business. As I stepped out into the street, I felt like I'd done so with a large sign above my head saying *'look at me, I'm a criminal.'* Every step made me feel nauseous. With Nicole by my side, we tried to imitate the cops. Move with purpose. Don't look around too much. Act natural, for God's sake. We headed for the closest unoccupied police cruiser. Like most, it was a Ford Crown Victoria. The most popular vehicle to be converted for America's finest. I looked through the driver side window towards the ignition. No key. Shit.

I shook my head to Nicole and heard a muffled swear behind her visor. I strode onwards to the next. There were cops close by, but they were busy with the crime scene. The club was looking worse for wear in the light of day. Gone was the brash decadence it boasted the night before. The tall, thin windows that had risen high had smashed, and the glass was scattered all around the sidewalk.

The next Crown Vic was only a couple of feet from a cluster of cops. I walked by it, aiming for one of the vehicles further away from the action. The cops looked up at me as I passed by. I could feel their unified gaze burning through my aviators.

No one stopped me. Act with confidence. Works every time. Well, maybe nine times out of ten. Closer to the far end of the block, three police vehicles were parked up side by side. I checked the first. No use. No key. Same with the second.

The third had the key in the ignition.

I climbed into the driver seat and fired up the engine like I was right at home behind the wheel of a police cruiser. Nicole climbed in beside me. I could hear her breathing through the helmet. She was just as scared as I was. A quick glance told me no one had found our actions overtly suspicious, so I did a steady J-turn in the street and headed back for the alleyway.

I didn't drive down. Didn't want to get stuck or scratch the vehicle on the wall. I parked up alongside the mouth, wheels on the sidewalk, and got out. Together, we hustled down the alleyway. Felix was still unconscious. The officer was not. She glared up at us, eyes full of conviction. Didn't help her none. Nicole jabbed her again with the butt of the shotgun, and she slumped down.

'Seriously, stop hitting the cop.' I hissed at her.

'I'm not risking it.' She hissed back.

We hauled Felix up, dragged him back to the cruiser, and threw him in the back. I climbed into the front passenger seat and twisted around to try and secure him in place. I settled with clipping one of the seat belts around his waist.

Nicole watched me.

'You finished playing with your dolly?' She mocked.

'You'll thank me if we crash.'

'Wasn't exactly planning on driving us into a wall.'

'Just get going, will you?'

She fired up the engine and turned the car around. She did it slowly. Carefully. Like a cop, not a fugitive. I watched out of the window, searching for any objecting faces. None jumped out at me. Nicole eased the cruiser forwards, towards the impromptu barrier and the crowd of civilians.

Three cops were on crowd control. Two spoke to reporters, who had already scuttled up out of the sewers to take snapshots of all the dead bodies and destruction. A particularly brazen and stout female reporter had her microphone wedged deep into one of the cops' nose, and from the look on his face, he was at breaking point. Upon hearing the approaching vehicle. He stepped away from the reporter and hustled over. He was dressed in his everyday work attire. Hat and badge. Smart black uniform. No protective tactical gear. He was low on the food chain. He bent down and leaned towards my passenger window.

'Sir?' He said. He was young, probably not long on the force.

I nodded and said in my finest American accent 'We've been called back to the precinct.'

The cop peered at Felix, slumped in the back seat.

'We were told to wait for DEA and Forensics before anyone is permitted to leave.' He said matter-of-factly. The new guy. Not willing to bend the rules.

'New orders, son.' I said, emphasising the hoarse tone to my already weary voice. 'This one needs taking in to be questioned.'

He looked at Felix again.

'Why isn't he secured?' He asked.

'He's unconscious.' Nicole interjected.

'Unconscious people wake up, ma'am.' The cop said, eyeing her outfit with an all too unpleasant air of suspicion.

'You getting smart with me, boy?' She snapped. 'What's your badge number.'

Reluctantly, he read it out.

'Now listen here,' she said. 'Unless you want to spend the rest of your career on the night shift, you better get those reporters out the way and let us through.'

He nodded apologetically and stepped back.

I wound the window up and whispered to Nicole.

'He doesn't trust us.'

'No shit. I told you bringing this guy was a bad idea.'

'I need him.'

'Enough to risk your life?'

I didn't reply. The cop moved over to the barrier. He began the arduous task of shooing the civilians out of the way. They moved reluctantly aside, taking longer than necessary. But then he stopped halfway, distracted by something. A voice on his radio shouted something. Through the closed windows, it would have been inaudible. But Nicole had a similar radio attached to her outfit and heard the same nine words as the young cop did.

'Officer down. I repeat, we have an officer down.'

TWENTY-EIGHT

THE IMPOSSIBLE

STATISTICALLY SPEAKING, I AM AN EXTREMELY LUCKY INDIVIDUAL. Luck has been in my favour every step of the way. After everything I have been through, every trial and tribulation, I have been through enough suffering and misfortune to last countless lifetimes. Yet somehow here I am, alive and kicking. My survival is a statistical anomaly. Every bullet, knife, fist or explosion that has been thrown my way each had the chance to end my existence. My luck had run way into debt, and one day fate would collect. For now, though, the reaper could keep his feet up.

So, statistically, I'm a winner. Hurray to me. I dodged every boulder, jumped every pit of fire, braved every storm. Here I was. The impossible James Stone. If luck was a commodity, I was rich.

But it wasn't. And statistics aren't worth shit when you've been caught with your hand in the cookie jar.

The young cop was tangled in a web of conflict. The scene before him and the panicked voice on the radio were two clashing versions of the truth. Neither one could be completely believed or discredited without further speculation. His mind ran through thousands of scenarios, searching for the right answer.

Nicole didn't give him the chance to reach a conclusion.

She stamped on the accelerator, and the cruiser exploded forwards with absurd ease. The reporters scattered like pigeons, and we shot through the vacant space, out into the busy road ahead. The young cop barely had the time to fall aside before he was in our dust.

'You idiot, why did you do that?' I snapped. 'We could have convinced him.'

'We couldn't, and you know it,' she snapped back. 'He knew we were lying the second he saw your best friend back there. I told you it was…'

'A bad idea. Yes, I'm aware.'

The early morning rush hour had already spread across the city like a bad rash. Nicole flicked a button on the dashboard, which turned the cruiser into a whir of flashing lights and wailing sirens. Cars and trucks pulled aside, unknowingly abetting our escape.

'We need to ditch the car,' I said. 'They've got to have a tracker in here somewhere.'

Nicole swore again and said 'We'll ditch it up ahead. Need to get some distance between us first.' She looked at me, dressed head to toe in battle gear like a twenty-first-century samurai. 'We'll need to get out of these clothes too.'

I chucked the police hat on the back seat. It bounced off Felix's head and fell into the footwell. Nicole powered through the intersection, narrowly avoiding a truck headed right towards us. The driver squeezed on his horn.

'How did you find me?' I asked.

'It's a long story,' she said. She swung the cruiser between two rows of stationary traffic up ahead and burst out into another intersection. 'This isn't exactly the right time or place for stories.'

I pulled off the police vest and looked behind me. Flashing lights in the distance. Lots of them. Nicole swung a hard right at the next intersection.

'I need to change,' she said. 'Can you take the wheel?'

'That seems like a good idea.' I snarled. 'I really fancy crashing into traffic.'

'I swear to God James, I'll punch you.'

She let go of the wheel and pulled her helmet off. I hastily grabbed the wheel and weaved between the slow traffic. It was hard to judge spatial awareness from the passenger seat. Nicole pulled off her tactical top, revealing a plain grey t-shirt beneath. She hoisted the trousers down and released the accelerator momentarily to pull them over her shoes. Underneath, she wore light blue jeans. She looked a damn sight better than me in my damp shirt and trousers. She took control of the vehicle again and turned sharply into an alleyway.

Halfway down, she stamped on the brakes.

'On foot from here.' She ordered, and before I could speak, she was out of the car.

I climbed out and opened the rear passenger door.

'What are you doing?' she said.

'I need him.' I said again.

'We don't have time for this.'

'Then go. I didn't ask you to help me. I can't leave him here.'

'Because he knows something? I know something too. If you don't leave him here, you'll get caught, again.'

I unbuckled Felix and dragged him off the seat onto the street. He flopped and bashed his head against the tarmac.

'Stay here with him.' I said.

'Why?'

'I can move the car. They'll track it here in no time. We need to get as far away from it as possible. Faster to move it than us.'

'I'm not staying here with him.' She snapped.

'Then you move the car.'

'I'm not leaving you.'

'I'm not going anywhere. I'll wait for you.'

'You think I trust you after what you did?'

I sighed and said 'Can we please talk about this later?'

'I'm not moving the car, and I'm not leaving you.'

I looked at Felix. He wasn't going anywhere.

'Right, we leave him and move the car.'

She helped me drag Felix behind a pile of trash, and jumped back in the car. I drove. I wanted to control how far we went. I didn't want to risk leaving Felix alone. If he woke up before we got back, or got caught, then it was all for nothing. The further we drove, the likelier that would be the case.

I floored the cruiser down to the end of the alleyway and turned left, heading back in the direction we came. I drove fast, adopting the same policy Nicole had taken for getting everyone to move. Blues and twos, all the way. It felt exhilarating to hold such power. I was Moses, parting the sea of sedentary traffic.

It didn't last for long. I didn't allow it to. I ducked right into a tight alleyway beside a bespoke jewellers store.

'Pass me that helmet you were wearing.' I shouted.

'Why?'

'Just do it.'

Nicole obliged, reached over to the back seat to grab it, and handed it over. I wedged it down onto the accelerator pedal. The engine roared.

'Get out, now.' I barked.

She did, and as I released the handbrake, I dived out of the driver side door and watched as the police cruiser rocketed away down the alley. With no one at the reins, the vehicle reared and weaved into a hefty industrial trash bin at the other end of the alley. It came to an almighty, devastating halt. As the helmet dislodged, and the car finally came to a standstill, we were already halfway down the street.

It took less than a minute for the cops to arrive. They swarmed on the store, barricading the street from all angles. At least fifteen cops climbed out, guns raised, pointed at the ruined cruiser.

Nicole and I kept walking. Long strides. Not running. Not strolling. Fast and confident. She took my hand. Just a couple going for a stroll. I knew it wouldn't last long. It would take seconds to scan the vehicle and register that it was empty. Then they would fan out in every direction, looking for two men in black suits.

'You need to change out of that suit.' Nicole hissed, coming to the same conclusion.

'No shit,' I whispered back. 'But I haven't got any money, do you?'

'No James, you stole all my money, remember? You better not have lost it.'

Up ahead was a large shopping mall, glistening in the morning sun like a beacon of hope. We ducked through the glass double doors. The shops were open, and the sleepy morning staff were acclimatising to the horrors of a new working day. Nicole hauled me further inside, into a gargantuan three-story atrium. The vast paned glass ceiling flooded the mall with light. Hundreds upon hundreds of people milling around across the three stories. Nicole led me to an escalator, and we rode up to the second floor.

Mixing in with the crowd, I felt much safer than I had on the street. It would be harder to spot a particularly soggy needle in a haystack of this size, and resorting to CCTV footage after the fact would do little to stop us right now. We strode casually into a retail outlet that looked both bland and cheap and was sparsely populated. The cashier stood behind the counter with his head bowed. Not an early-morning prayer. The guy was checking his phone. He didn't acknowledge us.

Nicole strode across to a line of t-shirts and picked out a plain white v-neck and a brown shirt from the next aisle. She passed me the tops, along with a pair of dark blue jeans and ushered me towards the changing room.

'If they have any security tags, rip them off,' she hissed. 'I'll distract the cashier.'

I nodded and headed for the changing rooms, grabbing a beanie hat off a rack as I passed. Inside the security of the changing room, I pulled off my sodden suit and discarded it on the floor. I pulled on the new clothes, tearing them slightly to allow for the security tags to slip free, and headed back out into the shop. Nicole was sat on the floor in the corner, clutching her ankle with a look of extreme discomfort on her face.

'I can't move it, oh God. It hurts so bad.' She sobbed to the nervous cashier who was bent down beside her.

'I just don't...I don't get how you fell.' He stammered, looking around for some mystery culprit to pin the blame on.

'I slipped, asshole. You should have put a sign down saying the floor was wet. I could sue...'

'Just...uh...keep it elevated. I'm sure it's not broken.'

Nicole's eyes flashed over to me, and with infinitesimal care, she nodded towards the exit. I hurried outside, holding my breath as I walked through the detectors. They remained silent. I turned to make sure she was watching, and headed right, out of sight of the shop front.

A minute later Nicole walked out, holding a light blue shirt of her own.

'He gave me this as compensation,' she said. 'To stop me from suing.'

'How thoughtful of him.' I said.

She pulled it over her top and pulled up the sleeves, and we headed back towards the escalators. But a second later I stopped dead in my tracks.

A sea of police officers had entered the atrium. Like a swarm of locust, they dissipated angrily throughout the ground floor. Weapons raised, they scanned the room with incredible efficiency. Standing at the top of the escalator, Nicole swore under her breath.

'This way.' She said, taking my hand and leading me up to the third floor.

We took the rising stairs two at a time, watching as officers on the floor below did the same. The third floor seemed to mostly consist of a food court. The restaurants weren't open yet, waiting for the busier evening hours instead, but interspersed between them were smaller fast-food stands.

Nicole hustled across to a burrito stand and waited patiently in the queue.

'What are you doing?' I whispered in her ear.

'Acting normal. What kind of criminal would queue up?'

'The British kind.'

But she had a point. The police were looking for people on the run, not a couple waiting patiently for a burrito.

Nicole pulled out a few notes from her pocket.

'I thought you didn't have any cash?' I said.

'I've got a couple of bucks, not enough for a costume change.'

The queue shortened and we took the next place. Nicole ordered for both of us, and we waited. Using the escalator at the far end of the third floor, six armed police officers emerged. They fanned out, checking every restaurant as they moved, carefully considering each and every person in their vicinity.

A young man wearing a baseball cap was stopped in his tracks by two officers with their weapons trained at the ground and forced to remove the hat, revealing a thick bush of blonde hair beneath. The officers moved on without a second's thought. The blonde man turned to watch them go. He didn't look anything like me.

'This isn't going to work,' I whispered as the young woman behind the counter prepared our burritos. 'They're checking everyone.'

Nicole glanced over at the officers. They were still a long way off, but they were approaching with sickening haste. Her face was solemn. The woman behind the counter handed over the burritos, which I took with a smile. We moved steadily away from the approaching officers towards the downward escalator, but as we drew near more officers appeared. They were just a few feet away, and we were the closest.

Nicole spun on her heel and clasped her hands around my face. She pulled me close and kissed me. Her lips were warm and soft. Her breath tasted sweet. She was almost a foot smaller than me, and I had to stoop to be at her level. Without thinking, I wrapped my burrito filled hands around her back and held her tight. I closed my eyes and sank into the moment. I let it absorb and warm me like a hot bath. Somewhere nearby, I heard footsteps hurry past me, towards the burrito stand.

She let go and looked into my eyes for what felt like an eternity,

THE FATE OF GLASS

but in reality couldn't have been longer than a second. Then she turned to locate the officers.

'Come on, let's get out of here.' She said. And with that, she turned around and headed for the escalator. I stood, momentarily stunned for a moment as the gravity of the situation caught up to me, and then followed suit.

'You taste nice.' I said, following her down the escalator.

'Said the married man.'

'Point taken.'

At the bottom of the escalator, I passed Nicole her burrito, and we walked casually towards the exit. I tore open the foil wrapping and took a bite. Nicole did the same. Through my sunglasses, I stared at the moving officers as they swept the floor, and the telltale flashing lights of stationary police cruisers outside. Nicole noticed, and directed me towards a different exit. In my pocket, Felix's phone began to buzz. I ignored it.

We hung left, following the wall around to stay out of the primary focus of the police, and ate our burritos as casually as one can when trying to amiably avoid arrest. Nicole scanned the scene for something, and when she found it, she turned and put her hand on my chest, stopping me in my tracks.

'Wait here, and keep an eye out.' She said. She left before I could question her.

I stood and ate the rest of my burrito while she hurried down across to one of the giant pillars holding up the first-floor walkway. Built into the pseudo-marble front was a small red box. She moved close, looked around for any witnesses, and pulled the toggle.

The fire alarm was deafeningly loud. A high pitch scream echoed out through the atrium like a foghorn with the pitch turned up to eleven. All around, the mall shoppers jumped as the deafening sound rocked them close to a heart attack, and like a pack of sheep, they shuffled towards the fire exits.

Nicole rejoined me, and we slipped into the throng as they flowed towards the courtyard. Hundreds of people slogged out into the morning sun, overwhelming the officers with their imposing size. We walked calmly, scanning the crowd for any officers directly in our path, and headed for the street.

Nicole took my hand and leaned in close again to uphold the façade of our relationship. It worked. The officers by the parade of stationary vehicles were focused on the swarm of shoppers that had appeared before them, not the young couple moving away.

Once we were past the worst of it, we broke into a fast walk. Getting back to Felix took almost ten minutes. What had taken seconds in a speeding vehicle was much longer on foot. As we walked, a stream of police cars screamed right past us.

'That's it,' Nicole said, pointing at the alley entrance. 'Just up here.'

'It doesn't look like the cops are here. That's a good sign at least.'

'Unless they're waiting for you to come back.'

'You're starting to sound like a horse.'

'What?'

'With all this nay-saying.'

She hit me in the arm. 'Dick.'

We rounded the corner and walked down the alley. All was quiet. Just as we had left it. I reached the spot and pulled the trash aside.

And found a whole lot of nothing where Felix had been.

'Where the hell did he go?' I snarled.

There were no signs of a struggle. No signs of the police. He had to have woken up and fled of his own accord. Figuring out which way he had gone was going to be impossible. Ditching the car and getting back to the alley had taken the better part of an hour in total. In that time, he could be anywhere in the city.

'At least you got his phone and wallet,' the Wolf said. He'd been characteristically quiet as I escaped. Like always, he was too cowardly to stick around when things got tough. 'And here I was about to compliment you for being proactive.'

'He could be anywhere by now,' I said, directly to the Wolf. 'A phone isn't going to change that. He was probably ready to ditch it anyway.'

'I'm sorry Nicole,' I said, looking at the spot I'd left Felix. 'I didn't anticipate this. I should have just left him.'

I turned to give her a sheepish *"you were right"* smile.

And came face to face with the end of a pistol.

TWENTY-NINE

CATCH TWENTY-TWO

Not for the first time did James Stone stare down the barrel of a gun. Nor was it the first time I had been the one to point it at him. The man was a hurricane. He would pull everyone and everything in, and cause utter destruction. Now he stood there like a deer in headlight with a look of dumb shock plastered across his face.

'Where's my money, James?' I asked before he could speak. 'What did you do with it?'

'Nicole…' He sounded hurt, as though I was the one who stole from him, not the other way around.

'Cut the shit. You took my money. I want it back. Tell me where it is now, or I'll show you what the inside of your stomach looks like.'

'You're not going to shoot me, Nicole.'

'Want to bet? How about two million dollars?'

'Catch twenty-two.' 'he said with a wearied smile.

'What?'

'Catch twenty-two. You know, the Joseph Heller novel? Surely you've heard of it before?'

'Enlighten me.' I snarled.

'The paradoxical situation in which both outcomes aren't in your favour. If you made that bet and didn't shoot me, the money would be mine, but if you did shoot me, I wouldn't be able to show you where it is if I was dead. Simply put, it means you're screwed either way.'

'Keep stalling, and I'll put a bullet through your foot. Tell me where the money is.'

'Why are you doing this?' he asked. 'You know not everything can be solved by pointing a gun at it, right?'

The sound of sirens resonated across the city. Circling like vultures. It wouldn't be long before they were on top of us.

'James, for the last time. Tell me where my goddamn money is.' I snapped.

He looked at me and sighed.

'It's not here.'

'No shit. Where is it?'

'It's locked in a secure location about fifty miles from here. You need the four-digit code to unlock the padlock.'

'Alright, then what's the code?'

Another pause.

'I'm sorry I took the money,' he said. 'I just want you to know, I didn't do it out of spite, or what happened at Salazar's.'

'I don't care.'

'I wanted you to come and find me,' he said. 'You know that, right? I couldn't exactly leave an address for you. Your uncle would have torn it up, not that I knew exactly where I was going in the first place. And I figured if I just asked you to come along, you'd say no. I like having you around. I think we make a good team...when we aren't trying to sell each other out.'

'So, depriving me and my brother of a secure future was more important to you than letting go?'

'I didn't say it was a *good* plan. I was high on painkillers at the time. I didn't think it all the way through. Besides, you do owe me after everything I did for you. Some of that money is rightfully mine.'

'I'm sure a court would disagree.'

'Oh, because you're the rightful heir to it?' he snapped. 'News-flash Nicole, you stole money from one of the most powerful drug lords this country has ever seen. Even if you'd managed to evade Derek and his merry band of gimps, Hector Salazar would have found you eventually, and he would have skinned you and your brother alive. Or at least, his son would have on his father's behest. Don't act like I didn't help you out by putting a stop to them.'

'And don't you forget I just saved your ass.'

'And while I thank you for it, that doesn't make us equal.'

'Like hell, it doesn't. You'd see the electric chair inside of a week if I didn't risk my life for you.'

'And you and Bobbie would be dead if it weren't for me. Everything you were trying to achieve would be dead in the water if you didn't meet me in that diner.' He shouted. 'Now put that gun down, and we can talk about this like a pair of reasonable criminals.'

I lowered the gun.

'And for your information, I've saved your arse once more than you have mine.' He said. 'The tally is five to four in my favour.'

'Bullshit. If anything, it's six in my favour.'

'You lose a point for selling me out.'

'Then you lose a point for trying to shoot me.'

'Agree to disagree. But we need to leave now.'

'You better take me to the money, James.' I snapped.

'I can't. Not yet.' I went to raise the gun, but he interjected, 'I will take you there, but I need to finish business here first. After what happened last night, things are going to move quickly. I need to find Ramiro Salazar before everything goes to shit. To do that, I need to find Domingo Reyes.'

'Who?'

'The guy who owns that club. The guy who this bloody deserter works for.' He pointed at the trash bins where the giant black guy we'd rescued had lain.

'Who is he?' I asked.

'Felix Jackson. Miami superstar, aparently. He's the right-hand man to Reyes from what I can tell. He can help me track Salazar. Hopefully, before the cops devour the whole city.'

'I don't care about all that.'

'Nicole, if you help me, I'll give you the whole thing. You can have two million dollars all to yourself, minus the couple of grand I've spent getting here. I won't object. I'll take you all the way to it and give it to you with a big old smile on my face. But I need your help. If you refuse, I'll take the location of the money to the grave. You can shoot me as much as you like, I won't tell. You've seen my scars, the only thing you can do that will make me talk, is give me your cooperation.' He looked me dead in the eye. 'There's no one I trust more than you with this, even if you have sold me out more times than a West End show.'

'How long have you been sitting on that one?'

'A while. Does this mean you'll help?'

'Well since I don't exactly have a lot of options, and now I'm as much a fugitive as you are, then I guess I have to.'

'You could sound a little more enthusiastic about it.' he grinned.

'Don't think I won't still shoot you for being a little bitch.'

'I never doubted you. Come on. We need to find somewhere a little more suitable to be.'

We ran to the end of the alleyway and scanned the street. The cops weren't nearby. Their search of the city hadn't yet reached us.

'And for the record,' James said. 'You're not as much of a fugitive as me. I've still got you beat on that one.'

'Are you seriously bragging about that?'

'It's just,' he paused. 'Never mind. Christ.'

He waved down a passing taxi. The driver weaved and stopped just short of us. James opened the door, and we climbed in.

'Where to?' the driver asked.

'Miami International Airport please.' James said without pause. The driver nodded and took off into traffic.

'How exactly do you plan on flying anywhere?' I whispered to him.

'What makes you think I would want to fly anywhere?'

'Oh, my bad.' I hissed. 'Here I thought that's where they kept all the aeroplanes.'

The cab raced across the city as quickly as it could trapped in the early morning madness. Occasionally, I caught sight of flashing lights whizzing past the window, or heard the spine-tingling echo of sirens in the distance. They paid our little taxi cab no mind, and as we turned on to the final stretch, I could feel the burdening weight on my shoulders ease up.

'Just here if you don't mind,' James said to the driver, gesturing to a spot a short walk from the gate. The driver nodded and came to a stop. 'You've got this, right?' He said, already halfway out the taxi door. I paid the fare with a false smile, climbed out, and followed James as he headed away from the gate.

'Where are we going?' I asked.

'The long way back.'

The long way back, as James saw it, was a long and tedious journey. From the airport, we walked a mile back into the city and hailed another taxi.

'Take your top off.' James said as the taxi pulled up alongside us.

'I'm not flashing the driver.' I snapped back.

'As fun as that would be, I just meant the shirt.'

I sighed and shrugged off the shirt the panicked store worker had given me. James took it and balled it up with his own. He took off the beanie and stuffed both shirts inside. He gave the driver a street address, and we set off back into the city. I watched the fare creep up on the display on the dashboard.

'Seriously,' I said. 'You know I'm not made of money, right? How long is this detour going to take?'

'We're nearly there. Thanks for paying.'

'Yeah because you gave me much of an option. You want to explain what we're doing here?'

'Losing our scent,' he said. 'It'll be harder for the police to track us back here now. They'll find us on the CCTV in the mall pretty quickly, and will follow us to the first taxi not long after. It'll take longer to track the driver and question him, then to follow us to here. Put it this way, a couple dozen tech geeks are going to have to spend a whole lot of time to track us down, and we'll be out of here by then.'

'Wow, check the brains on you.'

'Well, a wise woman once told me I didn't become a globally wanted felon by stumbling through life.' He grinned.

'I believe I followed that up with "like an idiot."'

'I was paraphrasing for the sake of my ego.'

The taxi came to a stop on a quiet suburban street, and we got out. I paid the driver most of my remaining cash and followed James down the street. The sense of urgency had gone. From his pocket, he pulled out a sleek leather wallet and flipped it open. It was flush with cash.

'Thought you had no money on you?' I snapped.

'It's Felix's. I didn't think to check.'

He pulled out the cash and split it between us. Two hundred bucks. Certainly paid for the cab fare.

'My car is this way.' He said.

The car James had picked was a Ford Country Squire. The kind of car a grandma drives to bingo every Friday night. It had the smell of residual damp that was as much a part of the vehicle as the engine or steering wheel. The seat was uncomfortable, and the ride bumpy, but it did the job. It gave us anonymity.

'Where to?' I asked. James replied with a shrug and pulled out the cell he'd taken from Felix.

'See if there's anything useful in that.' He said.

The cell was a Blackberry, one of the newer models. A flashy piece of kit. Too expensive to be a burner. But if it was his private cell, would he keep all the information that would tie him to his life of crime? I doubted it. I checked the address book first. Nothing saved.

I moved on to his texts. Felix was a smart guy. Either he had only started receiving messages in the last few hours, or he had developed the bad habit of deleting them after reading. I figured the latter. The texts that appeared on file were all from the last couple of hours.

The first to miss the cut from Felix was from an unknown number and came through at five am on the dot. It consisted of three words.

"China has landed."

I relayed it to James.

'What do you think it means?' I asked.

'Beats me. A deal maybe? Is there anything else to go on?'

I scrolled through the other messages, but all of them were from a single contact.

'Nothing for that.' I said.

'Leave it for now then.' James replied. 'It's too vague to go on for now. Might not have anything to do with Reyes. What about the other messages?'

'Gun to my head, I'd say they were from a woman. Probably his girlfriend or something.'

I scrolled down to the first text to come through. The time stamp told me it had come through at quarter past five in the morning.

"You done soon? xo"

Short and succinct. Sent from a woman. I'd never met a man who used *xo* at the end of a message. The follow up was just minutes later.

"Can you pick up food on the way back? xo."

After that, there was a gap of almost an hour and a half. Doubt had ignited. A response expected, none received.

"You okay? Call me. xo"

Again, nothing. The next message was automated. A call had come from the same number and not answered. The cell provider had sent a text stating the date and time. Nothing special. Except that the next three messages were the same, each five minutes apart. She was getting agitated. She was starting to panic. She had expected Felix to be done by now. Little did she know, Felix was up

THE FATE OF GLASS

shit creek. How long would it take for the news to spread? Local news stations would have jumped on the attack at the club, ready to broadcast it on the morning news. If she had a television or radio turned on, she had to know by now.

But what did that mean for her? What was the logical next step her mind would make? If she was Felix's lover as I expected, she had to bet the cops were on their way, especially if she thought they had his phone. They'd want to talk to her. They'd want to bring her in. The only problem was where she was. If she was at home, she was safe so long as Felix kept his mouth shut. But if she was at Felix's...

'You took his wallet, right?' I asked.

James fished it out of his pocket.

'You got something?' He asked.

'Maybe. The woman texting, she's worried what's happened to him.'

James hummed to himself and scrunched his face up in deep contemplation.

'What, you know who she is?' I asked.

'I've got a running theory.'

'You ready to share it with the class?'

'Lisbeth Quinn.'

'Who is Lisbeth Quinn?'

'We'll get to that. You think she might be at his place?'

'Either there or her own, but wherever that is I've got no idea.'

I flicked open the wallet and found Felix's license. The unsmiling face of Felix Jackson looked up at me next to the words *"Florida, the sunshine state"*. Apparently, the irony was lost on him. I found his address and typed it into the cell. A twenty-minute drive away.

Those twenty minutes were spent with a one-sided conversation. James filled me in on the details, starting all the way back as he drove out on Bobbie and me, right up to the moment I pointed a shotgun at his head. He told me about Eva, about Quinn, and his plan to get to Salazar through Reyes. The whole thing sounded about as farfetched as they come, which for James seemed about right. The guy had a knack for living his life on the edge.

His story filled the whole journey, and by the time he finished, I knew we were in the right place. The palm tree-lined streets were home to some of the most lavish houses I had ever seen. Back home in Nebraska, we had big houses with hundreds of acres of land, but the houses were built from locally-sourced wood cut down by some two-bit lumberjack with a drinking problem. These houses looked like twenty-first-century castles. No two were the same. One on the right looked like a princess castle supersized, while one across the road looked like a piece of contemporary art. In this neighbourhood, the Ford Country Squire stood out like a clown at a wake.

We found Felix's place easy enough. The enormous building looked like the product of an architect right out of college let loose with a huge budget and even bigger supply of coffee. It looked like a series of shipping crates stacked in a random formation, like some kind of bizarre game of Jenga, except the whole thing had been made out of fancy quartz brick, and floor to ceiling reflective glass.

But it wasn't the house that was the problem. It was what stood outside that was going to be a pain in the ass.

THIRTY

HOPE FOR THE BEST

An army of reporters had amassed outside Felix's home. At least thirty of them, cameras and microphones at the ready. No sign of the cops. Go figure the press got here first. They always could sniff out a lead.

James cussed under his breath.

'This complicates things,' he sighed. He took the car up the street a little ways, and spun it around to face the way we just came. The house was up ahead. The crowd of reporters looked like a set of miniature figurines. 'We need to get in there.'

'You're not going anywhere with them outside, so you better have a plan to make them scatter.'

'That's not the bit I'm worried about,' he said. 'How long do you figure before the cops show?'

'It's got to be minutes at most, unless they've already been and gone.'

'Hope for the best.'

'Plan for the worst. What exactly is our plan then?'

He shrugged.

'A place like this has got to have some pretty serious security,' he said, scratching the hair on his jaw. 'CCTV, motion sensors, maybe a guard dog or two. You're not getting past that in a hurry.'

'We're,' I said, correcting his mistake, but he shook his head.

'I'm not getting any closer than this.' James replied. 'Not with those cameras outside. I can't risk it. You can.'

'I'm wanted too, you know.'

'Yeah, in Nebraska and a couple of other northern states. No one even knows you're here yet. You could get in and out no trouble.'

'And how am I supposed to do that?'

'You'll figure it out. I have faith in you.'

'Throw me under the bus why don't you?'

'Try to think of it as a considered nudge towards the bus instead,' he said with a smirk. 'You can always say no and forge a new life elsewhere.'

'Dick.'

'Off you go.'

I looked at the building. James was right. From what he'd told me of Felix and his lifestyle, he wasn't about to slack off on the home-front. It was bound to have some unnecessarily complex security surrounding it. No way I was getting in around the back. It had to be the front door. The only problem was how. There were too many people there to distract all at once, and even if I did somehow manage to turn that many heads away from the thing they were being paid to hound, I still had to get through a locked door. And that was all before the cops turned up, which had to be any second now.

A lightbulb went off in my head. I dug my hand into my pants pocket and pulled out something small and hard. Glistening gold in the daylight, the Miami Dade County Officer badge sparkled up at me.

'Where the hell did you get that from?' James guffawed.

'Where'd you think? The cop whose clothes I stole. You didn't think I'd leave something like this behind, did you? It's a golden ticket, baby.'

'God, you're worse than a magpie. You don't have to take everything shiny.'

I punched him in the thigh.

'You're such an asshole, James.'

'So that's your plan, pretend to be a cop?'

'It's as good a plan as any.'

'Until the real cops show up.'

'I don't hear you coming up with any better suggestions. If you don't like it, you go get her.'

'No. By all means, go play cops and see where that gets you, I'll see you in prison.'

'Dick.'

In my current outfit, I hardly looked like a cop. My grey top was damp with sweat, and my pants and boots were scuffed with dried dirt. Not exactly a professional look. I unwrapped the bundle of clothes James had tucked into his beanie before we got in the second taxi, and tried to smooth out all the creases of the blue shirt I'd been given in the store. I threw it on and tucked the hem into my pants. With the aviators, I looked a little more intimidating.

'What d'you think?' I asked James.

'It's missing something.'

'What?'

'I don't know. A jacket maybe?'

But there was nothing in the car to fit the bill. I needed to get creative.

'If I'm not back in twenty minutes, assume it's all gone to shit.' I said, climbing out the car.

'I'd expect nothing less from you.' James smirked.

I stayed on the sidewalk opposite Felix's house and the crowd of reporters and walked casually. Hands in pockets. Not a care in the whole damn world. Some of the late-arrivals had been forced to park their news vans across the street. The early bird gets the best parking spots. The closest van was an old grey hunk of shit with its rusted ass pointed right at me. As I neared, I slowed my pace and glanced up through the passenger window. No one inside. I looked ahead to the next van. No one in that too. Good start.

With no one around to immediately spot me and call me out for being all kinds of suspicious, I moved to the van door. Cupping my hands to negate the reflection, I got real close and looked inside. All I needed was a jacket or coat that looked smart enough for a cop to wear. Even though November in Florida was warm enough not to need a coat, people were creatures of habit. Surely, someone had brought their winter coat, just in case the storm came calling a couple of days early.

Not van number one. The worn seats were empty, and I wasn't about to start breaking in without a solid lead. I moved on to van number two and repeated the process. Check to see if anyone could see me, glance inside for a coat.

Zero for two. Move on to the next.

Van number three had a bored guy in the passenger seat. Asian guy with glasses and messy black hair. He slouched over the dashboard, one hand squished into his cheek that caused his glasses to skew on his face. I walked by as slowly as I could without drawing attention and glanced into the window of the van.

There, beside the bored passenger was a black leather jacket. Didn't matter if it was male, female or unisex, I could make that work. All I needed to do was get the guy out of the van. And as James liked to say, sometimes the simplest answer is the right one.

'Occam's Razor.' His voice echoed in my brain. Jeez, the guy was even an ass when he was a figment of my imagination.

I walked up to the passenger window and knocked twice on the glass. The guy jolted like someone had shocked his ass with a Taser. He reshuffled his glasses and wound down the window.

'Uh, yeah?' He grunted.

'Hey there,' I said with a nauseatingly sweet voice. 'What's going on over here?'

'Oh, some guy lives here who has a club uptown. Got vandalised or something. I don't know.'

'Sounds pretty serious.' I smiled.

'You betcha, but I don't think he's here. We've been here for like, an hour or something and no one's shown up.'

'That's a pity. Bet it would be real exciting to see some action, don't you think?'

'Uh, yeah.' He wiped the drool off his face. 'Did you want something?'

'Oh, no. I was just curious is all.' I turned to leave and pretended to see something at the rear of the truck. 'Oh, sir. I think you've got a leak.'

The guy made a fuss of unbuckling his belt and scrambled out of the door.

'Where?' he asked, looking at the blacktop for some sign of a spill.

'Right down there, sweetie.' I pointed at a spot low down at the rear of the van. The guy bent down to look at the whole lot of nothing that was there. As he did, I swiped the jacket from the passenger seat and balled it up around my arm. As he stood up, I hid my arm behind my back.

'There's nothing there.' He grunted.

'Oh, my bad. Sorry for wasting your time.'

He grunted again, and climbed into the van, completely unaware he'd been played. I gave him a polite smile and hustled away.

The leather jacket wasn't a perfect fit, but I made it work. I pulled it over the shirt and tucked the pin of stolen badge into the breast pocket, so it sat loud and proud on my chest. I ran my fingers through my hair to give it a little volume, then strode as confidently as I could right into the crowd of reporters.

'Out of the way, police business.' I snapped at anyone who didn't move fast enough. A couple of microphones waved in my face, but I batted them away with a quick 'No comment.' It felt good to have power, even if it was fraudulent.

The crowd had formed a good few yards from the front door. Probably a considered action to stop themselves getting in trouble with the actual police. Probably a law to say you can't plant your ass on someone's front lawn without due cause. I didn't know, but either way, it gave me a little respite from the crowd as I pressed my thumb into the doorbell.

It took just under a minute for a response.

'Yes?' The voice didn't come from the door, but a small speaker just above the doorbell. The voice was male.

'I need to speak to Mr Jackson regarding an issue earlier this morning at one of his businesses.' I said, taking on the role of cop as much as I could.

'Mr Jackson is not here.' The voice said. 'Who is speaking?'

'Detective Green.' I said. Above the door, a camera was pointed right at me. I pulled my stolen badge free and held it up to the lens. 'Do you work for Mr Jackson?'

'I am his housekeeper.'

'Please open the door. I will need to speak to you too.'

The door opened a moment later. Lurking in the shadow was a man at least six foot tall. He kept the door slightly ajar, not wanting to show his face to the crowd of reporters, all of whom perked up like a group of cats that just spotted a mouse.

'Please, come in.' He said. His voice was quiet, calm. More like that of a child than a man of his size. I took the invitation and stepped through the door.

If the outside of the building was a sight, it was nothing compared to the inside. Minimalist didn't seem to cover it. Every single inch of the massive entrance was painted white, all except for the staircase, which looked like a series of planks levitating one after the next. There were no lights on, because there didn't need to be. A massive skylight stretched the length of the building, flooding the extravagant home with dazzling natural light. It was impressive for sure, even if it looked more like an artist's interpretation of a home for the year three thousand than somewhere a twenty-first century ape would live.

The housekeeper was thin, with a light tan and the hint of a moustache on his upper lip. Had the air of a cat-walk model. The way he moved only emphasised it. He wore a smart black shirt, pants and shoe combination. If I had to guess, I'd say he was in his late teens, early twenties.

'Detective Green,' I said again, extending my hand for him to shake. He looked at it but didn't take it. Too scared. 'What is your name?'

'Manny Garcia.' He said politely. 'I'm sorry, but Mr Jackson is not here. He has not been back since he left yesterday morning. I do not know when he will be back.'

'That's okay. I didn't expect him to be here. I'm actually here about someone else, and I think you might be able to help.'

'Oh?' Manny's composure simultaneously relaxed and tensed up at the same time, like he realised something much worse was coming.

'Mr Jackson has a girlfriend, yes?'

'I... I am unsure of the question. Mr Jackson has many friends. Many women friends.'

'But one is a little more common than the others, right? Girl by the name of Lisbeth Quinn?'

His face practically gave away the answer, but he shook his head anyway, desperate to keep up the pretence.

'I do not know anyone by that name.' He said, taking a step back into the closed door. 'I think you will need to come back when Mr Jackson returns. He does not like me talking to people on his behalf.'

'I know you're lying, Manny. Your poker face ain't worth shit.'

'I do not play poker, Detective Green.'

'It's a figure of speech. Now, I need you to tell me where Lisbeth Quinn is. Do you know her address, or is she here?'

Again, Manny threw all his cards down on the table for all to see.

'I do not know where Miss Quinn is.' He stammered. His eyes darted all over the place, too uncomfortable to leave in one spot for too long.

'So you do know Lisbeth? I thought you didn't know who she was?'

'I... I am just saying. I do not know where this person you want...'

But a voice cut him off. From somewhere far off in the house, a female voice called out.

'Manny. Have those fucking reporters left yet? I'm getting sick of this shit.'

At the top of the stairs, a woman appeared. She wore a long pink dressing gown over a pair of slacks and a tank top. Her jet black hair was tied back, and her face lacked any makeup, but even so, she was breathtakingly beautiful.

'Lisbeth Quinn?' I asked.

'Oh shit.' She said.

And turned to run away.

THIRTY-ONE

PLAN FOR THE WORST

I WAS HOT ON QUINN'S HEEL AS SOON AS SHE TURNED TO FLEE. Go figure she'd try and escape. They always try and escape. People who know they're in the shit. Hell, I was usually the one doing the escaping. Didn't make it any easier to forgive at that particular moment.

I bounded up the levitating staircase three at a time, reaching the top seconds after Quinn had picked up speed. She ran towards the rear of the enormous house, her dressing gown flowing gracefully behind her. Through the long glass wall to her left, I could see a pool the size of a basketball court. Christ, how much money did Felix have to afford all this?

Quinn darted right, away from the pool through an open door. As I reached it, it slammed shut in my face.

I threw my weight into it and met resistance. Not a lock, more like something heavy pressed up against it. Had to be Quinn, she didn't have time to push something in the way. I took a couple steps back, then ran full force into the door again, and barged my shoulder into the door. It gave a little, and behind it, I heard Quinn cuss.

'Lisbeth Quinn? I need to talk to you.' I shouted through the crack in the door. 'I'm not here to arrest you.'

'Bullshit.' She snapped back.

'Just let me in so we can talk.'

'No way.'

I hit the door again, and it pushed a little further, enough for me to stick my arm through and jimmy it open the rest of the way.

Knowing it was useless to resist, Quinn moved away, and the door swung open.

I could see why she'd tried to hide in here. The room was a large, bedroom. Everything was white. The walls, the sheets, the side tables, everything. Well, not *everything*. Lying on the bedsheet was a small tin cigar box. It laid open, revealing an old metal spoon, a needle and a tiny translucent rock.

Go figure.

Quinn was panting. Her eyes flashed back and forth between me and the drugs.

'That ain't mine.' She said.

'I don't care. That's not why I'm here. I came to help you.'

'Bullshit,' she said again. 'You want to know where Jackson is. I don't know. I haven't heard from him in days.'

It was my turn to call bullshit. I retrieved Felix's wallet from my pocket and held it up. The look in her lucid eyes told me she recognised it.

'What did you do with him?' she snapped.

'Nothing. I don't know where he is either.'

'Then why are you here? You can't prove those are mine.' She pointed at the drugs. It was a weak argument. Even I knew all it would take to prove she was using was a urine test. I'd had my fair share of them before when I was running with Redd and the boys.

'I didn't come here for that. I came to help you.'

'Oh yeah? How?'

'You do know what happened last night, at your boyfriend's club? You've seen it on the news, right? I don't have to explain who that was that came and attacked your man, do I? I figure you understand how serious this is, and know that hiding under a different name isn't going to mean shit when you shack up with your daddy's second in command.'

I watched her recoil.

'You don't know what you're talking about.' She spat.

'Oh yeah? Your pop isn't Domingo Reyes? Cut the shit Quinn, why else would I be here? You need to get out before someone figures out you're here.'

'I don't need your help.' She hissed, wrapping the dressing gown tight around her body.

'You can either come willingly, or I'm going to cuff your ass and take you anyway. It's your choice.'

She scowled.

Downstairs the doorbell rang.

'Look,' I said, lowering my tone to something a little calmer. 'I'm trying to help you here. Felix is in serious trouble now. He can't protect you, which means you have three choices. One, try and go it alone and see how long that lasts for you. Two, go find your father and rack up a couple dozen charges against you for aiding a felon. Or three, come with me, let me help you, and live to see the end of all this.'

Through the open door, I heard Manny the housemaid open the door.

And I heard exactly who was on the other side.

Even worse, Quinn heard it too.

Cops. Real this time.

They introduced themselves to Manny and asked to come in.

'Your officer is already here.' Manny's voice echoed up to us. The damn building was an acoustic wet dream. 'She's upstairs right now.'

'Sir, we are the first on the scene.' Said one of the cops. 'Nobody else has been sent out.'

And just like that, the game was up.

As fast as lightning, I pulled out the pistol stashed in the hem of my pants and pointed it at Quinn.

'Make a sound, and I'll put a round in your throat.' I hissed.

She looked at me in horror. I took the chance to snatch at her wrist and haul her dumbfounded ass towards the door. She tried to resist, but the combination of shock and narcotics gave her the disadvantage. I just wished I had some actual cuffs to restrain her, but the Glock would have to do.

I peered out through the door and glanced down the corridor towards the entrance. I could just make out the top of Manny's head beside the front door, and the caps of two police officers. The corridor continued along for another couple of yards in the other direction, at the end there was a door leading out to the pool.

'This way,' I hissed to Quinn. I pointed the Glock an inch from her head, which did the trick. She shuffled forwards out into the corridor.

'She went upstairs to speak to Miss Quinn.' Manny said. I saw his finger point up the stairs. 'She said she was a detective.'

They were going to move any second now. I had to get going, fast. I yanked Quinn's arm, and she stumbled after me. I hustled for the door. Like the whole wall, it was made of glass and overlooked the pool and yard. If we weren't quick, the cops would spot us making our escape as soon as they got up the staircase.

But Quinn was dragging her feet. She had to think I was here to kidnap her, which in a sense was true, but not as serious as her mind was making it. To her, her best bet would be to get arrested. And that thought must have crossed her mind a second later.

Because she screamed.

The high-pitch, visceral noise almost gave me a heart attack. I jumped and instinctively whipped the pistol into the side of her neck. It stopped the screech, but the damage was already done. I could hear the squeak of shoe leather on the marble floor downstairs. The cops were coming.

I ran towards the glass door as fast as I could with a useless, drug-induced weight dragging along behind me. Gun in hand, I pushed the door, but it didn't budge. Locked. No time to find the key. I pointed the Glock at the glass and pulled the trigger.

The sound of the shot made Quinn scream again. The bullet shattered the door, raining thousands of tiny glass shards out into the yard. Quickly, I checked Quinn's feet. She was wearing a pair of worn unicorn slippers. They would have to do. I hauled her reluctant ass through the new doorway as the shouts of the cops called out from the top of the stairs. They were so close. I couldn't give up now.

I sprinted out alongside the pool. The water glistened, reflecting the mayhem back up at me. At the end of the pool, the ground sloped away into a small valley. To counter it, Felix and his team of architects had built the decking up another couple of yards into an outdoor seating area surrounded by a small glass barrier. The drop over it was maybe the same as jumping out a second-floor window. But it was either that or turn myself in. And I still had shit to do.

I stopped only enough to hurl Quinn over the edge, then jumped over myself.

The ground came up to greet us real fast. I slammed into the grass with enough force to knock all the wind out my lungs and rolled blindly downwards. My head spun, my chest hurt, and I felt nauseous beyond belief. When finally I came to a stop, I gasped desperately for air. I glanced around, looking for cops, looking for Quinn. I spotted her a couple of yards away

She was getting to her feet.

She was making to escape.

I hauled myself up and snatched the Glock which I'd dropped in the tumble. Up above, I could see the two cops leaning over the balcony. No way were they risking their lives in that jump. Paycheck wasn't fat enough.

Quinn was running away into the trees. I chased after her. In her unicorn slippers and sky-high on crack, she was no match for me. My motivation was stronger than hers. I caught her seconds into the tree-line. I snatched her wrist again.

'You're coming with me.' I barked at her.

'Get off me you psycho.'

'Don't make me pistol whip you.'

'Who the hell are you?'

'Someone who wants to help you. I don't work with your pop, or with any of his rivals. I'm trying to help you.'

'Get away from me.' She tried to worm away, so I hit her with the Glock.

'You don't have a choice here. Now, get moving.'

We hustled through the trees, looking for somewhere we could get back to the road. If James had heard the gunshots, what would he do? The reporters were no doubt squawking all kinds of shit after three cops entered the house of a person of interest, and gunshots followed. My face was going to be all over the news now, just like James. Goddamn it.

The trees gave way to a row of houses. They were still lavishly expensive, but not as much as Felix's street. I followed the row of changing garden fences until I found a gap to slip through, and hauled the both of us through a thick hedge. We collapsed out onto a neatly trimmed lawn that ran between two salmon-coloured houses. Up ahead was the street.

No one had immediately noticed us, but that didn't give us much advantage. I slipped my hand into Quinn's and pulled her close. I stuffed the Glock into the pocket of my leather jacket, pointed in Quinn's general direction. Made sure she knew the score. Together, we set off at a fast pace for the sidewalk.

The street was fairly quiet. A cluster of wealthy elderly residents in shorts and shirts power-walked together up ahead on the other side of the street. They watched us re-join the path with curious expressions on their faces. No doubt they'd remember our faces, but there wasn't anything I could do about that. Had to act natural.

'Let go of me.' Quinn growled, trying to slip her hand free. I kicked her in the leg.

'Just trust me, will you?' I hissed back. 'I won't lose any sleep giving you a gunshot wound.'

I figured the street we were on had to lead back around to where James was parked, if he was still there after all the commotion. It'd be just my luck if he decided to jump ship on his own dumb plan.

But as soon as the thought crossed my mind, I saw the hood of his Ford County Squire nose around the bend ahead. He spotted me, and pulled over.

'What on Earth happened?' He hissed. 'What happened to going in quietly?'

I opened the rear passenger door and hauled Quinn inside next to me.

'Don't blame me. It's her fault.' I snapped.

'I think you need to look up the word subtle in the dictionary and spend a good long while reading what it means.' James said.

I thumped him in the arm, and he set off.

'Where are you taking me?' Quinn shouted.

James shrugged.

'Someplace quiet I guess.' He said, driving past the group of elderly walkers, all of whom were watching us like the crows they were. 'You must be Lisbeth Quinn, or do you prefer Isabella Reyes? I'm James. I've spent a long time looking for you.'

'I know you.' Quinn replied, watching James in the rear-view mirror.

'Doubt it. I've got one of those faces.' He said.

'You're that guy on the news. The British terrorist. You attacked Jackson's club.'

Before he had the chance to speak, Quinn leapt forwards in her seat and wrapped her arms around his neck. James tried to react, but her muscles were already at work. She squeezed as tight as she could, like it was life and death. James let go of the wheel, grappling at her constricting arms. I pulled the Glock out of my pocket and struck her in the side of the head.

'Let go of him.' I shouted an inch from her ear.

The car swerved and mounted the kerb. James slammed on the brakes, and as one we all lurched forwards. The sudden stop gave James enough room to slip free and turn around.

'Jesus Christ,' he gasped. 'You've got a hell of a grip.'

'Is that all you've got to say to her?' I shouted at him. 'She could have killed us all.'

Quinn scrabbled at the door, but I pulled her away and pointed the gun at her forehead.

'Try me, bitch.' I snarled.

'Lower the gun.' James said, rubbing his throat. 'We need her help as much as she needs ours.'

'Oh yeah?' Quinn said. 'I don't need shit from you.'

'I think you'll change your mind.'

'Like hell I will.' She barked back. 'I'd rather turn myself in than spend another second with you.'

James put his hand in his pocket and retrieved Felix's cell phone. He tapped away at the buttons for a few seconds and held the screen up to show Quinn something on the screen. An image. I saw Quinn's expression change from one of anger to one of total shock. The tension in her muscles disappeared in the blink of an eye. She stared at the screen in absolute shock. Her mouth fell open. Tears welled up in her eyes. I twisted my angle to look at the image.

A woman, bound and gagged on the tiled floor of a bathroom. A sheet of paper at her feet with four words written onto it.

The cherry on top.

'Who is that?' I asked James.

'That is Quinn's ex-girlfriend. Eva Marston.'

THIRTY-TWO

LITTLE BOYS AND LITTLE GIRLS

THE DAY I LEFT ENGLAND WAS THE MOST LIBERATING AND terrifying day of my life. I remember standing in the terminal with my luggage, mum by my side. Dad couldn't make it. He had business in Scotland. He had given me the biggest hug before he left the previous morning. He didn't want me to go. Neither did mum. Their only daughter was stepping off into the unknown to spread her wings. As we stood there, people bustling around on their way in and out of the terminal, she held me in her arms and told me she loved me. We both fought back the tears and just held each other.

I clung on to that memory. Not what came after. Not the separation. Not the flight. Not the farewell to my home country. Just that embrace. The warmth of a mother's love for her only daughter. It became my one glimmer of light in an otherwise horrible world.

The room was dark, but at least it was clean. I had come to several hours before and dared not move so much as a muscle. No one had come for me. No one had come to see if I was okay. As I lay there motionless, my eyes started to adjust. It was a bathroom. I could make out the outlines of a sink and toilet close by. I didn't dare move. Tears ran silently down my face. Wherever I was, it couldn't spell good news. I could barely remember what had happened after the kidnap. It all happened so fast. The figures that ran out of the darkness. Hands that pulled me away from safety. The bag that slipped over my head. Panic had blurred everything into one terrifying nightmare. I should have never left home. I should have never left mum and dad.

I just wanted to see their faces again. It didn't matter whether I'd succeeded or failed in my American voyage. All I wanted was for them to hold me and tell me everything was going to be alright.

The door opened, and light flooded into the dark space. A figure stood in the doorway, silhouetted by the light. The figure was male. Big in height and stature. He observed me silently for a moment before he reached down, removed the gag from my mouth and snatched my bound wrists in his hands.

'No, please. Just let me go.' I begged.

I could see his eyes. Cold and piercing. Short hair adorned his head and face, but other than that, I couldn't see his features. He didn't speak. Just hauled me out through the bathroom door and into the room beyond.

The room had the clean and calm look of an untouched showroom. Every inch looked like it was straight off the production line, and laid out like a new-age studio apartment. From the bathroom, an immaculate open plan kitchen hugged the back wall. A granite kitchen island had been installed to separate the kitchen from the living room. A corner sofa tucked up against the wall and what looked to be a wall-length window, with a flat-screen television the size of a small car sat adjacent.

Vast floor to ceiling vertical slat blinds fluttered gently before the unseen window, disturbed not by a breeze, but a commotion. Only the meekest of light escaped through the beige slats.

Standing before the blinds were three men. Two were massive, daunting beasts, standing like unwavering colossi on the flank of a much shorter man. Yet it was he that filled me most with dread. Even through the dim light, I could feel his eyes burning into me. I wanted to cower away, but with the other man still dragging me forwards, there was nothing I could do but stare right into the blinding light of his imposing glare.

The man threw me down at the feet of his boss. I fell to my knees, transfixed by dread, and looked up into the face of the man I knew to be Domingo Reyes. The Black Viper.

At first, there was silence. Reyes watched me like I was nothing more than a caged animal in a zoo. His clothes oozed with expense. A midnight blue tailored suit rested comfortably over his body. The jet black shirt beneath was slightly unbuttoned, revealing a mass of thick chest hair and faded tattoos. He knelt down and rested his hand on my chin, lifting it up to stare directly into my eyes.

'Did you know, the bomb dropped on Hiroshima was only one

hundred and twenty inches in length?' His breath smelt of stale smoke. 'It dropped from a Boeing B-29 Superfortress, and for forty-four seconds, it fell through the sky before it detonated over the city. An explosion with the energy of fifteen thousand tonnes of trinitrotoluene, eviscerated over sixty thousand men, women and children, and caused a further sixty thousand injuries through fire and radiation. It was the single most destructive event in all of human history. And the name they gave to this weapon? The Little Boy.'

His fingers coiled around my throat. His grip was light, yet I felt powerless to move.

'How strange.' He mused. 'That something so small could be so... destructive. Tell me, little girl, have you ever seen total, unwavering chaos?'

He watched me, waiting for a response that could never come. He smiled and stood up straight. His hand remained on my chin, pulling me up along with him. Only when we were both standing did he continue to talk.

'Imagine those terrified faces as the bomb dropped. Imagine the panic that swept across the entire city as they tried to escape the inevitable. Forty-four seconds from deployment to detonation. How far could you run in that time? Not far enough.'

His hand slipped from my chin. Instinctively, I raised my hand to comfort the patch of skin he had touched.

'The citizens looked up at a blinding light as their bodies turned to ash. A two-mile-wide firestorm that annihilated everything in its path. Nothing survived. Not even the cockroaches.'

With lightning-fast speed, Reyes spun around and struck me across the face with the palm of his hand. The force threw me off my feet. I landed with a crash on my back. The shock stole my breath away and left me gasping like a wounded animal beneath my assailants. Reyes knelt down again, right over me.

'You see, you went and kicked the atom bomb.' Reyes snarled. 'You walked right up to it and just went to town. Did you think you wouldn't feel the blast? Did you seriously think you could escape the devastation?'

His hands were around my throat once more. His fingers dug deep, blocking my airway like it was nothing. I scratched at his hands, desperately trying to relinquish his grip.

'I am the fire.' He roared. 'I am the white-hot storm. I have come to end you. You got in my way, and you'll pay the price.'

His fingers squeezed deeper. Tighter. Harder. Every fibre of my being screamed out in sheer agony.

'You deserve this fate, you fucking whore.' He snarled into my ear.

My vision faded. The ringing in my ears growing louder by the second. My grasp on life, slipping.

'But it isn't what you'll get.'

His fingers loosened. I gasped for air, wriggling free of his grip.

'No, you'll be begging for death before long.' Reyes said with a laugh. 'Now get back in that bathroom and clean up. I want you looking good before we begin. We've got one more surprise that I want you to see.'

I couldn't hold back the tears as I tried to scuttle out of his reach, but it was no use. Hands snatched at my clothes and hauled me back towards my cell. My execution on hold, my sentence stayed. I landed with a crash down on the tiled floor and wept.

Time passed at a different speed, like it knew that it no longer mattered to me. The cold tile felt good against my exposed skin. It manifested stability in my fractured psyche and soothed the headache that ruptured inside. I let it consume me like a drug, and fell victim to the stillness.

The tears had stopped long ago. There was nothing left inside to weep. I felt hollow. Null. A ghost. A prisoner. I stared at the sleek granite tiles that ran up the lower half of the bathroom wall at the meekest reflection that lay dormant in the dark.

From the moment the bathroom door had swung shut, I had heard little more than the muffled movements of his men outside my door. The silence was disconcerting. The dread lingered and devoured my sanity with every passing moment until I was little more than a shell. I slipped into a corner of my mind where time no longer made much sense. A place where I could be alone. Far away from my cage. Far from Miami and all the horrors it had brought me. A minuscule freedom for a lost cause.

But it didn't last. It could never last. Finally, something broke the mould. Movement outside my cage, stretching closer like a tsunami. I twitched my arm, bringing some sense of being back into my body. Slowly, I pushed myself up. My head swam as the blood began to pump through to my heart and brain. As the nauseating feeling passed, the sounds outside my cell grew louder. I heard the sound of a door opening, and something being dragged across the threshold.

THE FATE OF GLASS

The door to the bathroom was not locked. It was a bathroom, after all, designed to allow privacy for those inside. But even so, I didn't want to risk opening the door and being spotted. Instead, I pressed my ear against it and listened intently.

'Get him inside.' It was Reyes speaking. His Haitian accent was recognisable. 'And wake the son of a bitch up.'

There was more movement. I retreated away from the door, afraid that something was headed my way. But after a few moments, it ended, and my door remained closed. I slid back beside it, listening once more.

'Where did you find him?' Reyes asked.

'Trying to flee the city.' Said another male voice. 'We got him a couple of blocks from his house. Bags packed. On his way to pick up his family.'

'Was Jackson with him?'

'No, boss.'

A pause.

'Wake him up.' Reyes repeated.

There were muffled sounds which I took to be Reyes' men attempting to wake the mystery person. A brief thought flashed through my mind. If Reyes and his men were distracted by the new arrival, there might be a way for me to escape. If I could slip out, I could run for help. It was a chance I had to take.

I raised my hand up to the handle and twisted it silently.

The door slid open without a sound. I peeked through the slit. The kitchen was empty. As quietly as I could, I slid across the tiles out into the kitchen, using the island for cover. I closed the door behind me and eased across to the corner.

Domingo Reyes stood with his back to me, watching the scene from almost the exact spot he had been in when he had addressed me. His clothes were the same, but the blazer had gone, and the sleeves of his black shirt were rolled up. Tucked into the seam of his midnight blue trousers was a silver handgun. In one hand he held a glass of whiskey. In the other, he held a decanter. Two of his men busied themselves with a third man, who was crumpled on the floor at his feet. I couldn't see much of him, but the brief glance at his face told me he was not conscious.

Off to my left, the front door was closed. The nearest man was at least ten feet away from it with his back turned away. But of the remaining men, too many had the door in their peripheral. I stayed where I was, pressed up against the island.

Eventually, the man stirred. He was younger than the other men I could see. His lightly tanned skin was creased with stress and fear. His clothes were damp and dirty. He looked up at Domingo Reyes with a look of total, petrifying horror.

Reyes sniffed. A big, exuberant action, like he was performing in a pantomime before a crowd of eager children.

'Do you smell that? A foul stench in the air.' He hissed.

'No, boss.' The young man replied. Even from this distance, I could see his hands shaking.

'It is like a dog that has shit on the carpet. Do you have a dog that shits on the carpet?'

'I don't have a dog, boss.'

'Did you step in dog shit and walk it into my room?'

'I... no, boss, I wouldn't.'

'Check your shoes. Go on, check them, right here. I want to make sure you are thorough.'

He did, lifting each shoe up to inspect the soles for the foul mess Reyes had detected. Both times, there was nothing.

'They're clean, boss.' He stammered.

'Do you bathe in it?'

He opened his mouth to speak, but no words came out.

'Do you bathe in shit?' Reyes pushed.

'No, boss. I...'

'Then tell me, why do you reek of shit? Is it just your natural odour? Does your wife and child smell of shit too, perhaps your mother and father also?'

Again, words bested him. He stood before his boss, mouth open like a starved fish out of water.

'I asked you a question.' Reyes snarled. 'Why do you stink of shit?'

'I don't know, boss. I'm sorry.' His words shook like false teeth in a glass.

'You do. You know exactly why. We all do.'

He was right up in the trembling man's face, just as he had been with me earlier.

'Don't you, pig.' He taunted. 'That's what you are, right? A filthy, fucking pig.'

The man dropped to his knees, shaking like a leaf.

'Please, boss. I didn't mean to do you no harm. I... I didn't know what to do. Salazar's men threatened my family if I didn't do as I was told. I had to protect-'

'You do not speak a fucking word unless I tell you to.' The Viper bellowed. He towered over his prey with the air of a man twice his natural height. 'The only reason you still breathe is that I want to know one thing.'

'Anything, boss. Anything at all.'

'Where is Jackson?'

The young man swayed on his knees.

'I... I don't know. I didn't see him at the club. I thought he maybe got-'

Reyes cut him short again.

'You do not know. I ask you one thing, and you cannot do me the service of giving a useful answer?'

'Sir, I would tell you if I knew.' He begged.

'You betrayed me and let my enemy into my place of business. You almost destroyed everything to save your whore wife and retard child. You forgot one very important thing when you crossed me, pig. I do not strike to wound...'

From the room to the right, two men appeared. In their arms, they carried two heavy wooden crates not much bigger than a shoebox. As soon as the man on the floor clapped eyes on them, he let out a wail of horror.

'No, please, boss. I'll do anything. Just please, not them.' He sobbed.

I looked between him and the crates, a rising sense of dread building inside me. One of the crates was dripping. The liquid was crimson.

'I strike to kill.' Reyes finished.

In unison, the two men opened their crates and dropped the contents down onto the floor, right in front of the screaming man. As the two objects thumped against the linoleum, I caught a flash of strawberry blonde hair and the piercing blue of a young, lifeless eye, before my body gave way and I slumped into blackness.

THIRTY-THREE

A MUTUAL OBJECTIVE

IT HADN'T TAKEN LONG TO FIND THE PHOTO. AS SOON AS NICOLE got out the car, I turned to Felix's phone and started a search of my own. Mostly, I was curious about the "*China has landed*" text. If the search for Isabella Reyes went nowhere, Felix was my next best bet, even if he was uncooperative. The China text had to mean something to him. A business meeting, a delivery, hell, it could be a new album he was desperate to listen to. Whatever it was, it could lead me to him.

The thought died a quick death when I opened the saved images file. There was only one, and the second I saw it, my heart dropped into my stomach. Eva didn't look good. Her face was gaunt, her eyes hollow with trauma. I opened the image description. It had been sent as a picture message at two in the morning by a number not saved into the phone. I checked it against the text messages. Sure enough, it was from the same number as the China text. Which had to mean one thing. The sender and Felix were working together.

And I had a pretty good idea who fit that bill.

Minutes later, I watched Isabella Reyes for some kind of reaction. Behind the shock and exhaustion, she was incredibly beautiful. Eva had described her as a troublemaker. With looks like hers, that sounded about right. All eyes would be on her. I could see her father in her. The skin colour, the jet-black hair, the eyes. They were powerful eyes. The eyes of a viper.

Slowly, she reached out and took the phone from me. She stared at the screen, unable to tear herself away from the haunting image on the screen. Re-reading those four little words that made the whole thing a billion times worse.

The cherry on top.

'What have you done to her?' There was anger, a lot of it. She broke away from the screen and glowered at me with unbridled rage.

'Whoa, this isn't us okay? That's your boyfriend's phone.'

'You're lying.' She hissed.

'Check for yourself.' I said. 'Your messages are on there. It's his phone.'

She checked the texts, read through the messages she'd sent earlier in the day. Felt the blame shift from one man, to another.

'Motherfucker.' She snarled.

'Look, you don't know me, and I'm not in any position to make you do anything, but will you hear me out?' I asked.

'Start talking.'

I looked around. A group of power-walking pensioners were hustling towards us, some of them pointed at the car. I hit the accelerator and pulled back onto the street.

'We need to get somewhere safe.' I said.

'I know a place.' Isabella said.

She directed me out of the neighbourhood and away from the pandemonium.

'Let's start over,' I said. 'I'm James, and this is Nicole. Pleased to meet you.'

I glanced in the rearview mirror and saw Nicole nod to Isabella.

'Call me Quinn.' She said.

'Not Isabella?' I asked.

'Not unless you want to get your ass kicked.'

'Then Quinn it is.'

We headed north, back towards the city mayhem, but turned off before it got too intense. Quinn pointed at a car park beside an old cinema. The lot was almost full. A smart plan. The car could sit here all day without anyone noticing.

'Talk.' Quinn said as I pulled up. 'Where is Eva?'

'I don't know. But I think I know someone who does. Well, we both do.'

'If you've got Felix's cell, I don't know how to get in touch with him.' She said, looking at the phone clutched in her hands.

'Not Felix. Your father. I think he's the one who has her.' I said.

'What would he want with her?' She asked, looking between

Nicole and me for an answer. I knew I had to tell her the truth. It would come out anyway.

So, I started at the beginning. I told Quinn how I followed one of Salazar's men to the house, helped Eva escape, and together we had begun our search for Quinn herself. I told her how we followed the lead up to Ozello and came into contact with her father's men. I omitted the specifics of how we parted ways.

'As soon as I heard about Felix, I went in that direction instead.' I said. 'I guessed he would have been a little more receptive than he was.'

'What did he do?' Quinn asked.

'Oh, the usual. He tried to drown me in that big aquarium in the club. So I broke it.'

'That thing cost like a million bucks. Reyes is going to be pissed.' She said.

'Even so, Reyes can learn to forgive and forget when I get to Ramiro Salazar.'

'And that's your endgame?' Quinn asked. 'You want to get to this guy by using Reyes to flush him out?'

'Something like that.'

'You know that won't work, right?' She said. 'That's not how Reyes works. He doesn't work with other people that way. You know why they call him The Viper? He doesn't strike to wound, he strikes to kill. If this Salazar guy is still breathing, it's because Reyes is letting him, because he has a plan for him. If you're still standing, you aren't part of his plan. No offence, but you're nothing to him. He doesn't care about you, and that's exactly where you want to be. If he knows about you, it's because you're part of his plan, or about to die. There's no grey area with Reyes.'

'Why do you call him Reyes?' Nicole asked.

'You kidding? That asshole has never been my father. Never once tried to be. He wanted a son and got me instead. I'm his little embarrassment. He sends me money every month for expenses, and that's it. No contact. No brunch meetups. No thanksgiving dinners. Nothing.'

'So how do we get to him?' I asked.

'You don't. You're not getting anywhere near him. Why do you think he has Felix run everything for him? It's so he can stand back and avoid any risks. He's like a puppet master, running everything from behind the scenes. Nobody gets to him unless he summons them. I haven't seen him in years, and I'm his goddamn daughter.'

'How did Felix see him?' I asked.

'Like I know,' she snorted. 'Felix didn't tell me shit about all that. He knew I didn't want to know, which made this all really simple. No business at home, that was the rule.'

'He must have a way to see him face to face though. Where does he live?'

'You'd have to ask Felix that. Which reminds me, how did you get his cell?'

Nicole told that bit. She filled Quinn in on the escape, and how Felix was gone when we returned.

'Long story short,' I said. 'We don't know where Felix is. Could be locked up, could be with your dad right now.'

'Then you're shit out of luck I'm afraid.' Quinn said.

I leant back in the chair and rubbed my hands across my face. I was exhausted. My last proper sleep was on Eva's sofa, which felt like a year ago. But I couldn't give up. Not yet. Not while Eva was out there. She needed my help, and I couldn't shake the feeling the egg timer over her head was running out of grains.

'We need to think about this logically.' I said.

'You didn't say that out loud.' It was the Wolf. He sat in the passenger seat, looking at me through my own exhausted eyes. *'You need rest.'*

'No rest for the wicked.' I yawned. *'Eva needs our help.'*

'We're no good to anyone like this.'

'I don't care. I need to find her. She's in this because of me.'

'No, she's in this because of Quinn. She pulled Eva into this, not us. We saved her from Salazar's men. That's as good as anything we've done.'

'It's not enough. I can't let her die at the hands of that psycho just because I needed a nap.'

'You okay, James?' Nicole asked.

'I'm fine. Just a bit tired.' I replied. 'When did you last speak to Reyes?'

Quinn shrugged. 'A couple of months ago I guess. He called me on my birthday, but he didn't know it was my birthday. We argued.'

'What did he call you for?' I asked.

'He wanted me to go to rehab.' She said. Her eyes darted back down to the phone. An awkward subject. 'I told him to go to hell.'

'Why did he want you to go to rehab?'

She shuffled in her seat and ran her fingers through her hair. The sleeve of her gown slipped down, revealing track marks on her arm.

'I got into trouble with the cops. Felix managed to smooth it over, but they started following me around. Figure they expected me to be enough of a train wreck to lead them to Reyes. He wanted to make sure that didn't happen. He didn't care about my health, he just wanted me not to cause him any problems.'

'How nice of him.' Nicole said.

'Don't get me started.' Quinn replied with a sigh. 'He doesn't care about anyone but himself.'

'Sorry for intruding, but did you go to rehab?' I asked.

'What's that got to do with anything?' Quinn snapped.

'Did you?' I asked again.

'Hell no. I knew he wasn't asking for my safety so I told him to shove it up his ass.'

I didn't reply. Nicole watched me.

'What are you thinking, James?' she asked.

'What if you called and told him you were ready to go to rehab.' I said. 'If you told him you were serious about it and wanted to talk to him first, he might meet with you.'

'I just said, he doesn't care about me. He won't give a damn.' Quinn said.

'Yeah, I know, but are you saying that because you're angry at him, or because he told you he didn't care?'

Quinn didn't reply, but the answer was obviously the former.

'How would I even call him?' She said. 'He doesn't contact me on the same number every time.'

'But he contacted Felix on that phone earlier this morning. He's probably still got the phone he called from. It's got to be a mobile if he can send pictures from it.'

'Unless he thinks Felix has been arrested and dumped the phone.' Nicole said.

'Maybe, but that would have been on the news, right? High profile guy like Felix Jackson being pulled in for questioning. Someone would have reported on that. And surely the fact all those reporters were outside his house means they don't know exactly where he is?'

'That's a lot riding on luck.' Said Nicole.

'All for something that he won't agree to.' Said Quinn.

'If you made it sound serious, he might hear you out.' I said. 'Even if you're right and he doesn't care about you, he'll know that having you out the way will be more beneficial to him right now, especially after what we did at his club. He'll be thinking damage control. He'll want you out the way, somewhere the cops can't get to you. They know you weren't at the club, Manny can attest to that, so they've got no reason to pull you out of rehab for questioning.'

'He won't want to meet. Not now with all this going on.'

'He might if you ask him to. You are his daughter. There's got to be some residual part of him that wants you to be safe. It's worth the risk.'

'You don't know him. He's not like that. At most, he'll promise to come and visit when I'm there, and then he'll flake. He won't come, and he won't let me come to him.'

'Then we need a backup plan.' I said. 'If you can't get him to agree to the meet, then we need to find where he is without him knowing about it.'

'You develop telepathic skills since the last time I saw you?' Nicole mocked.

'No, but I know a fair few other things, like the fact you can locate a phone call by triangulating the cell tower signals. That's got to give us a location.'

'And you know how to do that?' Nicole asked.

I did not, nor did I know anyone within a four-thousand-mile radius who might know.

'I know someone who might,' Quinn said. 'But he's not the sort of guy you want to owe a favour to.'

THIRTY-FOUR

CALLING IN A FAVOUR

It took the better part of the next four hours for Quinn to set the meeting. Using Felix's phone, she started with a call, then spent most of the following hours staring at the screen, occasionally typing a response.

In the meantime, Nicole and I drove further out of the city. Quinn agreed to spend some of her father's hard-earned cash on a rental car. A sleek, white Honda something or other with a satellite navigation system built into the dash. Nicole drove while Quinn and I sat in the back. We stopped off at a fast food chain with a drive-through and ordered lunch, eating it in the car as we continued our steady counter-clockwise loop of the city. I didn't know how long it would take the cops to track us to the rental lot and find out what car we were in, but we figured it was in our best interests to stay on the move.

The exception to our rule was only brief. We all needed a change of clothes, and since Quinn was the least wanted of our little trio, we sent her into a bland clothes store near the bay to stock up. After a couple of anxious minutes waiting, Quinn reappeared with three bags full of clothes. She threw them at me through the open passenger door and climbed in the front passenger seat.

I had to admit, her taste was bang on for me. A thin grey hoodie over a maroon t-shirt with a cartoon surfer printed on the front. A New York Knicks baseball cap and some mirrored aviators. A pair of dark blue denim jeans and a pair of blue and white trainers to finish the look off. All a perfect fit.

I changed first, then swapped into the driver seat to let Nicole change. Quinn, seemingly unperturbed by the prospect of an audience, changed in the front seat. I kept my eyes dead centre on the road.

Finally, after what felt like a lifetime spent in Miami traffic, Quinn got the news she wanted.

'He can give us twenty minutes,' she said. 'He's texting me the address now.'

The address was in itself another hour's drive away into the shadier stretch of the sunshine state. Graffiti-laden multi-storey buildings closed in around us, robbing us of the spacious comforts bequeathed by Felix's neighbourhood. The white Honda trundled merrily along like an unbeknownst chicken amongst wolves, all watching, all waiting to strike.

'That's it.' Quinn said, pointing out a building up ahead. I pulled over right outside and parked up. We left the guns in the car and got out. The ground floor of the building was a pawn shop with rusted metal shutters over the windows, protecting an array of trinkets and treasures from prying magpies and monsters. Quinn took the lead. Out of her pyjamas, she looked a lot more in control than she had previously. She pulled the hood over her long hair and pushed open the shop door. A bell jingled as she stepped across the threshold. Nicole went through second, and I took up the rear.

The pawn shop was a dour and claustrophobic affair. A portly man clad head to toe in black leather sat on a foldout chair in the corner. He watched us as we entered, but said nothing. Probably store security. Probably needed it in a place like this. I gave him a polite nod. He didn't return the gesture.

Quinn strode right by him to the counter. A thick layer of bulletproof glass covered in marks and stains separated her from the store owner. A woman who could be the carbon copy of the security guy, albeit with a couple of minor tweaks to the genetics. She removed a cigarette from her fat lips and stubbed it out on the counter.

'Yes?' She said, not even attempting to hide her boredom.

'I'm here about a watch,' Quinn said. 'A nineteen eighty-five Rolex with an engraving on the back.'

Which I figured had to be some kind of code, unless Quinn had decided to do a couple of chores on the way to saving her ex-girlfriend.

'What was the inscription?' Asked the store owner.

'Kings are the slaves of history.'

The store owner said nothing. Instead, she pressed a button under the counter, and the door to the right buzzed open. Quinn walked through. Nicole and I followed. The door led to a narrow staircase that smelt of stale air and body odour. Up above, a heavy baseline thumped through the walls. Must be one hell of a soundproofing job. It wasn't at all noticeable downstairs.

At the top of the stairs, I felt the familiar itch of anxiety creep in. The world of drugs was not one I was used to. Those involved weren't always the most rational or forgiving of people, and I couldn't help but feel on edge anytime I found myself amongst their ilk.

The room was dark. Enough so that I didn't immediately notice that the room was not empty. Sunk into a tattered leather sofa were two women. Their wandering eyes latched onto us, and one raised a malnourished hand up at us.

'They're coming for you,' she croaked. 'The angels, they can see you.'

We left them to their prophetical hallucinations. Quinn knocked on the door at the far end of the room and waited for a response.

The man that opened the door made the two people downstairs look like Olympic athletes. It was strangely beguiling to look at. He had to be almost seven foot tall and had packed on so much weight that he was almost that big width-ways. I struggled to believe he could actually get through the door. Perhaps he lived inside, a permanent fixture to the unpleasant space. He stared down at Quinn like she was a tasty treat for him to devour.

'We're here to see Vinnie.' She said, stretching her head to look up at him.

The giant gave a grunt of disinterested recognition and shuffled out of the way, revealing the room behind him. I didn't know exactly what I'd expected. I'd seen films of hackers seen through the lens of Hollywood, injected with steroids to amplify the thrill factor, but I knew that couldn't be what the reality looked like.

Even so, I hadn't expected this. Besides the window covered in newspaper sheets, there was nothing in the room to make it stand out as the main base of operations for a twenty-first-century criminal. No bells and whistles. No bullshit. A thin black laptop sat atop a filthy metal desk, behind which sat a man that looked neither big or strong, yet was one of the most imposing people I'd ever crossed paths with. A concoction of faded tattoos stretched from his knuckles all the way up his arms before disappearing beneath the rolled up sleeves of his creased black shirt. They made a reappearance at his neck, where they were joined by a plethora of piercings and scars. But it was in the eyes where the darkness lay, all kinds of danger tucked away in them.

'Vinnie,' Quinn sang, her voice full of insincerity. 'Long time no see.'

'You've got ten minutes. Tell me why the fuck this was so important.' Vinnie kept his attitude like he kept his office. No bullshit.

'You said twenty minutes on the phone.'

'It's ten now.'

'We need your help finding a guy.' Quinn replied. 'It's a time-sensitive thing, you know?'

Vinnie said nothing. Just stared at Quinn with a look of mixed anger and disinterest. He didn't seem too fussed about breaking the silence, so I figured I'd do it for him.

'War and Peace.' I said.

Vinnie fixed me with his piercing eyes.

'Leo Tolstoy, right?' I continued. '"Kings are the slaves of history." Not the most common quote from the book, but I suppose the one about knowing nothing is the highest degree of human wisdom wouldn't fit on the back of a Rolex, right?'

Vinnie's cold eyes swept across Nicole and me. I stifled the urge to shudder.

'I guess you could knit it onto a pillow.' I mused.

Should have stayed quiet.

'Who the fuck are they?' He snarled at Quinn. His New York accent emphasised the fuck.

'They're my friends. They're helping me track this guy.' Quinn said.

Vinnie stared intently for a long moment, then nodded. Behind me, the giant heaved himself forward. With hands the size of dinner plates, he patted me down. He did the same to Nicole. Vinnie watched his companion the whole way, deviating only to pull a hand-rolled cigarette from his pocket. Using a match, he lit the cigarette and took a long pull.

The giant grunted and stepped back to his favourite spot. Vinnie blew a cloud of smoke in my face. It didn't smell legal. He held the cigarette out to me.

'I'm good thanks. I don't smoke.' I said.

'I didn't ask.' He growled. 'You want my help, you do what I say.'

'If this is some kind of test to see if we're actually undercover cops, I'll make it easier for you.' I said. 'Google my name and see what you get. James Stone.'

He typed the words into the search engine, and a fraction of a second later, he got his result. His face dropped. Whether it was shock or anger, I didn't know. But before I had a chance to explain, his giant picked me up and pinned me to the wall. Vinnie leapt up from behind the desk, and in a second, had a pistol pointed at my face.

'Look,' I gasped. The giant held me by the neck in one hand, about a foot off the ground. Not the best situation to be in. 'I know this looks bad, but we need your help. I can pay you.'

'You think I need your money? You should never have come here.'

'Fifty thousand.' I croaked. The giant's hand crushed my windpipe. 'In cash. I can get you it.'

'Fifty thousand won't do nothing for me in a cell.' Vinnie snarled. 'Your money is no use here. You think I trust you, you son of a bitch?'

'Let him go, Vinnie.' Quinn snapped. 'He ain't with the cops. He's wanted more than the rest of us combined.'

'He don't need to be with the cops. They smell filth like you. They could be right outside my door.'

'Go check for yourself.' Said Quinn. 'We weren't followed.'

'Since when does Isabella Reyes roll with scumbags like him?' Vinnie spat in retort.

'Since when do you turn down easy money? He says he'll pay fifty thousand, just take the damn money and help us out.'

'One hundred.'

'Seventy-five.'

'One hundred.'

My vision had begun to blur.

'Okay,' I wheezed. 'One hundred.'

The giant dropped me. As I hit the floor, my legs crumpled, and I fell to my knees. My ears rang like a thousand harpies had swarmed the room. My head felt like it had been tumble-dried. The last twenty-four hours had been too much.

I dug my hand into my pocket and retrieved the stolen phone, and held it up like a tribute to a king.

'The number we need to trace is on here.' I coughed. My throat burned white hot.

Vinnie shook his head.

'Money first. Otherwise, I get my boy here to sit on you till you burst.'

'No. You'll get your money, but we need this done now. We waste time, and this won't matter at all.'

'Then you better find some other fool who'll listen to you real quick.' Vinnie snapped. He sat down behind his desk and stretched his feet up over the top. He didn't give a damn if we got to Reyes. He didn't give a damn if I got caught. So long as he got his money, I was just another customer. He held all the cards.

From here to the gym locker where I'd stashed the money was about forty miles. Getting past the city limits was probably half that, but would take easily twice as long as the rest of the journey. There and back was maybe anywhere in an hour and a half to three-hour detour, depending on any number of factors, many of which could end up with me dead or arrested, and Eva at the mercy of a madman.

Not good.

But I had no time to waste.

'It'll take time.' I said. 'I can get it, but it could take hours.'

'I can wait.' Vinnie said.

'But we can't. If you could do the trace, I can get you your money. But we don't have hours to waste.'

'Not my problem. You want my help, you better get me my money. Quid pro quo.'

I thought it through in my head. Weighed up the pros and cons. If we left without his help, we'd be blindly searching a city of millions for one man. Those were impossible odds. If I went, Reyes would have a massive head start to get out of here.

If he hadn't gone already.

I made a move for the door. But the giant stepped lithely in my way.

'Not you.' Vinnie said.

'What, why?'

'I trust you as far as I could throw you.' He said. 'You stay here. Your girl here can go instead.'

I looked at Nicole.

Shit.

'Don't do it, James. She'll get it and scarper.' Said the Wolf.

'I have no choice.'
'You do. You can persuade him to let you go instead.'
'He won't listen, and we don't have time.'
'Then make the time.'
'And risk Eva's life?'
The Wolf didn't respond.

I handed Nicole the keys to the car. She took them without a word spoken. What was she thinking?

'You got a pen and paper?' I asked Vinnie.

He tore off a corner from a coffee-stained sheet on the desk and handed me a sorely-chewed ballpoint pen. I wrote the name of the gym down, along with the locker number.

Then the four-digit code.

My stomach churned.

I handed the note to Nicole. I held onto the paper for a moment, bound in internal conflict. She pulled it free and looked over the words I had scribbled, then back at me.

'Please,' I whispered. 'Come back.'

'What do you take me for, James, a thief?' She whispered back.

And with that, she left.

'Why do I feel like you just made a really stupid decision?' the Wolf sighed.

THIRTY-FIVE

A FRESH PERSPECTIVE

CHAVEZ PICKED ME UP SIX BLOCKS AWAY FROM THE CLUB IN A silver Chevrolet Tahoe an hour after I'd made the call. I used a burner cell, bought with cash from a wallet I'd managed to pick from a tourist. Some habits die hard I guess. I made the call, knowing that whatever came next was probably not going to be pretty. By now, every cop in the city would have their eyes peeled for Felix Jackson, and mine was not an easy face to forget.

Chavez was dry and fresh, having avoided the disaster at the club by running errands for Reyes. He fixed me with those dead eyes of his that let me know that he already knew everything. No surprise. No remorse.

'You want to talk about it?' He asked as I climbed into the Tahoe.

'No, Chavez. I don't want to talk about it.' I sighed.

I pulled the hood of the sweatshirt he had brought me over my head and leaned back in my seat. Last thing I wanted now was someone to spot me as we escaped. Two heavies sat on the back seat. I could feel their eyes burning into the back of my skull. The midday traffic had started to ease up, which made our journey that bit easier. Though every couple of blocks, I could see the flashing lights dart by in the blink of an eye. Preparing for the coming storm, or looking for a couple of felons.

I knew I couldn't go home. That would be the first place the cops would check. I just hoped B would be able to escape before they arrived and started asking questions. The fact she was Reyes's daughter would only escalate things, and make the target on my back all the more visible. *What a fucked up situation.*

'What's the plan?' I asked. I had to know something.

'You need to go underground. The boss doesn't want you exposed.' Chavez replied, not taking his eyes off the road.

But his answer didn't exactly inspire confidence. That could be taken one of two ways. Either Chavez was telling the truth, and he really didn't want me exposed, or he wanted me underground. Literally.

'Where are we going?'

'We've got a place in Biscayne Park that we can wait at.' Chavez said. 'We should be safe there.'

'*Should* be safe there?'

'That's what I said.'

Biscayne Park was an old residential area. Lots of prying eyes peeking through curtain slits for signs of anything out of the ordinary. It wasn't the kind of place you took a guy to be executed, not unless you wanted half a dozen eyewitnesses. Perhaps Reyes wasn't done with me. Yet.

But keeping me out of the way was as much as a death sentence as anything Reyes could offer. For over a decade, I had been in his inner circle, and like it or not, I knew I was important to the old man. He had trusted me. Relied on me. That trust had not been abused like so many other men in his employment, and while I had never truly wanted this life, I had grown accustomed to it. I'd relied on Reyes as much as he had on me. Being locked away out of sight was a sign of things to come. He was cleaning shop.

We pulled up in Biscayne Park a half hour later. The house looked like it would struggle in a light breeze, let alone a category four hurricane. No way were we staying here for long. Not unless the place had a bunker.

The door opened as we approached, and another of Chavez's men allowed us inside. The house was dank and unused. The smell of neglect hung in the air. An oil lamp sat on the worktop, the flame flickering in the miserable space. Chavez flicked the light switch. Nothing doing. The electricity had been shut off a long time ago. The water too, probably.

'I need to speak to the boss.' I said. Not a request. A demand. Had to assert some authority.

'What happened to your cell?' Chavez asked.

'I lost it in the escape. Must have dropped it somewhere.'

THE FATE OF GLASS

'Stone didn't take it from you?'

I fixed Chavez with a fierce glare.

'You trying to say something?' I snarled.

'Reyes doesn't want to talk at the moment.' He said, meeting my eyes. 'He's got a lot going on.'

'No shit, which is exactly why I need to speak with him.'

'He'll call when he's ready.'

'No, I'll speak to him right now, goddamn it. This ain't the time to let egos go unchecked, Chavez. This is about the bigger picture. I need Reyes to know the situation. He needs to know what's gone down.'

'He already knows everything he needs to.' Chavez said. 'He knows what went down at the club. He knows you let Salazar's guys in, and he knows you let Stone escape. He told you to deal with Stone, and you had him in the palm of your hands.'

'That ain't how it went down.' I snapped. 'I told the boss not to antagonise Salazar. If he'd listened to me, my club wouldn't be a bomb site.'

'You figure?' Chavez retorted, showing anger like I'd never seen before. 'The boss knows you fucked up. And he knows that if you don't shut your goddamn mouth, he'll cut out your tongue. You got that, Jackson?'

I squared up to him. So close I could practically taste the aftershave on his neck.

'Who do you think you're talking to?' I snarled. 'You, some two-bit street brawler, think you can talk to me like we're equals? Boy, let me get something straight, right here, right now. You do not talk to me like I'm one of your dogs. I am Felix mother-fuckin' Jackson, okay? My goddamn pinky is worth more than your whole family. So you better take a long hard look at this face, because the next time you talk to me like that, it'll be the last thing you see. And when I ask to borrow your goddamn cell phone, you give me your goddamn cell phone.'

I stared unblinkingly into Chavez's eyes. No way was I about to lose this fight. Son of a bitch needed to check who he was dealing with. Sure enough, the guy folded. With a grimace that told everyone in the room he'd lost - and wasn't happy about it - he handed me his cell. I snatched it from his grasp and dialled the only number that mattered right now.

I listened to the purr of the outgoing call, searching for a response.

Come on. Answer the phone.

No one answered. The call went through to voicemail. As an automated voice ran me through the transfixed narrative, I moved away from Chavez and his men. Didn't want them overhearing. The machine beeped, all set for me to talk. I whispered into the receiver.

'B, it's me. Hey, I need you to listen to what I'm about to say, okay? I need you to get out of town. Grab what you need, but don't stay at the house long, you hear? The cops will be on their way. I need you to find someplace safe and wait until the storm passes. Don't try to call me. I lost my cell. Just keep yours with you, and I'll call you when it's safe to meet.' I rubbed my fingers into the bridge of my nose and thought about her. 'Look, this ain't gonna be easy, but you've got to trust me on this, okay? Shit is about to hit the fan in a big way, and I can't let you get caught up in it. Just get out, and stay hidden. Don't talk to no one. Please, just do as I ask, okay? I… I love you, B. See you soon.'

I ended the call and looked at the cell. I deleted the call from the cell's history. Didn't know when I'd next get a chance to call again. Could be never. I prayed she'd get the message before the cops arrived, or worse. If something happened…well, it wasn't worth thinking on. Lisbeth had to be safe. She just had to be. She was a strong woman. Stronger than most, given her upbringing. She could handle anything life threw at her. My B.

I turned around and passed the cell back to Chavez.

'Good talk?' He smirked.

'Bite me.'

I pushed past him and headed for the next room. Needed space from that asshole. I found a foul, flea-bitten armchair and flopped down. Springs dug up into my ass, but I ignored them. Just being out of Chavez's sight was enough for me.

It didn't take him long to follow. Goddamn hound. With two of his heavies in close pursuit, he filed into the room and stood over me. The smirk had transformed into a smile. A big shit eating grin. The look of a guy who just got the promotion he'd always wanted. Guess I wouldn't be calling B again after all.

'What's the matter, Chavez, your periods all sync up at once?' I said, not looking up at him. What was the point?

'The call came through. Looks like you've played your last hand.' Chavez grinned.

'You know what, Chavez, you always were an uninspired asshole. Even now you can't think of something clever to say. I bet you were a real dunce in high-school, or were you kicked out for huffing glue?'

'You ain't got to worry about how I did in school.'

'Oh, I wasn't worrying. But the lack of a proper education can stunt a brother's mental growth. You've got to keep that shit active. Do a crossword in the paper every once in a while. In fact, I got a riddle for you. Something a guy told me recently that stuck with me. What's the one thing you eat that eats you back?'

Chavez smirked again.

'This ain't the time for riddles, Jackson.'

'At first, it got me thinking.' I continued. 'Looked at it literally. Like, is it some kind of small fish that works away at your stomach lining before it dies? Maybe. Perhaps it's a kind of acidic berry, or a rock, or hell, I don't know. But I started looking at it differently. Swapped out the literal for the lateral. Maybe it isn't a definable, quantifiable answer. Maybe it's something grander. Something you got to look at through the cosmic epoch to understand. You dig?'

It was clear from his face that he did not.

'Didn't think you would.' I shrugged. 'Glue-huffers never do. But I ain't like you. I figured it was maybe something different. Like a retrospective assessment of the human being. We take, take, take, and don't give nothing back. We are greedy motherfuckers. We don't understand this world. We've drunk from the well without giving thought about what happens when the well runs dry. So that's what I thought the answer might be. Not the answer they expect, but the real answer. We are the consumers, and in doing so, we consume ourselves. Killing ourselves on greed. I don't know, man. But it gives you a kind of fresh perspective on life, don't you think?'

Chavez didn't reply. I guessed he was still stuck on the word epoch to have paid much attention. It didn't matter much. I'd always known this day would come eventually. Chavez was cut from the mould. He didn't break it. He would live and breathe this life until the day he took his last. He'd feel no remorse for his actions. Which made it all the more satisfying to know that I'd got one over on him. Ernesto Chavez. Dumb as a rock.

What I wouldn't give to spend one more moment with Lisbeth.

Chavez opened his mouth to retort, but I cut through him.

'Listen, boy. I don't give a damn what you've got to say. There's nothing you could possibly say that I want to hear. I don't know if anyone's ever told you, but you've got a really annoying voice. Real fucking grating. So do me a solid and just shut the hell up and get on with it, will you? At this point, a bullet to the head would be preferable to hearing you speak.'

Slowly, the smile returned to his stupid face.

'Is that what you think this is, Jackson? You think we brought you here to execute you?'

'Am I wrong?'

'Oh, boy. I wish I could put a bullet through your head. But Reyes has got bigger plans for you. He ain't ready for you to die. You better get yourself nice and settled, because he ain't done with you, yet.'

THIRTY-SIX
TRUST ISSUES

I SAT IN THE ROOM NEXT DOOR AND WAITED. NOTHING MUCH MORE I could do. Vinnie refused to help without his eyes on his prize, and I had no desire to sit and make small talk until Nicole returned. *If* she returned. Perhaps sensing the discomfort hanging in the room like a corpse, Vinnie ordered the comatose women next door to leave, and gave us their spot. Quinn took the sofa. I took a lone wooden chair that had seen better days. It was uncomfortable, which was exactly what I wanted. No way was I going to doze off with Vinnie around.

'Relax, would you?' Quinn said. I didn't know how long she'd been watching me. I didn't know how long I'd been sat there in silence. It felt like hours. 'We'll find him.'

'It's not him that I'm worried about,' I said to myself.

'You're not worried?' I asked her.

'Of course, but what good does it do here?'

True, not that it helped much. I asked 'Can I ask you something?'

'Fire away.'

'What happened between you and Eva? The way she talks about you, it's clear she was mad for you.'

'That's a pretty big question to ask someone you just met.'

'You don't have to answer if you don't want.'

'I think I'll pass.'

'Fair enough.'

'What about you and that girl, Nicole? You two together?'

'Oh, so I can't ask questions about your love life, but you can about mine?'

'So, you are together?'

'No. We met a couple of months ago. It's a complicated relationship.'

'I can tell. She likes you.'

'You think? Most of the time we're trying not to kill each other.'

'Sounds just like Eva and me.' She said with a fond smile.

'I mean literally.'

A silence drifted over Quinn. She was lost in a deep chasm of thought. Vinnie's dreadful music thumped through the thin wall. Whatever he was listening to, I wished it would die a quick and painful death. Eventually, she pulled herself from her reverie.

'Do you think she'll be okay?' She asked.

'You know your dad better than I do.'

'You've got terrible bedside manners. You never heard of a white lie?'

'I'm just calling it as I see it. I guess it depends on what he wants her for. If it's all part of some grand scheme, then she's okay as long as she serves a purpose. If not, then it's anyone's guess.'

'Seriously?' Quinn snapped. 'Like I'm not worrying enough as it is.'

'Sorry. My people skills aren't up to scratch. I don't exactly associate with your so-called normal folk.'

'What happened to you?' she asked. 'I mean, what really happened. Everyone knows what they showed on the news, but that's not the truth of it, right?'

'I'll tell you if you tell me.'

'About Eva and me? It's… it's personal.'

'And my life isn't?'

'Why do you want to know?'

'Because the woman I met was broken. She tried to hide her scars, but she couldn't. Not completely. She's the first person I met since I went on the run who reminded me of, well, me.'

'She has that effect on people.' Quinn said. 'She connects with people in a way I've never seen before or since.'

'So what happened?' I asked.

She took a long time to respond. I could almost see the memories flashing before her eyes. A relationship is a lot like a living being. It's born from two people. It blossoms and grows into something truly unique. But eventually, sorrowfully it comes to an end, and what comes after is loss. Trauma. A broken heart. Quinn's eyes showed it all in a moment.

'It was never going to last.' She said finally. Her eyes were glazed with memories. 'It couldn't. What we had was like the explosion of a dying star. It wasn't sustainable. I loved her, more than I had anyone. She saw through everything and accepted me for me. Not for who my dad is, or who my friends think I am. It was special. Magical even.'

'Why end it then? If it's what you say it was, what Eva said it was, that doesn't come around often.'

'If only it were that simple.'

She ran her fingers through her long, black hair and exhaled.

'What you've got to understand is that it was never just Eva and me. It never could be, not when your pop is one of Florida's most notorious criminals. Whoever tried to step up was going to fall under intense scrutiny. Reyes wouldn't let just anyone date his daughter, even if he didn't give a damn about me in the first place. He always had to cover his bases. Some new guy shows up dating his little girl, he wanted to know why. Couldn't be just a simple boy meets girl love story. No, he figures the guy has to be a cop or DEA agent or rival dealer or some such shit. Anyone who got close got spooked or run out of town before they got to second base.'

'That sounds fun.' I said.

'Oh, you bet. High-school was a goddamn nightmare. I had a bodyguard at my own prom. But it was more than that. The way Reyes sees it, I'm his one chance of a legacy. Even if I am a massive disappointment, he's got to think ahead to what he leaves behind. He might be a ruthless asshole, but he wants his reputation to continue, and if it can't carry on with a son, then he wanted to make sure I got shacked up with the right guy. Someone Reyes could mould into his successor, as dumb as that sounds.'

'He sounds like a thirteenth-century king.'

'He sounds like an asshole because that's exactly what he is.' Quinn continued. 'So imagine his reaction when he found out I was dating a woman.'

'He kicked off.'

'To put it lightly. He exploded. I've never seen him so angry as when he found out. I thought he was going to kill me, or Eva. I thought he was going to vent it all, then cut me out of his life for good. I thought I was finally free.'

'But he didn't.'

'Pretty much the opposite. He took it as a personal slight that I was dating Eva. He had his men follow us everywhere. He tried to control everything I did in the hopes that I'd give in, and wait eagerly for whoever he picked as a worthy suitor. He ground me down, day by day, but I didn't let him win. I couldn't.'

'What changed?'

'Lots of things. Reyes doubled down. He went all in to break me, and to an extent, he did. But if it had just been him, I would have kept going. What made it unbearable was Eva. I could tell she knew I was starting to crack. I never told her about Reyes. Never told her we were being watched practically twenty-four seven. I couldn't expose her to all that. So naturally, she saw a problem and figured she was the cause. She tried to fix something that wasn't broken. Like tightening a screw in a plank of wood. You can twist it all you want, but eventually, it's going to cause too much pressure and splinter the wood. It was like I was fighting a war on two fronts. I couldn't take it, and I couldn't shake the fear that one day she was going to see these two worlds collide. It was inevitable. One day she would see a guy watching her across the restaurant, and realise he was everywhere she went. She'd put the pieces together, and I'd have to tell her the whole, ugly truth. I couldn't do that to her. It would kill her.'

'So you broke it off?'

'I did what I had to do to protect her, and as much as it hurt, I know I made the right decision. I knew she would fight it. I knew she would try to fix it. So I cut her out completely. It was the only way. She wanted me in her life, and I wanted her in mine. But Reyes would have killed her.'

Quinn's eyes were red. The memories were fresh wounds for her. 'I knew the only way it would work was if I hurt her. She had to know in her heart I didn't love her. That I never had. It damn near killed me, seeing her like that. She'd just got this tattoo...' She trailed off. There was a slight tremor in her hands. She didn't seem to notice it. Too consumed by guilt.

'You can't beat yourself up about it,' I said. 'Your dad is a dangerous man. You did what you had to. Trust me, I know what that's like. Nothing makes it easier. Not even knowing that you're doing the right thing. I still see my wife's face every time I close my eyes.'

'Tell me about her.' There were tears on Quinn's face. She didn't try to wipe them away. 'Your wife. What was her name?'

'Sophie.' I said, picturing her smile. 'She was... she's beautiful. She always knows how to calm me down, and kick my arse.'

'How did you meet?'

'At a New Years Eve party for the millennium. A friend of mine invited me to this party in London. I didn't know anyone and had no place better to be, so I went. I met her about an hour before midnight. Everyone was starting to freak out about if Y2K was real, but she sat in the corner and just said that if it was, then so be it. We managed before technology, and we could learn to live without it again. We got talking and nearly missed the big show. There was this massive fireworks display. We could see it from the party. It was incredible.'

'That sounds lovely.' Quinn mused.

'It was. I asked her to marry me a year later. A small ceremony, but it was the happiest day of my life. Then nine eleven happened, and that was the start of my end. I think it changed everyone. Opened our eyes to this new world of ours. I got a job covering news in Afghanistan and...'

I was my turn to trail off. Quinn looked at me.

'What happened to you?' She asked.

But I just shrugged.

'It doesn't matter now. It can't be changed. Just like you and Eva, you can't change the past. You can only learn from it.'

'But now she's in danger, and it's all because of me.'

'This isn't your fault.' I said. 'You just wanted to protect her. No one could blame you for this.'

'It doesn't make a difference though, does it? She's stuck there, with him, because of I let her into my life.'

'We'll get her back, I promise.'

'You can't make that promise. You don't know him. He's ruthless.'

'And he doesn't know me.'

'He's got the edge over you on experience.'

'And I've got the edge over him on good looks and charm. I'd say we're an even match, and if Felix is out of the way, he doesn't know I'm coming for him.'

'So, it all depends on whether or not he managed to get to Reyes yet.' Quinn said. 'If he did, Reyes knows you're after him. If he didn't, we still might have the edge. How long has Nicole been gone for?'

I checked the time on Felix's phone. The clock said it was two minutes to five in the afternoon. Nicole had set off around half three, which meant it was coming up on the optimistic side of my estimation.

'If she's coming back.'

'She's coming back.' I said out loud.

'Yeah, I know.' Quinn said, giving me a strange look. 'Why wouldn't she?'

'Honestly, I don't know. If I were in her situation, I don't think I would.'

'You wouldn't help Eva?'

'No I would, but it's more than that.'

'Spill the details.'

'I may have stolen the money from her in the first place.'

'Oh, wow. You really know the way to a girl's heart.'

'To be fair, she stole it first, and she tried to sell me out.'

'Why not go halves on it?'

'Because then I might never have seen her again.'

'So you do like her?'

'It's more complicated than that. I've got Sophie, and my son, Peter. I haven't seen them in, how long has it been? Over a year. I don't know where they are. I don't know if they're okay. But I've been lost and alone for so long, it feels good to have some company, even if it does come with a whole lot of baggage.'

'You know, until today I didn't know you were married.' Quinn said. 'The news coverage over here didn't go into the background much. All we knew was that you'd come back from Afghanistan a terrorist. Politicians used you as a prime example for why we need better border controls, as if everyone who leaves the country is going to turn traitor.'

'The news back home vilified her.' I said. 'They blamed her for me. It was awful to watch, and I couldn't do anything about it, which made the whole thing so much worse. I can't bear thinking about it. I just try to look forward and find a solution, because otherwise, what the hell am I doing?'

'If you're looking for a way to fix it, then why are you here in America?'

'Shortly after it all came out, I ended up in Spain. I thought I was getting somewhere with it all when I was attacked. When I woke up, I was packed in this wooden crate about the size of a small dresser with a couple of holes drilled in the side. I tried calling for help, but the only people there were those who'd put me in it in the first place. They squeezed bits of old bread through the holes for me to eat and threw buckets of foul water at me that I had to suck off the wood. It was awful. I don't know how long I was in there. When they finally let me out, I was here in America. That's when I met Ramiro Salazar.'

'And that's the guy you're looking for?'

'That's right. He tortured me for weeks, all for nothing. He never asked questions, he never tried to get me to confess anything. He just brutalised me, day after day for sport.'

'That's horrible.'

'That's why I'm here. After I escaped, I was going to try and get back to England, but then I met Nicole and things spiralled out of control. Afterwards, I knew I couldn't just let him go. What he did to me was awful, but if I left him alone to do that to other people, I couldn't live with that on my conscience. I have to know he's dead. I need to stop him.'

Another silence drifted across the room like a gentle breeze.

'I hope you find him,' Quinn said. 'And I hope you kill him.'

'Thanks. Hey, do you like riddles?'

'What am I, a child?'

'What's the one thing you eat that eats you back?'

'How the hell would I know that?'

'I don't know what you know.'

'And how is that a riddle? That's just a convoluted question.'

'I wouldn't say it's convoluted.'

'You know, I can see why nobody likes you.' She joked.

'I thought you said Nicole likes me?'

'I don't remember saying I liked you, James.'

I spun around in the chair towards the stairs. Nicole stood there, a small plastic carrier bag in her hand. Through the translucent plastic, I could see the jagged wads of dollar bills. Not two million dollars worth, but almost definitely one hundred thousand's worth.

'You took your time.' I joked.

'Smart ass.' She quipped. She tossed the bag across to Quinn, who caught it midair and, without stopping, headed for Vinnie's room. She didn't knock. No time for waiting around. Nicole and I followed, and as I closed the door behind us, Vinnie had already begun counting through the money.

'It's all there,' Nicole said. 'I double checked.'

'Sure you did, lady.' He snarled. There were ten wads of cash, each wrapped with a strip of mustard-coloured paper denoting the value. Ten thousand dollars a piece. Vinnie riffled through the notes, checking to make sure there weren't any blank papers tucked away inside. There weren't. I'd checked most of them myself. And considering where it had come from in the first place, I would bet on every bill being as genuine as they come.

Eventually, Vinnie came to the same conclusion.

THIRTY-SEVEN

CONNECTED

VINNIE PUT THE MONEY BACK INTO THE PLASTIC BAG AND TUCKED IT into his desk drawer. 'Here's how this thing is going to work. You give me the cell you'll make the call from, and I'll hook it up to this laptop. That way, when you make the call, I can trace it.'

'How long will that take?' I asked.

'If you think you've got to stay on the line for sixty seconds or something, that's all Hollywood bullshit.' He said. 'That's not been relevant since like the sixties when you had operators connecting the calls. Don't get me wrong, it'll still take some time, but it's not quantifiable, you know? I ain't exactly practising this in my spare time, if you know what I mean.'

'So how does it work?' Nicole asked.

'It'll go one of two ways, depending on how inept your man is that you're looking for. The FCC ordered phone networks to feature location-tracking technology to assist cops finding criminals, like GPS chips and that sort of thing. But that only happened a couple of months ago, so depending on how smart your man is, there are ways around it. I ain't going to get into the details of that because none of you is smart enough to understand it. Put it this way, either this happens, or it don't. I can use the software on my laptop to see which cell tower the call is originating from. The longer you stay on the line, the closer I can narrow it down. Understand?'

'Sure.' I said. I handed Vinnie the phone, and he plugged it into his laptop via a long black cable. Then he tapped away at his keyboard.

'Okay, I'm all set up on this end. You'll need to leave the cell plugged in, so it's best to put the call on speaker, so you don't accidentally disconnect it. When the call goes through, all of you better stay silent, so you don't spook the guy. Understand?'

We all nodded.

'Good.' He said. 'Ready when you are.'

I looked at Quinn.

'You got this?' I asked.

She nodded her head, but I could tell she wasn't confident about the prospect of speaking to her father. Nevertheless, she stepped forwards, twisted the phone around to her, and found the number in the phone log. She took a long, deep breath, and pressed the button.

The purr of the outgoing call filled the room, the rhythm ticking like a swinging pendulum. Every second that passed filled the room with an electric mix of anticipation and dread.

And then finally, the call went through.

There was a silence. An ear pressed to a mobile phone, somewhere in the city, or maybe further. Listening. Waiting. A game of chess. One in which Quinn must make the first move.

She whispered into the receiver, 'Dad?'

More silence. More listening. More waiting.

Then a response.

'Isabella, this isn't a good time.' His voice was what I had expected. Deep. Rasping. Impatient. The voice of power and experience. Of a man with decades spent on the other side of life. I could picture his face in my mind, standing by a window, looking out over his city, while Eva struggled with her binds close by.

'I know dad, but I needed to talk to you. It's important.' Quinn insisted.

I could hear his breathing, slow and heavy through the phone's speakers. How long had it been since these two spoke? Quinn had said months.

'What is it?'

'I… I think I'm in trouble.'

How long had it been since the last time they'd seen each other? Years. A father and daughter, fractured.

'What kind of trouble?'

'You were right. I… I need help. The rehab, I think it's time.'

Would he question why she was calling from Felix's phone? Would he wonder why she had picked this very moment to call?

He didn't respond.

'Dad, I'm scared,' she whimpered down the line. Either she was an excellent actress, or the fear was genuine. 'I need help. I can't eat, I can't sleep. It's getting real serious, and I can't do anything without a fix. I can't even leave the house.'

Was he buying it? Did he believe his daughter had a problem? The words had some truth to them, but there was something about it that sounded wrong. I'd only known Quinn for a matter of hours, but even I could tell this wasn't her.

Her father's silence amplified the fear.

'Dad, please. Can we meet? I don't feel safe here. I don't like…'

'How did you get this number?'

There was no care to his words. No compassion for his daughter's drug problem.

'I… It's Felix's cell. He told me to call you.'

More silence. More unease.

'Dad, he told me you could help. Said you would know what to do. You were right, I need rehab. I need help. If we could meet, I know I could…'

Reyes cut her off.

'Isabella, put James Stone on the phone.'

Another pause, this time it felt like an age. The game was up.

'What? Who's?...' She started, but again his words cut through hers.

'Do not play games with me girl. Put Stone on the line now.'

All eyes turned to me. Quinn shrugged. There didn't seem any point in keeping up the pretence. I stepped forward and spoke.

'Mr Reyes,' I said, trying to keep my tone light. 'You wouldn't believe how long I've been waiting to talk to you.'

Again, another pause. I had to check the phone to make sure the line hadn't gone dead. The call was still active, the time creeping up to a minute on the line.

'Have you ever crushed a bug, Stone?' Reyes growled through the speaker. 'Have you ever held one in your hand and felt its tiny little limbs squirming around in the palm of your hand, desperately searching for escape, only to find nothing?'

'I can't say that I have.' I replied.

'It's a powerful feeling, holding another creature's life in your hand, literally. Knowing it is at your mercy. Knowing it cannot do anything you don't wish of it. I could open my fist, and let it scuttle away across my fingers, let it live to fight another day. Or I could clench the muscles, and squeeze so tight that it has no place left to go. I could crush it in a moment. I could feel it crack, and feel the soft, warm innards trickle down over my fingers. In a heartbeat, I could give it life, or I could take it away.'

There was another pause. The game of chess progressed again. My move.

'They say cruelty to animals is the first sign of a psychopath.'

'Understand this, Stone. Right now you are in the palm of my hand. You scratch at my fingers, desperate for freedom. You are completely at my mercy.'

'You must have huge hands…'

'Do not mistake the meaning of my words, I am not offering you a choice. I know who you are, and what you have done. You are nothing to me, Stone. Your life means less to me than that of a fucking bug. I will squeeze the life from you. I will break your ribs and watch as you drown in your own blood. I will burst your skull and watch your beady little eyes pop right out of their sockets. I will crush every single atom in your body until there is nothing left of you but your destructive fucking legacy. I will end you.'

'That wouldn't be a good idea.'

'You should not have got in my way, Stone. Your days are numbered.'

The line went dead. The call severed. Unease spread across the room like a foul odour.

'Well, that was fun.' I said, looking around at everyone in the room. Vinnie tapped away at the keyboard on his laptop.

'Did you get the location?' Quinn asked him.

'Sort of.'

'What do you mean sort of?' Quinn probed.

'I got it down to an area about a block wide, but he hung up before I could get specifics.' Vinnie said.

'Where?' I asked.

To which Vinnie replied by spinning the laptop around, and pointed at a spot on the display. Filling the whole screen was a birds-eye view of what appeared to be a city. An array of pastel colours replaced the view an actual bird would have seen from that angle, with three long strips of colour representing land, sea, and what I assumed was a long beach separating the two. It didn't take a genius to figure out where it was.

'Miami Beach,' Vinnie said, confirming my suspicions. 'Somewhere between fifth and fifteenth.'

'There's got to be thousands of people in that area,' Nicole said. 'Can't you narrow it down further?'

'Not unless you want to call him up again, and even then, I'd have to start from scratch.' Vinnie snapped. 'You got what you came for, now get out of my sight.'

'You didn't give us shit,' Nicole barked back. 'You're not getting one hundred thousand bucks for giving us a zip code. You better do something before I climb over that table and feed you that goddamn computer.'

'You threatening me?' He snarled at her.

'You bet your ass I am. Now get started.'

The pair faced off, casting daggers at one another until one of them folded. Vinnie went first. He muttered something under his breath and started typing frantically at his computer. Nicole caught my eye, and I smirked at her. Never in my life had I met someone as belligerent as Nicole Green.

'What's in the area?' I asked Vinnie. 'Residential or commercial?'

'Why does that matter?' Quinn asked.

'He's got to be somewhere safe where he doesn't have a thousand pair of eyes on him. He's too smart to walk around in public. So, if it's residential, that means he's either got someone in that area he can stay with, or he has a safe house. If it's commercial, he's probably holed up a hotel room or warehouse or something.'

'It's a combination of both.' Vinnie said. 'There's a big shopping mall a couple of blocks north, but down there it's mostly holiday homes and hotels.'

'So, he could be in any of them.' Nicole said.

'Not necessarily.' I said. 'Holiday homes round there aren't going to be cheap. Anyone smart enough to buy the property back when they were built will either have kept hold of it or rent it out for a small fortune. If Reyes owns one, then you can be sure the DEA know all about it. They've been after him for decades. They would know if he owned a couple of properties around there. They've had the time to search. And while it's no crime to own a holiday home, I'd bet my life that they'll have people watching them now, especially after last night.'

'That doesn't narrow it down though.' Nicole said.

'It does, because the DEA has spent years gathering evidence. They won't just have checked on him, they'll have a pair of eyes on every Tom, Dick and Harry that has ever been unfortunate enough to build bridges with Reyes. He has to know he's not safe right now being Reyes. He has to be trying to camouflage himself, somehow. My bet is he's found the most expensive hotel and booked a room.'

'You think?' Quinn asked.

'It's what I would do.' I said. 'What's in that area that costs the most per night?'

Vinnie tapped away at his keyboard for less than a minute.

'The Grand Regent Hotel falls in that area.' He said.

'Then that's where we check.' I said.

'And if he's not there?' Quinn asked.

'What else is there?' I asked Vinnie.

'Nothing else that fits your suggestion. The Grand Regent Hotel charges three hundred bucks per night, and that's for the worst rooms. The penthouse goes all the way up to five thousand.'

'That's where he is.' I said. 'Can you find any photos of the bathrooms in there?'

'Why?'

'Can you do it or not?'

He could. Moments later, he turned the screen again and showed me a crystal-clear photo from the hotel's website. It was a shot of an open-plan kitchen and living area. In the back of the room, and open door led through to a tiled bathroom. The same style found in the photo Reyes had sent to Felix's phone. The same spot Eva had lay bound and gagged.

'He's there.' I said. 'We need to go, now.'

'Hold up,' Quinn said. 'Vinnie, can you find out who's booked in at the moment?'

'I can get into anywhere, for the right price.' He sneered.

'Vinnie. I will snap you in two if you so much as mention money again.' Nicole snapped.

Behind her, the giant moved forwards. His hand reached up for her shoulder, but before he could touch the fabric of her top, she spun around, caught his hand and twisted the massive slab of fat and muscle around his body, and brought it up his spine. The sheer ferocity of her movement was enough to bring him to his knees, and he let out a noise that sounded like a distressed rhino.

'You need to learn how to treat a woman.' She barked at the enormous man. 'Touch me again, and I'll shove your arm up your ass and use you like a puppet. Understand?'

The giant nodded enthusiastically, and Nicole let him go.

I resisted the urge to applaud her performance. Vinnie glowered at her with such rage, I thought he might burst.

'Can you do it or not?' I asked him.

He broke from his livid revere and smiled menacingly in my direction.

'Like I said, I can get into anywhere.' He leered.

The job took him longer than the phone hack, but when he turned the screen around for the final time, I could see why. The screen was lit up with the personal details of over three hundred people. Names, addresses and card details - all of which should have been secured behind the hotel's firewalls - exposed for a bunch of criminals to see. So much for security.

'Can you print that off?' I asked him.

Vinnie nodded and hooked the laptop up to an old printer in the corner of the room. He fed the machine a wad of paper and waited patiently as line after line of personal information was committed to print. When he finished, he passed the document to Quinn.

'There. Now get out before I turn you over to the cops.'

'You wouldn't dare.' Quinn said.

'Watch me. Leave, now.'

THIRTY-EIGHT

CHECK IN

JAMES SPLIT THE PRINT-OFF IN TWO AND HANDED HALF OF IT ACROSS to me. He sat in the centre spot on the back seat, hood up, and hat low to his brow, while Quinn and I sat up front. Smart move. What with his name being all over the news again.

We'd caught the story just as Quinn fired up the rental. I was too tired after my round trip to the gym to want to spend another minute behind the wheel, so I switched on the radio and got an earful of complications courtesy of Kelly the over-excited news reporter.

'Police are advising residents of Miami to be on high alert for signs of activity from one James Stone. Stone, who was convicted on multiple charges of terrorism in the United Kingdom and Europe, has been linked to a gang attack on one of Miami's most prolific nightclubs. The venue, Vivaz, which is owned by businessman Felix Jackson, was attacked in the early hours of the morning, resulting in the deaths of multiple workers. Police were called to the scene, and were able to bring the attack to a swift end. During a sweep of the building, evidence has been uncovered that suggests the British fugitive was on site at the time of the attack, and managed to escape with Mr Jackson and an as-yet-unknown accomplice by attacking two police officers, and escaping in a stolen police vehicle. The fugitives are still at large, but police are warning people to be on the lookout for the young man and a female of similar age. We will have more on this story as it progresses.'

It didn't come as much of a surprise. James was hardly the most subtle of fugitives, and his antics at the club had come back to bite him in the ass. What mattered now was that we stayed well out in front. We were in overtime, and running out of seconds fast.

'Turn that off, will you?' James muttered as he rifled through the papers. 'I don't need to hear it.'

'You're not worried?' Quinn asked.

'They've been onto me for ages. This is nothing new. And I wish they'd stop reporting me as a convicted terrorist. I'm suspected at best.'

'They might know about the car.' I said.

'Not yet, they'd have mentioned it in the report. They'll want every pair of eyes in the city looking out for me. But until I see flashing lights in the mirror, I won't hold my breath. Now come on, we need to find which room Reyes is in.'

'If he's there.' I said.

'Is that helpful?' He snapped. 'No, I don't think it is. Just look through those papers, will you?'

I spread the papers out on the dash. There were twelve sheets in total, with every line on the page corresponding to a different room. Not every line was full of data, probably because not every room was occupied. Some pages were busier than others, with the sparsest only being half full. All the same, if James had split it evenly, that meant there had to be over seven hundred rooms to the Grand Regent Hotel.

'What are we looking for?' I asked.

'Well, I'm going to go out on a limb and guess he didn't sign in under his own name.' James replied, his head burrowed in information. 'Look for anything out of the ordinary.'

'Like what?'

'Rooms booked out for longer, names that don't seem genuine, I don't know. Just use your imagination.'

So I did. The first page was made up of reservations on the first floor. Eighteen rooms to a floor meant every page was just short of two floors a sheet. I skimmed through the details on the first sheet, seeing nothing of interest. A woman from Idaho was staying for five nights in a room on the second floor. Nothing special about that, other than that the lady had some fifteen hundred bucks to spare on a room without much view.

Pages two and three were of no help either. Short stays made by uninspired names. The same could be said for pages four and five.

'Anything yet?' James asked.

'Not unless Reyes had a sex change or found someone to shack up with. What about you?'

'Maybe, but it's a lot riding on assumptions.'

'Tell the class.'

He took a moment before answering.

'What do we know about him?' He asked.

'He's an asshole.' I said.

'We know he's up to something. We know he's done with this city. That's what Felix told me. He's lived his entire life at the top of the mountain, and now it's crumbling under his feet. He wants out, and he's got a plan in place of how to do it.'

'If you're right.' I said.

'But he's a pragmatic man, and he wouldn't risk everything he's built without careful consideration. The only reason he's not in the wind is that something is holding him back. Some part of his careful plan is taking longer than he'd like, which tells us a lot more about him than the face value.'

'Does it?'

'Think about it. The money is all that's important to him. With no son to carry on in his place, it's the only part of his legacy that he can take with him. So the question isn't what he's waiting for, it's how much he's willing to sacrifice to get it. If it was a case of taking as much as he can possibly get his hands on, then would he be willing to spend a lot of it in the process?'

'How much are we talking here?'

Another pause.

'Say, a quarter of a million.'

'Then I'd say it depends on how much he's expecting to make.'

'Exactly. That's the key question.'

'I thought you said the key question was how much he was willing to lose?'

'It's the new key question. Don't poke holes in my logic.'

'Why do you think a quarter million?'

He held a sheet of paper up and pointed at a block of five lines.

'That's why.' James said.

I took the sheet from him and looked at the point of interest. The five rooms in question took up the whole of the forty-fourth floor. Not only that, but they were all booked under the same name. J. Underwood. And cost an eye-watering four thousand bucks per room per night. The higher the cost, the better the view. Better be one hell of a view.

'That's a lot of money to spend on a holiday.' I said.

'And the reservation finishes tomorrow.'

'And you think this is it?' I asked.

'I think it could be. Who else would book out an entire floor for two weeks? That's a staggering amount of money to waste just to stay hidden. The Feds won't be looking for him in a fancy hotel, they'll be looking for him with known associates. I don't think Felix was lying when he said he couldn't arrange a meeting. He's too much of a public figure to come and go so easily from wherever his boss is hiding.'

'But why would he rent out five rooms? If he's up there by himself, he won't be coming and going, regularly.'

'I think you've got it completely backwards.' James said. 'I think he is back and forth. Perhaps not so much now, but I think he has been. I think he's been showing his face, making sure the people know he's still around. He doesn't want his enemies or his allies thinking he's gone soft. And I don't think he's up there alone. I think he's got those spare rooms filled.'

'What makes you think that?' I asked.

James handed me another page. It was unlike the others. No customer records. No account details or room numbers. Instead, the page was full of vehicle information. The print off logged registration plates, vehicle makes, and intended duration.

'What am I looking at here?' I questioned.

'About halfway down the page. There are seven cars logged in within a five-minute window.' He said, tapping at the sheet in my hand. 'They all logged in the same day the reservation started.'

'It could be a coincidence.' I said.

'It could, but if we dismiss it, we don't have anything. I've got a good feeling about this. I bet Reyes rocked up at the hotel with a small entourage, signed in under some pseudonym, and has been up there ever since, barring the odd expedition to piss all over his territory.'

I didn't respond, but my silence spoke louder than anything I could have said.

'Look, I know it's a long shot.' James said. 'But we have nothing else to go on. We know the call came from that area, and this is the best chance we have. Sure, he could be hiding in one of the other rooms. Hell, we might bump into him in the lobby. But I've got a feeling he's up there, wasting thousands every day while he waits for the motherlode to come through. And if I'm right, we need to be prepared for some pretty heavy resistance. We've got two pistols between us, which isn't going to be enough to take them down with force, so we need to be smart about this.'

'Well that's optimistic.' Quinn said.

'Hope for the best, plan for the worst. Seven cars could easily hold four people a piece, which means we're looking at a force somewhere between one old man, and twenty-eight armed criminals.'

'We don't stand a chance against twenty-eight goons.' I said.

'Then let's hope there's just one guy up there.'

'And Eva.' Quinn said.

'Yes. And Eva.' He said.

The Grand Regent Hotel stood like a giant salmon-coloured monolith amidst a sea of smaller beige buildings. A pair of concierges clad in pressed black shirts and pants stood outside the entrance like eager guards, ready to snatch the chance to welcome a guest to the hotel.

'Park up around the block and we can walk the rest of the way.' James said.

'They won't let us in looking like this.' I said. 'And even if they do, we don't have a reservation.'

'We can make one.' James replied, as Quinn took the next right and weaved the car out of sight of the hotel.

'This isn't the kind of place you just make a booking on the door, James. They might not have any rooms available.'

'We know that's not true.' He said, holding up the print-offs. 'And with the storm coming, they'll want anything they can take.'

'Even if that is true, we can't pay with cash.' Quinn said as she pulled up. 'They'll want ID, credit cards, that kind of thing. Unless you've got a really convincing forgery, we're stuck.'

'Could Vinnie hack them again and get us a room?' He asked.

'You want to piss him off some more?' She replied. 'He's doesn't take too kindly to having his toes stepped on.'

'I just paid him a hundred grand for about five minutes work.' James said. 'He can push it a little further.'

So Quinn called, and Vinnie reacted. Even with the cell pressed to her ear, it was easy to tell how angry he was. For the most part, Quinn let him vent his frustrations without resistance. Perhaps the exhaustion of the situation was getting to her. Perhaps it was the withdrawals. If it was, she hid the discomfort well. She waited until

Vinnie finally calmed down enough to convince him, and when she ended the call, it was clear she had her way.

'He says to give him five minutes.' She said with a little smirk. 'He's going to put it in that you arrived two days ago. So, all you've got to do is say you lost your key.'

'Who's doing it then?' I asked.

"It's got to be you, Nicole.' James said. 'Me and Quinn can't risk it.'

'And I can?'

'No, but since my face is all over the news, and it's Quinn's dad in there, you're the one with the least chance of being spotted.'

'Vinnie said he'll book it under the names of Mr. and Mrs. Hartas.' Quinn said.

'What room number?'

'I don't know. He'll just get whatever he can find.'

'What if they ask me?'

'Just tell them you can't remember.' James said. 'Act flustered, and they'll take pity on you. Oh, and ask them for a block of cheese and this morning's newspapers.'

'Why?'

'Because I'm really hungry and want to catch up on the news. Just ask them, will you?'

'When this all goes wrong and they pull me out of there in a pair of cuffs, I'm going to tell them where you are.' I said.

'I'd expect nothing less of you.' James grinned. 'Now get going. We haven't got all day.'

I flipped him the bird and got out of the rental car. Six-fifteen in the evening, and the weather was starting to turn. The news reports were telling people to hold up at home and prepare for the worst, but where was I? Of course, I was breaking into a hotel to confront a deadly drug dealer. This isn't what I meant when I told my fifth-grade teacher that I wanted to do something exciting.

Clouds packed with a punch loomed over the hotel, shrouding the giant salmon monstrosity in an unshakeable gloom. The knot in my stomach did a couple of warm-up stretches, preparing for the worst. I wrapped my arms around my chest, and jogged for the entrance. I ignored the looks of the two concierges, both silently judging me. I gave them my patented Nicole smile, lunged for the doors, and stepped through into the cool, calm air of the hotel lobby.

A tall blonde woman behind the reception desk watched me

approach with a false smile. In my pullover and denim pants, I looked a good couple thousand bucks less than most of the other guests. Still, she was a professional and didn't hold her judgement beyond face value.

'Good afternoon,' she beamed. 'How may I help you?' Her heavy Florida accent elongated the last syllable of her question.

'Oh, I'm just having the worst day.' I sighed. 'My husband and I were out doing a bit of shopping for the holidays, and someone stole my purse.'

'Oh no,' the receptionist cooed. 'That's terrible.'

'I know. It was a gift from my mom last year. I loved it so much. It had all my credit cards and my room key in it.'

'Well at least we can help you with that. What room were you staying in?'

'I can't remember.' I said, feigning the aftermath of a traumatic event with all the finesse of an Oscar-winning actress. 'My head is just all over the darn place. My husband and I checked in two days ago. The reservation is under Mr and Mrs Hartas.'

'Just one moment.'

The receptionist tilted her head to the computer screen in front of her, and tapped away at the keyboard. As she waited for the results to return, she gave me another smile, this time a little more genuine. It didn't last.

'Oh, I don't seem to have anything on our systems.' She cooed. 'Could you spell Hartas for me?'

I did, and she retyped the surname into the system.

Same result.

'Do you have any identification?' She asked.

'It was all in my purse.' I said, shaking my head.

'What about your reservation number?' She asked. 'Perhaps your husband might…'

'He's unavailable at the moment.' I said, cutting her off midsentence. 'He told me to come back here and rest. It's been such a miserable day.'

'Unfortunately, without the reservation details or any identification, I can't find out which room you were in. Are you certain you have the right hotel?'

The conversation had drawn the attention of another receptionist. A man in his late thirties had pricked up his ears, and turned to involve himself involuntarily in our conversation.

'Is everything okay?' He asked.

'It's fine.' I said.

'I'm just having a little difficulty finding this woman's reservation.' The tall receptionist said. She threw me a look that made the knot in my stomach twist a little tighter. She didn't believe me. The ruse was cracking.

'Could you check again?' I asked, this time a little desperately. 'I'm sure it should be in there.'

The male receptionist leaned over his colleague with all the pretension of dominance he could muster. He typed the exact same six letter word his coworker had typed, and hit the search button.

His face lit up with glee.

'Here we are. Mrs. Hartas. Room nineteen twelve?' He asked, unable to hide the smug look off his chubby face.

'That's it.' I said. 'I knew it was the high teens.'

'Just one moment.' He said, moving away to retrieve the key to the room. He slotted a small rectangular plastic card into a black machine on the desk, and waited for the machine to write the data onto the card. After a beep, he handed me the card.

'If there is anything else we can help you with, please don't hesitate to ask.' He said, ignoring his colleague who stood awkwardly at his side.

I thanked them both, and headed for the pair of glass elevators. The door slid silently open, and I stepped inside, thumbed the button for the nineteenth floor, and watched the doors slide shut.

THIRTY-NINE

PREP WORK

THE FLURRY OF DARK, DESPOTIC CLOUDS LOOMED OVER THE OCEAN, extinguishing everything beneath. The people of Miami had scurried indoors seeking shelter from the encroaching doom. The rain had not yet come, but it was close. A treacherous storm was coming. Those remaining scuttled about like bugs. The three of us stood side by side from nineteen floors up, and watched them hustle about while they still had the chance. The once beautiful and serene ocean had turned sinister. Huge waves struck the withered golden shores. Gail-force winds whipped the dishevelled palm trees back and forth, relentlessly testing their waining strength. The worst was yet to come, and from high up on the nineteenth floor, we were going to see the whole damn thing.

The perfect view to see in the apocalypse.

'Did you get the cheese and newspaper?' I asked Nicole.

'You know, it must have slipped my mind.' She replied.

'Can you call down and get room service to send it up?'

'What am I to you, an errand girl? Why do you want it?'

'Why does everything have to be a big problem with you? Can't you just get it, then I'll show you. And I don't mean a few slices of that weird plastic shit you call cheese. I mean a full block of the stuff.'

She groaned.

'Fine. Gimme a minute.'

I suppressed the urge to chuckle as she called down to the receptionist.

'They'll bring it up soon.' Nicole said as she returned the phone to the cradle.

'I can't stand this,' Quinn groaned. 'If he's here, we should just go up and confront him.'

'We can't do that.' I replied.

'Why not? He's not going to risk a shootout here. Too many witnesses.'

'That's my point exactly. He can't risk using guns, so neither can we. If it comes down to a brawl, he's going to have us beat from the start.'

'So why are we just standing around waiting?'

'We're not. I've got a plan. Just remember, if you fail to prepare, you prepare to fail.'

'They teach you that in Boy Scouts?' Quinn asked.

'I didn't do Boy Scouts, I did Cub Scouts instead.'

'The hell is that?'

'The British version. I can still remember the Cub Scout promise.'

'What in God's name is the Cub Scouts promise?' Nicole teased.

'I promise to do my best, to do my duty to God and the Queen, to help other people, and to keep the Cub Scout Law.' I recited.

'You truly are unbelievable.' Nicole sighed.

'What was the Cub Scout Law?' Quinn asked.

'Something to do with always doing your best, thinking of other people first, and doing something good every day.'

'Really held up that law, didn't you?' Nicole muttered under her breath.

I ignored her slight and headed over to the small kitchen area to search through the cupboards. I found what I wanted pretty quickly. I pulled out a large non-stick frying pan and placed it on the oven hob. There was a knock at the door. Nicole answered. A young guy in his hotel uniform with the morning newspapers and a big old block of cheese. She took it and retreated inside before he could ask questions.

'Here's your cheese, dick.' She said, throwing the plastic wrapped yellow brick at me. I caught it and flipped it over.

'Cheddar cheese, just what I wanted.' I said. Using a knife from the cupboard, I cut it up into thin slices and dropped the lot into the pan. It sizzled angrily as it came into contact with the hot metal, but yielded quickly. I prodded the thin slices with the knife, moving them around in the pan until they had turned into a watery goo.

When I was satisfied it was ready, I took the pan off the hob and left it to cool a little. Nicole stood and watched me work, utterly confused just what I was doing. Another typical day with James Stone. I took the newspapers from her with a smile that she didn't reciprocate.

I tore the newspaper in half. Taking a page at a time, I pressed it into the pan of cheese, and let the warm substance soak into the paper. Then I draped the soggy page on a towel by the radiator. By the time I got to the sixth sheet, most of the cheese had soaked up and left to dry.

'What is it?' Quinn asked.

'That, is unfinished. I need more stuff.' I replied, looking at the cheese-soaked pages. 'Any chance one of you could nip to the shops?'

Nicole looked out of the window. The weather didn't exactly look enticing.

'In fact, Quinn, could you do it?' I asked. 'You should be safe. I doubt Reyes has men patrolling the streets.'

'Is it important?' She asked.

'Very.' I replied. I tore off a slip of newspaper and jotted down the items I needed. 'These shouldn't be hard to get. Get a taxi if you want. Just be quick, okay? The shops will close soon.'

Quinn sighed and took the slip of paper. Nothing on it would take more than a DIY store to acquire. She nodded and headed for the door. No need for kicking up a fuss. Eva's life was on the line. I watched Nicole relax as Quinn opened the hotel room door, and disappeared out into the hallway.

'Don't worry,' I smirked. 'I've got a fun job for you too.'

'Oh God, what?'

'If we are right, and Reyes has the whole forty-fourth floor to himself, anyone who goes up there is going to be a risk. He might have people guarding the corridor. Only one kind of person can go up there unnoticed.'

She pieced the rest together herself, and her face dropped.

'Hotel staff.' She sighed. 'You want me to get my hands on a uniform?'

'Bingo.'

'And you couldn't possibly do it because you're the worlds most recognisable face?'

'If I thought I could get away without any risk to Eva's life, I would.'

She sighed. No point arguing.

'Don't worry about it.' I said. 'You're better at this stuff than I am anyway.'

'I'm a better thief?'

'See it as a compliment.'

I sent her off on her way with a plan in mind and collapsed onto the sofa with utter relief. My eyes could barely stay open, but I didn't succumb to sleep. Not yet. I stared up at the chalk white ceiling. Somewhere up above, Reyes and his men busied themselves with preparation. For what, I didn't know. This was his last night in the hotel. I doubted he was planning to extend his stay. Right now, he could be sat in this very spot, twenty-five floors up, looking out at a view of the city he built. I could feel him up there. Like a sixth sense. His presence radiated like the midday sun.

Could he feel me? Did he have any idea he was being hunted? If he had taken the call at face value as a feeble attempt to arrange a meeting, then maybe he wouldn't. But Domingo Reyes didn't get to the top of the food chain by letting assumptions get the better of him.

'You've been wrong before.' The Wolf hissed.
'This time is different.' I replied. 'He's here. I can feel it.'
The Wolf scoffed to himself and vanished once more.

I ran through the plan in my head. A risky play, but circumstances weren't likely to change, and if they did, they would probably not be in our favour. Reyes was so close to his endgame, and I knew every second was tempting fate. The only variable that concerned me was just how many men he had up there with him.

The door swung open, and Nicole scurried inside. In her hands was a bundle of clothes.

'How'd it go?' I asked.

'Pretty certain I gave the receptionist a reason to sue the hotel.' She replied. 'She's going to have the mother of all concussions.'

'Needs must. I guess. Go get changed. Quinn should be back soon.'

Quinn got back forty minutes later with a white carrier bag swinging by her side. She dumped the contents onto the coffee table. A roll of duct tape. Three plastic lighters and a pair of pliers. Nicole, in her smart hotel uniform, looked at her reflection in the mirror.

'It suits you.' I said.

'Bite me.'

'What's that saying, dress for the job you want, not the job you have.'

'I don't want to be a hotel worker.'

'You'd rather be a criminal?'

'The pay is better. Now, are you gonna fill us in on what it is you're doing?' She asked.

'Wait and see.'

First up, I took one of the lighters and the pair of pliers. I clamped the beak of the pliers down into the metal covering of the lighter, and pulled it free, revealing the inner mechanics beneath. I did the same with the striker wheel. The flint and spring beneath sprung out and flew across the room. I scooped them up, dropped the pliers back on the table, and twisted the spring around the flint.

Satisfied that part of the plan was complete, I returned to my cheese surprise. I placed the flint and spring down beside the other two lighters and took the roll of duct tape. I peeled it into a series of strips, making sure there was still enough left over to work with afterwards. With the cheese paper dry, I applied the tape on both sides of the paper, then rolled it up into a thin pipe, and secured it in place with a final strip of tape. The finished product looked like a plastic pipe, no longer than a foot and a half in length.

I tossed the finished item across to Nicole. She caught it and looked at it.

'What in the hell is that?' She asked.

'That, my dear friend, is a smoke bomb.' I replied with a smile. 'We're going to smoke Reyes out of his hole.'

I filled them in on the plan. They held their questions to the end like the diligent students they were.

'I just have the one question.' said Nicole.

'Fire away.'

'Do you actually see this working? I mean, can you seriously believe we can get away with it, without the three of us, and Eva, all dying in the process?'

'So long as we do it well, yes. We've got a solid distraction. He won't expect it from us.'

'If you say so.'

'Have a little faith. We've got this.'

And so, with no reason to delay the inevitable, we got started. I gave five of the smoke bombs to Nicole, along with one of the working lighters. I pocketed the last smoke bomb, the flint and spring, and the final lighter. Quinn headed to the bathroom and returned a minute later with three damp face towels provided by the hotel. We each took one and tucked them into our pockets. When the smoke started, we would be grateful for the protection it could provide. I looked from Quinn to Nicole. There was doubt in their eyes, but they didn't voice their concerns. No point. Eva couldn't wait any longer.

'We all ready?' I asked.

'As I'll ever be.' Quinn replied. I picked the two pistols off the coffee table and handed one to her. I slid the other into the back of my jeans and tucked my hoodie over it for concealment. Hope for the best, plan for the worst. Hopefully, neither of us would have to use the pistols, but I would be damned if I was going to go up against Reyes without one. Nicole would have to do without.

Nicole took the lead, heading out into the hallway and summoning the elevator to our floor. We got in and thumbed the button for the fortieth floor. Four floors below Reyes. Picked for its lack of staying guests. Only two of the available rooms were occupied. Three were vacant. Wasn't going to get better than that.

The elevator juddered and whirred, then obeyed our commands. Twenty-one floors to go.

I looked at Nicole. In the time I'd known her, she'd come up against a lot. Yet I could see the nervous tension in her eyes. She felt my eyes on her and fixed hers on me.

'You've got this.' I mouthed to her.

She gave a meek smile and looked away.

The elevator pinged, and the doors slid open onto the fortieth floor. Quinn and I got out. I pressed the button for the forty-fourth floor.

'See you on the other side.' I said to Nicole.

'Or in hell.' She replied as the doors slid shut.

FORTY

EVACUATION

AND ONCE MORE, I WAS ON MY OWN, DOING THE IDIOTIC BIDDING OF James Stone. My heart raced. The cheese-soaked paper rolls felt warm in my hand. I had no idea if the ludicrous concoction would even work, let alone do so enough to smoke out a group of armed hostiles. Of all the dumb things James had ever done, I prayed that this was the time it worked correctly.

The elevator pinged again, and the doors slid open to reveal the forty-fourth floor. The corridor was the same as the others. Plush, embroidered carpets in the shape of maroon and cream diamonds stretched from one end to the other, so clean it could have just been fitted. Eight doors in total. Three on one side, five on the other. Five adorned with polished brass doorknobs and gold-plated numbers denoting the number of the hotel room. Two at either end of the corridor leading to the stairs, and the final leading probably to a linen closet. Eight doors, five of which were important. Potentially twenty-eight armed men inside. With odds like that, you count your chips, cash in and head home. Not this time though.

The corridor was empty. No poised sentries ready and waiting to make my day a little bit worse. The glow of the wall mounted lights stretched into every inch of the deserted space, creating an eerie, uncomfortable atmosphere, not unlike the feeling of a doctors waiting room, minus the other patients, or hygienic smell. Through the door on my right, room forty-four zero three, I could hear the faint sounds of a television show. I pressed my ear up against it, but no other sounds stood out. Maybe Reyes was inside right now, watching commercials. Maybe it was just a random holidaymaker waiting out the approaching storm. No way to tell, yet.

One hundred and twenty seconds on the clock until James pulled the alarm. Two whole minutes to get everything into place. Most of that first minute had dwindled away, and I hadn't even begun. I took the first stick of newspaper out and lit the end. The reaction was almost instantaneous. A thick cloud of smoke erupted into the corridor like a miniature erupting volcano. The smell reminded me slightly of caramel, for reasons I neither understood nor had the time to investigate. I hurled it back the way I'd come like a stick of dynamite ready to burst, and sprinted away in the other direction. I heaved the damp cloth from my pocket and pinned it against my face with my right bicep. Without stopping, I lit the second stick and dropped it on the carpet.

The third bounced against the wall at the far end mere moments before the scream of the fire alarm filled my ears. Even knowing it was coming wasn't enough to stop my heart nearly exploding in shock, but there was no time to stop. I barged through the door to the second flight of stairs and lit the last two sticks. The first I threw down the first set of stairs, the second I dropped at my feet.

The acrid fumes occupied the tight space with incredible speed. Visibility dropped in seconds, as the smoke seeped everywhere. There was no way I could stick around for long. I sprinted back down the corridor with my hands clapped over the cloth on my face. My eyes stung. Tears poured down my face. All the while, the smell of caramel filled my world. If I got out alive, I made a mental note never to touch the stuff again.

I could hear a commotion from the surrounding rooms. Smoke slithered through the cracks in the doors, giving those inside a brief taste of what lurked outside. This was no equipment test. This wasn't something they could shrug off and ignore. They were right at the centre of it all. Nose to nose with the problem.

I heard a door swing violently open and crash into the wall and the barks of big men as they lumbered out into the corridor. The closest was three doors up ahead. The rest were behind. The guy I could see was big. Maybe six feet. Two hundred pounds. Definitely not Reyes. Could be a bodyguard. Could be an accountant for all I knew. I darted past him and kept moving, and reached the door to the stairs before the rest of them. I swung it open and stepped aside. The smoke from the stick James had lit was billowing upward, but was far better than anything inside the corridor.

'This way,' I shouted, asserting my authority as a pretend hotel employee. 'Don't stop till you get outside.'

Through the smoke, I could make out six figures hustling towards me. All men. All about the same size and shape as the guy I'd skirted by. They shambled towards me like obedient little giants and were through the door and down the stairs without so much as a moment to stop and question the whole situation. Not one paused to check if I was okay. So much for chivalry. I waved them through and looked ahead into the dense smoke.

No old cartel leaders.

No angry bodyguards.

No one.

I hurried back down the corridor and pulled the employee key card I'd stolen up to the first receptor. The machine buzzed, and I heaved the door aside. The room was opaque with smoke, but it was empty. As was room two. My head pounded. My lungs, starved of oxygen, felt heavy with the cheese smoke. Every step felt like I was wading through day-old soup, and as the smoke flooded the empty rooms, I couldn't even take a breath of clean air inside.

I couldn't take much more cheddar punishment.

I threw myself at room three. The room the guy had stepped out of as I passed. The door bounced open again, revealing a room identical to that of one and two. The veil of fumes shrouded everything. Well, almost everything.

Four men huddled close turned to look at me. They wore pressed navy suits like some kind of acapella quartet, except I doubted they were going to sing me a song. As they turned, they realised I wasn't a threat, and four Glocks in four hands slipped casually behind four backs.

'You need to get out of here,' I shouted. 'We have to evacuate the hotel immediately.'

They looked at each other, passing responsibility around like a hotcake. They weren't leaders. They were followers. All waiting for instruction.

I gave them what they needed.

'This is not a request. This is an order, unless you want to go up in flames. Evacuate the building immediately.' I barked.

But something held them back. Like a hound told to stay, they were bound to comply. How far did that loyalty go? Were they willing to burn to death forty-four floors up for no reason? Or were they waiting for something? An order to go. The all clear from down below, perhaps? Whatever it was, they were going to be unconscious if they didn't act soon. With the door wide open, the smoke pummelled the room like water on a sinking ship. No time to stand around with your thumb up your ass.

'Move!' I shouted at them.

From a door in the back of the room, a figure appeared. Not a six-foot bodyguard. The figure was smaller by at least a foot. The build was that of a man. Broad shoulders and a confident stride. No panic, as though a simple burning building couldn't affect him. It was the stride of a man above it all. A man confident in his continued existence. A man of power.

Only one man like that I could think of.

Domingo Reyes stepped out of the smoke and pierced me with an intense stare. His eyes bore inside my very soul, searching for a reason for my presence. As though the immediate danger wasn't a case of urgency. His suit was cream in colour and fitted his small stature perfectly. He approached me in silence. Unperturbed by the nauseating smoke or screaming alarms. He got right into my personal space and raised his hand to my chin. Even over the noxious stench of the smoke, I could smell the unmistakable stench of cigar smoke on his breath. His eyes were small, but sharp, and carried all the joy of an endoscopy. His skin was aged from decades of sun and experience. What remained of his hair was grey and short. No stubble. No cuts. No scars. Experience won through. Experience had given him a lifetime of success.

'Why are you here?' He asked. His voice was smooth like whiskey, almost disarmingly so. Yet I knew he could command power if he wanted to. He was a man in complete control. Not just of himself, but everyone who came into contact with him. Including me.

'I have to check everyone is out.' I replied. The cloth to my mouth muffled my words slightly.

'It is hotel policy to send its employees to search room by room? To risk death for those who choose to remain behind?' His voice was calm, yet it carried over the din of the alarms with ease.

'Please, sir. We have to leave right now.' I insisted. My eyes felt like they were on fire. Was that the smoke, or his relentless stare?

Reyes watched me suffer for a long moment.

'The girl asks us to leave.' He hissed. 'Then we must do as she asks.'

I realised I was breathing quicker. The smoke burned my eyes like phosphorous.

'We need to leave, now.' I reiterated. My voice had changed. It was urgent. Scared.

'After you.' Reyes leered, gesturing for me to lead the way.

I turned to leave, taking in what little of the room was visible. Was Eva still here?

If she was, Quinn would have to get her out, fast. That was her role. I hustled back towards the door and into the corridor. I had no idea how long the improvised smoke bombs would burn for, or if their flames would ignite the carpet and cause a genuine fire. I headed right, back towards the designated staircase.

I glanced behind me and saw two of Reyes's men right behind me. Following up was Reyes himself. A handkerchief pressed to his mouth. As I watched, he barked an order to the last two men, but over the ring of the alarms, I didn't make it out. Whatever it was, they broke off from the pack, heading left into the smog. Five rooms. Possible twenty-eight people. Were they rounding up the rest of the men?

I didn't hang around to find out. I had the target and just two men. The odds weren't going to get better than that. At the door, I swung it open again and ushered the three remaining men inside. With their numbers halved, the two guards flanked the older man and hustled down the first flight of stairs in close proximity. I followed close behind, relishing the comparatively cleaner air that met us as we descended.

Together, we hustled down, past the forty-third, forty-second and forty-first floors. No movement from inside. No frantic guests joining the fray. Reyes turned onto the next flight of stairs. Below, the door to the fortieth floor was ajar, wedged open by the tail of a bathroom towel. Through the gap, I thought I could see a flash of movement. The first guy ran straight by, paying it no mind, and headed further down the stairs. Reyes noticed it. His pace slowed as his survivalist instincts kicked in, and he moved slightly aside to allow his other bodyguard to move up.

The door swung open, and something small flicked through the gap. The flint and spring, superheated by the second lighter. It hit the landing in the blink of an eye. Just enough time for me to prepare.

The flint exploded in a flash of blinding light. I saw the white flash through my eyelids and jumped into attack mode. I leapt forward and kicked the closer bodyguard square between his shoulders. Dazzled by the light, there was nothing to stop him from going head first into the adjacent wall. His own momentum was enough to send his consciousness on an impromptu vacation. He slumped down, a big old pile of skin and bones with his face smushed up against the wall.

By which time, everything had escalated. The first guard had his back to the flint blast, and - sensing shit had hit the fan - heaved himself back up into the battle. At the same time, James emerged through the open door, pistol raised, and pointed it right at Reyes' head.

Reyes was fast. Too fast. Too many years of people trying to get the jump on him. He batted the pistol out of James's hand and sent it clattering down the stairs. Out of sight, out of mind. Reyes followed it up with a swift punch to the face. James staggered sideways, reeling from the blow, and left nothing between Reyes and me but a truckload of bad vibes.

I pounced on him like an enraged alley cat, and caught him in the chest. He bounced off the wall and threw his arms up to attack. He caught my hair and threw me aside with ease. Two swift punches struck me in the gut and chest and knocked the wind right out of me. I gasped, which gave Reyes all the time he needed to sink his claws into me and throw me towards the handrail.

I caught it just in time to stop myself from falling head first over the side and twisted around. Reyes was coming at me again. As was his remaining bodyguard. James intersected, and caught the guard in the gut just as Reyes did the same to me. Were it not for the mess of brawling men behind me, I knew would have died. Instead, we glanced off the pair and tumbled down the stairs much slower than previously intended. My head ricocheted off walls and stairs and Reyes before finally coming to a stop on the lower landing.

Whether I was alive or dead or completely broken, I couldn't tell. My only thought was that Reyes had fallen too. His body lay still as a corpse right beside me, his face squashed against the wall. Like his bodyguard, he had brained himself. At least I hoped that was all. I struggled to my feet. Up above, I could hear hurried footsteps on the staircase directly above me. More of Reyes' men joining the fight.

'James!' I shouted, but he was too preoccupied to break free. He was locked in combat with the guard, both struggling for control. We needed to get out fast. I grabbed hold of Reyes' shirt and hauled him down the next set of stairs. His body flopped down and came to a stop right beside the pistol. I snatched it up and pointed it back towards the two men above.

But there was little I could do. There was a flood of movement right into the space Reyes and I had just vacated as James and the guard crashed down the stairs. James was on top. The guy was the luckiest son of a gun I'd ever met. He scrambled up, looked at his foe, and stamped on his face.

'Hurry.' He barked, seemingly unfazed. He leapt down, heaved Reyes up into his arms, and ran.

I grabbed hold of his legs and followed. We took the stairs two at a time. Reyes flopped and bounced and bashed into everything. The smoke had cleared. The clean oxygen fuelled me onward. I pushed my body to the limit. Adrenaline coursed through me like coal through a steam train. The same looked to be happening to James too. At the next landing, he kicked open the door, and sprinted through.

It wasn't our floor, but it didn't matter. We just needed to put some distance between us and our pursuers. We hurried down the corridor, carrying Reyes in our arms like firefighters with a survivor. I pushed myself. Faster. Harder. Further than ever before.

We took the door for the second stairs. I knew some of Reyes' men would be coming this way, but they weren't on high alert. Not yet at least. We didn't slow down. Didn't want to risk failure. I tried to focus my ears on any distinctive sounds, but the piercing wail of the fire alarms was too much to break through.

'Here!' James shouted over the deafening siren. 'This is it.'

He barged through the door and raced onto our floor. I spotted the door to our room. James dropped Reyes and fished the key out of his pocket. The card bounced off the receiver, and the light flashed green. He swung the door open, and together we hauled the unconscious man across the threshold.

Only once the door swung shut behind me did I breathe a sigh of relief. Every part of me ached. I dropped Reyes and rushed for the sink. Smoke had burned my eyes, mouth, nose and lungs. I splashed cold water over my face and swore.

'I thought we were screwed.' I gasped.

'You did bloody great.' James cheered. 'I knew you had it in you.'

'I'm glad someone did.' I gasped. 'That was cutting it close.'

'Too right. Now come here and give me a hand.'

Reyes was still out, but he wouldn't stay that way for long. Well, not unless he'd died. I checked his pulse. Still beating. Good.

'We need to secure him before he wakes up.' I said.

'Really? I hadn't thought about that.'

'Not the time for sarcasm, James.'

He grinned, euphoric from the win. Together, we heaved Reyes up and headed for the bathroom. But as we drew close, there was a knock at the door.

'It's me,' said the woman on the other side. Quinn. 'Let me in.'

I jumped over and pulled open the door. Quinn was standing there. Alone.

Alone.

'She's not here.' She said. The look on her face one of utter devastation. 'I… I looked everywhere.'

But that wasn't our only problem. Because Reyes had woken up.

FORTY-ONE

THE WOLF AND THE VIPER

THE OLD MAN PUT UP QUITE THE RESISTANCE, BUT A LITTLE DUCT tape and a pistol pointed to his face soon saw to that. Nicole retrieved the chair tucked under the dressing table in the bedroom and placed it in the bathroom. I taped his hands behind his back and wrapped the remainder of the tape around his torso, binding him to the backrest. By the time we had finished, the fire alarm had ceased. The threat eliminated. Quinn stayed out the way, agitated that Eva was still missing. She paced back and forth, absentmindedly picking at her nails, lost in a labyrinth of unanswered questions.

When I was satisfied Reyes was secure, we left the bathroom, and closed the door. Quinn looked up.

'What's the plan?' She asked.

'The short answer, get him to cooperate.' I replied.

'He's not going to talk.' Quinn said.

'He's not got much of choice. Trust me, we can get him talking.'

She leaned against the window and ran her fingers through her hair.

'God, I just can't think straight.' She said. 'I don't even know if Eva is alive. He could have done anything to her.'

'You're sure she's not upstairs?' Nicole asked.

'I checked every room. There was no one.'

'With all that smoke and noise, you could have missed her.' Nicole said.

Which got Quinn riled. She spun and glared at Nicole, channelling the inherited rage of her father.

'I checked everywhere. Every goddamn inch.' Quinn snapped. 'She wasn't there. Reyes must have spooked and moved her before we got here. If she was even here in the first place.'

'Then we've got something to work on.' I interjected, stepping between the two women before something happened. 'If he just moved her, we can find out. We've got his phone. Someone will contact him to tell him they moved her safely.' I placed my hands on her shoulders and looked her dead in the eye. 'There is still hope. Trust me.'

'I can't deal with this right now.' Quinn said, shrugging my hands away. 'I need to lay down.'

She stormed away to the bedroom. As a final act, she closed the door behind her.

'She needs to chill.' Nicole muttered.

'She's worried.' I replied. 'Hell, I'm worried. I was sure Reyes would keep Eva close. He could have her anywhere.'

'Then go find out.' She said.

I looked at the closed bathroom door. The man on the other side was no joke. He had decades of success under his belt. A man like that couldn't be underestimated.

'Okay,' I said. 'I've got this.'

I approached the door. Sweat on my palms intensified, like the threat on the other side was an unknown. Like it wasn't just one man tied to a chair. If he knew how I felt, it would only further his resolve. I couldn't let him know. I put my hand on the handle and took a deep breath.

And opened the door.

The eyes of Domingo Reyes were cold and unrelenting, like a lizard, or a viper. His face showed none of the emotion he was hiding under the surface. You could take a snapshot of his face and tell people he was just a miserable old pensioner waiting for the bus, and everyone would be none the wiser. Not unless they recognised the bloodlust. He made no attempt to break free from his restraints. No shouts, no slurs. The guy could be dead if it weren't for the steady rise and fall of his surprisingly toned chest. Quinn's words rung in my head. *He doesn't strike to wound, he strikes to kill.*

I believed her words one hundred percent.

'I guess we can skip the introductions.' I said, closing the door behind me. Just me and him. The Wolf and the Viper.

He didn't respond. A power play. One I had to match.

'You look thirsty,' I continued. 'This can go one of two ways.

Either you get a bottle of water or a bottle of piss. I'll let your good behaviour decide.'

Reyes said nothing. His eyes did all the talking.

'You know, I did initially want to help you.' I persisted. 'We have a mutual goal. Or *had* at least. I don't know what your plan is now, but mine hasn't changed. Ramiro Salazar is a problem. He should have been pushed in front of traffic when he was a child, but the powers that be didn't let that happen. So now we have a psychopath wandering around, maiming people and scaring kids with that face of his. I wanted to take him out of the picture. I was willing to do it personally. No costs. No rewards. Literally no downside for you. If you'd taken the time to hear me out, maybe we could have worked together and put an end to that problem sooner.'

Still nothing from the old man. His eyes burned into mine. I fought the urge to look away.

'But then you decided to be an uncompromising dick about the whole thing, so I had to take matters into my own hands.' I continued.

'You think this persona scares me?' He said. No menace in his voice. No anger. Just the smooth, treacherous voice Quinn had warned me of.

'He speaks.' I jeered. 'How clever of you.'

'Make no mistake, boy. This will not last.'

'I bet you wish you hadn't wasted that bug-crushing metaphor.' I smirked. 'That would have worked a treat right now, wouldn't it? Don't take it personally, a lot of people have threatened much worse. I usually just take it on the shoulder and beat them at their own game.'

'You can feign confidence all you like, child.'

'And you can name call till the cows come home, it won't loosen that duct tape any. But what are you if not a businessman, so I thought I'd offer you the chance of a lifetime. I don't care who you are, or what you've done. I don't care that you've ordered your men to kill me on more than one occasion. I want two simple things. Eva free, and Salazar dead. He tried to kill me, and I'm not exactly a happy bunny. Bollocks to bygones. So that's why I'm here, because the enemy of my enemy is apparently my friend, when he's not trying to murder me. Help me on those, and I'll let you go.'

'You think I give two shits what that fool does?' Reyes snorted. 'He thinks he can control his father's legacy. He's welcome to the ashes. You've wasted your time, I'm afraid.'

'I wouldn't be so sure about that. It's the only way you're getting out of this bathroom.'

'James Stone, the feared terrorist. How does it feel not to get your own way? You hide behind your title like a badge of honour, but you're just a boy. This is a man's world, son. You've got to earn respect, and right now you ain't got shit.'

'You just lost the right to a bottle of water.'

'You act like you have the moral high ground. You think you can make me feel ashamed of my actions? I have fought for my place in life. I have earned it. There is more blood on my hands than I can remember, but do you see them shake? Do you think I repent my actions? Must I seek some higher being's forgiveness? No, this world will swallow you up long before I see judgement.'

'That's ambitious for someone tied to a chair in a bathroom. I think you're going a bit senile in your old age, or can you not hear me properly? I'm starting to wonder if you need hearing aids? Or would you like me to speak up?'

'I won't waste my breath entertaining you. My men will find me before long.'

'Like hell, they will. What kind of idiot would kidnap someone and keep them in the same building? They'll check every inch of the state before they come back here.'

'Are you so sure of that?'

'He's bluffing.' Said the Wolf. He stood by my side, observing the threat before us.

'We sure about that?' I asked him.

'His phone is turned off. He doesn't have some secret GPS tracker shoved up his arse. He wants to spook us. Put him in his place.'

'You think they could get here before I cut off your arms and beat you to death with them?' I snarled at the Viper. 'You think they could check every single room, every single closet, before I make you regret marking me as your enemy? Like I said, I'm not about beating the horse when you can feed it a carrot. You might have the age on me, but don't ever underestimate what I'm willing to do to get my way. Ramiro Salazar was the last guy who did, and I burned him.'

'Your threats will do nothing to me, boy. I have faced far worse than you, and I have won. Every. Single. Time.'

'What did you do to Eva? Where is she?'

Reyes chuckled.

'Does it scare you, knowing that you are so far from her?' He smirked. 'Even as I sit here bound to this chair, she is under my control. I could have her skinned alive if I wanted. Does that frighten you? You stand here the big man, puffing out your chest, but you cannot command a bathroom. You will never be in control.'

I threw my boot into his ankle.

'Were you in control of that?' I snarled. I kicked him again. There was an unmistakable flicker in his eye. The embers of an undying flame. 'What about that? Do you like it when I kick you?' I felt the familiar tingle inside me. The Wolf. 'You've spent too much time close to the sun, old man. You don't even realise your wings are all burned up.'

I kicked him again, but this time he was ready. Even bound to the seat, he moved with incredible speed. With one terrifyingly swift movement, he trapped my foot under the chair leg and pressed down onto my toes. The wood dug into the bones, crushing them under his weight.

'I wonder how many people have seen that videotape,' he growled. 'Do you ever wonder that? Do you ever think about the millions upon millions of men, women and children who have been exposed to the real James Stone?'

My stomach twisted at the thought of the tape. No matter what I could do, it would haunt me forever.

'There is no escaping what you are.' The Viper snarled. 'You will suffer through this world a haunted man, reviled by everyone you met.'

I tried to pull my foot free, but his weight was too much.

'And what about your family?' Reyes continued. 'I bet they've seen it too. I wonder what they thought when they saw what you were capable of. Do you even know if they're alive? Or have they paid the price for your sins?'

My hands slammed hard into the Viper's chest. The force of the attack sent him tumbling backwards onto the tiled floor. But it was not me who had delivered the blow. It was the Wolf. Once more he had taken the reigns. Once more he had seized my body for his own agenda. His chest rose and fell as adrenaline coursed through his veins. Our veins.

Too much control.

Reyes let out a howl of laughter. On his back, he was as helpless as a flipped tortoise. But he didn't care. He knew he had won. I left him where he was and stormed from the bathroom, slamming the door shut behind me. Nicole jumped at the noise.

'Are you okay?' She asked.

I ignored her and strode to the window. The weather was getting worse. Wind whipped against the building. The golden glow of streetlights bobbed and weaved as the gale battered them into submission. Beyond their reach, a terrible darkness loomed.

'What happened in there?' Nicole was by my side, a glass of whiskey in her hand. I took it and finished it in one. 'Hey, that was mine!' She objected.

'He pushed my buttons.' I replied, handing her the empty glass. 'He's not going to tell us where Eva is, or how to get to Salazar.'

'You don't know that. Give it time.'

'He's right. He's got us beat on experience. There's nothing we can do to him he hasn't endured before. He knows we're on a time limit. We can't stay here forever, and the longer he is missing, the worse it's going to get for Eva.'

'Jeez, what happened to you? Get a grip, man. He's only human. He'll crack if you want him to.'

'Nicole, we can't start torturing the guy in a hotel room.'

'Then come up with another way to get what you need. Like you said, we don't have long.'

I rubbed my face with the palms of my hands. I was dog tired. More so than I had been in weeks. Exhaustion bore into my body like a pneumatic drill. I let out a long yawn.

'You need sleep.' Nicole said.

'Did you know in ancient civilisations, yawning was a sign of the devil trying to enter your body to steal your soul?' I deflected.

'Go to bed, James.'

I sat down on the sofa and stretched out. Nicole was right. I was no use to anyone in this state. But thoughts of the videotape plagued my fragile mind. There was no escaping it. I closed my eyes and tried not to think about it. I could hear Nicole moving around, pouring herself another whiskey from the minibar. Just the one had already started to have an effect on me. I could feel it warming my body.

'Get some sleep, James.' Said the Wolf.

'What happened there?'

'We can talk about it later. We need rest if we're going to beat Reyes.'

So I did. I fell asleep with the video fresh in my mind and

dreamed a series of disjointed, torturous thoughts. When I woke, the room was much the same. All was quiet, save for the howling wind outside. Nicole sat beside me, her head bowed to the screen of Reyes's phone. She was out of her stolen hotel clothes, and back into the items Quinn had purchased.

'How long was I out?' I groaned.

'Couple of hours, maybe. Quinn's asleep too. I checked on her. You missed all the commotion.'

'What commotion?'

'All the guests got evacuated outside while the fire service checked the building. Figure they've got to know by now what caused it. I say we get out of here before sun up.'

'Noted. What are you doing?'

'Figured I might as well be the useful one of the bunch and check for clues,' she said with a cheeky smile. 'If you were wondering, he doesn't have any blatantly obvious secrets hidden on here.'

'Shame.'

'I know, right? Least the guy could do is spill the beans once in a while.'

There was a comfortable silence. I shut my eyes and drifted in and out of consciousness until again Nicole spoke.

'After you get him to talk, do you really think you'll be able to lure Salazar out from whatever rock he's hiding under?' she asked.

'Hopefully.' I yawned. Eyes still shut.

'That's a lot riding on hope.'

'It's basic human nature. Reyes and Salazar are enemies. They hate each other. Always have, always will. It's a tale as old as time itself. Humans always try and murder one another when you put a common interest in their way. Salazar has spent the last few weeks playing the big boy, trying to gather all his headless chickens together long enough to lead a head-on assault. He'll want Reyes out of the way so that he can be king of the castle. He tried it at the club, but he wants Reyes gone, I can feel it. All we have to do is make him think that his time has come.'

'So dangling Reyes as bait is foolproof?'

'Oh, far from it. It's downright reckless. But as they say, it's the punch you don't see coming that knocks you out. Salazar will smell the trap from a mile off, but not from me. As far as I'm aware, he doesn't even know I'm alive. It only needs to be enough to make him stick his head up long enough to shoot it right off his shoulders.

That's what I'm counting on. Curiosity killed the cat, or in this case, the Salazar.'

'I hope you're right.'

'Me too. What time is it?'

'Nearly midnight. Get back to sleep if you want. I don't mind standing guard over you.'

I didn't need telling twice.

FORTY-TWO

THE NIGHT SHIFT

JAMES WAS OUT IN A MATTER OF SECONDS. I GUESS BEING WRAPPED up in a gang war can take it out of a guy. I watched his chest rise and fall peacefully. Whether his mind was at peace was a different thing entirely. *Why hadn't he asked yet?*

I whiled away the time sat beside him, flicking through the contents of the stolen cell. Like Felix's, there was nothing of note. All contacts, messages and files had been deleted long before I got my hands on the device.

I dropped the cell on the coffee table and got up to make myself another drink. The minibar was stocked, and I had no problem with abusing the hell out of it. It wasn't my money paying for the room. Wasn't anybody's if Vinnie had done his job properly. I cracked open another miniature bottle of whiskey and fetched a glass from the coffee table. Normally, I'd add some ice. Today, ice didn't seem to matter much. The alcohol tingled against the back of my throat.

'Any of that left?'

I jumped and spun on my heel to see Quinn standing by the bedroom door. She had found a complementary white dressing gown from the bedroom, which she had wrapped around herself. The gown ended just above her knees, revealing her bare, pale legs beneath. Her hair was tied back, although a strand had broken loose, and come to rest over her right eye. She rubbed her arm sheepishly.

'There's more in the minibar.' I replied, intentionally leaving it to her to retrieve. There was something about her I just didn't like. Maybe it was the drugs. I'd seen enough people in my life be destroyed by them to know it's not a good road to take. But no, I didn't think that was it. It was her choice what she did. We all have our vices. If she wanted to stick a needle in her arm, then so be it. It wasn't that which sent my lizard brain tingling.

She brushed past me to reach the bar and selected two tiny bottles of gin. She cracked the first open and swallowed the contents in one. Her whole body seemed to ease up and relax as the alcohol hit her system. The second bottle went in a glass, topped up with tonic water from the bar. She took a sip and ran her empty hand through her hair.

'I could kill for another ten of these.' She sighed.

'Call room service.'

She didn't respond. I let the air grow stale between us, content with my drink. Finally, Quinn cracked.

'You don't like me, do you?' She said. Not really a question. Not really rhetorical. Somewhere in between, where all uncomfortable questions lay.

'Is that important to you, being liked?' I asked.

'Isn't it to everyone?'

'Don't know. I can't speak for everyone. I only know me, and I could care less what other people think.'

'How do you do it?'

'Do what?'

'Not care what other people think.'

Was it her looks that irked me? Maybe. She had that appearance that would have men bend over backwards to please her. Women too, apparently. There was something inherently distrustful about people who knew they could get what they wanted.

'What does it matter?' I sniffed. 'Someone doesn't like you, you only make it worse by trying to change things. Best to just accept it and move on.'

'I could never be like that,' Quinn said, taking another sip. 'Maybe it was growing up in my dad's shadow that did it, but I just can't let it go. I don't want people to think I'm anything like him.'

'I'm sure that getting high on his product will change their minds.' I scoffed.

'Hey, you don't know anything about me.' She bit back. 'You think it's easy growing up with a guy like him as your pop?'

Was it her looks, or was it something else? Her life, perhaps? She had grown up with a golden spoon in her mouth. A tainted golden spoon perhaps, but golden nonetheless. No matter what her father was, she had still decided to piss her life away. She could have taken his money and done something good, or just bought a house in the Maldives and forgotten all about him. My dad had been a truck driver. He barely had a spare buck to his name. I'd got where I was on my own. Well, almost on my own. Redd and James aside.

'I don't know what it was like, but I know I would have acted differently.' I said. 'Everyone would. That's not a dig at you. It's just human nature. The improbabilities of life. Like rolling dice, no one gets the same outcome.'

That killed her flare. No point in fighting back with a general statement. Like water to a flame. So she just drank her drink and contemplated her life choices, and the awkward silence returned. I downed the rest of my drink and headed over to the sofa to kick James awake. I was tired. My body ached from the fall down the stairs, and I was done with polite conversation. But I didn't get that far. Because the cell on the coffee table was vibrating.

The small black device bounced around the glass coffee table like an upturned bug. I stared at the screen.

'Who is it?' Quinn asked.

'The number is withheld.' I replied, picking the device up.

'Should we answer it?' She asked.

I didn't know. There were pros and cons for both. If we did, it might result in a lead, or letting the enemy know exactly where we were. If we didn't, we were safe, but no closer to Eva. My head couldn't make the call. So, I went with my gut.

I accepted the call.

'What?' I barked.

There was a pause on the other end of the line. Even in one brief word, they could tell the person on the other end of the line was not the person they expected.

'Who is this?' The voice was male, and suspicious.

'Nicole,' I said.

'Where's Reyes?'

'He told me to answer.'

'Put him on.' The guy said.

'No, he's busy.'

'Then I'll call back when he's not.'

'You want to piss the boss off by disrespecting his decision?' I barked.

Another pause on his end.

'How do I know you are who you say you are?' He asked.

'You want me to fax you my birth certificate?'

'No, I...'

'Listen, shit bag. I don't have time for your bullshit. Give me an update before I shove my foot up your ass.'

A third pause. The guy weighed up his options. It didn't take long for him to fold like a pack of cards in a strong wind.

'Tell Reyes we've picked up the guests, but they're worried about the storm. They want to know if the meet is still on?'

This time it was my turn to pause. My mind whirred with possibilities.

'Let me ask,' I said. 'I'll check with him. Call me back in a minute.'

The line went dead. With the cell still pressed to my ear, I spun around and kicked James in the side.

'Argh,' He moaned as he woke. 'The hell was that for?'

'Someone just called.' I said quickly. 'They're calling back in a minute. I need help.'

He was upright in a flash, mind in overdrive.

'What did they say?' He asked.

As fast as I could, I relayed the call to him and Quinn.

'Who'd they pick up?' Quinn asked.

'Beats me,' I replied. 'Could be anyone.'

'No, it couldn't.' James said. His eyes were unfocused, like a man lost in his own mind. 'There's only one option it could be.'

'Want to let me know before the guy gets back on the line?' I snapped.

'Think about it. Reyes is planning something. Everything we've seen of him supports that theory. He's getting out of the business, but not before something big, something he's willing to put the entirety of his old life on the line for. A thing like that will be the sole focus of his mind. It has to be, right? Why else would he not care about the DEA seizing everything he owns, and Salazar's men picking apart the remains?'

The cell started buzzing in my hands. The number withheld.

'Get to the point, James.' I barked.

'It's got to be China,' he said, breaking from his reverie to stare at the phone in my hand. 'Whoever they are, or whatever they want, I don't know, but it has to be them.'

I looked at the cell.

'What do I do?' I asked.

'Wherever they're going, that's where Reyes wants to be, and

I'd bet my life that's where they've taken Eva. That text to Felix's phone said she was the cherry on top. I bet she's part of his deal now. Find out where they are.'

I answered the call.

'What did he say?' The guy on the other end said. Same guy as before. Same mistrust in his tone.

'How far out are you from the location?' I asked.

'Seven, eight hours, maybe.'

'Whereabouts?'

'Just out of Charleston, although the weather is getting real bad here. What did he say?' He asked again.

'Reyes says to keep going.' I said. 'We'll be there around the same time.'

'You're not there already?' He asked.

'We got held up. But it's nothing to worry about. You know how to get there?'

'It's not exactly hard to find. One road in, one road out. The guests were worried about getting the boat out of there in the storm.'

'Tell them it'll be fine. You sure you know where you're going?' I asked.

As soon as the words escaped my mouth, I knew it was a step too far. The line was silent for a long while.

'I want to speak to Reyes.' The guy on the line said. Not a request. A demand.

'He's busy.'

'Then we're done.'

And again, the line went dead. I tossed the device over to James, who caught it in both hands.

'What happened?' He asked.

'I think I spooked them. He wouldn't tell me where they're going.'

'But he told you where he was?' James asked.

'Just out of Charleston.' I said. 'He said he was seven or eight hours out, weather depending. He said the "guests" were worried about getting the boat out.'

'Where's Charleston?' James asked.

'Depends which Charleston it is,' Quinn said. 'There's practically a Charleston in every state.'

'You know your geography?' James remarked.

'I studied it in high school.'

'Which is closest to us?' James asked.

'South Carolina is the nearest, but even that's about a fifteen-hour drive.' I said.

'Is it eight hours from the coast?' He asked.

'It's right on the coast.' Quinn said.

'Are any of the others?'

'I'm not *that* good with geography.'

'If you had to put money on where they are, which would you go for?' James asked.

'South Carolina.' Quinn replied. 'But that's just because it's the closest to us. If Reyes planned to meet them, he would need to have set off a long time ago to get even close to any of the other locations. No way was he planning on flying in this weather.'

'But that still doesn't tell us where they're going.' I said. 'The guy on the phone said they were eight hours out, max. How far could you get in that time?'

'If you estimate they can push sixty the whole way, which is generous, they've got a five-hundred-mile radius. Or to put it in grim statistics, they got somewhere in the vicinity of just shy of eight-hundred thousand square mile playground to play in.' James mused.

'Have I ever told you, your bedside manner sucks?' I said.

'You have, but while the numbers don't lie, it's not as bad as that seems.' He said.

'Why?' I asked.

'Because you can add a whole bunch of variables to that.' Quinn said. 'Whoever that was on the phone has to know vaguely where Reyes is. This is his homeland. He knows it as good as anyone. So, if someone wants to meet him, it's got to be somewhere in this state. His ego is big enough to make it inconvenient for anyone else and not care about the impact on his image. If they are in South Carolina and are eight hours away, they must be heading south. You said the guy on the phone was worried about the weather?'

'Yeah.'

'Then they've got to be headed towards the storm, not away from it. Unless there's another massive storm elsewhere in the country, he's coming to Florida.'

'Which cuts the square mileage down massively.' Said James. 'If he's coming towards us, that means he's going somewhere in the top half of Florida. And no one can manage a consistent sixty in bad weather. Traffic jams, poor conditions, closed roads, there are tons of different things that will push his overall speed down. I'd say at most, he'll manage fifty miles per hour if he's really lucky.'

'So how far could he get in that time?' I asked.

'I'd scale it down to four hundred miles, maximum.' James said. 'Somewhere south of South Carolina. Do you have a map?'

'Astonishingly, I don't carry one around in my handbag.' I replied.

'Me neither.' Quinn said as James looked at her. 'There might be one in the rental? Sometimes they put them in for tourists.'

'Okay,' he said. 'I need to look at one and wrap my head around all of this. Can you get it from the car?'

'Hell no, I'm not going out in the storm.' I snapped. 'Get it yourself.'

'I can't go out.' He said. 'If someone spots me…'

'James, it's like two in the morning. No one is going to spot you.'

He groaned.

'Alright, fine. You got the keys?'

Quinn threw them to him.

'Okay, I'll be back in a jiffy.'

'A what?'

'Never mind, Christ.' He huffed.

'Have fun in the rain.' I jeered as he closed the hotel room door behind him.

Another silence descended over the quiet room. The uncomfortable feeling had dissipated some in light of the escalation, replaced by an uneasy sense of accomplishment. We were getting somewhere. I sat down where James had slept. His body heat lingered on the upholstery.

'He's quite something, isn't he?' Quinn said.

'Who?'

'James.'

'Oh, I guess that's one way of describing him.'

'How would you describe him?'

I gave it a long thought before saying, 'He's annoying, but his heart is in the right place.'

Quinn moved across to the window. She stared out into the blackness.

'What's the deal between you two?' She said, not looking at me.

'Me and James? Nothing's the deal between us. Our paths crossed, and now we're here.'

'Bullshit. I've seen the way you two look at each other. I can see the spark.'

'Wrong. No spark. Besides, James is married.'

'So, you don't want to step on any toes?'

'No, I don't give a damn about stepping on toes. There's no spark. No magical romance between criminals. Sorry to disappoint.'

'If you say so.' She said, smirking. 'Tell me one thing then, why are you here?'

'Cosmically or geographically?'

'Why are you helping him?'

I paused and thought.

'James… helped me. Me and my brother Bobbie were stuck in a dangerous situation. James helped us get out of there. This is just me repaying the favour.'

'That's it?'

'Not much of a big story. He helped me, I help him. Quid pro quo, you know?'

'If you say so.' She said again.

She turned to look at me, but as soon as she did, the grin on her face disappeared, replaced by a look of shock. She spun around towards the bathroom at the same time as me, because the same noise that filled her ears had filled mine too.

Through the bathroom door, the unmistakable sound of shattering glass broke the silence. I snatched the Glock and pointed it at the bathroom door. My heart was racing. Quinn recoiled. Fear etched into her face.

'What do we do?' She whispered. I handed her the other Glock.

'Take this, and point it at the door. Don't shoot if you don't have to, and definitely don't shoot me. We want Reyes alive, if possible.'

She took the pistol in unsteady hands.

'Is that safe?' She asked.

'We've got guns. He's tied to a chair. Chances are he's just bashed his head against the mirror.' I said. But I couldn't shake the doubt. Silence had returned to the hotel room, but it was different to before. Gone was the serenity, replaced by a rising, unbearable tension. Like the silence before a sailing bullet hits its target.

I crossed the room and stopped a foot from the door. Quinn stayed behind. She pinned herself up against the window, weapon pointed at the door. I reached out for the handle with my left hand, keeping the Glock pointed forwards in my right. My hand made contact with the cold, sleek handle. My ears rang with the sound of my racing heart. I counted down from three.

And turned the handle.

The door exploded open with unbelievable force like a bomb had blown it off its hinges. The force of it sent me spinning. The Glock flew from my grip, landing with a clatter out of sight. From the bathroom, Reyes darted forwards with the ease of a man half his age. He caught me from behind as I staggered away and pulled me tight to his chest. Something sharp pressed against my neck. A jagged piece of shattered mirror. I tried to move, but the old man's grip was too tight, and the sharp object nicked my skin. The Viper spoke into my ear. His breath was hot and rancid. His words true.

'Move, and you'll die.' Domingo Reyes snarled.

PART THREE

THE FATE OF AN EMPIRE IS TO FALL

FORTY-THREE

THE PUNCH YOU DON'T SEE COMING

THE RAIN HAD REACHED PRECARIOUSLY CLOSE TO TAKING-THE-PISS territory. In the brief stretch I was exposed as I ran from the underground car park exit to the rental car, I felt like I'd taken another dip in Felix's hanging aquarium. With the hotel reception out of the question for me, the car park was my only route in and out, adding further to my time out in the storm.

And of course, it was all for nothing. No map. No GPS device. Just a couple of company business cards in the glove box, none of which would help me locate the meeting. With a sigh and a groan, I heaved myself back out of the car and sprinted back towards the hotel.

The water beneath my feet was like a stream. Billions of raindrops pelted me like thrown stones. The gaps in between the rain seemed barely capacious enough to house oxygen. The shock was almost suffocating, so I held my breath and ran.

I crossed the threshold a bruised and battered man. The steady decline into the car park made for an impressive water slide. As I climbed under the barrier, I slipped and slid all the way down on my back. Not a graceful entrance. I was at least glad that nobody was around to see it. The last thing I needed now was to be spotted by a passing security officer looking like an upturned turtle.

Sheepishly, I got to my feet and tried ineffectively to rub some of the excess water away like stray crumbs. With my eyes on my sodden clothes, it was my peripheral that noticed it. A slight movement somewhere to my right. A shape moving in a shadow. I glanced up, not sure if I'd seen anything at all. The darkness looked almost too dark, like the light was actively trying to avoid that corner of the car park. Had I looked at it head-on, I couldn't have been sure I'd seen anything at all. But the back of my brain itched, and inside the Wolf stirred.

I ducked low and slid silently into cover between the wall and the rear bumper of the nearest car, and made my approach. Was it a guard on a late night patrol? Was it one of Reyes's men, still searching for his boss? Or was it someone else?

The thundering rain outside masked my approach under a cacophony of furiously beating drums. I was close. The figure hunched low beside a smart black Mercedes. The car door opened, activating the vehicle's interior lights and bathing the figure in lucid, white light.

Reyes.

My mind froze. A deer in headlights.

Quinn. Nicole.

I burst forwards with the power of a bullet and sprinted for the Mercedes. I didn't care if he saw me. Didn't care if he had a gun. I just needed to stop him, no matter the cost. He slid into the driver seat and closed the door moments before he saw me. But the shock of my appearance did little to slow him down. In the light, I saw a smile creep across his face, and heard the engine roar into life.

He stamped on the accelerator as I reached the passenger door. My fingers snatched at the handle, and I managed to swing it open as the powerful vehicle lurched forward. The momentum forced the door shut, but I didn't let go. My feet left the ground as the Mercedes shot forwards. It didn't last long. In the cramped, busy lot, Reyes couldn't build up speed before he reached the adjacent row of parked cars.

He swung the wheel left towards the exit ramp. I swung the door back open, and this time I didn't waste the opportunity. I clung onto the headrest of the passenger seat and heaved myself inside. My legs hung out the door, dragging like sticks along the concrete.

Reyes was ready. He slammed his elbow into the bridge of my nose, cracking the cartilage like ice on a puddle. My eyes blurred and watered as the flood of pain exploded out from the centre of my face. Blindly, I reached out and grabbed onto anything I could find. My hand found something solid. The steering wheel. With all the effort I could muster, I heaved it down.

The Mercedes lurched left and within a second met resistance.

The car came to a sudden, crunching halt as it collided with a parked car. My body slammed against the dashboard, and as the impact rocked through the vehicle, I tumbled free.

Every part of my body screamed out in sheer agony. I couldn't tell where I was. My brain lagged as the images from my eyes fought to come into focus. I was on my back, staring up at the bright hanging lights on the car park. Beside me, I could hear the Mercedes' tires fighting for control, squealing over a chorus of wailing car alarms.

I rolled onto my stomach and heaved myself up to my feet as the Mercedes broke free from the crumpled mess of a ruined stationary sedan and twisted back onto course. Once more, I heard Reyes stamp on the accelerator, and the vehicle shot forwards.

I ran. Ignored the pain. I didn't have time for it. The Mercedes was already at the foot of the incline, fighting against the incessant stream of rainwater that rushed down. The enormous engine made easy work of it and quickly doubled the distance between us.

Reyes reached the top of the ramp and smashed through the barrier like it was made of cardboard. In a second, he disappeared into the night. I sprinted up the incline and looked around. Searching the encroaching darkness for a sign of headlights. But there was nothing.

He was gone.

I was panting. My body heaving and convulsing in a wretched spasm. I couldn't stop. Couldn't give him more of an advantage. I set off at a run.

'Don't!' It was the Wolf. His hand latched around mine, pulling me back. 'He's gone,' he bellowed. 'You'll never catch up.'

'I have to try.' I screamed, yanking free of his grip. 'I can't let him go.'

'Think. Nicole and Quinn. They need you. You need to go to them.'

The Wolf was right. I looked out into the darkness.

Reyes was gone. I had let him go.

Without another thought, I turned and ran back down into the car park. The elevators were at the back. I reached them and stabbed at the button with trembling fingers. The elevator took an age to arrive. Surely it knew. Surely it was trying to prevent me from what I was about to see. The doors slid open, and I leapt inside. I jabbed the button for the nineteenth floor again and again, like it would recognise the urgency and do something about it.

The elevator slid upwards at a sickeningly slow pace. The small LED lights flicked lazily through numbers as the correlating floors went by.

Ten. Eleven.

My heart raced, numbing the pain in a blanket of shock and denial. I felt sick. Felt like my body was going to give in.

Seventeen. Eighteen.

I couldn't even bear the thought of what I would see. I wasn't ready for it.

Nineteen.

The doors slid open, revealing an all too peaceful hallway. It was a lie, surely. It couldn't be so calm. Not now. I staggered out and tumbled towards the room door. My mind felt drunk. Paralysed by an outcome that was beyond my control. My sodden clothes stained the carpet, but I barely noticed. I knew I had to open the door, I knew I had to see what was inside. But staying outside prolonged the illusion of hope. Before I opened that door, nothing was set in stone. I reached the door to the room and snatched clumsily at the handle.

It was slightly ajar.

Like Reyes wanted me to see.

I missed the birth of my son, Peter. Sophie had given birth while I was in Afghanistan, after everyone had thought I'd died. She had gone into labour without me by her side. She had held our son in her hands, unable to share the moment with me. A single woman about to brave the seas of parenthood alone. I had let her down. She had asked me not to go. She had wanted me there, by her side. Forever and always. And I had let her down.

When finally they had pulled me from that hellish land and brought me home, it was not the same James Stone that returned to her. War had changed me. Once, I had heard her describe it to a friend over the phone while she thought I was resting. She said it was like someone had blurred me around the edges. So much of me was there, but so much was missing. And there was no telling where I ended, and the darkness began.

I had never felt like such a failure as I did in that moment. My wife, my son. I had failed them both. That failure cut deeper than any knife. It tormented me more than anything the monsters in my life could. The two people in the world I cared for most couldn't see me. I had died in that cell in Afghanistan. James Stone was no more.

Quinn was motionless. Her lifeless body slumped against the

sofa I had slept on less than an hour ago. Her blood soaked into the fabric, turning it from cream to black in the sombre light. I moved forward. Every step automated. An involuntary response. Slow. Afraid. Towards Quinn. Towards her body. Barely noticed the tears falling from my face. I had let her down.

My hands shook. My head buzzed. Everything felt like it was a million miles away, on some far distant planet. Wherever I was felt empty. Void. Dead. I opened my mouth, but words failed me. What was there to say?

The Wolf lurked in the darkness. He was different. Placid. Not aggressive. I could feel some remnant of sorrow emanating from him. Now was not the time for an attack. What would be the point? He would blame me, but no more than I already blamed myself. I looked up at him, waiting for some form of response, but got none.

Her body was still warm, although I couldn't tell if it was just my freezing fingers fumbling against the tirade of emotion. I lifted her wrist and felt for a pulse. Nothing.

I had pulled her into this, just like I had with Eva and Nicole. Their deaths were on me.

I looked around, searching for a sight I didn't want to see. Nicole. She had been through so much. Everything with Redd, with Hector Salazar. She had made it through it all, just to end here. I didn't want to see her body, but I knew I had to. I had to know. I owed it to her.

I drifted away from Quinn and scanned the bloodbath for her body. I couldn't see her anywhere. There was plenty of blood. Quinn didn't look to have moved much, which only made my stomach sink further. There was a trail of blood leading towards the bathroom where I had left Reyes. The door was closed.

I followed the trail and pushed open the door.

Nicole was there. Slumped down beside the toilet, head bowed, sat in a pool of blood. Her skin was pale and damp with sweat.

But she was alive.

There was a towel wrapped around her arm, turned crimson with pulsing blood. She held it in place with her other hand. Slowly, she lifted her head up to look at me.

'You took your time.' She whispered.

Her face was gaunt and hollow, her eyes sunk deep into her skull.

I dropped down beside her and held her in my arms. She winced from the movement.

'Jesus, are you okay?' My voice was hoarse. 'I'm so sorry.'

'He broke the mirror and cut himself free,' she croaked. 'He's a quick son of a bitch for a senior. Did you get him?'

'No. Nicole, I need to get you to a hospital. We need to get out of here now.'

'Like hell. I'll be fine.' But she knew it was a lie.

I helped her up to her feet. The act took its toll on her, and she winced.

'Take it easy,' I said. 'I can carry you.'

But she shrugged me away.

'I'll be fine. This ain't the first time you've got me injured. I'm made of stronger stuff, you know.'

Unaided, she moved carefully forwards. Her arm was the biggest problem, but she had a wound down her chest that had been left to bleed. Her clothes had torn where the blade cut through, exposing the wound, emphasising her weakness.

I caught her before she could fall.

'I can carry you.' I said again.

'I'm fine. Get off me.'

'You lost the right to make that call.' I said. I ducked down and picked her up like a large baby cradled in my arms. Even in her weakened state, she wasn't happy about it. I wasn't sure whether it was her condition, or the adrenaline coursing through my body, but she barely weighed an ounce. I looked into her eyes, slow and glazed. But alive.

'If you're done swooning, I'd quite like to get some sedatives.' She groaned.

I nodded and carried her through to the main room. My eyes fell over Quinn. Her body was so still.

'We can't leave her here.' Nicole whispered.

'But you need help.'

'I can walk.' She said again, a little more confidence in her words.

I put her down. She took a moment to regain some control before she moved towards Quinn. Her body looked so shrunken and crumpled where she had fallen. Her soul escaped like the wind from a balloon. Nicole knelt down beside her and stroked her face with the back of her bloodied hand.

'He was so fast.' She said, more to herself than to me. 'He caught me off guard. I told her to shoot him, but she couldn't. He was her father. He... he didn't hesitate.'

I had been the one to bind him. I had been the one to leave him alone. It was my fault they were dead. All my fault.

Tears ran down her face. She barely knew Quinn, yet her absence haunted us. I knelt down beside Nicole and put my hand on her shoulder. I couldn't shake the static from my head, but it had lessened. We couldn't stay. I would pay for my sins, but Reyes would suffer first. Nicole ran her fingers down Quinn's still body and around her wrist.

And her expression changed.

'James, there's a pulse.'

FORTY-FOUR

SURVIVAL

Lisbeth Quinn swayed in his arms. Her eyes rolled into her skull. She was in a bad way. Life or death. James held her as tight as he dared, and ran. I was behind. Didn't close the door. No point. Everything had already gone to shit. I pushed myself as hard as I could. Fought through the pain and weakness. Didn't have time for that either. My head felt like it was on a delay. Like when the audio is out of sync with the visual on a movie. James was already at the elevator. He hammered the button and bounced on his heels as the number ticked dreadfully slowly up.

'Stay with me, Quinn.' He whispered into her cradled head.

The doors opened, and he leapt inside, already punching the button for the basement car park before I'd hauled my ass inside. The doors slid shut. Quinn's head rested against his arm. Her skin was clammy and cold. He used his jacket as a makeshift tourniquet. A feeble attempt to stop the flow of blood, but anything was better than nothing.

'Don't you die, Quinn. Don't you dare.' He begged.

The ride down to the parking lot was awful. Every second felt like the lifespan of the universe. Creation, existence and destruction, all right there in a second. Again and again. A torturous loop of life and death. The doors pinged and slid open, revealing rows upon rows of stationary vehicles parked neatly side by side. All except for a cluster at the back that looked like they'd been dropped out of the sky and left in a crumpled mess, alarms blaring like a dying scream.

So many cars to choose from, but all locked. We didn't have time to hot-wire one.

James ran past the lot, heading for the exit. Water cascaded down the ramp. He stopped right before it.

'Wait here,' He gasped. 'I'll get the car.'

Carefully, he lowered Quinn down to the ground.

'Keep the pressure on her wounds.' He said. His voice sounded distant. Like a floating balloon in an empty night sky. I did as I was told. Pressed both my blood-soaked hands down into the tourniquet. She looked so empty.

I looked up, but James had already gone. Sprinting away into the night. The barrier at the top had been smashed, no doubt from Reyes in his escape. My arm throbbed where the blade had cut through it. Even the adrenaline couldn't hold it at bay. I wanted to do something. I wanted to find that son of a bitch.

The rental car burst through the gap in the barrier. It skidded down the ramp and came to a screeching halt inches from me. James staggered from the car and threw open the rear passenger door.

'Come on.' He yelped, snatching up Quinn with shaking hands.

James drove. He had to. I was too weak to focus on the road. I sat in the back and cradled Quinn's head in my lap. Her wounds were extensive, and the blood was relentless. I pulled back the borrowed gown and bloodstained top to see the extent of the damage, and immediately regretted it. Her stomach was a mess. The skin had torn in multiple locations, each bleeding profusely. The sight of it made me feel nauseous. How was she still alive? How long did she have left?

The roar of the engine echoed through the dank basement as James raced for the exit. We bumped up the ramp and out into the Miami storm. The streets were dead.

'Where's the nearest hospital?' I asked.

'No idea.' He replied.

'Get back to the city.' I said. 'Better chance than by the beach.'

James nodded and pushed the car onwards. The rental handled the slippery tarmac better than I'd expected. Either that or James was a better driver than I gave him credit for. But his knowledge of Miami was bound to be minimal, and mine was no better. We needed directions. We needed time.

I glanced around the car, desperate for something of use. Sewn into the back of the two front seats were elasticated pockets. I thrust my hand into the first, recovering a handful of crumpled pamphlets.

I threw them aside and snatched at the second pocket. There was something inside. Something useful. A map.

I held it out to show James.

'Where was that?' He asked.

'In here.' I pointed at the pocket. 'Didn't you check?'

'Not well enough apparently. Open it up.'

And so I did. I flicked open the booklet and scanned the pages for our location. Through the rain, I spotted a sign for the causeway. Our ticket back to the mainland.

'That way.' I shouted to James, before returning to the map. I found the causeway, followed it with a bloodied finger back towards the city, and searched the streets for signs of a hospital.

And there it was. The Jackson Memorial Hospital.

Eight miles away.

Eight miles on an open road was an eight-minute drive, probably less with some healthy speeding. Amidst the mother of all storms, it would take twenty minutes at least. The only mercy was that it was a relatively straightforward drive. Over the causeway, then off at twelfth avenue. Simple.

I told James, who responded with a list of expletives. Up ahead, the traffic had slowed at the intersection. Not lots, but even one car in our way was bad news. We didn't have time for intersections. The same thought had registered with James. He swung the rental out into the oncoming lane and leaned on the horn as we approached the lights. They just changed, and James flew across and swayed back into the correct lane.

But it was just one of many crossings. Already I could see another swarm of stationary vehicles up ahead. Their red lights shone through the evening light like a beacon of issues. This time, there was no quick alternative, so James had no option but to stamp on the brakes. We came to a reluctant halt behind a small coupé. The lights changed to green, and before the coupé could get in gear, James swerved around and cut it off.

Quinn's breathing was weak. With every passing second, I could feel her slipping away, and there was nothing I could do to fix it.

'This isn't working,' I said. 'We can't risk her losing any more blood.'

'I'm going as fast as I can,' James barked as he flashed by another busy intersection. 'I can't move traffic with my mind.'

He threw the rental hard right. The wheels screeched, and the rear of the vehicle spun wildly out as it caught the flood. I winced as my wounds stretched, feeling like the blade was cutting through me once more. James fought the over-steer and course corrected. Another round of angry horns pierced the storm.

'Turn there,' I shouted. 'Onto the causeway.'

James did as asked.

Two miles down. Six to go.

Traffic started to speed up as the bridge rose. James used every horse the rental had to offer and shot past the steady traffic like a bullet.

The causeway expanded out into six lanes of traffic separated down the middle by a row of blustered palm trees. Mercifully, traffic was light. James ducked in and out of every available space with frenetic urgency. The weather was only going to get worse, but that fact seemed to push the citizens of Miami out onto the road. Every single driver drove with impatience, desperately seeking respite from the downpour. And up ahead, it only got worse. Traffic had slowed to a standstill. It made James's job almost impossible, and before long he was forced to concede to the will of the road.

'This is useless,' he shouted. 'We don't have time!'

'Take the hard shoulder,' I said, pointing at the empty stretch of tarmac. 'It's our only chance.'

James twisted the wheel and scraped the bumper of the car ahead to squeeze through the gap. Quinn's head lolled in my lap.

'You're going to be okay,' I told her. 'Just hold on.'

'How is she?' he asked.

I had no idea. Her pulse was weak, but her heart was still beating. Blood pooled on the leather seats. I could feel it soaking through my clothes. I could smell it with every panicked breath. I felt dizzy. I wanted to vomit or collapse or scream or all three. But Quinn needed me to be strong.

James gunned it, taking the rental up to sixty in seconds. The rental scrapped against the barrier, but James held it steady.

Three miles down. Five to go.

The causeway crossed over a small island that according to the map was named Jungle Island. The traffic slowed as more cars pulled onto the road, and James was once more forced to stomp on the brakes. He came to a screeching halt just inches from a semi.

'Watch it!' I snapped, as the seatbelt dug into my wounds.

'For the love of God, I'm doing the best I can, okay?'

The second the semi was out of the way, he stamped on the accelerator again and shot in front of a giant Range Rover. But the hard shoulder ahead was no longer an option. Cars had spilt out, taking the same liberties that James had taken, but had opted for a maddeningly slow crawl instead. James leaned on the horn. A couple of cars ahead reluctantly retreated back into lane, perhaps mistaking the rental for some sort of governmental vehicle. James kept his hand on the horn and lurched forward into the newly vacant space.

The tactic worked. More and more cars pulled back into the throng of traffic, allowing us more space to push on. The causeway twisted around to the left, revealing the first signs of central Miami through the torrential downpour.

Five miles down. Three to go.

'Pull off there.' I said, pointing at the off-ramp just after we crossed back on to the mainland.

Again, the hard shoulder closed up as the traffic corralled into a separate lane, and James was again forced to oblige. The line inched forward, and no matter how much James leaned on the horn, it wasn't going to budge.

It took minutes for the traffic to ease up and split into three lanes, each headed in different directions. Way past the eight-minute mark, much closer to the dreaded twenty-minute deadline. I told James to head straight, and he did. He shot through the intersection and darted around another row of rain-soaked vehicles. Up ahead, the next section was blocked up with parked cars. James skidded, and bumped up onto the kerb, and cut across the sidewalk.

I put my hand against Quinn's throat, feeling for a pulse.

But there was none.

Six miles down. Two to go.

No.

'There's no pulse.' I yelped. 'Put your foot to the floor.'

'It already is.' He barked back. 'Do something.'

But what was there to do? I'd learned first aid in my teens, but it wasn't exactly the best of circumstances. I didn't know what to do. My head was a wreck. My wounds draining everything from me. I glanced up at James. My vision was blurred, but I could see the panic on his face.

'Stay with me, Nicole.' He begged.

'I'm trying.'

One mile left to go.

The final stretch was like a lucid nightmare. Nothing felt real.

The blood on my hands looked more vivid. The smells and heat and rain all amplified to a nauseating degree.

James screeched to a halt outside the entrance to the accident and emergency ward. A male nurse who had been casually smoking dropped his cigarette and ran across to us. When he saw the extent of the damage, he ran back inside and returned a moment later with a stretcher and another nurse.

Together, we transferred Quinn from the back seat to the stretcher. James climbed out through the open door. His clothes were stained with her blood. The nurses hurried Quinn towards the entrance.

'Go with her,' James said. His face was gaunt. Hollow. Like a part of him had died in that hotel room, and what remained of him hung in the balance. 'You've got to make sure she's okay.'

Like I had any other option. I needed help too.

'You need to get out of here.' I wheezed. 'Someone's sure to recognise you.'

He pulled out the Glock he had stashed in his pants and held it out to me.

'What are you doing?' I hissed, pushing the weapon out of sight. 'You can't go waving guns around at a hospital.'

'She's not safe.'

'A gun isn't going to change that.'

'You've got to protect her.'

'She's going to be okay, James. The doctors know what they're doing.'

'No,' He was scared. Shell-shocked. I could see it in his eyes. 'If Reyes finds out, or Salazar, they'll send someone. You can't let that happen. You've got to make sure she's okay.'

'I can't carry a pistol inside. They won't let me.'

'Then make sure the cops know she needs protection. Please, Nicole. I can't let her die. I can't.'

I held his hand. He was shaking. Deep and internal. He was ruined.

'I promise. They won't get to her.'

With all I had left, I hugged him tight.

FORTY-FIVE

WHERE GHOSTS LINGER

I watched the sky turn from a concrete grey to an impenetrable blackness from the boot of the four-by-four. Just moments before Domingo Reyes had sent me away, his men had bound my arms, legs and mouth with duct tape. All the while, he had watched. Those sharp, piercing eyes sucking any warmth from the room. He didn't care for me. I wasn't a woman to him, wasn't a living being. Just another obstacle in his path.

His men dragged me away. Out of the hotel room, down in the elevator, and across the parking lot. With no care, they threw me in the boot and set off without so much as a word spoken. Panic had riddled my mind. Where were they taking me? Were they going to kill me? Would anyone ever find my body? I willed my mind to focus. To recalibrate from fear onto something else, something more positive. But it was a task easier said than done.

But not impossible. From everything I had learned about Domingo Reyes, he was nothing if not methodical and pragmatic. He had held me against my will for the better part of two days in a hotel room. His manner had been for the most part calm. Right up until the very end. He had ushered me out hastily. Like a reaction to something. Like a cheating husband with a lover. Not in control.

Which meant he was exposed. And exposed people make mistakes.

All I needed was to use it for my advantage. And if I'd learned anything from James Stone, it was to seize opportunity, even if it wasn't there to begin with. The men in the car with me were not placid. They did not drive calmly into the storm. They were anxious, each smoking or drinking or complaining to ease their nerves. They talked at length about the situation, and it was clear from their incessant ramblings that they were as in the dark as I was. Wherever we were headed, I knew I had to make my escape before level heads prevailed.

And as if it were a sign from God, when finally we started to slow, I had a pretty good idea where we were headed.

The rain had been relentless for most of the ride, and as such, the bayou was much deeper as we approached. The four-by-four struggled through the groves that James's van failed at, forcing our approach to little more than a crawl. Two of the men jumped out to push, returning only when the vehicle was free, caked in the foul stench of mud.

By sheer miracle, they made it through the point James had conceded defeat, and up the other side. The ground rose up, and as a fresh gale crashed into the vehicle, I guessed we were up by the fence. I pictured James making his way down the abandoned space towards the old structure at the basin. Was that our destination? The night was darker here. The light pollution of the city all but a forgotten memory. We made our way slowly around the outskirts, heading for the gate. The two mud-ridden men got out and cleared the way, and finally, we began to descend the weathered land.

I resigned myself to play my part a little longer. The vehicle came to a stop, and the engine died. Our journey finally over. I heard four doors swing open, and four men climb out. A moment later, the rear door opened. A gust of bitterly cold wind swept over me, alerting my senses. Outstretched hands snatched at my legs and heaved me out into the night.

Outside, the world was impossibly dark. One of the men switched on a flashlight, casting a thin beam of light down at the thick, sloppy mud beneath our feet. The hands grabbed my arms, and dragged me along. My feet trailed along behind in the mud.

Rain lashed down like furious whips on my face. I kept my eyes on the beam of the flashlight. The holder moved away, with the two men holding me following close behind. It was so dark, I couldn't see the man in front, even though he could only be a matter of feet in front of me.

The beam of light flicked up, illuminating the old structure I had seen from afar just a few days earlier. Up close, it looked much larger, and in serious disrepair. The aged wood groaned and wailed in the fury of the storm. Patches of rotten timber lit up like a wart on the face of the beaten old structure. I could make out two large barn doors ahead. The man with the light moved closer, and after a minute of struggled unlocking, heaved the right-hand door open enough for us to move through.

The weather inside was better, just. Rain fought its way through cracks in the roofing, whipped into a frenzy as it caught in the prying gale, and drenching everything that sought shelter beneath. The man with the flashlight moved around, lighting a series of hanging gas lamps that looked as old as the building itself until some semblance of light stretched across the blustery space.

The barn was not empty. Far from it. Remnants of the old mine had clung on across the decades. Ancient steel carts lay abandoned beside what looked to be the makings of a ruined track. Some upright. Some tipped on their sides. A series of pulleys and chains swayed in the wind, chattering together like a message from the damned. What little remained of the cart track snaked away into a darkness so absolute, it felt like I was looking directly at the end of the world.

Across the barn, a battered old staircase led on up to what looked to be a decrepit mezzanine balcony that stretched over our heads along the front of the structure. The man with the flashlight looked up at it, then at me.

'Take her up there,' he barked at the men still holding onto me. 'Make sure she's secure. I don't want her doing anything without my say so.'

'She's just a whore. What could she do?' The guy beside me laughed.

'A lot more than I'm willing to allow. Don't underestimate her.'

With a snort of disbelief, the man beside me hauled me forwards. His grip was vice-like. His manner that of a worker, hauling his load where it needed to go. No thought for the life he was condemning. No consideration for the thoughts running through his victim's mind. No idea of the plans that were formulating.

The stairs wailed their complaints as we made our way up them. The wind was ever more fierce at the top. The cracks were much more extensive, which allowed free passage of strong, unconquerable wind. Massive wooden beams propped up what remained of the roof. Time had not been kind to them. Wood rot had worked through every inch of the ancient supports, rendering them practically obsolescent. My captor eyed them cautiously. One wrong move and they would tumble down like matchsticks. *Don't underestimate her.*

He listened to his colleague's words and chose the only other option at his disposal. To the right of the closest support was an old cable drum. The wire that had spooled around it was long since gone. His hand still clutched around mine, he edged forwards and gave it a kick. It didn't fall apart. Made of stronger stuff.

Surviving his meagre examination, the guy smiled and yanked me forwards. Once again, my legs trailed behind me. The tape around my ankles robbed me of any dignity, and I fell down beside the drum.

'Hurry it up.' The man with the flashlight called out from down below. 'They'll be here soon.'

His colleague snorted at the comment and pulled me up so that my back was up against the drum. The wood was soaked through. I could feel the bitter cold seeping into my back, sending shivers up my spine. The man looked around. In the dim light, he looked young, maybe not far off my own age. He wore a grey woollen hat pulled low to cover his hair and ears, leaving only his eyebrows, and a pencil-thin moustache across his upper lip to determine what colour his hair was. Dark brown, or perhaps black. The light was too dim.

Pencil-lip looked around, searching for something. I guessed he wanted something to tie me up. *Don't underestimate her.* But the old abandoned barn left little to satisfy his demands. With my arms and legs bound, my chances of escape were slim. And with my mouth covered, I couldn't let him know that fact either. On the wall beside me, a pair of rickety wooden shutters clapped enthusiastically against the window frame. The noise was loud enough to infuriate the young man, which only served to sever his patience.

Eventually, Pencil-lip settled on a length of rusted chain. It dangled precariously from one of the pulleys up in the rafters. He heaved the remnants of the chain up, and wrapped them twice around my waist, finishing off with a simple loop of the chain. Maybe he wasn't taking the job seriously enough.

'Don't go anywhere.' He said with a smirk.

I played along to his game, pretending to struggle against my restraints, before conceding defeat. He gave another, obnoxious snort, then hustled back downstairs to his band of brothers.

From my position, I could make out what was going on down below. All four of Reyes's men hurried about in preparation. An overturned table was recovered, along with three chairs. The gas lamps were moved strategically around the barn in an attempt to dispel the darkness.

As they busied themselves, I got to work. Mercifully, my captors had not tied my hands behind my back. An error on their part. Even though the wind raged noisily, I moved with as much care as I could muster. Quietly, I raised up my legs, tucking them up towards my arms. As soon as they were in range, I began to pick at the tape. It was robust, industrial stuff. Designed to hold together until the bitter end.

But I couldn't wait for the bitter end. I had things to do.

Down below, the men talked. Their voices were lower than a shout. In normal circumstances, their words would have carried with ease. But over the constant racket of the storm, I could barely make out a single word. I kept my eye out on Pencil-lip. His body language was more excited than the others. His attention kept falling back to the caves, and their enticing, intoxicating blackness. The man with the flashlight caught him gazing and slapped him on the arm. The pair talked quietly. Pencil-lip looked agitated. Obviously, not getting his way.

A flash of light caught my eye. Not from indoors. It was only momentary, but as I turned to inspect it, I saw a pair of distant headlights disappear through a gap in the barn wall. I moved my head, trying to get a better look, but the vehicle had already moved out of sight.

My fingers had made some progress on the tape. Working at a minuscule pace, I worked the thick adhesive apart with my nails. A small tear appeared. I stretched it out until there was enough leeway to rip the rest apart in one go. I pulled my feet free and stretched them out in relief. The tightness had forced my ankle bones to rub, and the skin was painfully sore.

The headlights appeared again, this time much closer. Beams of light pierced the multitude of cracks in the barn's defences, drawing the attention of the men down below. Pencil-lip moved to look through the door as the others hastened to finish their tasks. The vehicle came to a stop as close to the barn as it could get, and over the howling wind, I heard the engine shut down.

Below, the barn door was forced open once more, and the whole structure shook as another strong gust forced its way inside. Seconds later, it closed, and I could make out the sounds of several new guests reeling from the assault of wind and rain. I peered down over the side of the mezzanine to see who the newcomers were. They wore large raincoats with hoods pulled up tight.

They shuffled over to the hastily prepared table. Whoever they were, I figured they were the guests the man with the flashlight had mentioned. Accompanying them were a further two men. They were similar to the guys Reyes had sent me with. Their clothes were dark and casual and all too ill-prepared for such a tumultuous storm. The coats of the three guests looked new. They were big, bulky items that had not yet been worn in. The hoods restricted the movements of those wearing them. With robotic movements, they lowered themselves into the three chairs. They shivered with a near pantomime level of eccentricity. They were not used to this.

With my legs free, I moved to my hand restraints. The chains tied around me were loose enough that I felt confident I could break out of them easily enough. With only my hands bound and my mouth tied, I could at least conjure up some form of escape should I need to. Layer after layer of the black tape bound my arms together just above the wrists. Again, it was tight, but it's positioning granted me an opportunity. I pressed my hands together like I was praying, and worked my elbows outwards. It made short work of the restraints, unable to fight against the might of an adrenaline-fuelled body, and soon I had enough space to wriggle one hand free.

I cast the tape aside and propped myself up on my knees to improve my view of the ground floor. The guest seated in the middle had pulled back his hood. He was Asian. His short, greying hair appeared wiry. As he turned to survey his surroundings properly, I caught sight of his face. Like the barn he sat in, time had worn into his features.

'How long will he be?' He snapped to no one in particular. Even his voice showed signs of age.

'He is coming.' Said the man with the flashlight, matching the volume of the Asian. 'The storm has complicated things, but I assure you he is on his way.'

The Asian spat something in his native tongue. It seemed to rile Pencil-lip.

'I assure you,' the man with the flashlight said again. 'Everything is on track. The storm is working in our favour. The cops will be too busy cleaning up the mess to worry about us.'

'I would have expected a better reception from a man with such experience.' The Asian yapped. 'Don't you Americans know how to treat your guests?'

'If you would like, we can move deeper inside?' Flashlight man said, gesturing towards the mouth of the cave. The Asian eyed it suspiciously.

'Is it safe?' He asked.

'Safer than here. And you can spend the time inspecting the cargo.'

That elicited a grotesque, perverse smile on the Asian's face. Like a child in a sweet shop, he nodded, and shook his colleagues to stand. They did so, removing their hoods to reveal two more Asian faces. Both were younger than the man in the middle. Both lacked the same level of grandeur and commanded less respect from the other men.

With a nod, they followed Pencil-lip and the Flashlight man towards the foreboding cave entrance. The flashlight penetrated the still blackness. Its light cast off jagged, dripping stone walls, revealing its contents, but not its secrets. The five men, followed by another two of Reyes' goons set off into the shadows, and within seconds they were gone.

FORTY-SIX

CLEANING UP

CHAVEZ WOKE ME WITH A KICK TO THE SHIN. I DIDN'T REALISE I'D fallen asleep. The day had been a long and torturous one, but I'd suffered worse before and managed to stay alert. Perhaps it was the lack of coffee. Maybe the shock that my pride and joy had been destroyed in a firefight. No. The club was replaceable, and coffee didn't have that kind of hold on me. It was the uncertainty that had drained me. I needed to know she was safe.

I rubbed my eyes and looked up at Chavez's stupid smirking face. Didn't want to think about how long he'd stood there watching over me.

'Had enough beauty sleep?' He sneered. His mood had lifted since his impromptu promotion. No longer was he the obedient dog that had eagerly lapped up every command I threw his way. The man that stood before me was the real deal. The resentful snake. Darkness flickered in his eyes.

'Didn't your momma ever tell you staring is rude?' I snarled, stifling a yawn. 'Or was she too busy turning tricks to care about you?'

'The boss has a job for you. He wants you to clean up.'

He was damn near euphoric with joy, like a schoolyard bully preparing their latest victim. So was that the plan? Embarrass and demean until I begged for death. It wasn't beyond what I'd seen of Reyes in the past to imagine that was exactly what he wanted. I'd seen him force a man to eat raw sewage straight from the pipe. It had not been a sight I quickly forgot.

I climbed up out of the armchair and stretched my aching muscles. Chavez clapped his callused hand around my arm and pushed me towards the door.

Somehow, outside was much, much worse. No sooner had one of Chavez's goons swung open the side door did I feel the full might of the storm. Feeling as dead as a dog, it was almost enough to knock me off my feet. Without Chavez's unwilling support, I might just have. The sky was completely black. Even the near permanent light pollution that radiated into the atmosphere had subdued. Rain plummeted out from the darkness. Every last drop felt like being pelted with footballs.

The Chevy was parked in the same spot. Chavez flung the rear passenger door open and thrust me inside and climbed in behind the wheel, with one of his goons taking the passenger seat. A final man slid in beside me, shuffling close like an overeager teenager on a first date.

'You going to tell me where it is we're going?' I asked as I slid away to regain some space, and dignity.

'Don't be so impatient.' Chavez snorted. 'You'll find out soon enough.' He was hiding something, and whatever it was, I knew it wouldn't be good.

Chavez reversed the Chevy out into the empty, rain-swept street, and headed off into the blackness. I checked the time on the dash. Quarter to five in the morning, and the city was quiet. People weren't stupid. The warnings had been there, and they'd listened. Everyone with half a brain would bury deep. Only the brave would venture out. The brave and the stupid.

Chavez certainly fell into that latter category. He twisted through the empty streets toward his destination. I just hoped wherever that was, it was someplace indoors. I couldn't take another minute of this goddamn rain. The radio crackled and hissed as the antenna struggled for some reception. Nothing doing. Chavez switched it off and we all tuned in to the endless beat of a billion tiny drums.

I tried to switch off again. The feeling in my gut was one I'd worked hard to suppress. Fear did nothing in this business. I zeroed in on the sound of the rain, trying to force my mind to make some kind of sense of it. But it was useless. My mind was stuck on one thing. Lisbeth. Wherever she was, she was in danger. Whether it was the weather, or what lurked in it. Both were just as dangerous as a bullet to the head.

THE FATE OF GLASS

I wasn't sure how long the journey took. Time made little sense in the eye of the storm. A currency best spent in the light of day. Even as Chavez pulled over behind a row of abandoned, stationary vehicles, I couldn't tell where exactly we were. Didn't take long to rectify that.

The Jackson Memorial Hospital was dead ahead. Illuminated windows glowed like dying beacons in the treacherous night. Through them, I could just make out the moving shapes of hospital employees, no doubt dealing with the ensuing chaos. What the hell were we doing here?

Chavez could practically read the question on my face.

'Like I said, we're cleaning up a mess. Your mess. Come on, let's go.' He said as he opened the door and climbed out. The goons followed suit, leaving me to climb out. I chose to get out before I was forced out. Needed the win, however small it may be. The wind and rain got right back to it, hammering down on me like rounds from a Kalashnikov. I raised my hand to block what I could from hitting my face and followed. Chavez headed for the main entrance, unfazed by the weather. I figured this was as good as any time to make a break for it, but curiosity won through. Whatever reason they had for bringing me here, I wanted to see it for myself.

We crossed the threshold to be met by the immediate turmoil of an emergency service buckling under some serious pressure. The waiting area was packed to the limit, with more bustling in, in a near constant stream. Hospital staff hustled around like headless chickens. Too few for too many. The commotion offered us the perfect disguise. Four men amongst fifty hardly stood out. I followed Chavez as he led his men through the reception and into the beating heart of the hospital. The corridors were no less busy. Chavez came to a stop and turned to address his troops.

I cut in before he could speak. All about the little wins.

'Listen, Chavez,' I started, savouring the flare of anger in his eyes. 'I've had enough of your shit here. I'm not one of your precious goons. You better tell me exactly what it is we're doing here.'

Chavez smiled again. I wanted to slap it right off his face.

'Always so impatient,' he sneered. 'I was just about to tell you.'

'Then get on with it.'

Another pause from the younger man. He drank the moment up like a hot coffee.

'You know what? I think I'll wait and let you see for yourself.' He said. 'What with it being *your* mess.'

'Listen here you little shit...' But I stopped as soon as one of Chavez's goons slapped his hand on my chest. He was a huge guy, like Bigfoot. Looked as smart as Bigfoot too.

'Jackson, you better get this straight before you get yourself into trouble.' Chavez said. From the hem of his pants, he pulled out his Beretta and pointed it right at my gut. Bigfoot kept his hand on my chest. 'You ain't in charge no more. That ship has sailed. If you do as you're told, you might see this night through. If not, you're going to get real acquainted with your guts when I cut them out and make you hold them.'

I didn't doubt his threat was anything but genuine. I'd seen the guy do much worse. My silence was all the answer he needed. Chavez put the Beretta back in his pants. Bigfoot removed his hand and stepped away.

'Good.' Chavez smiled. 'Now, all we need to do is find Jackson's mess. You two, go that way.' He said, gesturing to his goons to head left. 'I don't want this punk out of my sight.' He looked right at me. 'If you find anything, you call, okay?'

The two men nodded and shuffled away, leaving me with Chavez. They knew the deal too. The deck was rigged, and they were waiting to drop a royal flush on my ass. I'd seen it before. I'd played the hand myself in the past, which meant I knew what the score was.

A hunt.

How wasn't my concern, yet. But the realisation did fill me with a little more confidence. While I had always tried to keep myself clean, Reyes had forced me to get my hands dirty. Their faces still haunted my dreams from time to time. But if I needed to pull the trigger, then I could pull the trigger. What bothered me was the who of it.

We followed the flow of the building around until we came to a directional map. Coloured lines snaked along the floor, navigating lost souls to their destination. Chavez studied the map and decided on the yellow route. As we moved away, I glanced up at the map. Yellow led to the intensive care unit. Intensive care?

The deeper into the hospital we moved, the worse the situation got. Doctors, nurses, and in some cases, patients raced around, lost in their personal traumas. Very few gave us so much as a glance as they rushed by. The show had only just begun. How much worse would it get as the world turned to shit?

We found the ICU in minutes. The yellow line led us all the way to the swinging double doors. The room was a large space about the size of a gym hall. Green curtains surrounded busy beds, creating small secluded areas for the sick and dying patients inside to suffer in solitude. Their coughs and cries set my skin on edge. The smell of death, decay and disinfectant hit me like a right hook and left me reeling. Chavez scrunched his face up, making him look more like a pit-bull than usual. It was not an improvement.

He glared at me.

'Make a scene, and I'll slit your throat.' He snarled.

A limp threat. I wasn't planning on drawing attention to us by throwing a damn hissy fit. And there was nothing he could throw my way that would make me give a damn. He moved right, and I followed. We headed straight for the first curtain. Chavez peered through, but whoever was inside wasn't his concern. We moved on to the next, and the next. Each getting the same level of disinterest from the psychopath. We checked every cubicle. Nothing doing.

At the end of the room, another set of double doors led on to the central ICU area. Through the windowed doors, I could see permanent fixtures built with bricks and mortar. Another wave of busy staff hustled around, tending to the sick. Chavez lumbered through, and the search began again.

The first room we came to had the blinds shut, but a quick look through the door was all Chavez needed to know it wasn't the room he wanted. He moved on to the next room.

That was when everything changed. Like a binary switch. Ones became zeroes. Light became darkness. A sudden and irreversible shift in my entire goddamn life. The cruel, twisted smile that crept across Chavez's face was all I needed to know that my life would never be the same again. He beckoned me over and pointed towards the figure resting on the bed.

I had known her almost her entire life. She had grown up right before my eyes, transforming from the awkward teenage girl into a beautiful, confident woman. I had lived seventeen long years with her in my life, yet only one with her by my side. I'd seen every side of her, felt every struggle, rode the highs, and suffered the lows.

But there she lay, still as a corpse. My Lisbeth. My B.

FORTY-SEVEN

PURGATORY

I SAT IN THE RENTAL CAR ACROSS THE STREET FROM THE HOSPITAL. Seat reclined. Engine off. Alone in the dark. Practically invisible. The sheer ferocity of rain distorted the vehicle's windows. No one was going to spot me lurking there in a hurry, not that there was anyone about to be offered the chance. The weather was far too unpleasant to warrant so much as a single person outdoors without significant purpose.

'She's not safe in there. Neither of them are.'

The Wolf was worried. His agitation buzzed like a swarm of angry bees off in my peripheral. It was a new shade to his personality. The fear. The need to protect. For the first time, he was more like a Wolf than he had ever been before. I channelled my fear into him. Let him soak it all up like an emotional sponge. If he knew, I couldn't tell. He sat beside me in the passenger seat and anxiously eyed the entrance to the ER ward. His fear focused my mind. It became his responsibility, not mine. It freed me up to stay alert. It widened my field of view. For once, we worked together. We shared the load.

'Don't get used to it, James.'

By now, the police would know what had gone down at the hotel. They would probably have the license plate, and the doctors would have alerted them to their new patient. The dots would eventually connect, and once more the hunt would resume. But for now, a little part of me felt safe.

But was Quinn? It had taken a long time for me to climb out of the static swamp in my head. Quinn would be in surgery. A team of surgeons working to undo the damage her psychopathic father had done, and it would be some time before her fate would be sealed. Until then we were trapped in the space between spaces. A purgatory of uncertainty.

I tried to take my mind off it. A task that was easier said than done. I needed a distraction, but in a stationary car rocking in the tumultuous weather, there was little to occupy a preoccupied mind. I fiddled with dials, hoping that something would beep or whir or send me through a magical wormhole where all my problems didn't exist. But there was nothing. Even the car wanted to punish me with my thoughts.

'You can't blame yourself for this.' Said the Wolf. 'You'd have never left Reyes alone if you thought he was capable of this.'

'I didn't think you were capable of empathy.' I replied, not moving my head. 'That's certainly a new colour on you.'

'There's that classic James Stone avoidance technique.'

'What am I supposed to say? I absolutely should have expected this from Reyes. It's what he does. It's what everyone warned me about. I shouldn't have just left him alone. I should have never let him out my sight for a second. I underestimated him. That's on me.'

I looked at the dash. The time was quarter to five in the morning. Had I really been here that long? I wasn't sure if that was too much time, or too little. How long does it take to stitch a person back together? Quinn was no doll. You couldn't just sew the surface and leave the stuffing beneath well enough alone. I had no idea what kind of internal damage she had suffered. I didn't even know if she was still alive.

'We did everything we could,' the Wolf insisted. 'Nicole and Quinn are alive. They're going to survive. I can feel it.'

I let out a long, exhausted sigh. Nothing made much sense anymore. Not in my personal purgatory. Not life. Not time. I felt like I was trapped at the epicentre of a ticking clock, right where the hands joined. Time had no meaning there. Quarter to five was the same as twenty past eight, or five to three, or bang on midnight. It was just another bullshit concept. Right next to the clock on the dash was the odometer. The number displayed was at forty-nine thousand, nine hundred and ninety-nine miles. Of course it was. What a wonderfully irritating coincidence.

'We need to start thinking about the next phase of the plan.' The Wolf continued to no avail.

Just one mile off a nice, clean round number. Fifty thousand. Probably less. Probably half a mile. Probably a quarter.

'James, stop looking at the numbers and talk to me.'

Probably not even a quarter. Probably right on the turning point. Teetering on the edge. The car was parked on a slight hill, leading down to a T junction right outside the entrance to the ER ward. I could coast down and tick it over.

'And what will that achieve?' the Wolf snapped. *'Just leave it alone and think. We can't wallow in the past, we need to figure out where Reyes has gone.'*

I pulled the handbrake and lifted my foot off the brake. The car inched forwards, picking up a little momentum the further it rolled.

'Or is the plan just to let him go? Are you finally admitting defeat?'

We reached the turn. The clock didn't budge. I squeezed the brake and swore.

'James, Eva is still out there. We need a strategy. We need to figure out how to save her.'

I fired up the engine and reversed back up the hill to the spot I'd parked. Then I repeated the roll down the hill.

'Have you lost your fucking mind?' The Wolf shouted in my ear.

The clock ticked over. Fifty thousand. I stamped on the brake.

'Obviously, I have.' I said, not looking at the figment of my imagination. *'But it doesn't help to have you berate me.'*

'Then think.' He snapped. *'Stop indulging these small delights and think.'*

But I wasn't listening to him. I was looking at the car that had just pulled up alongside the hospital. It was a silver SUV. Four men got out and moved to the hospital entrance. Three of the men I didn't recognise. One of them I did.

Which could only spell bad news.

Felix Jackson didn't look my way. Nor did any of the other men he was with. He just raised his hand up to shield some of the rain from his face and marched onwards like the good little soldier he was. If Reyes had sent him here, I had a pretty good idea what their purpose was. Reyes wasn't in the business of giving second chances.

I wished Nicole had a phone. I needed to know what was going on inside. I doubted she would be sat right by Quinn's side. Not in the condition either woman had entered in. Nicole was just too weak. My actions had nearly killed both of them. I couldn't stand by and let it all be for nothing.

I had to warn someone. I had to save Quinn.

I waited until the last man was through the automatic double doors before I leapt out and ran. The rain was relentless, and in a matter of seconds I was completely drenched, again. I slowed to a furtive stride only as I neared the door. Didn't want to arouse suspicion by sprinting into the building. My clothes were bloodstained, but if I was going to walk into anywhere looking like this, an ER ward was about as ideal a locale as I was going to get. Second only to a busy street on Halloween.

The first thing to hit me was just how busy the hospital was. The main impact of the storm had yet to arrive, but already the hospital was packed to breaking point. Signs on the walls warned that antisocial behaviour towards staff would not be tolerated. I wondered what the policy was for people coming to murder patients. Probably equally frowned upon.

I felt exposed. I had to be all over the news. Between the events at the nightclub and ensuing getaway, I had given the news outlets plenty of chances to revisit my story. Luckily for me, there was no television in the lobby, and the patients looked too consumed in their own issues to care about a newcomer.

I scanned the crowd for Felix and his cohorts. I spotted one of the bigger guys up ahead. For men of such large stature, they had weaved through the throng of sickly stragglers with ease. I kept my eyes locked on the giant guy's head as I attempted to replicate their passage, but it would have been easier to imitate Moses in the red sea. There were just so many people, all of whom seemed completely oblivious to my unheard requests to pass by.

I squeezed and slithered my way to the other side. Naturally, Felix and his men had not waited for me to catch up. The hospital narrowed down into a series of interwoven corridors. I looked around, searching for the big guy. His size made him a useful beacon. I thought I saw him duck through a door down the corridor to the left.

I followed suit. The hospital was full of activity. Doctors, nurses and patients shuffled about like the living dead, busy with a myriad of problems. No eyes rested longer than necessary on my weary face. No flash of recognition on their faces. A hospital had to be pretty low on the list of places a hunted criminal would go. Nevertheless, I couldn't stay dressed in my current state for long. Bloodied, sodden clothes stood out enough to get noticed eventually, and the stench was nauseatingly potent. I hustled over to the door the big guy had taken and slipped inside.

I tried to piece together a narrative in my head. We had dropped Quinn off hours ago. Depending on the severity of her wounds, she could still be in surgery. If all had gone well, she could be in a room under supervision. At worst, she was in the morgue.

Only two of those places would be worth my time, and only one would be easily accessible. Established, respectable men Felix's goons were not, which meant they weren't getting into the surgery room without drawing maximum agro.

They had to have come to that conclusion too. They weren't dressed to impress, so that option was off the table. That would also explain the timing of their arrival. No reason to linger around causing a scene while Quinn was patched up, when they could arrive afterwards and clean shop.

I followed the duo through the busy corridors, trying to stay as inconspicuous as possible for a wanted man drenched in blood. They weaved to and fro, occasionally stopping to peer through the reinforced windows built into patient room doors. Wherever Quinn was, she wasn't there.

The itch to change clothes was too much. It was damn near suicidal to keep wandering around in such an obvious state. Someone could have easily called the cops by now. That would certainly put a dampener on the evening.

I scanned the plaques dotted around for signs of a staff room. It wouldn't be the first time I'd fooled the world as a doctor. It stood to reason it would work again. Felix's men didn't seem to mind. They idled along, glancing around for Quinn. The fact they had split up was a worry. It made sense from their perspective to cover more ground faster. But it meant my chances were down by precisely fifty percent. Not good odds in any situation.

Up ahead, a sign hanging from the ceiling detailed the points of interest. Down the corridor was the Intensive Care ward. To the left was the cafeteria, and to the right was one of the wards. Felix's men had headed right. I went left.

'What are you doing?' the Wolf snapped. *'You got some secret shortcut you want to share?'*

I ignored him, not wanting to draw any more attention by being a crazy person. The cafeteria meant food, which meant people, and the last time I'd checked, doctors were people. It stood to reason that some form of staff room would be nearby. No need to waste the precious time of the busy doctor by making him walk further to the cafeteria than necessary.

Sure enough, I found it adjacent to the cafeteria doors. The sign by the door was small. Probably a design choice to deter needy patients from loitering around outside, and it was unlocked. I pushed it open and slid in. The room inside was long and thin, with a row of back to back lockers almost spanning the width of it, and benches running from wall to wall along both sides. At the far end was a tiled washroom. The room was maybe forty foot wide. Not huge, but manageable. Down at the far end, a man wrapped in a towel was busy checking his phone. He paid me no mind, so I scuttled around to the other side of the lockers before I piqued his interest.

A woman dressed in grey scrubs lay flat across the bench with her arm over her head. She looked completely exhausted. Tuckered out from what was undoubtedly a rough evening. Tucked in the corner, a hamper rested on top of a trolley. It was about half full of dirty scrubs of varying colours. Or half empty, depending on your frame of mind.

Either way, it was perfect.

Carefully, I picked out a pair of purple scrubs that looked to be about my size and rested them on the bench. I pulled off my hoodie and dumped it in the basket under the scrubs.

'They're getting away,' the Wolf said.

'Then keep an eye out.' I replied, pulling the purple top over my head.

'Newsflash, genius, I'm part of your subconscious. I can't see anything you can't see.'

'Astonishingly, that revelation had dawned on me.'

'Just hurry up, will you?'

I pulled the purple trousers over my own to save time and took one final search in the wash basket for a scrubs cap. I found one coloured grey that barely fit my head, but it would do. Anything to mask my appearance. I tucked my damp hair up inside it and headed for the door.

I hustled back to the crossroads. Now the ICU was on my right, and the ward was straight on. Felix's men had headed in that direction, but in the interlude, they could have gone anywhere. By now, they could be racing out to their car, satisfied with a job well done.

But until I had confirmation, I wouldn't give that thought any traction. I had to assume they were still inside.

But which way? Just because they had gone to the ward, it didn't mean they were still there. It could have taken seconds to realise the error, and turn back and head in another direction. I didn't know where Quinn was, nor Nicole. Either could be resting in one of the many patient wards the hospital had to offer on any of the numerous floors. Every decision I could make was a gamble.

I made a snap decision and headed forward in the direction I'd last seen Felix's men. Yet the itch of uncertainty remained.

FORTY-EIGHT

FIGHT BACK

THE SMELL OF CHLORINE HUNG IN THE WARD LIKE A CRIMINAL. The stench put me on high alert. The Wolf too. I could feel his presence stronger than ever, like a fellow soldier right beside me in battle. It felt good to have him there, for once. We marched, side by side, toward our enemies.

Once a long, narrow room with a dozen or so beds spaced evenly out along the walls, the ward had transformed to meet the needs of demand. The number of occupants looked to have doubled, at least. Bed-ridden patients separated only by thin green curtains packed in tight like large, sickly sardines. Doctors and nurses jostled about, tending to their patient's needs. Their moans and sufferings echoed out over an insufferable and unending rhythm of beeping machines and ringing telephones. It was an anxiety-sufferer's nightmare.

In a sea of people, I was invisible.

There were no signs of Felix or his companions. Only a handful of curtains were shut, but I doubted Quinn would have been left in such an exposed location after extensive surgery. Even so, I couldn't keep wandering around like a lost lamb. I moved through the ward. Eyes searching.

In a small gap between the line of beds to the right was a cluttered nurse's desk. A panicked male nurse tapped at a computer keyboard like his life depended on it. Behind him was a small alcove. Shelves of bottled drugs lined the small recess. An idea flickered into my mind.

'I like the way you think.' Said the Wolf.
'Just keep a lookout.'
'Still can't see anything you can't, genius.'

The trick to getting in places is confidence, and never is that fact more prevalent than in a hospital. Doctors and nurses are the most hard-working people I'd ever met. They were quite literally the best of the best, but that kind of commitment came at a price. They don't have time to deal with the cascade of trivial problems continually falling their way, and I am a master of the problematic.

In my scrubs, there was little else I needed to do to uphold the façade. With a doctorly haste, I strode confidently towards the counter and slid in behind the male nurse. His attention was split between the phone stuck to his ear, and the spreadsheet open on his computer monitor, neither of which looked to be a treat. I squeezed into the recess and glanced over the selection of drugs available.

Despite my appearance, my knowledge of medical mumbo-jumbo was seriously lacking. I don't know my 'oralites from my 'odeines, so I stuck to what I did know. I looked for the coup de grâce. Can't go wrong with a bit of good old-fashioned Morphine. Named after the Greek God of dreams, Morpheus. It was easy enough to find. There were dozens of patients on the ward that would be doped up on it right now. I snatched a bottle from the shelf, and picked up a sterile syringe packet from a lower shelf, and drew up a dose. I pocketed the bottle and sheathed my syringe, and moved back out from behind the counter.

Back on the hunt. I scanned the face of every doctor, nurse and patient I could see. None were recognisable, and with every passing moment, the sense of unease grew. I turned the syringe in my pocket, feeling the clammy warmth from my palms on the plastic casing. I followed the narrow gangway along and into another room. It too was packed to bursting point, and it too showed no signs of progress.

I kept going, because turning back felt like failure, and failure meant Quinn's death. I picked up the pace. Through the ward and out the other side. Another corridor, at least this time I only had one available route. I broke into a run. Every step felt like I was moving further and further away from my goal. I hadn't been that long getting changed. The two men couldn't have searched the ward and moved on, could they? And what about Felix and the other guy. They had to know where Quinn was. They had to be there already. Thoughts bubbled up and over the surface until I could barely think.

I came to a stop and planted my back up against the wall, desperate for so much as a shred of clarity.

'You need to get it together.' The Wolf snapped.

'I don't know what to do.'

'Then take a breath and think. You can't let fear get to you.'

He was right. I took my hand off the syringe and ran my fingers through my hair, closed my eyes, and took a deep breath. Counted to five in my head. Then opened my eyes.

A shred of clarity. More than a shred, actually.

Across from my spot on the wall was a door. Through the meshed glass porthole I could see another ward, and through the swarm of people was one big, lumbering beacon. The giant. Not many people of his height and size would casually wander around a hospital at this hour. I kicked off the wall and pushed open the door.

He was not alone. The second, shorter man waddled along nearby. Their apparent nonchalance distinguished them from every other person in the room. They worked in unison, on either side of the ward. One taking the left, the other the right. They moved from curtain to curtain, checking those who rested inside. Searching for Quinn.

'They don't know where she is.' The Wolf whispered in my ear.

And if they were still checking, surely it meant Felix didn't know either. Maybe luck was still on my side.

I didn't wait around for that to change. I crossed over to the bigger guy. Figured he was best to take down first. The taller ones were always the problem. He was enormous, nearly pushing seven foot, and broad enough to pull it off. Practically a giant. The guy was a statistical anomaly. Only a couple thousand people in the world fit that bill, and I was staring one in the back.

A swarm of doctors burst into the room, surrounding a gurney. The patient was not Quinn, but instead an overweight teenage boy. His face was blue and scrunched up in agony. I watched the giant turn his attention to the boy, saw a smirk dance across his face.

The doctors raced across the room to the far end where there was a vacant space. I ducked in behind and ran after them as a disguise, breaking off just behind the giant. He had his hand on the curtain of a closed cubicle. As he swung it open, revealing an elderly lady asleep in her bed, I withdrew the syringe and stuck it into his back. He barely had time to register before I plunged the entire syringe's contents of morphine into his body. He was a big guy. He could take the whole thing.

'What the fu…' he started, before his eyes drooped and he toppled forwards into the cubicle. I caught a fistful of his jacket just in time to stop him going down like a felled tree. He weighed about the same as one though, and dropped in a hurry. The biggest guys always had the worst falls. There was no way he was getting up from that any time soon. The fall didn't wake the woman. She was out for the count too. I heaved the giant onto his side and stuck him in the recovery position. His head was massive. You could cut it off and pretend it was a newly-discovered Easter island artefact and no one would be any the wiser.

I swung the curtain shut and stepped back. The giant's feet were just visible under the curtain. I pushed them in with my foot. I glanced around, checking to see if anyone had heard, but the ward was too busy for my antics.

I skirted around another gurney and filled the syringe up halfway with the bottle of morphine. The fat man had moved on. To where, I wasn't sure. I strode over to the point I'd last seen him last, and drew open the curtain. A young boy attached to a machine sat on the bed. He looked at me with innocent curiosity.

'Hi.' He said.

'Hey there. You feeling okay?' I responded, using my best American accent.

He nodded.

'Good stuff,' I said. 'Keep it up, okay?'

He smiled, and I ducked back out. I checked the next partition, and the next, and the one after that. No signs of Quinn, Nicole or Felix's men. And in the time I'd been on the lookout, the fat guy hadn't reappeared. I moved on to the next room. Again, the curtains were closed. I eased open the curtain, and peered inside. A heavily bandaged patient rested in the bed. Standing beside him was a doctor. He looked up at me inquisitively.

'Yes?' He asked.

'Oh, sorry, wrong patient.' I ducked back out and closed the curtain again. As I closed the door, I saw the flash of suspicion on his face. I didn't want to draw attention to myself. With one criminal unconscious, and at least two wanted felons lurking around, the police were bound to smell action. Time was running short.

I abandoned the cubicle-to-cubicle search and dashed towards the end of the room. Another door led through to a larger, busier room. It was, in many ways, similar to the one before, except that instead of hastily-erected partitions, a series of smaller rooms had been built, each of which had a door, and glass window separating them from the main hall. A glance through the first window told me all I needed to know.

This place was for the severe cases. The people who weren't in for a quick fix, but would need their mail forwarding. The man in the bed before me was hooked up to a dozen machines that staved off the cold hand of death. The chart at the foot of his bed looked thicker than most novels. I left him be and moved on.

Which was when I spotted something strange.

He was standing in the doorway of the room across the ward looking directly at me. The remaining goon. Shorter than the giant, wider around the waist. There was something off about his expression. For a moment, I thought he had recognised me, but in the scrubs, I highly doubted that. Besides, the look on his face was not one of recognition. It was one of shock. His eyes bulged out like a squeezed frog. His mouth wide open like a starved fish. Caught in a petrified rapture. Something dark wrapped around his neck.

That was when I saw her. Standing behind him. Hands gripped tight around her belt.

The anger in Nicole's face was palpable. She squeezed the belt with such ferocity, I could barely believe the guy's head remained in place. She was pulling back, but the sheer size of the man was too much to control. He didn't want to die, and his best chance of survival was to get out in the open.

Unluckily for him, I was in his way. Channelling my inner rugby player, I shouldered the guy in the chest. He tumbled back, throwing Nicole off her feet, and the pair crashed down to the floor. I shut the door behind me with one swift kick and gripped him by the chest.

But there was no point. He was already dead. He stared blankly into the great beyond, never to return. From beneath his large mass, Nicole groaned.

'What the hell?' She gasped.

'You alright?' I asked, heaving the dead man off her.

'Why'd you push him?'

'He was practically out the door. Someone would have seen him if I hadn't.'

'I had it under control.'

I looked her over. Her arm was bandaged, as was her chest. Her hospital gown had patches of blood on it.

'Are you okay?' I asked her.

She nodded. 'The docs gave me something. The good stuff. I

can barely feel my own mouth. They said I came off lightly. If the wound was much deeper, I'd be dead.'

'That's a relief.' I sighed.

'Oh yeah. I'm so relieved I only got stabbed a little.' She snarked. 'Makes everything so much better.'

'That's not what I meant. I'm glad you're okay.'

'Bite me.'

I looked from her to the dead guy. 'How'd you know about him?'

She looked down at the corpse. 'I got a bad vibe.'

'You killed a guy over a bad vibe?'

'No, of course I didn't. Dude burst into my ward a couple of minutes ago with a gun on his belt. I figured he wasn't a cop, so I followed him here. I think he's got a partner.'

'Had a partner.' I corrected, holding up the syringe. 'I was going to do the same to him before you beat me to it.'

'Is that morphine?' she asked. I nodded. 'Can I have some?'

'Maybe later. I need to see Quinn. Is she okay?'

'I haven't seen her. I don't know where she is.'

FORTY-NINE

FINISH THE JOB

CHAVEZ STOOD BEHIND ME, BLOCKING THE DOOR. I FELT HIS HAND on my back push me closer.

Her body was so still, just the meekest of movement in her chest as the mask strapped to her face fed oxygen into her lungs. Her skin, usually so vibrant, was pale and ghostly. An image I had imagined so many times. Too many sleepless nights as I lay beside her and feared that the day might be her last. That she could overdose, and I wouldn't be there to save her. I had tried to help her. I had done everything I could. But she was an addict, and she was unwilling to change. She said she was young. That one day she would kick it for good. But not today. Never today.

She was so small in the bed. Like a balloon left to deflate, she had withered beyond comprehension. I moved closer, so that I was right beside her bed. My mind was a hive of raw emotion and visceral torment that all I could see was her, lying there, so close to death.

'What happened?' I gasped.

'She picked the wrong side.' Chavez snarled, channelling his employer. 'You know the game. Blood is thicker than water. She made her choice.'

Somehow, I pulled my focus from Lisbeth and locked eyes with Chavez.

'What happened?' I asked again, this time slower.

'You failed.' He said. 'You were supposed to kill Stone, but you let him get away. You let him find her, and she helped him find

Reyes. She always was a gullible little bitch. She drank it all up, played her part, and betrayed her pops along the way. But you better be glad Reyes got out of there when he did, otherwise we'd be in a much worse situation right now.'

'I won't ask you again.' I snarled. 'Tell me what happened.'

'They jumped him at the hotel.' Chavez said, looking from Lisbeth to me. 'Faked a fire to flush everyone out. Stone and his bitch got him out of there before the boys could stop them. Locked him up in the bathroom like some fucking prisoner. But he got out, and she got in the way. You don't turn on family. Not unless they ain't your family anymore. Like I said, she made her choice, and you made yours. This is the consequence.'

Reyes. Reyes did this, to his own daughter?

No. Even he couldn't go that far.

Chavez saw the doubt in my eyes.

'He thought you should be the one to come,' the young man leered. 'Given your... history.'

And suddenly, it all made sense. The smug looks. The veiled comments. The reason I was here, all as clear as day.

'How long has Reyes known?' I asked.

'Long enough. You should have known you couldn't hide it from him. Didn't no one ever tell you not to shit where you eat?'

I floated back to her side. Her hand, so frail and fragile, rested atop the sheet. An IV protruded from it, pumping fluids straight into her delicate body. I touched her fingers gently. She was so cold.

'There are two ways this goes. One body bag or two.' Chavez said. He moved away from the door to stand right by my side. 'Reyes is willing to forgive your mistakes, but you got to pay the price, okay?'

To see her like that was more than I could bear, but to know who had caused it filled me with a rage I had never felt before.

And what he expected of me.

Clean your mess.

Oh, I'll clean my goddamn mess.

'You get a parking ticket, you don't ignore the fine, right?' Chavez continued. 'You suck it up and pay your dues. Don't overthink it. Besides, she's dead either way. Why give her a couple extra minutes at the cost of your own life?'

He put his arm on my shoulder like a friend consolidating another. Before the shit eating grin stretched across his face, I gave him all the reason he needed to wipe it straight off. Channelling every single atom of pure, unadulterated power I had, I reached up and snatched his hand from my shoulder and twisted it far beyond the breaking point. The snap of his wrist sounded like a gunshot in the quiet space and dwarfed the gasp of surprise and shock that dribbled from Chavez's mouth.

But I was far from done. With my right foot, I flicked up and kicked his legs out from under him, and like a pair of mighty oak trees, I went crashing down with him.

My hands were around his throat as he hit the ground. Squeezing. Tearing. Ripping him apart. I could feel his trachea through the flesh. I forced my thumbs in deep, crushing everything they came in contact with. With only one working hand, Chavez scratched at my hands. Nails digging into the skin. Not good enough. Nothing would be good enough. No fucking way. I squeezed harder and tighter and stronger and deeper until there was nothing left to work. I glared into the man's eyes. Watched them bulge and panic and slip out of focus. His nails eased up. His hand fell, and slapped lifelessly against the floor.

I didn't let go. Couldn't let go. Didn't care if anyone had heard us fall. Didn't care if anyone was watching me crush his throat. Rage thundered through me. My chest heaved in the pure fury. The jet-stream of oxygen powered in and out until there was nothing left in the room but anger and hatred and fear.

Somewhere a million miles away, I could sense someone standing in the doorway. A doctor or the cops or anyone, I didn't care. Nothing mattered but Chavez's death and Lisbeth's life. The figure didn't move. Just stood and watched.

Finally, I broke away from the corpse and looked up. Not a doctor. Not Bigfoot. Not the cops.

Not who I was expecting.

'Sorry, were you having a moment? Would you like me to come back after you've choked that guy to death?'

It was Stone. James fucking Stone. Beside him was a woman I didn't recognise. I relinquished my grip on Chavez's neck. There was no movement from him. He'd already checked out.

'What do you want?' I snapped, unable to hide the embarrassment at having been caught in such a compromising position.

'I'll cut the sarcasm because you don't look in the mood, and I don't want to end up like that guy,' he replied, looking at Chavez. 'I wanted to make sure she was safe.'

'She will be.' I snapped, standing between them and Lisbeth.

'Are you so sure about that?' He asked. 'It doesn't take a genius to figure out what went down here.'

'I won't let anyone near her,' I snarled. 'You included.'

Together, the pair moved into the room and closed the door behind them.

'You should be thanking me.' Stone persisted. 'I'm the one who brought her here. I saved her life.'

'You put her in danger in the first place.'

'Right, because I was supposed to assume Reyes would try and kill his own daughter, was I? You know what they say about assumptions.'

'You should have kept her out of it.'

'That's pretty rich coming from the man who was dating his boss's daughter on the sly.'

I hit him with a ferocious glare and returned to Lisbeth's side, running my finger across her perfect face. Whether it was the adrenaline running out, or her presence, I didn't know, but I felt the anger trickle out.

'What happened?' I asked. My voice was weaker. Not by choice.

'Reyes got the better of us.' Stone said. 'We had him tied up, but he managed to break loose while I was busy and, well, you can guess the rest.'

Anger burned through me. How could he do that, to his one and only daughter?

'Fucking monster.' I snarled.

'That would be one name for him, yes. But look, Felix, I need your help. You know the guy. I need to know where Reyes is going.'

I looked back up at him. Stone looked like I felt. Dog tired and beat. Yet he wasn't ready to give up. Guess that's how he'd lasted so long.

'You won't catch him.' I said. 'This is his endgame. If he would do this to Lisbeth, after everything he's done to protect her, it means he's finished with this place. Only thing he cares about now is getting his money and getting out of here.'

'From his deal with China?'

That was a shock. Even Lisbeth hadn't known about China.

'What do you know about China?' I asked.

'Not nearly enough.' Was his response. 'I know whatever he's got planned goes down today. I know he's got Eva Marston there, and whatever he's selling is going out by boat. I just need to know where he's meeting.'

I looked up at the clock on the wall. Twenty past five. I shook my head.

'You're too late.' I conceded. 'The drive up there is six hours at least. Longer in this weather, and he has a head start. He'll be out of there before you got close.'

'Where, Felix?'

'Ozello. Hell, you got so damn close I figured you'd have this whole thing worked out already. For all your talk, you a dumb son of a bitch, aren't you?'

I could see him running the numbers through in his mind. A six-hour drive. Reyes was at least four hours ahead. In this weather, that drive could be much longer, for both of them. Was it doable?

'I don't have a choice,' said Stone. 'I need to know everything you know about the deal. How many men has he got there?'

'I'm the wrong guy to ask,' I said with a shrug. 'Got kicked out of the inner circle the moment your little stunt ruined my club. But if Reyes is sending this sack of shit here,' I kicked the corpse on the floor. 'He must be running out of manpower. I'd say six, maybe seven guys, give or take. China only has a small consulate. Three men, although they won't be armed. They might have hired some local clowns to handle the shipment.'

'What about the deal, what is it? Guns, drugs, what?'

But I just smiled.

'Brother, you're better just seeing for yourself. I'm washing my hands of the whole thing. We're all taking the fast track to hell. Least I can do is spend my days repenting.'

'What has he got there?' He pressed.

'You better get going. The end is nigh.'

Stone looked at his girl. She just shrugged. The pair had a silent conversation, just like I used to with B. I turned my attention back to her. I was done. With Stone, with Reyes, with the whole damn world.

'Keep her safe,' Stone said. 'She deserves better than all this.'

You're goddamn right.

Stone and the girl left. I just stood and watched them leave. With three bodies scattered around the hospital, news would quickly spread. At some point, they would find Chavez's body, and that would be it. No point in trying to escape. The world had caught up with me. It was time to take my lumps. And I wouldn't leave her, alone and exposed.

I hauled the visitor's chair around to Lisbeth's side and slumped down in it. This was our moment. Nobody else's. And it was likely our last. At least for a long time. I weaved our fingers together, mine warming hers. I watched her rest. She looked at peace. I was glad. I didn't want her to suffer. Not anymore. Never again. She was here because of me. Because I had failed her.

But I was not the sole proprietor of that blame, and I would not accept full responsibility. Two others shared it. Two others would pay for it.

Domingo Reyes, and James Stone.

I let go of Lisbeth's hand and leaned down to Chavez's body. I fished out the cell from his pocket and dialled a number from memory. Not Reyes. Not any of his men. I pressed the cell to my ear and waited for a response. None came, but that was expected. I knew he wouldn't answer an unknown number. The automated voice asked me to leave a voicemail.

'Ramiro Salazar, this is Felix Jackson. I work… worked for Domingo Reyes, and I've got a way you can settle the score.'

FIFTY

THE STORM

I drove through the night, leaving the city of Miami in our dust. Come what may, I doubted I would return. There was nothing here but bad memories and lost souls. I needed no reminder of that. Beside me, Nicole fidgeted. She twisted the same dials and pushed the same buttons on the rental car's dash that I had earlier. Something was on her mind.

'If you've got something to say, we've got a long drive ahead.' I said.

'Are you sure this is a good idea, going to Ozello? She asked.

'I don't think I've made a single good idea in my adult life. Today isn't the day to change that.'

'I'm being serious, James.'

'It's got a delightful poeticism to it, don't you think?' I said, weaving out into traffic. 'Fighting a nemesis in the heart of a storm. They could make a movie about it.'

'This isn't a game,' she snapped. 'I don't know if this is some kind of coping mechanism for dealing with Quinn, but you have to stop, okay? The storm will tear through the state. Chances are they'll get caught up in it, and then we don't need to worry. We can watch the whole thing on TV from a nice, warm motel room.'

'We can't be sure. Reyes tricked death before. I won't let them do it again. And I can't leave Eva there. I need to help her.'

'But not this way. There's a better way to do it. I know we can figure it out.'

'If you don't want to come, I'll drop you off somewhere.'

'You know I'm not going anywhere,' Nicole huffed. 'Reyes tried to kill me too, remember? I want him dead, just as much as you do.'

'If you did, you wouldn't be trying to stop me.'

'Hey, I've put just as much blood, sweat and tears into this as you have. Probably more.' She said, holding up her bandaged arm. 'Not everything is about you, James. If you want to put your life on the line, at least do it with a plan that's not half-cocked.'

'I can't leave it anymore,' I said. 'This is a golden opportunity. It's not going to come round again. Reyes will burrow himself under a mountain. I'll never see him again. Never. I've suffered too much to let this slide.'

The rain was unrelenting, as was the wind. It buffeted the rental car with incredible strength and forced most of the traffic off the road. I preserved. I had to. Because I couldn't live another day knowing Domingo Reyes walked the Earth.

'You're not thinking straight. There's only two of us, remember? Reyes has at least half a dozen armed guys waiting there. We can't take on an army.'

'She's not wrong, you know.' Said the Wolf.

I thumped the horn and beeped at no one in particular.

'I can't let them win.' I sighed.

'They won't, alright? I won't let them. But we need to do this the right way.'

She fiddled with the radio, searching for something to lighten the mood. There was mostly static. The storm had knocked out all the good stations. She settled on a news broadcast. The female reporter's voice crackled in the poor reception. The biggest story was, of course, the storm. The weather warning had been jacked up to severe, especially across the north of the state of Florida. Citizens who hadn't already evacuated were advised to call a designated hotline. Hundreds of thousands of people upended by Mother Nature. Millions of dollars worth of destruction predicted. Houses decimated. Businesses devastated. Lives lost.

And we were headed right into the centre of it.

'You can't cheat a hurricane,' Nicole said. 'If Reyes is where you think he is, it will get him too. There's nothing like it. It doesn't differentiate gender, race, or power. It will pick him up and throw him into space.'

'He'll find a way.'

'I'm sick of arguing with you. Do what you've got to do, but if I die, I'll haunt your ass into oblivion.'

'Duly noted.'

And with that, the conversation died away. Hours passed. Nicole rested in the passenger seat. With the heater on to the max, our rain-soaked clothes slowly dried. The heat helped Nicole to doze. Her wounds were too fresh to put up much of a fight.

We drove into the darkness. Wind buffeted the car to and fro across the road, making every mile a struggle to stay on course. The only thing in my favour was the fact that almost every citizen of Florida had taken the hint and hidden indoors. Occasionally, I spotted the flashing lights of stationary police cars. Some were tending to roadside accidents, some parked in a meagre attempt to block traffic from continuing. I paid all no mind. No one was going to chase an idiot in this kind of weather.

Dawn came, although you'd be hard-pressed to notice. The thick blanket of black clouds masked any attempts the sun could make to break through. Unless it was actually gone. Perhaps it was the apocalypse. The end wasn't nigh. It was now. The rain was so thick, it hung like a dreadful fog in the air, reducing visibility down to a couple of metres in front of the car. I kept the rental steady, using the map Nicole had found to guide me back up the state. With every passing hour, the weather grew worse, growing from treacherous into downright suicidal territory.

When we were an hour away, Nicole woke. I watched her rub the sleep from her eyes and look around, lost in the momentary lapse of recognition. It came back to her soon enough.

'You okay?' I asked her.

'Fine and dandy.'

'How's your arm?'

'Hurts like some lunatic stabbed me. Are you going to give me some of that morphine?

'Maybe after we win.'

'You better do. How's the nose?'

I'd almost forgotten about my nose. My last interaction with Reyes. The bleeding had stopped before I made it to the hospital. The pain was little more than a dull ache. Pretty low on the scale of other injuries.

'I hear chicks dig a scar. I'll be fine.'

'They don't dig broken noses.'

'Too bad. They don't know what they're missing out on.'

'How far out are we?'

'Another hour and we should be there. The roads have been

dead. Managed to stay over the speed limit for most the way. Hopefully, it's enough.'

'Hopefully.'

I glanced over at her. Saw the look on her face. She was biting her lip, deep in contemplation.

'What is it?' I asked.

'Why haven't you asked about the money?'

'What about it?'

'You haven't asked if I moved it. I was gone for hours getting the money for Vinnie. I could have done anything with it. Anything at all. Why didn't you ask?'

I bit my tongue.

'I wanted you to find me.' I said finally. 'That's why I took it. I wanted to see if you could track me down.'

'Bullshit.'

'It was never about the money. I didn't come to America by choice, and I didn't help you by accident. I wanted to help you. I wanted to do something good for a change. After everything that happened, I wanted to ask you to come with me, but I knew your uncle would never allow it.'

'You could have just asked me if you wanted me to come.' She said.

'Like you'd have come with me otherwise. I know what that money means to you, to Bobbie. I knew that by taking it I was going to be on your shit list. I knew it would spur you to come and find me. I'm not going to say that a couple million dollars wouldn't help my cause, but it was you who I wanted to see again.'

'That is one convoluted way of asking a girl on a date.'

'Look, whatever you've done with the money, I just want you to know that I'm glad you're helping me. It really means a lot to me knowing you're by my side.'

'I'd blush if I had the blood to spare.'

We laughed. It felt good to do something fun. The next few hours would likely be some of the hardest either of us had ever seen.

'Hey,' I said as the laughter subsided. 'You want to hear a riddle?'

'Sure.'

'What's the one thing that you eat that eats you back?'

She looked at me.

'You're kidding.'

'What?'

'A pineapple. It's the Bromelain enzyme in them that breaks down proteins in your body after you eat them. You know I was the one who taught you that, right?'

'Did you?'

'You ass. I absolutely was the one who told you. How many people have you been using that on like it's your own fact?'

'I completely forgot.'

'Dick.'

The radio crackled into life again. The female reporter's voice broadcasting intermittently through the storm. Only fragments made it through, but they told the story well enough.

'...the scene of a brutal attack in the early hours of the morning... a woman stabbed repeatedly... James Stone was sighted... still at large...'

'They think you're responsible.' Nicole sighed, switching the radio off.

'Let them. It doesn't change anything.'

'You can't let them put it on you,' she said. 'They have to know it was Reyes.'

'Why, what difference will it make? They think I'm a terrorist. I've got enough blood on my hands.'

'That's a horrible way to think.'

'Reyes will pay. He won't see the inside of a courtroom. There'll be no one left to stand and testify.'

'Quinn will. She won't let them put this on you.'

'But it is my fault. I didn't do the deed, but she's in hospital because of me. I dragged her into all this.'

'James, speaking as someone who's seen a whole lot of the shit you get yourself into, I can promise you, it's not your fault. She is a grown woman. She wanted to find Eva for her own reasons, not yours. She would have kept going to the ends of the Earth. She'd be right here in this godforsaken storm if she could. Stop blaming yourself, because you didn't hurt her, okay? Reyes did.'

'That doesn't change...'

Nicole thumped me in the arm.

'Christ, melodramatic much?' she snapped. 'Quinn is in hospital because a lunatic stabbed her with a broken mirror shard, not because she took life advice from the world's sulkiest terrorist, okay? If you blame yourself again, I'm going to kick you in the nuts.'

'Is that a threat?'

'You bet your ass it is. We've got enough problems to deal with, without you spitting your dummy out. Get over it, and focus on the road.'

'We're nearly there,' I said. 'An hour tops.'

'Whoopee.'

The intermittent crack of lightning lit up the sky, followed seconds later by an almighty boom. Nicole winced.

'I hate lightning.' She shuddered.

'Good job we're in a Faraday cage then, isn't it.'

'A what?'

'A Faraday cage. To put it simply, it's an enclosed space that can be used to block electromagnetic fields by having an earthed metal screen around the subject. In this case, the metal shell of the car absorbs the electricity, and the rubber wheels negate it. That's why people don't die from lightning when they're in a car. It's named after the English scientist Michael Faraday, who invented them in eighteen thirty-six.'

'That's putting it simply?'

'Trust me, I could wax lyrical about this stuff for days.'

'Does knowing that kind of stuff ever actually help you in the real world?'

'It comes in handy for pub quizzes.'

Visibility dropped even lower, forcing me to slow. There could be anything on the road. Abandoned cars. Fallen trees. Bodies. If I smashed into anything, it would be game over.

And I couldn't rid the itch that was growing in the back of my mind that there was something out there, hunting me like a pack of wolves. What it was, I couldn't tell. Paranoia had done much worse to me in the past, and men like Reyes and Salazar had only made it worse. They were monsters. And monsters had no place in this world.

'Here,' I said, gesturing to a sign up ahead. 'We're close.'

'You said that an hour ago.'

'And I meant it. Now we're even closer.'

Nicole looked at the sign.

'What does that say?'

'Ozello,' I said. 'Reyes's final resting place.'

'What the hell is in Ozello?'

'Nothing fun.'

'And you're sure he's here?'

'When am I ever sure? Felix said he was. I came here a few days ago. Reyes had the whole place locked up, and as soon as he found out someone was snooping around, he sent two men with rifles to come and deal with us. He had the whole town under his thumb. No police presence for miles. Whatever his plan is, it has to be there.'

I turned the rental car up onto the track I'd taken just a few days before in my beloved van. The rental was lower than the van, and the grooves in the road were harder to traverse. I pulled the car out of the grooves, attempting to carve my own path through the bayou. Huge mistake. It didn't take long for the car to grind to a halt. The wheels spun uselessly in swamp water.

'Damn it,' I said, switching off the engine. 'Looks like we're on foot from here.'

'I wish I'd brought a coat.' Nicole said, looking at the downpour outside.

'I can offer you a pair of used scrubs.'

'I'll pass thanks. How far is it from here?'

'A mile maybe. Hopefully less.'

I looked at the clock on the dash. Five minutes to eleven. Not too bad. But the rest of the journey was going to be as tough as anything I'd been through before. Nicole knew it too. She fixed me with a look of sheer determination and utter reluctance. Classic Nicole.

And with that, we climbed out of the rental, pistols in hand. Headed for battle.

FIFTY-ONE

THE KILLING BLOW

The Asian guests did not return. Nor did Pencil-lip or the other men. Hours went by in near complete silence. The wind's war cry our only soundtrack. The two remaining guards positioned themselves at the table. They made quiet conversation, breaking off occasionally to peer up and make sure I was still there. I didn't dare move further. The rattle of the chains would cut through the quiet if I made any attempt to escape. I knew my time would come. I just had to be patient. Finally, the meekest glimmers of dawn broke through the canvas of foreboding, dark clouds, giving way to a brand new day.

And all the horrors that came with it. They towered over the horizon like a terrible omen. A swirling monolith of total devastation. Never in my time in America had I seen one first hand. Only reports on the television, and scenes of the aftermath. But here it was. Mother Nature at her most ferocious. The hurricane was real. And it was coming right for us.

God help us all.

The onslaught was insane. To its very core, the barn rocked back and forth as though it was made of little more than paper. Like a tortured soul, it wailed in agony. Yet there was no respite. I was exhausted, unable to get so much as a wink of sleep. I wished for the storm to subside, or for someone to come and take me deeper inside where the noise may be subdued. Or for an opportunity to present itself, and a chance for escape.

'Dwight, get ready. He's nearly here.'

I looked down and saw one of the guards at the table. The other man, Dwight, had moved down towards the mouth of the cave. Beneath his feet, a steady stream of water washed over his boots.

'You think we should warn them about this?' He asked, kicking up the rainwater around his boot.

'That ain't my problem, man. They got all they need down there anyway. I need you outside.

'I ain't going out there.' Dwight complained.

'You ain't got a choice. You got to wait for the big man. You know how he gets.'

'Why can't you do it?'

'Because I make the damn call, alright? Get out there and wait. He won't be long.'

Dwight huffed and trudged through the rising water towards the barn door. A strong wind broke through the gap as he opened the door, and slipped out.

I had to take the chance. With only one man down below, I knew I'd unlikely have a better opportunity. With my hands and feet free, I wiggled out beneath the rusted chain. It clinked and rattled as I shuffled down, but far less so than if I'd tried to unwind it. As my head wriggled loose, it chattered against the coil, then came to a rest.

Through the gap in the barn, I saw more lights. Bright, halogen beams slicing through the dark. Even as it approached, the noise of the storm masked any sounds made by the vehicle. Unlike the car that had brought the Chinese guests, this one didn't stop outside. Instead, Dwight and the remaining guard pushed open the doors, and the vehicle drove straight in.

It was a large SUV, grey in colour, although a heavy coat of mud had covered most of it. The driver pulled into the centre of the barn and switched off the engine. The barn door closed, restoring the ambient groans of the rickety old structure as the main source of noise.

Domingo Reyes climbed out of the driver side door. He wore a black parka coat that packed some considerable heft to his short stature. His trousers were waterproof pullovers. His boots like that of a soldier. He shut the door behind him and looked at his men. Another two men climbed out of the SUV. Both were armed with assault rifles.

'No,' He snapped, looking at Dwight. 'I want you outside. You stand guard, understand?'

'Yessir.' Dwight said, hiding the obvious disappointment in his voice, and ducked back through the barn doors.

'Where are they?' Reyes asked Dwight's partner.

'They're already inside.' He said. 'They were complaining about the weather. We thought…'

'And that was your mistake,' Reyes snapped. 'Thinking without permission. They were not to go down there without my supervision.'

'Sorry, Boss. It's just…'

'Save your apologies for someone who gives a damn.' He was angry. Much more so than I'd seen him before. 'Get them up here. I want to do business here, where I said we would.'

'Yessir.'

The guard rushed away accompanied by one of the newcomers, heading for the mouth of the cave. Reyes watched them go. An unpleasant silence descended on the barn. Made all the more uncomfortable by the man below. His aura was sickly. The air he expelled felt toxic. Instinctively, I held my breath and recoiled away from view.

'Where are you, little girl?' He hissed.

It was as though he had sensed me watching. My heart began to pound, so loud I was sure he would hear. I ducked down, just in time to avoid his wandering eyes. But he knew where I was. Slowly, he began to make his way toward the foot of the staircase.

'You cannot hide from me.' He leered.

I slid back into place by the coil and snatched up the torn restraints. With trembling fingers, I replaced the tape around my legs, hiding the tear at the back, and slid my hands into the stretched tape that had bound them before. I didn't have time for the chains. Instead, I pressed my back up against them and prayed he wouldn't notice.

Reyes reached the top of the stairs and cast his eyes around slowly. When finally they rested on me, a wide smile slid across his face.

'There she is. The whore.'

He walked across to me and knelt down by my legs. I tucked them up as close to me as I could, hoping it wouldn't disturb the ruined tape. He rested his hands on my knees, and carefully pushed them apart. Had it not been for the tape over my mouth, I would have screamed.

'You are like a lit match.' He said as his eyes wandered down my legs. 'Dangling precariously over a pool of gasoline. Waiting to fall. Waiting to make everything go...' He ran his finger down my thigh. 'Boom.'

I snapped my legs shut and forced him away with my shins. He laughed and stood up.

'You know, I met a friend of yours.' He continued. 'Mr Stone. He told me you were helping him find my daughter before you got cold feet.'

He looked me in the eye. Cold and soulless. I looked away.

'He thought you might like to know that he found her. She was sleeping with an old associate of mine. You taught her well. She was quite the whore too.'

I wished I could speak. Wished I could tell him just how vile he was, that he would talk about his daughter with such distaste.

'The thing is,' Reyes continued. 'I have no place in my family for whores. I have a reputation to uphold. A reputation that you besmirched. That's a problem for me. A problem I had to fix myself.'

He kneeled down again and pressed his face close to mine. So close I could smell his breath again. I scrunched my eyes shut and shied away. The stench of stale smoke filled my nostrils.

'There are no whores in my family anymore.'

I opened my eyes and stared into his. And understood. I felt everything slip away, like reality had gone and the nightmare had taken over, and there was nothing I could do about it, nothing at all. The grin that stretched across his face was like no other. The malice in his dark eyes cut through everything I had ever wanted. And there was nothing left. He had taken it all from me.

Tears ran down my face. Like kindling to a fire, they only served to fuel his glee. He let out a loud howl of laughter and got up. My vision blurred as he moved away. Why hadn't it been me? It should have been me. Not her. Not Quinn.

I fell back against the coil and wept. All I'd ever wanted was for her to be happy. Now I would never see that look again on her face as she smiled. The tattoo on my wrist burned. The letters ABYB searing as though they had been branded onto my skin. I slumped down and forced my eyes shut. I just wanted to see her face. I just wanted to see her smile.

But it wouldn't come, no matter how hard I tried. I willed her back to me, and was met with a void. The wind and the rain seemed like an afterthought on the stage of despair I had found myself on. I was only faintly aware of the movement going on down below. Reyes and his nefarious plans were all but a fallacy to me. In a world without Quinn, nothing mattered anymore.

No. That's not what she would want. She would want something good to come out of this. She would want her death to mean something. Lying here would accomplish nothing but the continued survival of Domingo Reyes. I couldn't let him get away with it.

I picked myself up off the floor and pulled my hands free. The tape came away with ease. In his determination to hurt me, Reyes had not noticed my binds. I threw the tape aside and wiped the tears from my face. They had crusted into my cheek. How long had I mourned?

I looked over the balcony, down at the man I was determined to kill. He stood by his SUV, smoking a cigar like the world wasn't going to shit all around him. He had taken off the parka coat, revealing a tight-fitting black sweater, amplifying his villainy to stratospheric heights.

The barn door scraped open again, and the man named Dwight stuck his head through the gap. He looked like a drowned rat.

'Boss, I just saw lights up on the way. Think there's someone up there.'

Reyes stormed across to the door and stared out at the dark. I did the same a floor above, peering through a gap. There were no lights.

'Where?' He snapped.

'Up there. Three of them. They turned 'em off a couple seconds ago, but I couldn't see nothing without them.'

'Stay on guard. Shoot anyone you see, understand?'

Reyes pushed his subordinate back out into the rain and shut the door behind him, and slid the bolt lock into place. He walked back over to the SUV and swung open the trunk. Out of it, he pulled a large rifle.

He slung it over his shoulder, pocketed a box of ammunition, and carried the rifle across to the stairs. For an older man, Reyes seemed unconcerned about carrying the heavy weapon up to the mezzanine. I ducked down behind the coil. The size of it hid my frame well. When he spotted I was missing, I could use the element of surprise to attack.

But either he didn't notice, or he didn't care. Stopping at a spot inches from where my feet had been, he unbolted the shutters and swung them open, causing a torrent of wind and rain to decimate the balcony.

THE FATE OF GLASS

It didn't bother Reyes. He rested the rifle's bipod on the sill of the open window overlooking the front of the barn. He didn't look around to see what else was near him, and nestled into the butt of the rifle. He slid his finger over the trigger. He moved his right eye over the scope and closed his left to focus.

My heart skipped. This was my chance. My chance for escape. My chance for revenge. The bastard had to die. By my hand. For Quinn.

I looked around for something to use. I wished for a gun, or a knife, or something that would put him down for good. The best I could find was a broken plank of wood. It looked like it had once been part of the bannister. The wood was soft from years of rot and decay. I couldn't be sure it wouldn't crumble on impact.

I looked at the chain Pencil-lip had used to bind me to the coil. Even though it was old and rusted, it was still strong. With the open window blowing a fierce gale into the barn, the chain rattled noisily against the pulley system in the rafters. But unwrapping it would make too much noise.

Reyes slid the round into the chamber and took aim.

That was when I saw it. Not a chain or a piece of rotten wood, but something much stronger. With a coat of rust so dark it blended in with the surroundings, the ratchet was almost unrecognisable. Tucked away and forgotten to time, it lay beside a piece of moulded, termite-infested wood that had long since given up hope of salvation. I reached out and wrapped my fingers around the tool. Flecks of jagged metal sliced my skin, but I didn't make a sound.

For Quinn.

Reyes squeezed the trigger and fired. The boom of the rifle was nearly enough to knock me off my feet. I gasped, feeling like the round had hit me square in the chest. As I struggled to recover, I saw him load the second round into the rifle and take aim again. Whoever he was firing on, I hoped they would keep him distracted for long enough.

I eased out from behind the coil, heading for the old man's blind spot. I raised the tool up over my head. One swift attack was all I needed. He took the second shot. The noise was just as loud as the first. But I was prepared for it. He wasn't going to get off a third.

With everything I had, I brought the ratchet down on the back of the Viper's head. The attack caught him off guard, and he slumped to the side. Blood trickled out over his short-trimmed hair.

But it was not the killing blow I wanted. No sooner had I brought the ratchet back up for a second attack did Reyes react.

'You'll regret that.' He snarled.

And with one quick movement, he flung the butt of the rifle up. It caught me in the chin, and knocked me off my feet. Blood filled my mouth as my teeth clenched down into my lip, and my vision went suddenly white.

No, I couldn't let him win.

But he was already standing over me. Rifle raised again.

'You aren't worth the bullet.' He snarled.

The rifle came crashing down, and my world went black.

FIFTY-TWO

FOOLS RUSH IN

THIRTY SECONDS OUT OF THE CAR FELT LIKE THIRTY SECONDS IN A damn ocean. The rain wasn't just fierce, it was suffocating. It thrashed me like an abusive drunk. Darkness had swamped the world, turning visibility into a fallacy. Never before had I wanted to be in the Bahamas so much. Sneakers, it would appear, were a bad idea.

'You know that feeling you get when you've made a stupid ass decision,' I shouted across to James. 'This is one of those times.'

'Wait in the car if you're going to be a wimp about it.' He bellowed back. He was only a few feet from me, but his voice was barely audible.

'And miss all the fun? Like hell.'

The cold bore deep into my body. It tore at my face, tightened my muscles, and froze my bones. James looked no better. His clothes were muddied and torn and soaked from the last twenty-four hours of mayhem. He hadn't slept properly in days, and it was clearly taking effect. Every squelching, exhaustive step sapped a little more of his soul. His face was gaunt, like someone had wrapped a layer of skin over a skull, and then vacuum-packed it tight. How he was still moving was beyond me, but there was no point in arguing. He would keep going until he had nothing left to give.

And I couldn't shake the feeling that moment was approaching fast.

My arm throbbed. In the car, I'd looked it over. The damage was not as bad as I'd thought. Some of the stitches had given way when I'd choked the guy, but not torn entirely. A bit of handiwork and some clean bandages had seen to it. But mixing fresh wounds with my surroundings felt like the dumbest decision I'd ever made.

'Son of a bitch!' James barked.

'What?'

'We have to go through that.' He pointed up ahead at what could only be described as a lake. 'There used to be a path. Bloody storm has flooded everything.'

'I'm pretty certain we're about as wet as we're going to get.'

'It's not the water that bothers me. It's the snakes.'

'You're joking, right?'

He shook his head. My skin crawled.

'Crocodiles too, probably.'

'Fuck off.'

'I'm not giving you a piggyback.' He said.

'I didn't ask you to.'

'Do you want to give me one?'

'Oh sure, hop aboard. Do you want a sponge bath as well?'

'If you wouldn't mind.'

'Bite me.'

'You going to be okay with your arm?' He asked.

'I'll be fine. I'll try and keep it above the surface.'

'I will actually give you a piggyback if you want. If it'll help.'

'Just concentrate on all the other things trying to kill us, okay?'

Reluctantly, we waded into the swamp. The water was thick and full of floating objects. I kept my arms raised like I had surrendered to the horrors that lay beneath. The stitches stretched, but there was nothing I could do about it. More than once, I felt something below the surface brush against my leg or midriff and made me shudder.

'This is literally the worst thing ever.' I shouted.

'Worse than being stabbed?'

'It's a figure of speech.'

'Then it's not literally. It's figuratively.'

'James, I will drown you right where you stand.'

The water rose higher and higher until it lapped against my ribcage. Seconds later it was at up to my chest. Freezing water clung to my chest, stinging the wound. With every step, my sneakers sank deeper into the sludge. It seeped into my socks and tickled my toes. We were less than halfway across.

'Be careful where you step,' James shouted. 'There's a pretty big drop on either side of the path. You'll be in over your head if that happens.'

'You're telling me this now?'

'It seemed appropriate.'

'This is actually a nightmare.'

'Shush.'

'Don't tell me to shush. I'm doing this because of you and your…'

James shushed me again, but this time I knew why. The sound of an engine permeated the storm. It was unmistakable. The low growl rustled like thunder. Growing with the might of a god.

'Get down.' James shouted.

He grabbed me around the waist and threw me aside into the repugnant swamp. And not a moment too soon. The second we hit the surface, a pair of bright white lights cut through the rain behind us. Through closed eyelids, I saw the beams raise up and crash down into the swamp. Thick, foul fluid flooded through my pursed lips and rolled over my tongue. I wanted to vomit. James held me tight. The first set of lights slithered past from right to left, headed in the same direction as us. Followed by another pair, and another after that. Only when the final vehicle had passed us did James let go.

I scrambled to the surface and gasped for air. Sludge trickled down my face and into my mouth, and I wretched.

'Are you okay?' He asked.

'Swell,' I gagged. 'Next time, give me a warning.'

'It's foul, isn't it.'

'You betcha. Who was that?'

'I don't know. Surely it isn't Reyes.'

'Maybe the guests from China?'

'They should have beaten us all here. It could be more of Reyes's men. Backup, in case the worst happened.'

'Or in case Felix ratted us out.'

'Well, either way, we're lucky they didn't spot us.'

We swam back over to the higher ground and crossed the rest of the swamp without any more spontaneous dives. Incredulously, taking a swim had achieved the impossible. I was even wetter and colder than before. But now, the vile, putrid water had worked its way into the wounds on my chest and my arm. I couldn't fight the thought that billions of deadly bacteria were now snaking through my veins. As we scrambled back onto land, a crack of lightning flashed through the sky. A second later, the boom of thunder followed. I shuddered.

'We're okay.' James yelled to me.

'We're not in a Faraday Cage anymore though.'

'Just don't wear a tinfoil hat and you'll be fine. It can't be more than a mile. We better be careful.'

'Oh yeah,' I shouted back. 'Because up until now it's been a breeze.'

The lightning intensified as we hustled onwards until it was practically on top of us. The stark bolts of light dazzled and temporarily blinded me, and the thunder shook me to my core. The whole scenario was as close to my worst nightmare as I thought possible. If a pair of clowns jumped us, I was sure I'd die on the spot.

I felt exposed and vulnerable, which were bad traits to have when walking into a war zone. The wind was unbearable. Every step forwards felt like I was playing tug of war against a battalion of soldiers. I buckled down and leant into the gale to stop myself toppling backwards. It was my only choice.

Another flash of lightning smashed into the ground up ahead. Much too close. I screeched and fell back, but not before I caught sight of one of the pickups that had driven past earlier. A group of men stood nearby, but the light had already dissipated before I got a clear view of them. James noticed them too.

'Over here,' he shouted across to me. 'We can't let them see us.'

We trudged across into the surrounding dense undergrowth and approached the stationary trucks. With every bolt of lightning, the picture changed. The men moved about, preparing for something. Flashes of assault rifles silhouetted against the stormy sky sent waves of panic through me.

James and I had a pistol each. Both Glock 37s. I'd checked them over on the drive up. Large barrelled. Bevelled slides. Not that that made much of a difference when push came to shove. Capable of ten rounds, but a quick stock check on the drive up had told me we have sixteen rounds between us. A fifty-fifty split. Eight each. We shoot to kill, and take what we can off anyone who gets in our way. But even so, sixteen bullets split between two pistols were not going to bode well against upwards of a dozen men armed with assault rifles.

We crept closer, using the gale's dance through the shrubs to mask our approach. There were nine in total. Eight men, armed with assault rifles, and one with a pistol the size of a house. All nine men wore tactical gear. Dark Kevlar vests strapped over thick black overcoats. No messing around. No games. They were here to kill.

Not Reyes's men. But if not, then who?

But it was the man with the pistol that drew my attention. He stood with an authoritative stance, and ordered his men into position. Like his men, he was coated in Kevlar, yet he kept his head exposed. Another bolt of lightning lit him up like a performer on a stage. His twisted, ruined features ablaze for all the world to see. Only one man I knew who could fit that bill. Ramiro Salazar.

Beside me, I felt James tense up. Felt the shock and horror hit him like a bullet.

'It's him.' He gasped. His eyes wider than I'd ever seen before. It wasn't anger I saw on his face. It was fear.

I reached out and grabbed his arm, sure in the knowledge of what he was about to do next.

'Take it easy.' I shouted, my face just a few inches from his, yet my voice barely escaped my own mouth. 'Don't do anything stupid.'

Sure enough, he tried something stupid. He leapt forwards. Pistol raised at his enemy. Ready to fight. Ready to die. I tugged him back with everything I had.

'James, not like this.' I yelled. 'Not while he's surrounded. You need to listen.'

The last time I'd seen him was when the skin on his face burned. The skin melting right before my very eyes. The anger in his eyes had been as palpable there as it was on Stone's face now.

'Let go of me.' James hissed. He had his prey in his sights, and he was ready to strike. I didn't let him.

'We do this the smart way, yeah? No guns blazing bullshit.' I pulled him away and stared into his striking blue eyes. 'If you go in there now, you'll get yourself killed. Eva too, probably.'

But the look on his face was not one I'd seen before. His eyes darted back and forth furtively. His lips moved silently, like he was speaking a lost language to the dead. And the dead were talking back. He bowed his head to the left, as though to better listen to a whisper in his ear. His eyes narrowed. His brow furrowed. His lips moving in response. What the hell was wrong with him?

'James, I need you to focus before you do something stupid.' I shouted. 'You're freaking me out.'

With one hand clutching at the scruff of his clothes, I slapped him across the face. The shock snatched him away from his thoughts. Brought him back to the land of the living. His eyes fixed on mine, and there was life behind them once more.

'I can't let him escape.' He said, like even the possibility of failure would be the death of him.

'He won't. We won't let him. But you need to keep your shit together, okay?'

He nodded, but there was no mistaking the unyielding desperation in his face. I stared into those eyes of his. Beautiful and blue. Fractured and fearful. A broken man.

Salazar's men began to move. A large fence ahead had crumpled and fallen. The group split up in two. Four men moved first. With their weapons raised, they pushed forwards. A few seconds after, Salazar followed. He walked confidently, pistol down at his side, as though he thought the precautions of his men were unnecessary. He stomped through the storm, and a moment later he was out of sight. Taking up the rear, the second group followed suit with the first. Weapons raised, eyeballs scouring for signs of movement. They followed their commander into the fray.

The moment they were over the rise, James sprinted forwards. Taken off guard, I had to push hard to keep close behind. He ran with purpose, like a wolf after its prey. He sprinted to the pickups and ducked down. As I reached him, he brought the pistol up and pointed it into the window of the driver's door. Empty. He gestured for me to check the next one, while he searched the last. Both were empty. Salazar had sent all his forces in one.

'What do we do now?' I bellowed over the storm.

'I'm taking this.' He shouted back, pointing at the pickup. The one Salazar had climbed out of.

'Don't you think that's a bit dumb, what with them having enough guns to take out a bank?'

'I don't care anymore. I just need him dead.'

I thumped him in the arm as hard as I could. Not nearly as hard as I'd hoped. Another strong gust of wind hit us and knocked me off my feet. I landed on my back in the thick mud. Flecks splashed across my face, in my eyes and mouth. James grabbed me and pulled me back to my feet.

'We need to get out of the rain.' He shouted.

And on that, I agreed. Together, we staggered across to the pickup and hauled the doors open. I clambered inside and slumped onto the faux leather seat like it was a gift from God. As the door swung shut, the near deafening howl of the storm was muffled. Not by much, but enough for it to be a mercy.

'This is unbelievable.' I gasped. My voice hoarse from shouting. 'How can weather be this bad?'

'I know, right? I heard category four hurricanes were usually a tea party.'

'Have you ever thought about not being sarcastic twenty-four seven?'

'I did. It didn't suit me.'

I rubbed some of the mud off my face. Didn't work. My hands were as caked as the rest of me.

'What do we do now?' I asked.

'I guess we improvise.'

'I thought that was what we were doing already.'

'You thought that was improvising?'

'I don't know dude. Your plans rarely make any sense to me.'

'Clearly, you haven't spent enough time improvising.'

'Well, can your careful consideration factor in that we've only got sixteen bullets between us?'

'What did you think I wanted the pickup for?'

He gave me a smile, and pulled the console underneath the steering wheel apart. He pulled apart the wires and connected together the ignition, and in under a minute, he had the thing running.

'Fools rush in, you know.' I said.

'What better way is there? At least we'll be dry.'

'Until they start shooting at us. Then we'll be dead.'

'Are you ready?' James asked.

'Hell no, are you?'

He shook his head and smiled.

And stamped on the gas.

FIFTY-THREE

THE RIDE OF THE VALKYRIES

I STOMPED ON THE PEDAL, AND THE PICKUP POUNCED FORWARDS. The tyres had already begun to sink into the mud, the texture of which was closer to custard than it had any right being, but the sheer power of the vehicle quickly resolved the issue. The chain link fence that had blocked my path before crumpled with ease, and we shot forwards with the force of a fighter jet.

The radio was off. No point in trying to find a signal out here, and the rain would have drowned it under its own battle cry. But that didn't matter. I imagined the speakers were booming with music. The Ride of the Valkyries. The soundtrack of war. A fitting song to drive into the end of the world with. Time to see if we were worthy of Valhalla.

What became immediately clear was just how much the blanket of trees and overgrowth had done to dampen the effects of the storm. As the pickup breached the crest, everything came into devastating clarity. What felt like invisible steam train slammed into the side of the pickup. The wheels lifted up into the air, and sent us hurtling sideways.

Nicole swore. I forced the wheel right, trying desperately to counter the storm and get back on track. Reluctantly, the tyres obeyed, fighting the powerful gust and landed with a splash back onto all four wheels. I aimed for the barn, and stamped once more on the pedal.

The world outside looked like some kind of confused dream state. A fumbled mixture of swirling shapes and loud, distorted

THE FATE OF GLASS

noises cascading around us. I switched on the main beams. I didn't want to use them. The element of surprise was better, and the ferocity of the storm would likely mask my location. But it just wasn't feasible. Above all else, I needed sight, lest I hit a stray boulder and bring my fight to an abrupt end.

There was no point with the windscreen wipers. The rain came down too fast, hard and sideways for it to make a difference. It formed a heavy, waving sheen across the windscreen, like a river had decided to carve its way across the glass. It deformed the view ahead. Twisted shapes into disfigured monsters. A reality into a nightmare. The headlights cast over a group of objects directly in front of me. People. They turned, reacting to the disturbance behind them. The nearest was barely a couple of yards away, and getting much closer by the second.

He had just enough time to raise his weapon, but not enough to shoot. The pickup ate him up and spat him out like a light salad. His body disappeared beneath the enormous vehicle. Whether he was alive or dead, it didn't matter. He wasn't walking away from that in a hurry. I couldn't tell who it was, but I knew it couldn't be Salazar. He wouldn't let a rogue pickup get the better of him.

Before the tattered body came to a rest, his comrades retaliated. A volley of bullets bombarded the pickup from both sides. Metal punctured like paper. Glass smashed, and whipped into the air as it was caught up in the storm.

'Floor it.' Nicole screamed.

'I'm trying.'

I jumped up a gear and mashed the accelerator into the ground. More bullets hit the pickup, but this time they were closer to the rear. A loud bang told me they'd shot out one of the tyres. The pickup dipped, slowed, and weaved as the mangled tyre dug into the mud. But I held it in place. Nothing was going to stop me now.

Through the darkness, the barn loomed into shape. From a gap in the roof, a small flash of light pierced the gloom. A nanosecond later, I knew what it was. The crack of a rifle muzzle. Whatever its target was, it wouldn't hit. The weather was far too powerful to make a weapon like that accurate. It was a show of force, nothing more. It had to be Reyes. This was his final stand, and he wouldn't walk away from it.

In my head, the song rose to a crescendo. I flicked up another gear, and forced the pickup faster. I didn't care for the vehicle. It could fall apart for all I cared, so long as it got me to the barn. It bounced and crashed and bucked and kicked as the ruined tyres fought against the land. My head bashed against the roof, and slammed into the window. Beside me, Nicole flopped around like a rag-doll. There was no point retaliating with gunfire. It was a waste of bullets.

More small, distorted figures appeared through the darkness. More of Salazar's men. They were prepared, weapons raised to counter the approaching threat. No way was I going to be able to use the element of surprise to wipe them out, but I did have one thing on my side. The wind. With terrifying strength, it battered the squad to such a degree, they could barely remain upright. I watched as they buckled and fell to their knees, bending to the wall of the hurricane. Those that remained upright fired their weapons. The bullets went wide, missing their mark. And before they had the chance for a second volley, we were already out of their range.

We were closing in on the barn. The epicentre of a war zone was not a fun place to be, but the pickup had nothing more to give. It was at the breaking point. The constant barrage of bumps and bullets was literally tearing it apart. The surviving windows smashed to smithereens as the pickup crashed back down, and we were showered in rain and glass fragments. The terrible wind disarmed me, and for a brief moment, I let go of the steering wheel to protect my face. Huge mistake.

As my hands let go, Reyes let off another round. Whether he aimed for it or not, I would never know. The tremendous, unstoppable force of the bullet cut through the pickup's front tyre like it was less than nothing. The rubber exploded, which forced the pickup into a sharp, irreversible twist. My hands snatched desperately for the wheel, and fought for control. Too little too late.

The remnants of the tyre ploughed deep into the mud, forcing the pickup to an abrupt halt. But the momentum was too much. No graceful stop for us. Like it had been ejected from a catapult, the rear of the pickup launched into the air.

Strapped to the seat, I was powerless to stop it. I shut my eyes and willed my body to relax. I wasn't sure which part of the pickup hit the ground first, or second, or third. All I knew was that with every sickening crash, I thought I was done for. My life was about to end. Nothing flashed before my eyes. My life remained where it belonged, in the past.

It seemed never-ending. Every crunch, crash, smash and tumble continuing on for an eternity. I didn't dare open my eyes. Didn't want to see the rush of destruction. My limbs bounced back and forth, colliding with everything in reach. Each impact surely my last.

Then suddenly, it was all over. The pickup stopped. I opened my eyes, and glanced around in the darkness for something, anything that I could use to recalibrate. The pickup's lights had died, as had the engine and everything else in the vehicle. The only thing I knew for certain was that the pickup had come to a stop on its roof. Beads of water trickled up my neck, over my chin, and towards my forehead. Blood pulsed in my head, building pressure on the back of my eyes. Blindly, I grappled with the seatbelt and released the clip. I crumpled down onto my head and flopped awkwardly onto my side.

There was a momentary calm inside the ruined pickup, but I knew it wouldn't last. Salazar's men were fast approaching, and Reyes wouldn't let up his retaliation anytime soon. We needed to get out while we still had the advantage, if that's what you could call the situation. Every inch of my body felt bruised and sore, but nothing felt broken, which was about as good an outcome as I could expect to get.

'I feel like I've just been tumble-dried.' I groaned. 'Are you okay?'

There was no response.

'Nicole, are you alright?'

I reached out and fumbled around for her. I felt her arm, cold and motionless. I scrambled around and shuffled over to her. I unclipped her seatbelt and moved her around. With my forefinger, I checked for a pulse. Even through the severe chill, I felt the beat. It was strong and resilient.

'Nicole, wake up!'

'Urgh, you drive like an ass.' She groaned.

'We've got to move. We're sitting ducks out here.'

'At this point, I think death would be preferable.' She huffed.

I kicked open the driver door and crawled out into the storm. A torrent of water raced across the deep, squelching mud. I scrambled to my feet and pulled Nicole out behind me. The severe darkness hid our position, but so did it for Salazar and Reyes. Somewhere out there, a small army was headed right for us.

I grabbed Nicole's hand, and together we ran. The wind was intense. At any moment I felt it could sweep me off my feet and claim me its victim. I doubled over and ran as fast as I could downhill. Another crack of lightning illuminated the barn ahead. It was close. Another flash of the sniper rifle pierced the dark. This time, I heard the devastating clap as the round exploded out of the weapon. I had no idea whether he was aiming at us, or at Salazar. All I knew was that the bullet didn't hit me.

'Don't stop.' I shouted, but I had no idea if Nicole could hear me over the chaos.

Rain pummelled my face like a million tiny fists. The ground beneath my feet was horrendous. It felt like I was running through wet cement, yet somehow also on ice. The rain made it almost impossible to stay upright. More than once, I was pulled back as Nicole stumbled. I had no idea if she was alright. But if she gave up now, it was game over for her, and I couldn't let that happen.

We were close. I could feel it. The massive rock face that had been mined all those years ago sheltered a little of the wind from claiming us. The barn was yards away. With nowhere else to go, the rainwater collected at the base of the mine. I splashed through the freezing water, and covered the final stretch in seconds.

The door to the barn was shut. In the pitch black, I grasped around, searching for a handle. To my right, I heard a single gunshot cut through the storm.

'Nicole?' I shouted.

'Christ, there was a guy right there. I could barely see him!'

'Get his weapon.'

I heard her splash around for a few seconds. I found the handle on the door and gripped it.

'Did you get it?' I bellowed.

'Yeah. It's an AK.'

'You know how to use it?'

'Yeah. It's an AK. A kid could use one of these.'

'Great. Are you ready?'

'Just open the damn door, James!'

I swung the handle and heaved open the door.

FIFTY-FOUR

WHEN WORLDS COLLIDE

A SERIES OF OIL-FILLED LANTERNS LIT THE BARN. THEIR SOMBRE orange glow barely reached the corners, but it was enough to illuminate the contents, dangers and all. A row of steel carts lay abandoned along the side of the barn. Each covered in rust and looked heavy enough to withstand the might of the hurricane.

A parked SUV sat in the middle of the barn, between the door and the entrance to the mines. A large chain hooked around the SUV's tow bar, shackling it to one of the barn's main supports. Reyes might be a dangerous man, but he intended to survive the encounter, and he didn't want to resurface after the storm with his vehicle halfway to Mexico.

Standing beside the SUV was a man. He stared bemusedly at us as we scrambled inside, caught in a flux of indecision. In his hands, he held an AK47. That was all the decision I needed. I raised the pistol, but Nicole beat me to it. A small burst of gunfire was all it took to down the goon. He crumpled where he stood, and floated face down in the knee-high water.

I swung the barn door shut behind me. I had no idea how far off Salazar and his men were, and I didn't want to give them an easy route inside. Although judging from the decrepit state of the barn, and the ease with which the storm shook it about, I doubted it would hold much longer. Every single piece of wood groaned and cracked under the incredible pressure, and it was about to get much worse.

From somewhere high above, I heard footsteps. Before I had the chance to look, an onslaught of gunfire smashed down around us.

Instinctively I ducked and raced towards the SUV. With Nicole close behind, I hurled myself down into the water beside the corpse and snatched his weapon. The gunfire ceased.

'Give it up, Reyes,' I shouted. 'You can't win.'

He fired again, peppering the roof of the SUV, and smashing the windows. Glass showered down on top of us, but none of the bullets hit. Nicole ducked out and let off a burst of rounds up in his direction.

It was enough to stave off another immediate attack. I heard Reyes move position. I pushed off from the SUV and dived across to one of the abandoned mine carts. On its side, the cart was semi-submerged. The thick steel shell had to be strong enough to carry massive weights over and over again. A bullet was never going to penetrate it.

Nicole took the next one over. They were easily big enough to hide inside, but they left us exposed on one side. Our only saving grace was the dim light. Hidden under the cart, we were shrouded in darkness.

Using the brief respite, I checked the AK47. The magazine was full, which was a bonus. As I slotted the magazine back in, a volley of bullets came at me from my right. A lone gunman, standing in the mouth of the cave, rifle raised. His calculated pot shots forced my head back down out of range, and he used the advantage to close in.

A loud splash nearby confirmed my suspicion. Reyes had descended. They were trying to surround us. I stuck the rifle out of cover and fired blindly at the spot I'd last seen the advancing henchmen. To my glee, I heard a cry of pain, and a splash. Another one bites the dust.

That changed Reyes's tactics. Instead of advancing towards me and putting himself in danger, he moved away, skirting around the SUV. Only one place he could be going. Into the mines. I followed his trajectory in my head and pointed the gun towards the rear of the SUV. I squeezed the trigger.

Seven shots in total. Six of them hit the cave wall and splashed down into the flood. But one hit something else. Reyes swore and fired back. His bullets went wide, and the sound of his escape ceased. Wherever I had struck him, he struggled to recover.

'Sorry, did I get you there?' I laughed. 'My bad, I'm not good with guns.'

'Does it hurt to know Isabella died because of you?' Reyes shouted. 'Can you feel her blood on your hands?'

'Oh, I've got a lot of blood on my hands, but not hers. You should check your sources first.'

Nothing from Reyes.

'Haven't you heard?' I shouted. 'You've got a terrible problem with subordination. First your daughter, now Felix. I mean, I applaud you for trying to make it poetic, getting Felix to choose between his love and his life, but it backfired massively.'

'You're lying.'

'Am I? Who'd you think told me you were here?'

His silence radiated with rage.

'You might as well give it up,' I continued. 'You've lost. You won't get out of here alive.'

That solicited a laugh from the Viper.

'Two against eight. I think my odds are higher than yours.' He bellowed.

'It's two against five at best,' I replied. 'After your man on the door, and these two gimps swimming in their own misfortune. And I don't know if you'd checked outside, but Salazar has come to play. Don't feel bad if you didn't see them. I hear sight loss is common in old men.'

But as I spoke, I caught more movement out of the corner of my eye. The cavalry. Five men, all armed with assault rifles, came marching up out of the cave. Their clothes were drenched, but they seemed no less determined to fight for their boss.

'What were you saying there, Stone?' Reyes jeered.

I didn't respond. Didn't want to give away my position to the newcomers. They'd be busy enough when Salazar arrived.

And as if on cue, the barn door opened once more.

* * *

I opened my eyes. Gone was the image of Quinn, radiating her love and warmth into me. It was replaced by the dark, cold realisation that I was still alive, and still in her father's company.

Slowly, I moved my head around, searching for the vile being that had robbed me of the one bright spark in my life. My Quinn. But he was nowhere to be seen. The gale billowing through the open shutters where he had been stood was somehow worse than before. It savaged the barn with such hellish abandon, that it was a miracle the ancient structure remained intact.

Below, I could hear voices. Over a chorus of splashing water, at least three men could be heard.

And it was with a stab of horror that I realised I recognised all three.

'You're late to the party, Rami.' Domingo Reyes barked.

'Aww, you call him Rami?' James Stone cackled. What on earth was he doing here? 'That's so adorable. You should have told me you had a nickname. It might have made our time together more bearable.'

'I've missed you, James,' Ramiro Salazar hissed. His words elongated by his terrible scars. 'I've missed that look in your eyes as I slit you open.'

The conversation was cut short by a burst of gunfire. The ceaseless racket of an assault rifle echoed through the barn. The muzzle flash lit up everything like an array of fireworks. I ducked low, praying no bullets would ricochet up towards me. None did, and just as soon as the fighting had started, it died a death.

I crept across to the side of the mezzanine and peered down, overlooking the battlefield.

Five men were directly beneath me. They took shelter behind the rear of the enormous SUV, weapons scanning for a target. The man in the centre with the most coverage was the burned man. Ramiro Salazar. His damaged skin glistened in the light of the lanterns.

'What happened to the rest of your men, Rami?' James heckled. I couldn't see him, but his voice seemed to be coming from one of the overturned mine carts. 'They get tired in the storm and stop to have a nap?'

'It will only take one man with one knife to cut you open.' Salazar snapped.

'It's going to have to be a hard pass on that one I'm afraid,' James called back. 'I've got dinner plans. Need to be in one piece for that.'

Another bombardment of bullets enraged the battlefield. Shadowed figures near the entrance to the cave fired at the mine carts, and two sets of returning fire highlighted those two which were occupied. In the fragmented light, I could see James's head. All that protected him from Salazar's men was the cart to his left. Their bullets went wide, and one of the shadow-clad figures darted between cover. As he passed through the glow of one of the lanterns, I saw his face. Reyes. He was making a break for the mines.

The distraction of the two parties gave the third chance to advance. Four of the five men pushed out from their cover, weapons raised and returning Reyes's fire as they spread out. Only Salazar stayed behind. Too cowardly to risk taking a stray bullet.

He was directly beneath me, oblivious to my presence.

The rusted chain swayed beside me, chattering in the fierce wind. One end attached to the pulley high above me. The other wrapped around the large, heavy coil.

* * *

I was painfully aware of armed men advancing. With Nicole focused on Reyes and his men, there was little I could do to stop the progression the Salazar tribe made towards us. I knew Salazar himself would not move. Not until the battle was won. Coward. Tucked inside the cart, I aimed the gun left, finger poised on the trigger.

I fired the moment someone moved into view. A man, but that was all I managed to register as I squeezed down on the trigger and cut a hole straight through the spot his face had once occupied. I moved on before he dropped, swivelling the weapon back to help out Nicole. She had taken down two, and had a third lined up in her sights. As she squeezed the trigger, a fourth figure appeared mere feet from her, weapon aimed to cut her apart. It wasn't Reyes, but that didn't protect them from my weapon. The bullets caught him in the chest and throat, and he went down like a discarded rag doll.

Outside, the storm was reaching new heights of raw power. What had before felt like an imposing force, now felt timid. The world was tearing apart, and we were at the goddamn centre of it. An almighty crack above splintered a large portion of the roof. A section about half the size of a car was there one moment and gone the next, sucked out into the descending oblivion.

The SUV creaked and groaned as the wind whipped underneath it. An old table flipped and smashed against the wall, right beside one of Salazar's men. The shock stunned him, and Nicole took him down with a well-timed burst. Seizing the opportunity while it lasted, I saw out of the corner of my eye the figure of Reyes on the move. From his hidden position, he staggered away and disappeared into the mouth of the cave. The last remaining man to fight for him watched him go, then followed suit. I fired. The bullets caught the man in the back, as he ran into the eerie blackness of the cave.

The battle had shifted. No longer were we the only combatants, duelling it out for first place. Now we were survivors, all prey to the biggest foe of all. But with Salazar and his men within spitting distance, any chance I had of escape was in their hands.

* * *

The snap above me sounded like a bomb going off, and the ensuing wind was nearly enough to pull me off my feet. I gripped onto the coil for dear life and prayed I had enough time to succeed. It wasn't about whether I lived or died. Nor was it about the lives of anyone left in the barn. This was about Quinn. This was for her.

I threw my weight into the coil and knocked it onto its side. The thud as it smashed down onto the floor was masked under the sheer chaos that infiltrated every inch of the barn. The top of the coil splintered as the rotten core toppled, but the bulk remained intact. And that was all I needed.

I pressed my shoulder up against the coil and pushed. It was so heavy. It creaked forwards an inch, then another, and another, towards the dilapidated edge of the mezzanine, towards the unsuspecting victim below. I pushed and I pushed and I pushed past every barrier my mind and body threw at me. Past everything the storm could offer. I wasn't going to let it go. Wasn't going to let failure defeat me. This was my chance.

The coil reached the edge of the mezzanine. The rusted chains rattling around it like unwilling shackles. The pulley hanging onto the rotten beam above. Now was my chance.

And I pushed.

* * *

'You were so weak, James. So powerless.' Rami screamed over the storm. 'It was such a beautiful sight to behold. You, writhing beneath my blade. You will always be my toy. My dog. I defeated you, James. No matter what happens, you are mine. You will always be mine.'

'How's the face Rami?' I shouted back over the pandemonium. 'I bet you can still feel the flames. The same fire that burned your father to a crisp. Does it wake you up in the middle of the night? Does it make you scream like a child?'

I saw the top of his head move. Out from behind the protection of the SUV. Out of cover. He raised the enormous handgun up, pointed right at me, and in that moment I finally saw the damage I had done. The burns, the scars, the resentment. It was all there. His scars and mine, not just skin deep, not just superficial. He wore his pain just as I did. He wore his mistakes for all the world to see.

He looked deep into my eyes, and I saw the man who had tried so hard to break me.

But he had failed.

He had not broken me.

I was still here.

We fired our weapons at the same time.

Two rounds, drifting through the chasms of the apocalypse in opposite directions. Both obeying their masters. Both hitting their marks. I felt the thump in my shoulder as the round buried deep. I felt the kickback as it cut through flesh and bone. And I felt the satisfaction as I saw the same reaction on the face of Ramiro Salazar.

His wound was lower. Somewhere in his stomach. He dropped the handgun and took a step back. His hands moved instinctively towards the blood oozing from his gut. He looked down at it, then up at me. And he smiled.

But the words on his lips did not come. From a balcony above, something large came crashing down right beside him. Splinters of wood exploded outwards like ball bearings in a grenade. At the same time, a thick chain that wrapped the large projectile snapped tight. Like a tendon pushed beyond its limit, something had to give. High above, the strain found its weak point. A large, rotten beam up in the rafters took the punishment and buckled.

And in one fluid motion, the ceiling collapsed.

The barn was done. The structure reduced to ruins. Like a ravenous pack of piranha, the storm decimated the remains of the structure. My eyes flashed up to the spot the object had fallen from, and I felt my heart stop. Looking down on me was a woman. Eva.

No.

I screamed out, begging for her to do something, to move, to escape. But it was too late. I looked into her eyes as the blackness swallowed her up. The front of the barn jerked up and disappeared into the storm. In the blink of an eye, Eva Marston was gone.

With nothing holding it back, Reyes's shackled SUV became the next victim. As though controlled by a giant, invisible hand, the huge vehicle shifted sideways and flipped onto its side. A lone figure held onto its side. Salazar. Like a terrified child, he clung to the bumper, legs crumpled beneath him. His men were gone. Claimed to the storm. He was the only man left alive.

But not for much longer.

I fired again. My bullets wouldn't hit, but I had to. I had to. And as the final round burst from the spent magazine, the SUV reared up like a stallion and was sucked into the terrible blackness.

And with it, Ramiro Salazar too.

FIFTY-FIVE

SUFFOCATION

I felt a hand on my arm pull me away. Up and out of the mine cart, away from the storm, away from Salazar, and Eva. The ravenous gust snatched at my feet, desperate to claim me it's victim, but the hand on my arm was stronger.

The barn was a ruin. With the front half all but a memory, the rest came crashing down. Tonnes upon tonnes of battered, rain-soaked timber smashed down to the ground. Some of it flicked up into the sky like a balloon in a breeze, but most of it thundered down around us. The hand on my arm pulled harder, urging me to move, but my eyes were transfixed on the spot he had been.

As the final supports toppled like dominos, the barn was no more. I barely had a chance to move as the last beam landed at my feet, bringing with it a cocoon of ruined timber. The devastation provided a small windbreak and shattered my distractions like a pane of glass. I climbed free from its quagmiring thoughts, back to the real world.

Nicole had not let go of my hand. Aware that our respite from the tumultuous onslaught would likely only last a matter of moments, she powered onwards. Sure enough, the hurricane was already at work on our defences. One by one, it snatched at the rotten wood and threw it aside, as though some enormous giant searched the pile for its next meal. We had seconds at most.

I turned away from the devastation and ran. No thought for the throbbing bullet wound in my shoulder. It would have to wait. With Nicole by my side, we sprinted down into the depths of the mine.

With every furtive step we took, I could feel myself growing closer to Domingo Reyes. The darkness was absolute. It was suffocating. Water gushed down by my feet, easily reaching my knees. It had to be going somewhere, but whether that would be a place safe enough to survive was anyone's guess.

'Are you okay?' Nicole gasped. Her voice was much louder and clearer as we moved deeper.

'Eva. She's… she was there.'

And as though summoned by her name, the rush of emotion hit me like a punch to the face. My legs buckled and I fell down into the stream. Eva, the kind, broken girl. It shouldn't have happened that way. She shouldn't have done that. Not for me. I wasn't worth it.

Nicole placed her hand on my shoulder. Exactly where the bullet had cut through. I winced, and she recoiled in shock. 'You're hurt.'

'I'm fine.'

'What happened?'

'Salazar got me.' The words like barbed wire in my throat. 'Just before I… the bastard shot me.'

'We have to stop. You can't go on with a bullet wound.'

'I'll be fine.' I insisted. 'I have to find him. I have to kill Reyes myself.'

'James, it's suicide.'

'You want to go back and see if the storm has subsided? Be my guest, but I'm not turning back. Not until I know this is over.'

'You are one stubborn son of a bitch, you know that?'

'Takes more than a category four hurricane and a gunshot to stop me.' But it was a lie. There was nothing in me, save for the need to keep going. I consoled myself to push onwards, to find Reyes and to put a bullet through his skull. I still had the pistol tucked in my pocket.

The storm had made easy work of the debris. Air whistled by my body, trying desperately to pull me back.

'This goddamn storm is going to finish me.' Nicole growled.

'No it won't. Just keep going.'

'That's easier said than done, James. I'm at my limit. I don't think I can keep going.'

'I'll drag you if I have to. We're so close now.'

The tunnel was horribly claustrophobic. Even without light, I could feel the walls closing in on me. The grooves from the old mine cart track at least provided some stability, but they were slippery and uneven.

'Damn it, fine. But if you complain about your one bullet wound, remember I went through worse and didn't whine like a baby about it.' Nicole barked.

'You're much stronger than I ever was.' I said. But as I spoke, my voice wavered. A knot formed in my throat.

She wrapped her arms around me and hugged me. Not tight. Neither of us could manage it. I put my arms around her and dropped my head onto her shoulder. Tears trickled down my face and onto her shoulder. I closed my eyes and let the torrent of thoughts cascade through my mind for just a moment. That was all I could give. Then we let go.

Back to the fight.

With the wind struggling to drag us back, I felt like I was running through an endless series of massive spider webs. A fatigued Nicole didn't help. With every step, she seemed to lose a little bit more of her strength. I quickly took the lead, blindly venturing forth into the dark. Where she had helped me, now I took the mantle. I could feel her behind me, lagging and stumbling.

'We're going to be okay, I promise.'

'Don't make promises you can't keep, James.'

We struggled on through the tunnel. I had no idea where we were going. For all I knew, I could have passed right by another path, completely unaware that we were headed in the wrong direction. If that were the case, I was certain we would die in here. I shooed away the thought. It could do nothing for me.

The water was rising. With every step, I sank deeper into the water. Deeper into the unknown.

'It's a dead end,' Nicole cried. 'We must have missed a turn somewhere.'

'We didn't. It's this way.'

'James, it's flooded. We have to turn back.'

'You can if you want, but Reyes is definitely this way.'

'How can you be certain? If this does go anywhere, you'll drown before you make it.'

I pointed down into the water, before realising Nicole couldn't see my arm, let alone my extended finger.

'Look down there,' I said instead. 'Can you see it?'

'Last time I checked, we were stumbling around in the dark.

Unless I've had a massive brain injury and gone blind, I'm pretty certain there's nothing to see.'

'Look closer. There's light down there.'

It was faint. More so because of the water. But there was no mistaking the faint glow of light somewhere in the depths.

'That could be a flashlight floating around by itself.' Nicole said. 'We can't go swimming around down there without proof.'

'That's about the only proof we're going to get I'm afraid. Unless you've got some magical sixth sense you've been keeping secret.'

I took another step forward, but Nicole didn't budge.

'You okay?' I asked. 'We don't have any other options.'

'I can't.'

'Why not?'

'Swimming around in the dark, it's literally my worst nightmare – yes literally, James. Just thinking about it is making me freak out.'

I squeezed her hand.

'Hold on tight to me, and I'll get us through this, okay? I used to do competitive swimming in school. I was the fastest in my class. I'll have us in and out in seconds. All you have to do is hold your breath and my hand. If it's a dead end we'll be back before you know it.'

'Did you practice with a bullet wound?'

'I practised with a backpack once.'

'That's not the same thing, jackass.'

The water was still rising. It lapped at my chest.

'Can't you go and check first?' She whimpered.

'I'm not leaving you, Nicole. We're in this together. I did tell you, you didn't have to come with me.'

'Yeah and if I'd known this was on the itinerary, I might have sat this one out.'

'So you'll take on a hurricane, but a little bit of water makes you piss yourself?'

Through the darkness, she punched me in the arm.

'Don't be an ass, James.'

'I promise you we will get through this. Do you trust me?'

'Like hell I do.'

'Good, because you either go with me or you can go see how strong that hurricane is.'

'Alright, fine. If you let go of me and I drown, I'm going to come back as a snake and bite you.'

'I would expect nothing less of you.'

Nicole wrapped her arms around my shoulders and clung on tight. I gritted my teeth as she pressed up against the bullet wound, but there was nothing to be done about it now. Together, we took a long, deep breath, and I dove down into the darkness.

The water was bitterly cold, and far from calm. The constant flux was immediately disorientating. It sucked me down into the depths before I had the chance to take my first stroke, and bashed me against the cavern walls with the careless abandon of a child with its toy. Nicole's grip loosened, and I had to forfeit one of my hands to ensure she didn't slip away.

Flotsam from above ground filled every available space. Rocks and dirt and sticks and god knows what else scratched at my face and arms. I wanted to keep my eyes open, but I knew that doing so would likely blind me, and that was the last thing I needed. I opted for short squinting bursts. It was enough to keep some vague idea of which way I needed to go. The faint glow was a little stronger underwater, but there was no telling how far away it was.

Using my legs to propel and my free hand to steer, I pushed myself as hard as I could. We had been under for around thirty seconds. It was no problem for me, but I could tell Nicole was beginning to struggle. Fear did that. It robbed them of the one thing that would make the situation easier. Calm.

I squeezed her hand again and kept going. The ache had started to kick in. My lungs craved fresh oxygen. My heart rate accelerated. My mind had registered the problem, but it knew that the one thing it needed was inaccessible. It was a snowball effect. As the tension rose, so did the need to breathe.

The light was growing. There was no way it was a flashlight. It was too bright for that. It flickered like a fire, and no fire I'd seen could burn underwater.

My lungs were really starting to hurt. While I had swum at school, I'd never been in it for the competition. I wanted the lie to sooth Nicole, but it did little to assuage my doubts. Had I been alone, the dive would be easier. It certainly had been simple enough for Reyes with a bullet wound. But Nicole was a lead weight, dragging me down. She squirmed against my back. The burning starvation consumed her. I felt her exhale a lung-full of carbon dioxide and felt the bubbles rush past my ear.

And then she inhaled.

Filthy water flooded into her lungs. As she realised her mistake, she tried to expel the foul liquid, but it only made things worse. She needed oxygen, but there was nothing to give. Panic had well and truly set in, and there was nothing she could do but hold on and survive. I let go of her hand to give myself the maximum amount of forward momentum, and cut through the water as fast as I could. Her hands slipped, and she let go.

No.

I twisted in the water and flailed wildly for her hand, but already she was out of my grasp. The current carried me further along, and as I struggled, I felt myself drifting into the darkness.

Don't make promises you can't keep, James.

I grappled with the cave wall for something to hold on to. My fingers bounced off the jagged surface, unable to grip. I gave up, and tried to force myself back with a powerful breaststroke. The current was strong, and progress was pitiful, but eventually, I started to make headway.

I pushed myself beyond the limitations my mind had set in place. I couldn't let her go. I just couldn't. I'd promised Eva I would protect her, I'd promised Sophie I would make it back to her. I'd promised Nicole I'd keep her safe.

I couldn't break another promise.

My hand brushed against something cold. I kicked further, and stretched out with both arms, gripping on to what I had found. It was an arm, small and lithe. It had to be Nicole. I tugged her towards me, and swam as hard as I could towards the light. It had to be close.

It was. As I opened my eyes, I saw the distinct orange glow high above me. I twisted, and kicked off the rocks, and propelled myself towards the light. It was so close.

I burst through the surface with a large gasp and opened my eyes. I pulled Nicole up beside me, and looked at her face. Her eyes were closed. Her lungs were full of water. She needed CPR.

We were in a large cave. A hearty fire close by illuminated the room in a warm, flickering glow. I swam towards it, keeping Nicole's head above the water. As I reached the shore, I heaved her up onto the rock, and scrambled up beside her.

Without pause, I tilted her head back to open her airway and began compressions on her chest. I'd learned CPR when I was in college. Thirty compressions followed by two rescue breaths. I worked on her chest, counting the compressions in my head.

One, two, three, four.

Her body rocked under my compressions. Her skin was cold and sodden and deathly pale. Her eyes remained closed.

Ten, twelve, thirteen.

Come on Nicole.

'She's dead, James.'

Twenty-two, twenty-three, twenty-four.

'Give it up. You need to find Reyes.'

At thirty, I pinched her nose and breathed twice into her mouth. Her chest rose and fell, but she remained still. I began compressions again. One, two, three, four.

'James, I need you to focus. We aren't safe here.'

I ignored the Wolf. I wasn't about to give up on Nicole. I couldn't.

Fifteen, sixteen, seventeen.

'James. You've got to stop. It's not...'

Something solid pressed into the side of my neck. The barrel of a weapon.

'For a moment, I thought you might have actually beaten me.' Domingo Reyes leered.

I kept up the compressions. Twenty-three, twenty-four, twenty-five. Reyes jammed the rifle into my skin.

'Let go and stand up now.' he barked.

I looked down into her beautiful face. The face of the only person in America I trusted. If the tables were turned, would she give up on me?

'I won't ask you twice.' Reyes snarled.

With great reluctance, I stopped the compressions and got slowly to my feet. I lifted my eyes away from her body, cold and still. Betrayed by the person she had put her faith in. *Don't make promises you can't keep, James.* I had let her down, just like everyone else, and I couldn't even bring myself to look at her. I picked my head up and looked away. And that's when I saw them.

Children. Hundreds of children.

FIFTY-SIX

THE VIPER'S LEGACY

A SEA OF TERRIFIED FACES LOOKED AT ME ACROSS THE CAVERN. They cowered together, shepherded by the last of Reyes's men. The goon didn't look good. The bullets I'd fired earlier had caught him in the back. It was by sheer will that he hadn't collapsed. He kept his weapon raised at the mass of innocent bystanders. From the faces I could see, the children couldn't be older than twelve. Some looked as young as five or six. Most were white, with just a handful of faces black or Asian. Almost all of them were girls.

'What is this?' I stammered.

'A product in high demand.' Domingo Reyes said. The rifle still pressed into my neck. 'A business deal worth millions of yuan, to the right buyer.'

Standing close by, I spotted them. Three Asian men, all clothed in heavy black parkas. They eyed me with the curiosity commonly found in visitors at a zoo. The guests from China. The buyers.

'You're a monster.' I snarled, looking at Reyes.

'Don't lecture me, Stone. We both know the score. We're both businessmen at the end of the day.'

'I am nothing like you.'

'Are you so sure about that? You have survived because of your tenacity. Men like us are all the same. We see an opportunity, and we take it. These kids will join millions just like them all across the globe. It's nothing new. It isn't going to change. They are a product, just like dope, coke or corn. You find the market, and you make your mark. Simple as that.'

I looked at the children. Their clothes were torn and dirty. Most looked like they were on the cusp of starvation.

'Admit it, Stone. You've failed. You fought your way here for nothing. No one beats me, understand? No one. I've crushed bugs bigger and stronger than you.'

'Again with the bug crushing. You must have big shoes.'

'What?'

'To crush bugs the size of a grown man. You must have big shoes.'

'You're stalling. I can understand why. You fear death, but there is nothing you can do. Even your little bitch is dead. You can follow her to the grave, not that anyone will ever find your bodies to dig you one.'

I looked down at Nicole. She was so still.

The Wolf knelt down beside her and stroked her face. Then he looked at me. His bright blue eyes mimicking mine.

'Make it count.' He said.

'How many kids you got here?' I asked. 'One, two hundred maybe? That can't be much of a profit surely?'

'What you see here is just the start of a long and profitable business deal. Every day thousands of children go missing. Not all make it back home.'

'That seems like a lot of work though. Surely more so than manufacturing cocaine?'

'People will always pay extra for American-made.'

'And you're okay with destroying their lives, just so you can make a quick buck?'

'Business is business. If it weren't me, it would be the next guy. You can't stop it.'

'And how much do you stand to make off all this?'

'Enough to leave this place for good. Perhaps I should thank you.' Reyes said. 'None of this would have been possible if you hadn't blown Hector Salazar to hell. You forced me to open my eyes and adapt to change. This world has no place for old dogs like Hector and me. Not anymore. People don't want their cocaine by the pound. They want the new craze. Drugs are a fashion accessory. They change faster than the seasons. It's exhausting. It's a young man's game. And because of you, I finally have my way out.'

'That way out won't be worth much when all these kids are burnt to a crisp.' I said.

Some of the children looked on in horror.

'And just how exactly would that happen?' Reyes sneered. 'There are no tricks up your sleeve, and even you don't have it in you to kill everyone here just to get the better of me.'

'You'd be bang on the money there, but I didn't pack everyone here inside a combustible cavern.'

'That fire isn't going to light shit in here. It's all rock and water.'

'True, but that water's got to be at least ninety percent phosphate. That's what they mined here, right? Back in the day when this place wasn't used for acts of pure evil. The rocks will be coated with the stuff. It'll bleed out of them like an open wound. All that water in here will be contaminated now.'

'You're full of shit, Stone.'

'Can't you feel it? My nose and eyes are burning from the stuff. The second that flame hits it and this place is going to light up like the fourth of July. That's a term you guys use, isn't it?'

'Phosphate isn't explosive.' Reyes snarled.

'Since when? No offence mate, but I studied chemistry a lot more recently than you. And I've not gone senile. Well, not entirely yet. I've got news for you. It's massively volatile. And it's all mixed up in that water by our feet.'

I could almost feel him glance down. The curiosity would be too much. It was instinctual. He had to see for himself, even if all he would see was the dark, chilled fluid lapping against his boots.

It had worked on Jorge the gangster. It would work on Reyes the Viper.

He had made his first mistake pointing the weapon into the side of my neck. He should have put it in my back. I'd have more space to move through before he squeezed the trigger. But he hadn't, and all I needed to do was to twist a couple of degrees to be inside the rifle's barrel and be out of harm's way.

I flicked around like a fox. My neck spun just out of the way of the rifle as the first bullet fired. Reyes had the reactions of a man half his age, and had already begun to squeeze the trigger as the first steps of my plan were in their infancy. The bullet sliced through the air by my neck. Close, but no cigar. The rest of the rounds shot off into the darkness, slicing into the rushing torrent of water.

But the spin was just the beginning. I wrenched my right arm up and slung it over the rifle, and brought my left fist smashing into the side of his head. If my injuries were hurting, I couldn't tell. Nothing else mattered now but beating Reyes. The Viper, versus the Wolf. I forced the rifle down and threw my weight into Reyes's midriff. He was fast, but I was faster. As he squeezed the trigger again, I sent him tumbling backwards onto the slippery rocks. We landed with a crash, locked together in a struggle. With one hand desperately on the rifle, Reyes threw his other fist into my face. The blows landed with devastating force and knocked me aside.

As I keeled over, I brought my knee up and caught Reyes in the groin. He swore and fell backwards as the wave of nausea rolled through him. Both kept our grip on the rifle. I was the first to recover. As I scrambled to my feet, I flung my forehead down onto the old man's nose. His head smashed back against the rocks, blood spurting everywhere. I raised my head for a second attack.

But it was a huge mistake. With his free hand, he gripped my throat and squeezed. His fingers like viper's fangs, piercing deep with unrelenting force. I let go of the rifle and grappled at his hand, but his fingers were dug in deep. I punched him in the face. His bloodied nose had bent to the side, yet the rage numbed him. Anger amplified him. He let go of the rifle and wrapped his hands around my throat. It made everything a thousand times worse. I dug my fingers into his, scratching and clawing to subside his attack. Though it only seemed to egg him on. My eyes bulged in my head. Blood thumped against my temples. He was going to snap my neck in two. He could feel the life seeping out of me, and it fuelled his bloodlust.

He rolled me over and positioned himself on top. With all his weight he pressed down on my throat, pinning me to the ground. I punched him, again and again in the face. My fists bounced off him like he was made from marble. Blood trickled down into his eyes and mouth, but all he did was smile. It grew wider and wider across his face. He knew he would win, and that thought terrified me more than anything.

My whole world was going black. My starved brain couldn't register his face as a whole. I saw only his eyes, then they faded into darkness as his leering, bloodied smile swam out of the fog. My ears buzzed. So loud, I couldn't comprehend anything. I watched his mouth move. I couldn't hear the words, but I knew what they said.

'I've won.'

From somewhere in the blackness, a flash of light appeared. It was infinitesimally brief, like the bolts of lightning on the surface. A final spark before my world ended. Reyes's smile faded from my view, and my whole world went dark.

'James, get up.'

The voice called out from somewhere. I couldn't place it. Was it Sophie? Peter? The Wolf? Or was it Fadhil? My mind was a mess of light and noise. Nothing made sense. Nothing came into focus. Here I was, trapped in a state of unknowing.

'I know you can hear me. Quit lying around and help.'

It was none of them. It was Nicole. With great effort, I raised my eyelids and tried to focus. Nicole was standing over me, her face illuminated in the glow of the fire. She looked half dead, but the smile she gave me was full of life.

'I knew you were faking it.' She beamed.

She grabbed my hand and hoisted me up out of the water. My head spun as the blood flooded back into place, and I felt dizzy.

'Easy now, I think Ass-face over there had you at the pearly gates.' She said. 'You looked like you needed a hand.'

I looked around and saw Domingo Reyes lying on the ground. He had a large, gaping hole in the side of his skull. It didn't take a genius to realise he was dead. His last remaining man stood nearby, too weak to retaliate. As I looked at him, I realised Nicole had deprived him of his weapon. Through sunken eyes he watched us wearily, perhaps hoping his lack of resistance might grant him a free trip home.

Behind him stood the three guests from China. Two looked just about ready to break down in a fit of hysteria, but the man in the middle was something different. There was anger in his eyes. Whether he planned to act on it was a different matter, but the possibility was more than I was willing to allow. Nicole was watching him too.

'What should we do? She asked.

'I want to talk to him.' I croaked. My throat felt broken.

With care, Nicole pulled me to my feet and handed me the pilfered rifle. I gripped it in my left hand to let the right rest. My shoulder pulsated where the bullet had cut through.

I took a step towards the guests from China. My legs felt jellied. If the three men put up a fight, I hoped Nicole was alert enough to drop them where they stood. The man in the middle watched me approach. His lips tightened with every step. When I was just feet from him, he pulled back his hood and looked me dead in the eye.

'You speak English?' I asked. My voice was hoarse.

The three men watched me. The man in the middle didn't reply. I knew he understood me. The look he gave was not one of incomprehension. It was pure, unfiltered hatred. His eyes burned into mine as the silence elongated.

I shot him in the chest. A chorus of petrified screams echoed around the cavern.

He fell back against the wall, hands clutching at the hole in his chest. No way was he walking away from that. His engaged face glared at me for just a moment. Then he was gone.

'James, what're you…' Nicole shouted, but I raised my hand, and she fell silent.

'I'll ask one more time,' I snarled. 'Do you speak English?' This time it was slower, clearer. My voice returning.

The two remaining men cowered away, looking at their deceased companion. The man on the left said nothing either. His body shivered through a mixture of cold and fear. If he could understand my request, he didn't make any attempt to respond.

Finally, the man on the right nodded. It was just the briefest of actions, but it was all I needed.

'Good,' I growled. 'Then you better listen if you want to get out of here alive. Whoever you work for, you tell them they just made one serious enemy. What happened here ends today. Right goddamn now. You tell them that if they ever take so much as one more child away from their families, I'm going to come for them, and I will cut through them like a hot knife. I do not care how long it takes. I do not care how many people get in my way. I will find them, and I will fucking ruin them. Understand?'

He nodded.

'Attaboy.' I smiled, patting the man on the cheek.

Nicole was nearby. Her gun pointed at the last surviving man on Reyes' team. I went to him next.

'You got any rope down here?' I asked.

He nodded his head towards a pile of boxed munitions near the children. Blankets, food and water for the journey to China. And rope too, for those who stepped out of line.

'Mind tying up our guests?' I asked Nicole.

'Not like I have a choice.'

She retrieved the rope and tied together the two men from China. Arms, chest and legs for good measure. Once she was satisfied they were secure, she came back to me.

'Is there another way out of here?' I asked the wounded guard.

He nodded.

'Up there,' he whispered, nodding towards a pathway near the pool we had emerged from. 'It leads out back.'

'Good lad. How are you feeling?' I asked.

'Screw you.' Was all he could muster.

Nicole tied him up too. Again, there was no resistance from the dying man. The restraints were merely for show. I had little doubt he would survive the storm. With the rope finished, I hurled the rifle into the water, along with any other weapons I could find.

'What now?' Nicole asked as she threw her pistol into the water.

'You think you can calm down those kids?'

'Probably better than you can. You shouldn't have shot that guy.'

'He wanted to buy children. I couldn't let him walk away from that.'

'Even so, next time think it through, yeah?'

'Next time,' I snorted. 'You make it sound like I do this sort of thing often.'

'You do. What do you want me to tell the kids?'

'Tell them to eat and drink whatever they can, and that help is coming. Get them wrapped up and tell them not to move till the cops come.'

'You want to leave them here, with those men?' She asked, unable to hide the surprise in her voice.

'So long as you tied them up well enough, they'll be fine.' I replied, feeling the exhaustion more than ever. 'We need to get out of here as soon as possible. And it's safer here than anywhere else right now. It's dry, calm, and hurricane-free. Besides a bunker, you can't get much better than a cave. Just make sure they know not to move, okay?'

'Will do.' She said, turning to leave. But I stopped her just before she could go.

'Hey, I don't suppose you know if phosphate is flammable do you?'

'What kind of question is that? How should I know?'

'Never mind.' I replied, and she moved away to deal with the children.

She knelt down near one of the older girls. She spoke softly, and with great kindness. She radiated the vibe found in older sisters talking to their younger siblings. A trick she'd no doubt learned from helping out her younger brother, Bobbie. It worked almost instantly. The girl stretched out her hands and hugged Nicole tight.

How long had she been away from her family, and how long would it be till they were reunited?

I hoped it would be soon. At least the man responsible was dead. I left Nicole to it and walked over to Reyes's corpse.

The smile had gone, as had most of the top right quadrant of his face. What remained was a sore sight to behold. Brain matter and skull fragments littered the ground beside where he had dropped. Dead in an instant. He probably didn't even know it was going to happen. The last thought on his mind had surely been victory. It was a mercy he didn't deserve. After all he did, he should have drowned, slowly and painfully in the horror that he had finally been defeated. I wanted to see the fear in his face, but there was none.

He had got off lightly, but he was dead. He couldn't hurt anyone else.

And that would have to suffice.

EPILOGUE

END OF THE LINE

Blood oozed out onto the hard, lumpy mattress. I stared up at the ceiling fan, willing it to start spinning. No dice. Nicole flicked the light switch on the wall again and again. Nothing.

'Power must be out.' She mused.

'Yeah, I figured that.' I grunted.

'How're you feeling?'

I opened my mouth, but I barely had it in me to speak. Getting to the motel had taken every ounce of willpower I had. My shoulder was in sheer agony. Salazar's bullet had not cut clean through, and the tiny object burned inside me like wildfire. A final present from the burned man.

We had waited out the storm in the company of the Viper's guests and victims. Nicole divided up the remaining rations amongst the children. Nothing for the Chinese guests. They'd forfeited the right to eat when they decided to buy another human being. As soon as the weather subsided, we followed the directions given to us by Reyes's final employee, and ventured out into a brave new world.

The damage was hard to comprehend. Felled trees and scattered debris stretched far into the distance in all directions, and as we neared the first signs of civilisation, it got a whole lot worse. Every building we passed looked to have suffered significant damage. Roofs had ripped free, leaving buildings exposed like gaping wounds. Walls had caved in, and smashed windows scattered into the street. Flipped vehicles lay on their sides, and in some cases, hurled into buildings.

Then there were the bodies. Coats and sheets rested over the still remains, granting a shred of dignity in a cruel and unforgiving world. Those that had survived trudged around like the living dead, too tired to deal with their new reality. I did not envy them, rebuilding their lives quite literally from the ground up.

Nicole found an abandoned car with the windows smashed. She hot-wired it and we headed off in silence for someplace to rest up. The first to fit the bill was a weathered motel that looked to have survived the worst of the storm. The lady on reception gave us a room with no charge, incorrectly assuming the hurricane had destroyed our homes. We didn't correct her. Figured we needed the help as much as anyone. The kindness of strangers won through.

I headed for the room while Nicole used the reception's landline to make a call. There were two hundred children in need of rescue..

The mattress springs dug into my spine, but I didn't care. The pain from it and my shoulder just didn't seem to matter. It wasn't what occupied my mind. It was Reyes and Salazar. Two powerful rivals wiped off the board. The world had just got that little bit less terrible, and yet I felt numb from it. Their deaths didn't bring me solace. Didn't bring Eva back, or save Quinn from her suffering. It didn't recalibrate my mind back to fixing my life in England. It didn't do anything.

'I know you're going to hate me for this,' Nicole said. 'But we need to get that bullet out.'

'You got a plan there, or are we just stating the obvious?'

'As it turns out, I do have a plan, and I feel a little less guilty about it with you being such a smartass.'

'And that is?' I asked, but she just smiled and told me to wait.

And so I did. Nicole headed back outside, leaving me to do little else than keep the makeshift tourniquet she'd fashioned in the caves held to my chest.

Why did I feel so empty at their deaths? It was a question I just couldn't seem to answer definitively. Ramiro Salazar was gone. His body was probably floating somewhere off the Gulf of Mexico, waiting to be devoured by the fishes. He couldn't hurt another soul in the world. I had accomplished what I set out for, and yet here I was, clutching a bloodied rag and lying on a bed in Florida, unable to shake the feeling that somehow, I had failed.

Nicole returned with just a bottle of vodka and a pair of long-nosed pliers. Her plan became pretty bloody apparent in that moment.

'You're kidding me.' I groaned.

'The bullet needs to come out,' she said, matter-of-factly. 'It's either this or you take a fun little trip down to the nearest hospital and see if the cops are okay giving you a free pass.'

'Fine. Hand us the bottle then.'

'Oh, that's not for you, it's for me. Got to calm the nerves somehow.' She smirked. 'I'm kidding. Just don't drink the whole thing, yeah?'

She passed me the vodka, and I took a long swig. I hated vodka, but I hated pliers inside my shoulder that much more. I handed her back the bottle, and she took a swig, then poured some onto my shoulder. The alcohol seared my arm, and I couldn't contain the explosion of profanities that escaped my mouth. Nicole ducked down and picked up the television remote.

'Might want to bite down on this,' she said, handing me the device. 'It's going to hurt like a bitch.'

'Oh, don't mince your words, will you?' I looked at the grubby remote. 'I'm not putting that in my mouth.'

'Don't then. But when you bite your tongue in two, don't come crying to me about it.'

I looked at the remote, tried not to think of all the people who had touched it, and wedged it in between my teeth.

'Try to think of it this way,' Nicole said as she splashed a little more vodka onto the open wound. 'At least this won't be the most painful thing you'll experience.'

'What could possibly be worse than this?' I asked through a mouthful of plastic.

'You'll see. Now lay back and relax. I used to be ace at those arcade claw games.'

'Not the same thing.'

The alcohol stung my flesh, but it was nothing compared to what followed. The moment Nicole pressed the pliers into the wound, I knew I was in for one of the most excruciating experiences of my entire life. The long metal pincers dug deep into the tissue, sending every fibre of my being into meltdown. I clenched down into the remote and felt the plastic snap into a dozen little pieces.

I scrunched my eyes shut and tried desperately to think of something, anything positive. But only one image burned into my mind's eye. Salazar. It was not Nicole piercing me. It was him. He was tearing into me, picking me apart, determined that this moment would be my last. There was no escaping him. Even in death, I was at his mercy.

'Stay with me, James.'

But I didn't know if I could. After everything, not just over the past months, but the preceding years. I didn't have the strength to carry on. There was still so much ahead of me. So many obstacles. So many monsters. And so much at stake.

'I've got it.'

The pain intensified, going from catastrophic to damn near apocalyptic. The pliers retreated, dragging with it the small metallic tumour. I crunched down through the plastic fragments, turning them into a fine dust. I wanted to be free of it, through any means necessary.

And mercifully, it ended. The pliers worked free. I opened my eyes and looked up at Nicole. In her hand was the bullet.

'See, it wasn't so bad, was it?' She smiled.

'You've got a funny definition of the word bad.'

She threw aside the tool and snatched up the bloodied tourniquet.

'Keep that pressed tight,' she said as she forced it down on my wound. 'We need to stop the bleeding.'

I nodded and took the rag with my working hand. The pressure stung the wound, but compared to what had come before, it didn't seem to matter, like getting a scratch on a recently-severed limb. I kept my eyes open. Didn't want to see Salazar's face again. Instead, I watched Nicole. She picked up the Glock, and ejected the clip. Then she prised one of the bullets free.

'What are you doing?' I whimpered.

But she didn't respond. Instead, she used the bloodied pliers to carefully pull the end of the casing from the rest of the bullet, and pour the contents into the palm of her other hand. A substance like black salt. Gunpowder.

'Please tell me that's not what I think it's for?' I moaned.

'Look at it this way. It won't hurt for long.'

'You saying that from experience?'

'Hell no. You think I'm crazy enough to do something like this?'

'No, of course, what was I thinking?'

She ignored me and moved closer. I eyed her cupped hand and recoiled.

'Don't be a baby about it.' She said. Gently, she poured the gunpowder into the wound, and with a delicate finger, moved around the clumps. Then she struck a flame with her lighter. I stared at the flickering flame and tried to ignore the pterodactyls in my gut. 'And try not to pass out or die on me, okay?'

Turned out that was easier said than done. Whether I was dead or unconscious as my fresh wound exploded, I didn't know. Could have been either. And in many ways, death would have been preferable. That kind of pain is hard to describe. It felt like an atom bomb had gone off on my torso. And in a nanosecond, my brain shut up shop.

* * *

The smell of cooked meat filled my nose and made me wretch. James's eyes rolled into the back of his skull, and his body went limp. Typical. The guy couldn't handle a little gunpowder. The wound looked sore, but at least the bleeding had stopped. For how long, I didn't know. It was a short-term solution at best. James was going to need medical attention, which for a guy like him was going to be hard to come by.

But that was tomorrow's problem, and I needed rest. I slumped down on the bed and closed my eyes. Immediately, I felt the warm clutch of sleep on my shoulders. I didn't want to, but I didn't have much choice. My wounds were as bad as Stone's, and weighed on me like a mountain. In seconds I was out of it, drifting into a deep, dreamless sleep.

I wasn't sure how long it lasted. Could have been minutes. Could have been hours. Hell, could have been days. But when I woke, the light through the curtained windows was low. My throat was bone dry. I glanced over at the bottle of vodka. No, vodka wouldn't cut it. I needed something refreshing.

I glanced over at Stone. Poor guy was beat. Even after the victory, he just wasn't the same. He'd put too much faith on the prospect that revenge would somehow plug the hole, and now he was stuck in the void that lingered. Not the first guy to fall for it, and not the last. Nothing filled it. Nothing replaced it. Wounds like that never healed. That was the horrible truth of it.

I put my hand on his chest and felt the steady thud of his heart beating strong. Attaboy. I moved my hand up his chest to his forehead. Hot. Too hot. He was burning up. I cussed and got up. He needed cooling down. Fast. I hustled to the bathroom and flicked on the shower. It made a noise like a petulant child, then barked, but nothing came out. Pipes must have bust in the storm. Shit.

I tried the sink taps and the toilet. Nothing doing. I headed back to James. We didn't have much with us. Didn't exactly plan on this outcome. And the last thing I wanted to do was pour vodka on the guy. I leaned over him and tapped him on the face. Out of it. I shouldn't have fallen asleep. Should have stayed awake to see when the fever started. Could be his brain was already a mess. But I couldn't think like that. He needed help.

I wondered if the motel had an ice machine. Most did that I'd stayed at, which was more than I was willing to count. Could be it had stayed cool enough to do the job. Hell, even if it had melted, at least I'd have someplace to dunk him in. I headed for the door and swung it open.

And felt my heart sink like a stone.

The parking lot had been about half full when we arrived. Some of the vehicles had been too damaged to move. Some were owned by those who had needed shelter after the storm, just like us. They had scattered across the lot, along with a whole bunch of random debris.

It was a lot busier now. I counted seven police vehicles. A mix of different makes and models. No two the same. No two any less of a problem. The cops spilt out into the parking lot, some taking up watch at either end, some talking on their walkies. Others scanned the scene. For what, I had a pretty good guess. No way was this a coincidence. One or two, maybe, but not seven.

I retreated back inside before anyone spotted me and cussed again. Had they traced my call about the kidnapped children, or had the receptionist ratted us out? Either way, it wouldn't take long for them to find us.

I ran back through to the bathroom. We needed a way out. Couldn't risk making a break for it out the front. A small frosted-glass window above the toilet was our best bet. It looked just big enough to squeeze through, hopefully. I snatched the complimentary motel towel off the rack, and wrapped it around my fist. Then I punched right through the glass. Fragments scattered outwards, how loud was anyone's guess. I knocked out the remaining shards and draped the towel over the ledge. Outside was a row of dishevelled trees. What lay beyond them, I didn't know. Hopefully a way out.

I headed back to the bedroom. James looked so still. Almost too much so. I checked for a pulse. Still there. So was the fever. Moving him would be problematic. *If* I could move him, that is.

'James, I need you to wake up for me, buddy.' I called, voice raised like an irate parent. 'Come on. We need to get out of here.'

Nothing. I slapped him across the face. Hard enough to stir a drunk. Still useless. He was practically comatose.

I ran back to the door and opened it a crack. Huge mistake. The cops were closer. Much closer. And moving in my direction. Their heads turned to focus on the movement, and in unison, they all perked up.

I swung the door shut and slid the chain through the latch. As soon as it clinked into place, a flurry of fists hammered on the door.

'Police, open up.' One of them shouted.

I ignored them and ran back to James. Didn't have time for games. I slapped him across the face.

'Come on, James. I need you to wake up.'

But it was no good. There was just no waking him. He was a dead weight, and I needed to make a choice. Let go, or sink.

What would he do?

Something solid smashed against the doorframe. Boot or battering ram, I wasn't sure. Didn't have time to find out. It was followed by a louder, harder crash. The frame splintered and cracked. I was out of time.

I looked down at James once more. Then I ran. I sprinted back to the bathroom and squeezed through the window. As my shoulders jostled through, I heard the door burst open. Cops flooded into the motel room like a tsunami. I didn't turn back. They kept going. I kept going. As I wriggled loose, I felt hands scratch desperately at my ankles. Not today.

I hit the ground and rolled away.

'Hold it right there.' Shouted one of the cops.

I didn't stop. Just kept going.

There were more cops around the back. They'd come prepared. But they weren't close enough. They were on my flanks, but far enough away to give me a head start. I set off at a sprint, through the trees, and into the great beyond. I could hear something. Running water. Lots of it. Sure enough, as I pushed through the tree line, I spotted a river up ahead. The water level was high. Stormwater and debris powered along in the mighty current.

It was my only option. The cops were closing in on me. Their shouts grew louder, their threats all the more dangerous.

I didn't stop. I hurled myself towards the river as the cop's bullets soared over my head. I hit the surface and went under. The current sucked me in, and pulled me away. Away from the motel. Away from the cops.

Away from James Stone.

JAMES STONE WILL RETURN

ENJOYED THIS BOOK?

PLEASE CONSIDER LEAVING A REVIEW

When it comes to getting attention for books, reviews are an important and powerful tool for any writer. While I don't have the financial muscle or worldwide ubiquity of a big name publisher at my disposal to hurl my books into the face of every literary lover, I do have something far more important.

You. The most wonderful reader to have ever graced this planet. I beg of you just a morsel of your time.

If you've enjoyed the book, please just hop over to your local Amazon store and leave a review. It might just encourage a random stranger to click the Buy Now button, and it would mean the world to me.

Thank you so much for your support.

WANT MORE?

KEEP GOING WITH THE JAMES STONE SAGA!

I'm a new author, and one of the most important things to me is spreading the word of James Stone to the world. With that in mind, I want to offer you a free James Stone novella - entitled "Aftermath" - available right now!

At midnight she tried to end her own life
At ten minutes past, she found the body

All you need to do is pop over to my website and join the mailing list. You'll get an email with the link to the book right away.
Go to www.robertclarkauthor.com
and get your free copy today!

Don't worry, I won't spam you with garbage. Joining the mailing list will just allow me to send the odd update with new book news!
What more could you ask for?

ALSO BY ROBERT CLARK

No More Shadows
Aftermath

ACKNOWLEDGMENTS

For all the people of Florida who got together and collectively agreed to let me write a novel based in their magnificent state.

For Felix, who helped shape No More Shadows enough for me to steal his name.

For the wonderful people of the Self Publishing Formula community who kept me going.

For Matt and Sue, who gave invaluable help with the editing of this book.

And for Poppy, Xena, Kya, Ziggy and Milly who kept me sane.

ABOUT ROB

Robert Clark is the author of the James Stone thriller series.
By day, Rob desperately tries to avoid working for a living or talking to strangers, but by night he furtively types away at the keyboard to bring James Stone to life.
Rob's dream is to continue doing this so he can buy the nice biscuits for his lunch.
Rob is on the social medias (because it seems to be pretty much impossible not to these days)

The Fate of Glass

Copyright © 2018 by Robert Clark

All rights reserved.

No part of this book may be used or reproduced in any form or by any electronic or mechanical means, including information storage and retrieval systems, without written permission from the author, except for the use of brief quotations in a book review.

This book is a work of fiction. Names, characters, businesses, organisations, places, events and incidents either are the product of the author's imagination, or are used fictitiously. Any resemblance to actual persons, living or dead, events or locales is entirely coincidental. Such is the way of life.

Book and cover design by Robert Clark

Printed in Poland
by Amazon Fulfillment
Poland Sp. z o.o., Wrocław